CANDL ECstasy

"I'VE BEEN ON MY OWN FOR YEARS NOW. I LIKE IT THAT WAY."

"I see," Brian answered.

"What do you see?"

"That you are a beautiful woman who's been going to waste."

"Oh, thanks." Kelly propped herself up on one elbow and glared at him. "You make me sound like an undiscovered natural resource."

"No man in your life?" he asked, ignoring the bite in her words.

"No one I'd buy an emerald for," she said with forced reserve, remembering only too well the beautiful stone that had thrown them together.

He laughed.

"What's so funny?"

"You are. If you want to know about my love life, ask."

"I don't."

"You don't care if I'm engaged, married, living with someone?"

Of course I care, you fool, she wanted to say, tightly clamping her lips shut instead.

Brian rose a little stiffly, hurrying over to the pile of supplies, then dashing back under the covers with her. He held out the brilliant green jewel, offering it to her. "Here, it's yours now."

EMERALD FIRE

Barbara Andrews

A CANDLELIGHT ECSTASY SUPREME ™

Published by
Dell Publishing Co., Inc.
1 Dag Hammarskjold Plaza
New York, New York 10017

To W.C.A.
for years of negotiating

Dell ® TM 681510, Dell Publishing Co., Inc.

Candlelight Ecstasy Supreme™ is a trademark of
Dell Publishing Co., Inc., New York, New York.

ISBN: 0–440–12301–1

Printed in the United States of America
First printing—-August 1983

To Our Readers:

Candlelight Ecstasy is delighted to announce the start of a brand-new series—Ecstasy Supremes! Now you can enjoy a romance series unlike all the others—longer and more exciting, filled with more passion, adventure, and intrigue: the stories you've been waiting for.

In months to come we look forward to presenting books by many of your favorite authors and also the very finest work from new authors of romantic fiction. As always, we are striving to present the unique, absorbing love stories that you enjoy most—the very best love has to offer.

Breathtaking and unforgettable, Ecstasy Supremes will follow in the great romantic tradition you've come to expect *only* from Candlelight Ecstasy.

Your suggestions and comments are always welcome. Please let us hear from you.

Sincerely,

The Editors
Candlelight Romances
1 Dag Hammarskjold Plaza
New York, New York 10017

CHAPTER ONE

"One thing, Cheryl, don't take any orders for nose rings."

Kelly Valentine checked the deco-style wall clock behind the counter for the third time in as many minutes and smiled at her shop helper.

"You're kidding me."

"I wish! Last year a man had me make one with his old fraternity pin hanging on it. It was so tacky I mailed it in a plain brown box."

"I know football Saturdays in Ann Arbor are wild, but that man must've started his tailgate party the night before. Did he expect his wife to wear it?"

"I preferred not to ask. At least his check didn't bounce. Which reminds me: Be sure to clear all personal checks through me. I've been stung twice in the last three years by the football crowd."

Sliding open the door of the case that held her handcrafted bracelets, Kelly arranged several, polishing one on the sleeve of her camel blazer before positioning it on the velvet-covered tray.

"I like the emerald-green against the silver, don't you?" she asked absentmindedly, glancing out the window, then back at the clock.

"I like all the pieces you make," Cheryl said enthusiastically. "Duane came in once and really liked your Big M design. He said your jewelry has class, not like the gung-ho preppy stuff that most places sell."

"Bless Mr. Washington! I hope his touchdowns knock State off the field," Kelly said, pushing aside long raven-black hair, reminding herself for the hundredth time that she should have it cut. It was starting to get in the way when she worked at her jeweler's bench.

"He's a defensive back, not a ball carrier," Cheryl said with a giggle, "and they're playing Notre Dame today. Weren't you a football fan when you attended the university, Kelly?"

"Far from it! Remember, I only took a few design courses, not even enough hours to qualify for a student ticket."

"You must have gone to some games."

"One. Michigan-Ohio State. The bands were great, the crowd was crazy, and the time clock moved so slowly I thought I'd freeze to death. The highlight of the day was the man in front of me throwing up about a gallon of whiskey sours."

"Not a football fan? That's scandalous!" the willowy black student teased. "How can you live in this town and not watch all those magnificent men doing their stuff?"

"You forget, they're all too young for me."

"Poor old lady. You must be all of twenty-five."

"Twenty-eight, Ms. Johnson, and before we open, I want you to know I really appreciate your working this morning. When Krista phoned in sick, I nearly panicked."

"If she's sick, I'm Snow White," Cheryl said grumpily, arranging the last tray of rings she'd taken from the safe and closing the case with a swish of irritation, "but I'm glad to get a few extra hours."

She was by far the most efficient of the three students who clerked for Kelly at odd hours as their schedules allowed, freeing her to work on the jewelry she designed, made, and sold. Even though her store, Valentine's Treasures, carried pieces made by other artisans, her own creations gave the business its reputation.

"Just be sure you leave in time to make the kickoff," Kelly said.

"No problem. My roommate owed me a favor, so I borrowed her bike. Do you think we'll get a lot of people before the game?"

"Mostly lookers, I imagine. Old grads who come early to wander around the campus or fans who leave early to beat the traffic. People like to stroll through Campus Town before a game."

"It's a great day to be outside, almost like summer. You want me to unlock the door now?"

"No, there's still seven minutes. Do we have enough boxes on the wrapping counter?"

"Enough to last till Christmas."

"Did I tell you about Officer Michaels' ring?"

"Twice. It's in the silver box, his name is on it, he's the adorable cop with the handlebar mustache, and he's picking it up this morning. Lucky girl, that fiancée of his, but why are you so jittery, Ms. Valentine?" she asked with mock formality.

"I'm not jittery, but I'm going to hold you hostage in the john and make you miss the game if you call me Ms. that way!"

"What way is that?"

"Like your tongue is stuck on your bottom teeth!"

They both laughed, but Cheryl arched her sharply defined brows and frowned, not easily put off.

"You don't usually pat your hair every ten seconds, and I saw you primping in front of the mirror in the back room. I do believe you're expecting a man."

"Not the kind of man you mean!"

"What kinds are there? They come in different sizes and colors, but far as I can tell, they've all got the same basic equipment. How long have you been divorced, Kelly?"

"Since you were in elementary school. And stop being a missionary."

"A missionary?"

"You're in love, so you want to spread the good word and infect everyone."

"Would that be so bad?" Cheryl grinned.

"It's the last thing I need just when this store is beginning to make it. I think we can open up now."

"I'll unlock the door. It looks like we've got somebody waiting. Did you notice that man with the beard? He was across the street looking over here when I came. Weird, a brown beard with blond hair. He looks like a customer with some strange request."

"Let's hope not! Oh, Cheryl, I did forget to tell you I have an appointment at eleven."

"I knew something was up!" she said triumphantly, tossing the keys back to Kelly. "Let me guess. A man."

"A potential customer."

"With an appointment?"

"A little unusual, huh? But he called earlier in the week to make sure I'd be here. He has a stone he wants set."

"This is getting interesting. Uh-oh, look. Our customer is slipping away. He just went into the pizza place across the street. Pizza for breakfast? Yuck! I'm glad he isn't coming here. Now what about this appointment that's making you so nervous?"

"Are you sure you're not a psych major?"

9

"Dental hygiene. I love sparkling white teeth. Don't change the subject."

"I might as well tell you. Since you're from Detroit, you might recognize him."

"Henry Ford is coming here?" Cheryl joked.

"Close. Brian Fort."

"Brian Fort? Hmm. Not from my neighborhood."

"Nor mine! His family is to finance what Ford is to cars."

"Of course. Fort. Owns a basketball team or something."

"That's his older brother, I think. I don't know what this Fort does, but he probably doesn't have to do anything. For some reason he's coming here this morning."

"Why? I mean, I know you make terrific jewelry, and Ann Arbor knows you sell great stuff, but how does Brian Fort know?"

"Good point," Kelly agreed, not at all offended, because she'd been wondering the same thing herself. "I guess he's coming here for the game, but I don't know why he'd bring a gem to me. There are hundreds of qualified jewelers closer to his home."

"Where's that?"

"One of those Grosse Pointe specials, along the waterfront. You know, a mansion on Jefferson Avenue hidden behind a high fence and a small forest. Ford country."

"So Brian Fort is the reason you're as edgy as a quarterback stuck with the ball."

"I'm not nervous about meeting him," Kelly denied emphatically. "It's just a professional challenge. I don't get many chances to work with precious stones."

"Is he having something made for his wife?"

"According to articles from time to time in the *Free Press,* there is no wife."

"I knew it! He saw your picture somewhere, and he's coming to check you out."

"That's highly improbable."

"But not impossible. You've won enough awards for your jewelry. He could've seen your picture."

"In some obscure jewelry trade journal? Be serious."

"Well, he had to hear about you somewhere."

"Probably a friend recommended me."

"Was that nose-ring customer from the Detroit area?"

10

"Yikes! He was. Now I *am* nervous."

"So am I," Cheryl said, suddenly serious as she moved closer to the display window, staring thoughtfully out at the street. "That guy with the beard is back, and he keeps looking over here."

"Does he look spaced out?" Kelly moved to the door so she could see.

"Can't tell. Do you think we should call the cops?"

"What would we tell them? That there's an odd-looking character on the street? They'd laugh. Every other person in Ann Arbor is a little strange."

"Well, he's walking away, so I guess we don't have to worry about him."

A portly middle-aged couple came into the store, and Kelly backed off to let her assistant help them. Selling was the part of her business she enjoyed least, and Cheryl was a natural, putting the customers at ease and making sales to the least likely prospects. She watched happily as Cheryl made a substantial sale.

"Thank heavens you came today," Kelly said some time later when they both had a brief moment of respite. "I would've been swamped here alone."

"The nice weather has everybody out walking, I guess. Say, that guy with the beard is back."

Slipping over to the front door, Kelly caught a glimpse of his face before he walked away. His clothing was ordinary enough—faded jeans and a hooded sweat shirt, one of the navy ones with a gold M that were seen everywhere on campus—but instinct told her he wasn't a student. He was too old to be an undergraduate, and he didn't have the intense, harried look of a graduate student. In fact, his expression was pretty vacant. He gave her the creeps, but unless he crossed the street, he really wasn't her concern.

"Your 'appointment' is late," Cheryl said after the next wave of customers had milled around, surprisingly purchasing several expensive pieces including a pendant Kelly was delighted to get rid of. It had been in her original stock when she opened three years ago, and she'd been worried that the unusual quarter-moon design would never sell.

"I can stay longer if you need me," Cheryl offered. "You can't talk to Fort and handle the mob we've been having."

11

"It looks like he's a no-show. Anyway, I won't have you miss any of the game."

"Underneath my self-sacrificing exterior, I was praying you'd say that. I just gotta make sure that man of mine doesn't get himself all bruised and achy. I've got to look out for my love life."

"Go, go, go."

"I can work another half hour and still make it."

"No, I'm sure the rush is over, and Mr. Fort probably forgot about coming here. I'll just stick around until Officer Michaels picks up his ring, then close up. Once the game starts, this street is deserted enough to bowl down the middle. Thanks again for coming on such short notice, Cheryl. I really appreciate it."

A woman looking for screw-on earrings distracted Kelly for a few minutes, and she sold a sterling pair fashioned in three interlocking rings. The customer was so pleased Kelly made a mental note to make a few more of the same type. Many older women didn't have pierced ears.

Making change for the customer, she noted with satisfaction the stacks of bills; sales had been good for a Saturday morning. In fact, she had too much cash on hand for her own peace of mind. As soon as she was alone, she pulled out most of the larger bills and rolled them into a wad. Until she could check the register and get the receipts ready to drop in the night depository at the bank, the money could stay in her secret hiding place.

Shortly after opening her store, when every dollar could have meant the difference between staying open or going under, she'd painted the inside of an empty glass jar with dull gray paint. She put the bills in it now, putting it back on a shelf that held the chemicals of her trade. Sitting between a jar of powdered pumice and one of potassium sulphate, the hidden money would probably escape the notice of even clever thieves. She took all the precautions possible on her shoestring budget. Her supply of silver and gold was housed in a safe-deposit box at the bank, and she rarely took out more than she'd use in a week.

A young couple wandered into the store, gave a few disinterested glances to her stock, and left hand in hand, obviously interested only in each other. Young lovers were habitual browsers in the Campus Town shop, but today they made Kelly feel old and out of touch.

If she'd ever been young enough to kill time making eyes at a boy, she'd forgotten it.

Why did she feel so irritable? Business had been great that morning, Cheryl was fun to work with, and the prospect of a whole afternoon catching up on jobs that needed doing in her little apartment above the store was a pleasant one. So what if Brian Fort had stood her up? Kelly sighed.

"So much for ego trips," she said aloud, smiling ruefully.

The thought of designing a setting for a member of one of Detroit's wealthy old families had been exciting, a professional coup that could've led to even better commissions. She had a right to feel disappointed that Brian Fort hadn't come. Over an hour late now, he'd undoubtedly gone right to the stadium, forgetting all about her.

Well, her self-confidence wasn't so fragile that Mr. Fort was going to ruin her day. She usually closed at noon on Saturday, and it was past that. Where was Officer Michaels? He'd been in a frenzy all week, checking in several times to make sure the ring would be done in time for the big evening he was planning.

Figuring that he'd pick it up when his job allowed, Kelly decided to wait. She liked being alone in her shop; it gave her a chance to stand on the customer side of the counter and view the displays with a supercritical eye, checking for details that weren't up to her standards.

Not bad, she thought, trying to take in the effect the store might have on a stranger. She'd tried for an art deco look, using more imagination than cash to achieve it. The shop had housed a used-book dealer before she leased it; the walls had been unpainted for at least a quarter of a century and the floor covered with cracked tiles. She'd torn out shelving, filled holes in the plaster, and painted the walls herself, using an off-white shade. With the help of a friend she laid carpet remnants in three shades of gray ranging from a soft dove to dark charcoal, arranging them in wide stripes on the floor. Another friend, an instructor in the art department, had painted a silhouette of a flapper on the center wall, using the same shades of gray with marvelous success. The clock, a geometric shape bought in peeling but workable condition at an auction, was repainted in charcoal, giving the finishing touch to the decor. Even after three years, it was still chic.

She'd been fortunate to find used display cases for sale in a small

13

neighborhood grocery store in Wyandotte, her hometown. She'd been delighted to get the battered pieces. The glass was still clear and uncracked, responding well to her energetic polishing. The wood she painted with gray enamel; the original surface was too rough to warrant stripping and varnishing.

This season her jewelry was set off by velvet draping in her favorite shade of emerald green, but it would be changed several times during the year. A piece that sat for months on a dark background might sell immediately displayed on pastel. The shelves weren't as full as she liked them; tomorrow had to be a work day. Her supply of men's rings was greatly diminished, and there was so little time between the fall rush and the holiday season.

Noting the time with a renewed twinge of irritation, she decided to begin the closing process while she waited for the policeman. She knew he was on duty and could only drop in when he had a spare moment, but she didn't want to stay open until his shift ended at three o'clock. She'd carry all the trays of better jewelry back to the safe, tally the receipts, and vacuum the carpet. If he still wasn't there, he'd have to buzz her apartment to get his ring.

Starting with a tray of rings, she began transferring her stock to the safe. Although she thought of herself as a silversmith, the lure of gemstones was growing stronger, and her jewelry included as many as she could afford: spinel with rubylike color; zircons, the poor man's diamond; turquoise; golden topaz; amethyst; pink tourmaline; and opal with bits of fire locked in the stone. Her bookshelf was crowded with books on gems, and she never missed a chance to learn more about them. The opportunity to set a stone for a member of the Fort family had been too good to be true—now literally so, since he hadn't kept his appointment.

What kind of boor didn't even bother calling to break an appointment, she wondered, growing more angry as she hastily deposited trays of jewelry in the safe. She'd called Cheryl to work because of that appointment, and she'd worn an overly warm blazer with lined flannel slacks just to look more professional for her thoughtless patron. Now she was hot and annoyed, all because one of Detroit's ruling class didn't have an ounce of consideration. She slammed the heavy door of the old-fashioned steel safe, twirling the dial with a vengeance.

Looking over her workroom, larger and even more satisfying

than the public section of her business, she felt a familiar eagerness to finish a silver bracelet that only needed a final buffing. Not for the first time she wondered if she had a split personality. In the store a piece of lint on the carpet or a smudge on a glass case was a personal affront, but here in her workshop an outsider would think a cyclone had hit. The room was roughly divided into three areas. The business area held the safe, her desk, files, and a layout bench with materials and patterns she used in designing. The largest working space was allotted to her workbench and the special equipment for casting, drawing wire, forging, hammering, rolling, and pressing. The third section was walled in with a vented fan for safety in polishing and finishing. Financing the equipment she needed to be a jeweler had been a harder struggle than building her stock, and she was proud of her workshop, however chaotic it might look. It did need a good cleaning and reorganizing, though, and she sighed at the thought of yet another demand on her time.

The buzzer on the door sounded, and she grabbed a little box from her desk, snapping it open for a last glimpse at the delicate engagement ring.

"It's about time you got here," she teased, rushing out.

It wasn't Officer Michaels.

"Sorry," the rather surprised man in front of her said, smiling at her discomfort as blood rushed to her cheeks.

"Oh, I thought you were—I have a ring all ready for—well, I'm sorry. I was expecting someone else," she said, as close to a stammer as her habitual composure allowed.

Sometimes when she designed a piece of male jewelry, she imagined the man she'd like to see wearing it, and now here he was, standing in her store, amusement and curiosity flickering across his face. His hair was as dark as hers, casually styled around a strong face, his eyes also dark under arched brows. He was so wholly male that he could wear a medallion around his neck and look like a knight groomed for combat, but his fingers were long and agile-looking, perfect for the exotic bloodstone ring she'd once designed. The ring's buyer had been an obnoxious man who reminded her of a weasel; after six months she still regretted selling it to him. This man could have worn it like a badge of honor.

"I'm late, but I think you were expecting me."

15

"Expecting you," she echoed, feeling like a total idiot when he held his hand out to her.

She had to switch the ring box to her left hand, extending the right one awkwardly, aware that her palm felt sweaty against his cool, hard grasp. Knowing that limp handshakes were bad business, she'd taught herself to clasp hands firmly, but she wasn't at all sure what to do when a person didn't let go. That's exactly what he was doing, keeping her hand locked in his while he looked her over with a thoroughness that made her even more uncomfortable.

I hope you like what you're seeing, she wanted to say, but instead forced herself to be courteous.

"Can I help you with something?"

"Oh." He seemed to remember that he had her hand and released it. "Sorry, your eyes surprised me."

"My eyes?"

"They're green. Authors like to write about green eyes, but it's unusual to find someone who actually has them, especially with black hair."

She laughed a little nervously.

"My driver's license says hazel. They seem to change color."

"Well, I like today's color."

"Thank you."

Damn, her cheeks felt hot! Was she actually blushing? Thank heavens Cheryl wasn't still working. The scheming little matchmaker would never let her hear the end of it.

"I had a business problem this morning and got a late start. I thought I'd get here on time, but an accident on I 94 really snarled the football traffic. I hope you still have time for me."

"You're Mr. Fort," she said weakly. "I'm Kelly Valentine."

"Yes, I recognize you. I saw your picture in *Jewelry News* when you got the Crafts Council award. Your bracelet reminded me a little of Anna Lustead's early work."

"You've heard of her?"

"Don't look so stunned. Some of us amateurs know a little about the jewelry field."

"Of course, there's no reason why you shouldn't. I didn't mean to imply . . ."

"That a Fort can't appreciate anything that isn't green and crinkly?"

16

His sudden defensiveness rattled her even more.

"I'm sorry," she said quickly. "I don't know enough about you to imply anything."

To her relief he laughed.

"We're off to a great start: I apologize, you apologize. Can we skip the next round? I'm still hoping to get to the game by half time. Some people are meeting me there."

"Of course, Mr. Fort. You said something on the phone about a gem."

She tried not to be so aware of him, his chest looking broad and muscular in a deep burgundy sweater, the navy jacket draped over his arm, his square white teeth that Cheryl would have adored.

"Let me show you."

He pulled a small cloth bag from his pocket and loosened the drawstring, carefully placing the gem on the glass top.

"An emerald," she said, awed in spite of her determination to appear nonchalant.

"It's only a little over a carat," he said casually, "but it's high-grade Colombian."

"May I?" she asked, picking it up when he nodded approval.

She wasn't as expert as she'd like to be, but with her small lens she couldn't detect the slightest tinge of yellow or blue.

"It's lovely," she said, holding it in the palm of her hand, almost consumed with eagerness to design a setting for such a beautiful stone.

"What I have in mind is something sentimental, but not fussy," he explained earnestly. "There's a rush on this, I'm afraid. Before we talk designs, can you clear your schedule to have it done for me by October nineteenth?"

"Yes, I'm sure I can manage that," she said with forced reserve. "Do you want it delivered, or will you be picking it up?"

Why was that question important? she asked herself impatiently. He was only a customer, and she could easily send the finished piece by registered mail.

"I'll come for it," he said with a grin that was almost mischievous. "What I have in mind is a pendant."

Women wore pendants. Her eyes flickered involuntarily over his strong, tanned fingers resting on the counter, angry at herself for the stab of disappointment she felt. She should be thrilled at the chance

17

to set such a gorgeous gem. It was silly to stand there imagining how it would look on his hand instead of paying attention to business.

"I have a design book. Would you like to look at it?"

"Actually I have a few rough sketches of my own. I was hoping you wouldn't mind looking at them and offering some suggestions. You can probably interpret what I want better than I can draw it."

He took some folded sheets from his jacket pocket and extended them to her.

"It's for a gift," he explained. "I don't want the stone to get lost in a lot of elaborate gold work, but it should have a certain sentimentality. No, that's not the right word. You'll think it's for a doddering old woman. I guess what it needs to show is deep feeling, love."

He wants it for a woman he's in love with, Kelly thought, startled by her own disappointment. Here was the professional opportunity of a lifetime. She was an idiot to care who'd wear the thing.

"I'd prefer yellow gold," he said, thoughtfully fingering the gem that lay between them.

His sketches were surprisingly good, taking into account the square shape of the emerald and wisely avoiding a circular pendant. His design would call for some skillful wire work, but she was sure she could handle it.

"I do have one question," she said thoughtfully, brushing aside a strand of hair that fell forward as she bent over the paper. "Would you consider a few changes to make it more delicate? Here, I can show you better with a pencil."

"Please do. I didn't expect my sketches to serve as a working design, or I could have gone to any jeweler."

"It's nice of you to say that. I'll need all the encouragement I can get to work with such a beautiful stone."

I don't believe I said that, she thought angrily to herself. For years she'd worked to get away from the awful habit of putting herself down, and now that she had a great opportunity, she was sounding like an insecure beginner.

"There," she said, finishing some changes and pushing the sketch toward him. "I think that may be what you have in mind."

"Incredible," he said, smiling. "Just like that you improved my drawing a hundred percent."

18

"It was a good design before I touched it," she said, knowing this was true.

She couldn't resist picking up the emerald again, holding it on her palm while she tried to visualize it in the setting sketched on the paper.

"I can't wait to start working on it."

Her enthusiasm slipped out, but it seemed to please the tall man leaning with one elbow on her counter.

"I have to meet my friends," he said, "but maybe after the game we could . . ."

The door banged inward, startling them both, and Kelly instinctively clutched the gem in her fist. Before either of them could react, two men were inside the shop, pulling down the shade on the door, waving heavy black handguns in a threatening way.

"My God," Kelly gasped, too stunned to know if she was afraid.

"Don't make a move," a tall beanpole of a man in tattered tan pants and a dirty yellow jacket warned.

Kelly doubted if she could.

"All we want is a little contribution," the second man said, fingering his beard and chuckling as though he'd said something clever.

His beard! He was the man with the beard, the blond with the odd brown whiskers.

"You were across the street most of the morning," she blurted out. "All morning."

"You didn't see me no place around here."

"You idiot!" his partner snapped. "I told you to stay out of sight."

"Hey, I had to case the joint!"

"Stop talking like you're playing Al Capone and check the cash register. You two, move very, very slowly toward that clock. Keep your hands in sight in front of you."

Kelly was moving, but her legs weren't acting on her orders. What happened to people when they got too scared? Heart attack? No, she had to be too young for that. What if she wet her pants? She'd die—of embarrassment. Brian Fort was moving slowly toward the wall, his face guardedly wary. She hoped his calmness was catching. Hands extended, she kept her fists tightly clenched, frantically aware that she had ten thousand dollars worth of emerald biting into her palm.

19

"I'd better search 'em," the whiskered one said, still fumbling with the register, trying to figure out how to open it.

"Search them for what, you jackass?" his partner snapped. "Get the money."

"I just thought it'd be fun."

He laughed through his teeth, making Kelly feel a little nauseated. If that foul creature touched her, she'd kick him where it mattered the most. The thought of his beefy hands anywhere near her made her so mad she almost forgot how scared she was.

"Can't you do anything right?" the tall robber asked, moving over to release the cash drawer himself. "Now empty it."

"Hell, there's not much here, Fred."

"Call me by name, why don't you! Get what there is. What we really want is the gold and silver."

"Easy," Fort whispered so softly Kelly just barely heard him. "Do as they ask."

"Damn, there ain't fifty dollars here," Whiskers said.

"Get on with it!"

Brian Fort was beside her, so close their elbows brushed. With so little in the cash drawer, he must think she had a poor business. He couldn't know she'd hidden most of the day's receipts. Would she ever get a chance to explain that to him? It was a ridiculous thing to be worrying about during a robbery.

"Okay, miss," the thin man said, "we don't want trouble. Just tell us where your bullion is, and we won't have to hurt you."

"My bullion! You make it sound like I'm a bank."

"Where?" he insisted.

"In the safe, but there's a time lock. It won't open until Monday at eight."

Was that a sigh she heard beside her? It was a reckless bluff—one that could backfire if these men knew anything about safes—but she was getting angrier every minute. She wasn't going to hand her jewelry over to them. It was insured, but it'd take months to build up her stock again.

"You two, get down on your knees slowly."

She sensed the man beside her slowly bending and reluctantly did the same, hoping he didn't hear her knee creak as she did.

"Now lie flat on your faces. Benny, watch them while I check the safe."

"Thought you said not to use names," the other thief complained.

"Get over here."

The carpet would make her slacks look like a cotton field, she thought, then wondered why she kept thinking about piddling little things. Was it a defense mechanism her brain used to keep her from passing out with fear? She looked up and saw the bearded Benny gazing at something outside the window. Impulse more than reason prompted her to slide her hand under her breasts, quickly shoving the emerald between two blouse buttons into a safe pocket made by her bra. Unless the thieves really did search her, they wouldn't get the gem.

The string of obscenities coming from the back room did nothing to quiet her fears.

"Get that broad in here. Time locks weren't invented when this safe was made."

"You'd better do as they say," Fort urged.

So much for heroes rescuing damsels in distress, she thought unfairly, knowing she didn't want him to risk getting shot. Her slacks had more lint than she'd expected, she noticed as she stood, again amazed that her mind kept noting useless facts right in the middle of a catastrophe. She should be memorizing the thieves' appearances so she could identify them in a lineup and testify against them in court. Was the brown beard real? Had she seen a mole on the other crook's neck? Why didn't they have enough sense to wear nylon stockings or ski masks over their faces? Didn't they know witnesses could recognize them later?

Or didn't they plan to leave any witnesses? That was it! They planned to kill both of them as soon as she opened the safe. She'd never find out what Brian Fort had started to ask her.

"Just open the safe, lady, and there won't be any trouble," Fred said, gesturing with his gun.

"Yes, yes, I will."

Her mind was racing in circles, all concern for her property gone. He was going to kill both of them, but now that she knew it there had to be some way to stop him. Any other day the shop would've had customers; only on football Saturdays was Ann Arbor's campus area a ghost town. One more customer was coming, she remembered: Officer Michaels. After an instant of relief, she felt worse than before. They might kill him too, and he was supposed to give his fiancée a ring that evening.

Standing in front of the massive black safe, she was so nervous she really did forget the combination for a moment. Trying to rally her thoughts, she let her fingers move the dial at random, pretending distress when it failed to open.

"Unless you want that pretty nose punched in, you'd better get that box open," the thief threatened.

"I'm trying!"

She really did try, but her hand was shaking and twice she failed to open it, having to start over as his snarls became more and more menacing. He grabbed her shoulder in a viselike grip and shook her so hard she expected the emerald to drop from its hiding place between her breasts.

"I'm really trying, but you've made me so nervous I absolutely have to go to the restroom," she explained desperately, giving the performance of her life as she partially doubled over and squeezed her legs together.

It wasn't all acting. Her only experience with robberies had been watching police shows on TV, and they didn't show how fear caused bladder problems. When he looked a little uncertain, she gave it another try.

"I can open it in less than a minute, but not when I have to go so badly. It's right over there, and there's no window."

"All right, but make it quick and don't shut the door."

"I have to shut the door!"

"Leave it open two inches so I know you're not going to lock yourself in. Any tricky stuff from you, and your customer will regret it."

"No funny stuff," she said with forced meekness.

As long as the safe was locked, the thieves needed her alive. She made her now-urgent call last as long as she dared, washing her hands with elaborate care afterward, cringing when she heard an angry demand that she come out immediately. The brief delay hadn't given her a single practical idea; she definitely couldn't use the lid of the toilet tank as a bullet shield.

"Nice workroom you have here," Fred said, scowling. "I bet we could get the safe open a lot quicker if I used some of these tools."

"I don't think jeweler's tools will work on the safe."

22

"They will on you."

The tumblers seemed to fall like the hands of fate, and all too soon the lock released the heavy steel door.

"Pull everything out," the thief ordered.

She obeyed, noticing as she bent down to remove the trays that he was wearing heavy suede hiking boots, well worn but obviously an expensive brand. Was he one of the desperate unemployed, a habitual criminal, or a kook out for kicks? Which would be better for her?

"Do you do this for a living?" she asked, trying for a normal everyday tone but squeaking a little.

"Where's the gold you work with?" he asked impatiently, ignoring her question.

"Here, in this box."

"That's it?"

"What do you expect when you rob a small operation like mine?"

"I expect to get away with it," he said sarcastically. "Unless you want me to leave you stuffed in the safe, dump those bracelets in this bag."

He handed her a heavy-duty plastic lawn sack.

"You must have thought you were robbing Cartier."

He only ignored her.

"What's that?" he asked when the buzzer on the front door sounded.

"My shop door," she answered without thinking, a cold dread stabbing the pit of her stomach.

Closing her eyes, expecting to hear a gun go off, she realized that Fred had run to the front of the building, leaving her alone. With blind haste she threw the partially loaded bag into the safe, tossed in the trays that weren't in the sack, and slammed the door. They could force her to open it again, but she wasn't going to make the robbery easy for them.

"Get out here," the bearded Benny yelled at her from the doorway.

The back exit was closer to her, but he was waving the gun, gesturing with a kind of wild-eyed frenzy that terrified her. When she moved too slowly, he took a step closer and yanked her in front of him.

Officer Michaels was standing by the door looking angry and

ineffective, and Brian Fort was still on the floor with Fred's knee on the small of his back and a gun touching his head.

"Make her get the bag," Fred hissed frantically.

"I don't see it," Benny shrieked.

"It's by the safe."

"The safe is shut. The damn broad shut the safe, Fred. What do we get out of this now? Tell me that, what do we get out of this now?"

"Shut up and keep the broad in front of you. Mr. Policeman, we're walking out with two hostages. You make a move to follow, and they're dead. Now get up very, very slowly, mister. One wrong move and the girl is dead."

Kelly believed them. They were acting like hoods in an Abbott and Costello rerun, but she was scared witless. With a slowness that showed he was trying to find a way out, Fort rose to his knees and then to his feet, looking powerful and dangerous beside the tall but scrawny thief. He glanced in her direction with a resigned expression and walked slowly toward the door with the barrel of the gun pressing against his kidney.

Would he have done something foolish and heroic if she hadn't been in danger? Kelly didn't know, but she hoped not.

The strong stench of her captor bothered her more than the gun poking against her spine. Did the man ever wash? No wonder he ate breakfast at the pizza place. He must live on garlic and beer.

Suddenly she felt sorry for Officer Michaels. All he wanted was his ring, and he was being forced to watch a crime being committed. There wasn't a darn thing he could do, either.

"They didn't get it," she whispered hoarsely as Benny steered her toward the door, his grip almost cutting off the circulation in her arm. "The box beside the register. Take it!"

His curiosity piqued, Benny stopped and almost went back to see what he'd missed, but his partner snapped at him furiously.

"Get going! If you try to follow, cop, you'll have two bodies on your hands."

This wasn't really happening. She was having a vivid dream, she tried to convince herself. On the far corner, a town character was talking to himself staring into space, oblivious of the world around him. Of all the people in this neighborhood who could have been out on the street now, it had to be him. She shook her head, trying

24

to grasp that she really was being pushed along a familiar but strangely deserted sidewalk, past the Oriental novelty shop, the windows of a large textbook store, the corner sandwich hangout, and beyond the branch bank where she should be making her deposit.

Their van was a nondescript dark blue, the paint powdery on her hand when she tried to steady herself beside the door. The other two men, hostage and thief, were already inside, and a third sat behind the wheel. Benny ordered her into the vehicle, pushing so roughly on her rear as she climbed in that she stumbled forward on her hands. More furious than fearful now, she crouched defiantly, determined never to cower in front of an animal like him.

He laughed at her.

"What the hell's going on?" the driver yelled. "Who are these people?"

"Just get going. Fast!"

"Not with them in my van, I won't. Are you two crazy?"

"Go! The cops know. They can't touch us as long as we have them."

"That's kidnapping. Heavy stuff, FBI."

"We'll throw them out when it's safe. Drive!"

CHAPTER TWO

Partly pushed by Benny and partly thrown by the motion of the vehicle, Kelly went tumbling toward the rear of the van, her fall broken by the most welcome pair of arms she'd ever felt.

"You don't have to get rough with her," Brian said tensely.

"Sit there and shut up, both of you," Fred snapped, his face pasty white as he crouched and tried to keep his balance.

"We gotta get rid of 'em," the driver insisted, careening around a corner so recklessly the two hostages were thrown together.

"Stay cool," Brian whispered, cushioning her from the jolting ride by holding her against him.

"Slow down!" Fred screamed.

"We gotta get out of here and dump them two."

"You stupid creep, the cops aren't looking for this van. You're gonna get us busted on a traffic rap." He stood and glanced at the road ahead for an instant. "Stop for that light!"

He did, nearly throwing Fred off balance. Kelly felt the man holding her ready himself to act, but there wasn't time.

"Use your head, Mack," Fred said, trying to reason with the driver and watch them at the same time. "Just go the way we planned."

"Is that what you were doin' when you grabbed 'em?"

"A cop walked in on us. Do you think he'd tip his hat and let us walk out? We had no choice."

The driver gunned the motor, but after the light changed he started driving at a legal speed.

"Where's the money? I don't see no bag fulla gold. Some crappy idea. Hit a little store, you said. Go in when everybody's off at the game, you said. No sweat, you said. Well, I'm sweating, Dibble. I'm sweating a whole lot."

26

"That's all you're doing! You're sure as hell not thinking. Why don't you give them my address too? It's not bad enough you brought your pea-brained brother-in-law with us. You know what he did? Take a guess! He hung around across from the damn store all morning. How many people saw him, do you think? How many will remember that beard of his?"

"We needed another man," Mack alibied halfheartedly.

"A man, not a moron!"

"Hey, we ain't all college men," Benny protested, turning around in the seat beside the driver to hurl a mouthful of contempt at the crouching would-be thief. "You're the jerk who let the broad lock all the stuff back in the safe."

"Shut up!"

Fred eased himself into a sitting position on the floor, warily watching his two hostages and keeping the weapon braced on his jutting knee. The front seat was the only seat, the van apparently serving as some kind of handyman's carryall. Several corrugated cardboard boxes were pushed against one side, and a long gray metal box, probably holding tools, was against the opposite side. A pair of greasy overalls were wadded up in a back corner near Kelly.

"You mean you had all the gold and stuff and lost it?" Mack asked.

"Sure, the smart college boy blew it, how's that?" Benny jeered. "Had us a sack fulla gold jewelry, and he let it get away. I'm the only one who got anything. Cleaned the cash register."

"How much?" his brother-in-law demanded to know.

"Fifty bucks or so."

"Fifty!"

He turned his head, and the van strayed toward oncoming traffic, barely missing a pickup truck.

"Watch where you're going!" Benny shrieked. "You call *me* dumb!"

"We could do five to twenty hard time, and you jokers tell me we got fifty bucks!"

"Hey, maybe the guy's loaded," Benny suggested.

"With our luck, he only has credit cards," Mack moaned.

"Toss your billfold here," Fred said, sounding a little less gloomy. "Move slowly. I can't miss hitting one of you at this range."

"I'll do better than that," Brian offered. "All I do have are credit cards, but this ring is worth at least five thousand. Take it and let us go."

"I'll take it, all right, but I'll say when you go. You can't bargain with this, mister."

Fred gestured with the gun, running the other hand through thinning, nondescript hair. "Toss it here," he hissed impatiently.

The ring was a golden lion's head with two small emeralds as eyes, apparently snug-fitting because it took a while for Brian to work it off his finger. When he did toss it, the ring went far to Fred's right. The thief didn't grab for it, instead letting it bounce against the back of the seat and fall to the ribbed rubber flooring.

"Now your watch," he ordered sharply, "and no cute tosses. Slide it this way with your foot. Slowly."

The heavy timepiece had traditional hands, not a computerized quartz movement, and Kelly felt his reluctance to part with it.

"My grandfather's. Accurate to within two seconds every thirty days. The Swiss know how to make watches, but it mostly has sentimental value today. You'll want my chain too, I suppose?"

Not waiting for confirmation, he slipped his sweater over his head and unbuttoned the top buttons of his white shirt, sliding the chain, obviously solid gold and valuable, over his head rather than releasing the clasp.

He wants them to forget about his billfold, Kelly realized, wondering what it contained that was more valuable than the expensive pieces of jewelry he was giving up.

His identity! If they looked at his driver's license, they just might be smart enough to recognize his name. Judging by the way they'd operated so far, it was a fifty-fifty chance, but she sensed Brian's concern. While he pulled the sweater back over his head with a lot of unnecessary squirming, she pressed hard against his side, reaching behind him to grope for the billfold in his back pocket. Running her fingers along his waist to let him know what she was doing, she felt his weight shift, making it easy for her to slip her fingers into his pocket and palm the leather case.

Now that she had it, what could she do with it? Hiding it under the greasy overalls was the best possibility, but she couldn't reach them without the risk of being seen. While Brian talked and straightened his clothing, she slid the billfold under her bottom, feeling like a chicken sitting on a turkey egg.

"Now the billfold," Fred demanded.

"Okay," Brian said casually agreeing and reaching for his back pocket. "Oh, no."

He brought his empty hand back in sight.

"I must have lost it during the robbery, maybe when you had me lie on the floor."

"Don't give me that crap."

"Well, check for yourself. It was in my back pocket, and now it isn't."

"Benny, get back here."

The bearded thief maneuvered his chunky body over the seat with obvious enthusiasm. "Told you we should search 'em," he said with anticipation.

"Stay here, you idiot," Fred said. "Don't get between my gun and them. You, mister, lie on your belly and don't make any funny moves. The gun is on the girl."

Kelly squirmed uncomfortably on the billfold as Benny searched Brian, then she forced herself to be motionless, hoping they wouldn't search her.

"It's gone."

"It can't be. I remember seeing the bulge on his hip when he climbed in the van. It's here in the van somewhere. Check the broad."

"Give it to them, Kelly," Brian said quickly.

His use of her name startled her. Well, if this situation didn't put them on a first-name basis, nothing would.

Benny was standing over her, bits of spittle clinging to the whiskers near his mouth. Remembering the lump of emerald between her breasts, she didn't doubt that he'd find it if Fred let him loose on her.

"Don't let him touch me. I'll give it to you," she said reluctantly, extracting the billfold from under her.

"When are we getting rid of 'em?" Mack asked angrily, turning his head to see what was happening in the rear.

"Watch the road!" Fred yelled.

"Well, I gotta know, do you still want me to go to Dexter?"

"Yes, do just like we planned." To his hostages Fred said, "No fast moves. Just slide the wallet towards me, same as the watch. Let's see what kind of bundle you were trying to hold out."

29

Brian pulled himself back into a sitting position beside her.

"Fifty-dollar bills," Fred said with some satisfaction. "Let's see. Fifty, hundred, one-fifty, two, two-fifty and a couple of tens. Not bad, but worth a lot less than the ring and watch. So why were you so eager to hide this?"

Fred began ripping it apart, searching all the compartments, making a pile of the credit cards and other contents.

"I don't get it. You play games with a coupla hundred bucks, but point out how much the ring's worth. Look at these, Mack."

Mack glanced at the cards, then pulled off the road and stopped so quickly Benny lost his footing and narrowly missed crushing Fred under his bulk.

"Do you know what you idiots have done?" Mack asked. "You've snatched Brian Fort!"

"Who?" Benny asked.

"Fort. Owns a basketball team. Big money."

Mack seemed to be hyperventilating, staring back at them with eyes that bulged out under a heavily ridged forehead. Kelly wouldn't have trouble spotting that face in a police lineup, but would she ever have a chance to do it?

"You're mistaking me for Bradford Fort. A lot of people do that."

"Let me see those cards again," Fred said, reaching for them with one hand while he scratched his ankle with the nuzzle of the gun.

"Hey, I hearda him," Benny said. "There's a street named after his ol' man or someone."

"If you mean Fort Street, it was the western border of the old British fort, nothing to do with our family's name," Brian said with resignation.

"What do you do for a living?" Fred asked, still thoughtfully fingering the cards.

"I have a traveling job."

"He probably travels from bank to bank counting his money," Mack said bitterly. "I used to know a cook who worked in one of them fancy Grosse Pointe mansions. I know who this guy is: Damon Fort's son."

Fred whistled between his teeth.

"Get this wreck going. I've gotta think about this."

"Let her go," Brian said. "One of us is all you need."

30

Their captor didn't bother to answer. He did that a lot, Kelly noticed, all her untried liberal leanings put to the test. She'd always thought of the inmates behind the massive walls of Jackson's prison as victims of their poor environment. But now that she was a real victim of criminals, she had no interest in their psychological make-up and only wanted to survive. What were the chances of getting away alive? In the store things had happened so fast, she'd reacted without really believing they'd be harmed. Now she wasn't sure.

Benny was pawing through the contents of the billfold now, making Kelly wonder if he could read. He scratched his bearded cheek with a gasoline card, then bent another between his grimy-nailed thumb and forefinger until it snapped in half.

"Give me those," Fred said impatiently.

"My cousin is gonna be mad if I bring these two to his garage," Mack warned nervously. "He only said we could hide the van there for ten percent of a clean operation. Hostages are heavy, man, too heavy for me."

"So the chicken wants out," Benny said. "Geez, I told my sister you was worthless, but she had to marry you anyway. She always was stupid."

"Shut up, Benny. I don't want any family fights," Fred said.

They obeyed Fred. Everyone always obeyed Fred. Was that good or bad, Kelly wondered. It was good if he kept Benny away from her, bad if he decided not to let them go.

Brian's arm was around her shoulders, his fingers lightly caressing her arm as though trying to give her a message. She imagined the two of them rushing the crooks, fighting it out the way super-heroes did in cartoons, bullets flying but missing them, of course, as they zapped the bad guys with devastating punches. Considering that she hadn't punched anyone since Bud Warsky had tried to steal her jump rope in the fourth grade, it was a pretty ambitious fantasy. Feeling the weight of Brian's arm made her believe for a few soothing moments they were an invincible team. He was a man who'd fight when cornered, but not without provocation. She felt a protectiveness in his nature that might have challenged her independence if they hadn't been thrown together in such a hazardous situation.

The van was traveling on a rougher surface now, the old springs failing to cushion the bone-shaking bounce in the rear end. Kelly's

31

old enemy, motion sickness, started to assert itself, the faint nausea beginning in her head and gradually getting a grip on her innards.

"Please, please, please," she prayed aloud, hoping against hope that she wouldn't be sick.

"Are you all right?" Brian whispered anxiously.

"I get a little carsick sometimes," she confessed, feeling she'd better warn him.

Just in time the van slowed, eventually coming to a complete stop. If the dimness was any indication, they were inside a garage, but Kelly could only partially confirm this by glimpsing what looked like bare boards in front of the windshield. Benny hustled out, and the sound of a heavy overhead door banging shut made her jump. Unfortunately he returned to the van.

"I have to use a bathroom," Kelly said emphatically.

"You just went at the store," Fred said angrily.

"I was only stalling there," she said miserably. "Now I really have to."

"Too bad."

"I'm going to be sick."

"That's your problem."

"You can take me to a bathroom or scrub out the van."

The three men's argument was heavy on obscenities and light on compassion, but Mack finally agreed to take her into his cousin's house.

"He'll nail my hide to the wall if he finds out," he said gloomily.

"Any tricks, lady, and I'm going to let Benny work on your friend here for a while."

That Fred had an answer for everything, she thought angrily. Why didn't he go on a TV game show instead of playing cops and robbers?

The house, little more than a shack, wasn't in a town at all. It sat by itself against a background of fields and woods, although the main crop, if it was a farm, seemed to be wrecked autos and parts. The siding on the house had long ago been painted a particularly bilious shade of green, peeling now to show the pink underneath. Mack gripped her upper arm and hustled her through a side entrance into a kitchen that reeked of stale beer and cigarettes. Here dishwashing seemed to be a lost art, and she tried not to notice the litter of crusty dishes covering all available surfaces.

32

She slammed the bathroom door before her escort got any clever ideas about leaving it open two inches. The only good thing about the facility, aside from the lock on the door, was that it had ample supplies of soap and cold water, both of which she used liberally.

Mack was banging on the locked door, trying to find a threat potent enough to dislodge her, but she took time to look around for possible weapons. A cartridge of razor blades on the edge of the sink wasn't promising enough to make her extract it from a blob of used, whisker-specked shaving cream.

When she finally came out, Mack pushed her ahead of him at a trot, through the small side door of the garage and into the van, as though they were being chased by invisible gangbusters. It was so dark, she stumbled over Brian's foot, but he caught her in his arms, pulling her down on his lap and cradling her head against his chest so her ear was close to his lips.

"Are you all right?" he whispered.

"Yes, much better, thanks."

"Your hands are like ice."

"I washed in cold water."

"You're not ill?"

"No, it was only motion sickness. I'm not a good traveler, but I'm fine now."

Well, not quite fine, she thought, but cuddling on his lap was doing a lot for her mental health. She snuggled a bit closer to him, reveling in the warmth of his broad chest under her chilled fingertips.

"I don't think they'll let me go," he said, "but I'll try to get them to free you."

"They won't do it."

"No, probably not, but we'll think of something. Just follow my lead. Don't try anything rash."

"No."

She wrapped her arms around his back, wondering if that counted as rashness. Outside the three were debating heatedly, but just for a moment it didn't matter. She felt secure in Brian's arms, sinking against him with a warm, tingly feeling. How long had it been since she'd leaned on a man?

His chin brushed against her forehead, and she sighed deeply, amazed at her contentment. After Larry she'd been determined never to depend on a man again, but this didn't count. She was trapped in a terrible spot with this stranger, and three dangerous criminals could be planning to kill them. If his arms were momentarily reassuring, why shouldn't she stay where she was?

Tipping her head just a little, she met his lips descending on hers, their kiss as unreal as it was exciting. Any moment one of their captors might intrude on their solitude, but for a few precious seconds, she welcomed the distraction he was creating.

"This is so crazy," she whispered as his hands slipped beneath her blazer to sensuously massage the tense muscles of her back. Heat seemed to course from his fingertips, and she sighed with pleasure at the sensation.

"Yes, it is," he answered, then his mouth fastened on hers, his tongue flicking against the roof of her mouth, sending shivery tingles down her spine.

Kelly remembered reading somewhere that fear could be a potent aphrodisiac but she hadn't believed it, certain that danger flushed away that kind of urge. Now she wasn't sure. Here she was in a dark, stuffy van with a stranger, and she couldn't get enough of his kisses.

"Oh, Brian," she said when a sudden silence made them pause. "I didn't know being scared could affect me this way."

"I'd like to think I have something to do with it."

He trailed soft kisses across her forehead, brushing against each lid until she caught his lower lip with hers, nibbling gently. His kiss grew more ardent, and she could feel the vibrations all the way to her toes. Only when the door of the van was yanked open did he release her, easing her off his lap to the hard floor beside him.

"I still think it's a mistake," Mack grumbled.

"You're an old woman," his brother-in-law sneered.

"You don't have any objection to being rich, do you?" Fred asked.

"You said that about the jewelry shop too. You blew that, and you'll probably blow this," Mack said morosely.

"You can back out, but we're taking the van. If we get caught, the cops will hear whose it is and who drove it away from Ann Arbor."

Fred sounded confident, not even bothering to make his threat sound menacing.

"He's gotcha there," Benny said chuckling.

"I can make it worth your while to leave the girl behind," Brian said.

She wasn't crazy about being called a girl, but she had to admit Brian's voice carried authority. The three men stopped wrangling and listened.

"We've got everything you had with you," Fred sneered to cover his interest.

"I have a credit card that's as good as cash with my signature. I can get money at any time in any large city in the country."

"We ain't exactly in no large city," Benny said.

"Twenty-five thousand cash if you let her go unharmed."

"Make it seventy-five, that much for each of us," Fred said skeptically.

"I can manage that," Brian said, "but only in Detroit. I don't have the connections here to put my hands on that much on a Saturday afternoon."

"Shit, there ain't that much cash in the whole town of Dexter," Benny said. "I'd rather keep the broad anyway."

"Shut up," Fred warned.

"Which card is gonna get you that money?" Mack asked.

He took the billfold from Fred and palmed all the cards, including the one Benny had snapped in half.

"The gold one."

"Sure, you're safe saying that," Mack said glumly. "The damn thing's broke."

"The number is still legible. That's all I need."

"You're putting us on."

"No, I can raise seventy-five thousand if you take me to Detroit."

"Well, we're not interested in no piddling seventy-five," Benny jeered. "We're goin' for a cool million from your ol' man."

"You'll never get it," Brian said flatly.

Kelly believed him. The others didn't.

"Let's quit talkin' and go," Mack said nervously. "I can't trust my cousin no farther than I can throw him if he comes back and sees these two."

Brian's hand was on her knee, his squeeze meant to be reassuring, but Kelly felt overheated and agitated, a condition his touch only aggravated.

"Can you tell me where we're going?" Brian asked, his tone too courteous to arouse their anger, but his contempt still obvious to Kelly.

"You'll find out when I want you to," Fred said arrogantly.

Benny stepped outside to close the garage door, then climbed into the van, settling down with his back against the empty passenger seat, facing Brian and Kelly with malicious pleasure visible on his pushed-in features. She decided the beard had to be real. No false whiskers put on for the day would be so scraggly—unless of course they had been bought in a costume shop as part of a werewolf outfit. His gun was stuck in a wide belt, but when he sat a roll of fat overlapped it, the discomfort forcing him to draw it out.

Fred's gun was in his pocket, but Kelly wasn't forgetting it. In her mind she schemed to get possession of it and suspected Brian was doing the same. It was hopeless. Even if Mack wasn't armed, Benny was a blubbery arsenal, far too dangerous to tackle.

"Where are you going?" Fred asked, standing and bending over the driver's shoulder.

"Thought I'd pick up I 94 west. Save time."

"Are you crazy? We agreed to stick to the back roads."

"I was gonna as soon as we got to Jackson."

"If anyone saw this van near the shop, the freeway cops will be looking for us. That strip will be buzzing with them."

"Well, it's gonna take forever to get that far north on county roads."

"I can't steal no boat till it's dark anyhow," Benny said complacently.

The road wasn't as dippy as before, but Kelly worried about getting sick again. Fortunately she seemed to be all right, but an hour of riding on the floor make her squirm uncomfortably. Her back ached from sitting upright, but when she leaned back, the vibrations made her queasy. She changed position every few minutes, but her rump was getting tired of the hard floor, and she couldn't manage to look prim and be comfortable at the same time. Worse, she was acutely aware of every breath Brian took, every move he made. Her lips had a memory of their own, tingling from his very distracting kisses, and she restlessly shifted her limbs.

"Put your head on my lap. Try to get some sleep," Brian offered.

"No, you'd be too uncomfortable."

"Not as uncomfortable as I am watching you wiggle around like a Mexican jumping bean. Come here."

"Oh, baby, I got a nice soft lap," Benny jeered.

Ignoring him, Brian cautioned her with his eyes, patting his lap invitingly. Could she actually fall asleep in the middle of this mess? It was worth a try.

His thighs were firm under her cheek, and she tried not to be aware of how intimately she was resting against him. He brushed a strand of hair from her forehead, a muscle quivering slightly when she shifted her head. She wiggled some more, trying to be comfortable without bothering him, finally resting her hand between his leg and her cheek.

"Lie still," he said with gentle firmness.

How was she supposed to sleep with Benny's obscene leer behind her and Brian so invitingly close and masculine? Next time she was kidnapped she hoped only women were involved. No, she didn't, because then she wouldn't have this strange, giddy feeling to make her forget how frightened she was. At least his hand on her shoulder made her feel secure, and gradually she began to doze.

"We're stopping for food."

Brian's voice was pleasantly close, and she slowly shook off her grogginess.

"I was sure I wouldn't be able to sleep. How long have we been driving?"

"I'm not sure. They have my watch."

She glanced at hers, an inexpensive timepiece that hadn't tempted the thieves. No wonder she felt so hungry. It was nearly dinner time.

"I need gas," Mack said glumly.

"Stop at that station up ahead. Benny, you walk across the road and get us a bag of burgers and shakes while we fuel up."

"I ain't your errand boy."

"If you want food, get it. We're not stopping again."

"Gimme some money."

"Use what you got from the store."

"Hey, that's mine."

"Stupid, it's nobody's until this is finished, and then a few bucks won't mean anything."

"Yeah, I'll believe that when the money is in my hand," Mack said.

"I have to use the women's room," Kelly said, lying this time but hoping against hope that she might think of some way to get help if they let her go into the service station.

"Again!" Fred swore at her angrily.

"Women! Pains in the neck," Mack said unhappily.

"You have to let me go," she pressed.

"Go," Fred said looking at her with eyes that were drawn into narrow slits, "but if I think you're taking a minute too long, I'll let Benny do a little carving on your friend here."

She ran awkwardly, her legs stiff from riding on the floor, first to the outside door of the room then back to the tiny office to get the key hanging by the register. The only attendant was on duty outside servicing the van. Wherever they were, they'd left self-service stations with computerized gas pumps behind.

The tiny cubicle was surprisingly clean, only a sink and stool with no stall. An oval bar of hand soap was lying on the sink, her first break. The message she scrawled on the mirror was crude, but hopefully legible:

HELP KIDNAPPED
BLUE VAN NORTH
FORT AND VAL.

There wasn't room or time to smear her full name with the soap, but surely their abduction was on the news by now. Anyone within range of a radio should be able to figure out the message. The only trouble was the station didn't seem to have a booming trade. How long would it be before someone came into the restroom? The attendant wouldn't come at all unless he cleaned it before closing, and it looked clean already. Local customers wouldn't bother to use the facility, and the station surely wasn't on a major route for travelers.

What if someone did come and ignored the greasy scrawls on the mirror? She had to be sure her message attracted attention. A fat, full roll of tissue was on the roller, the only one in the room. Working with desperate haste she unrolled long ribbons of it and draped them liberally on the plumbing, the paper towel holder, and the doorknob. Anyone walking into the mess would be sure to yell for the owner. As final insurance, she flattened what was left of the tissue roll as well as she could and walked out clutching it tight under her armpit between her blouse and skin.

"About time," Fred snarled.

She couldn't look directly at Brian; the temptation to let him know what she'd done was too great.

The hamburgers Benny brought were greasy but filling, and when Kelly picked off the raw onions, discarding them on the paper wrapping, the bearded man instantly called for them. Mack ate as he drove, swerving over the middle line as he tried to unwrap a straw and poke it through the plastic lid into a chocolate milkshake. The tiny slit wouldn't part for him, and the lid flipped off, spilling the cold mix on his lap. Benny was the only one who laughed at his outraged cries.

"How can we get a note to your old man?" Fred asked Brian.

"You expect me to tell you that?" Brian asked, his tone making Kelly think she'd hate to have him mad at her.

"No, you don't have to," Fred said unpleasantly. "I can use the U.S. Postal Service. Just means you'll be freezing your ass a little longer. I'm patient. This is going to be worth waiting for."

"I'll tell you whatever you want to know after you let Kelly go. Just stop at the next service station and let her out."

"To call the cops. We ain't that dumb," Benny said.

"She doesn't know where you're taking me."

"Neither do you, hot shot. I like it that way."

"Fred, there's a little grocery store on the corner up there. Why don't I stop and get the stuff?"

"Okay. But no trips to the john for you, lady. This is a quick stop. Don't give me any trouble, or I'll forget to buy you a can opener."

Fred went up to talk with Mack in whispers, while Benny eyed her lecherously.

"Don't know why we can't have a little fun with the broad," he complained, but the others ignored him.

"It won't come to that," Brian assured her, covering her hand with his.

For some reason she believed him.

Nightfall came early in September, but the day already seemed a hundred hours long. Brian kept his arm around her, cushioning her head on his shoulder, but she'd never been more wakeful. Her eyes felt glued open, and she found herself counting seconds between winks, wondering how often her lids flickered when she wasn't paying attention. The air in the van was getting cold, and when she failed to repress a shudder, Brian insisted on draping his nylon jacket over her.

Even though Fred and Benny sat facing them, their eyes wary and their weapons at hand, the darkness made Kelly feel less like a caged animal. She was like a balloon exploding inside a papier-mâché shell, she thought, remembering the masks her troop made in Girl Scouts, puncturing the rubber skins with long hat pins and hearing the muffled pops. She was exploding inside, but she couldn't shatter the nerves of her captors with the noise.

Hating them was something entirely different from the way she'd come to despise Larry. With her ex-husband her hatred had been mixed with regrets, self-pity, lingering affection, and hurt. She hated the kidnappers with a razor-sharp, undiluted wrath, feeling violated by their eyes and words.

The ride went on and on and on, darkness the undoing of her vague sense of direction.

"Do you have any idea where we are?" she whispered.

"A long way from Ann Arbor." Brian patted her hand. "We've been traveling north and northwest. We shouldn't be too far from Lake Michigan, but I can't be sure exactly where we are."

"Benny, you'd better get in front and give directions," Fred said. "You're the one who knows this area."

"Damn right I do. Ain't a woods around here I ain't hunted. Crooked Lake, Larks Lake, I fished 'em all."

"I wish to hell you'd stayed in the woods," Mack mumbled.

"Me and a buddy heard they was hirin' at the Rouge plant. Never did get me no auto job though, but I liked working at Little Joe's okay."

"Until he threw you out for bothering his waitresses," his brother-in-law said.

"Knock it off, both of you. Benny, you'd better be damn sure you can find a boat, or I'll strangle you."

"Strangle Benny Strang. I like that." Mack sounded cheerful for the first time.

"Hey, you told 'em my name, *MacIntyre.*"

"It doesn't matter!" Fred said, grabbing Benny's sleeve when it looked like he'd go over the back of the seat and get the driver of the van. "In a few days we'll scatter and disappear."

"Right on. I got me a little piece up in Canada. I'm gonna build a cabin way up there, hunt all day and . . ."

"Forget that and show Mack where to go."

"This isn't a road. It's a cow path," Mack complained minutes later.

The hamburger was doing little tricks in Kelly's stomach, flip-flopping around in a bag of acid as the van jolted her from side to side, up and down.

"It's a dead end!" Mack screamed, slamming on his brakes and pitching all his passengers forward.

Brian reacted the fastest, throttling Fred and forcing him to drop the gun, using him as a shield.

"We don't much care what you do to ol' Fred," Benny said, "but the broad is set up for me like a pheasant in a rifle sight."

Unfortunately he was right.

"Tie his hands," Fred ordered when Brian was forced to release him, the rage in the thin man's voice making Kelly realize he was the most dangerous of the trio after all.

Benny ripped a strip from the greasy overalls and chuckled while he secured Brian's hands behind his back, shoving him down to the floor of the van.

"Dumb try," Brian whispered apologetically.

"Worth a shot," she assured him, fear running icy fingers down her spine.

"Now what?" Mack wailed. "You've got us lost, you cretin."

"I just gotta find the lake is all."

"How can you lose Lake Michigan?"

The van scraped a tree backing up, the only way to get out of the dead end.

"Where the hell are we?" Fred asked.

"I ain't been here in eight years. I'll get us there."

"If you know Lake Michigan like you know the woods, they're gonna scrape us off the beach next spring," Mack predicted.

"I can navigate them islands with my eyes closed."

"Keep them open," Fred warned dryly.

"If it wasn't for me, you'd hafta hole up and watch 'em day and night."

41

"Okay, you've had the one good idea of your life," Fred said impatiently. "Now let's get to the boat."

"Take a left," Benny said.

Gravel sprayed against the van as Mack took the corner, going only a short way before he was ordered to turn again.

The kidnappers were too busy arguing about the route to pay attention to anything she said, so Kelly didn't even bother to whisper.

"Why do they want a boat?"

"From what they said while you were gone, they intend to maroon us on one of the islands in the Beaver Island archipelago."

"Don't people live there?"

"On Beaver Island, yes, but some of the small islands only have summer homes, and a few are just small chunks of sand and rock, uncharted and largely deserted."

"But why take us to an island?"

"With the state police looking everywhere it's easier to abandon us than guard us. It's the off season. We could be stuck on an island for a long time."

"Meanwhile they ask for ransom?"

"Yes."

"Will your father pay to learn where we are?"

If his chuckle was meant to be reassuring, it wasn't.

."He may negotiate."

"Oh, great."

"I ain't getting into no rowboat," Mack was protesting loudly. "No way."

"Summer people are loaded. We'll get us a cabin cruiser," Benny said, sounding more and more excited. "There, pull off in the woods there. We gotta walk from here."

At Brian's insistence, Kelly kept his jacket, rolling the cuffs to free her hands; then she rather ineffectively helped him out of the vehicle.

Benny led the way, carrying the metal toolbox. The other two were right behind them, Fred's gun prodding Brian with wicked jabs. The paving gave way to sandy beach, filling Kelly's neat low-heeled pumps before she took three steps. She struggled along, sensing that this was the wrong time for delaying tactics.

"The dummies ain't got their dock out yet," Benny said with delight.

"Lucky for us." Mack sounded even more sour and unwilling.

Whitecaps were slapping against the shoreline, and the lake seemed to press forward, creeping closer with each rhythmic swell. It was late, past midnight, and the absence of lights on the shoreline and horizon were doubly ominous to a city girl used to the all-night glow of streetlights. The word *alien* took on a new meaning as Mack shoved her down the white pier and onto the boat.

Even a landlubber could tell it was a sturdy boat, the cabin protruding above the level of the deck. The kidnappers didn't give her time for sightseeing, though, ordering her down some steep steps into total darkness.

"Untie my hands," Brian whispered urgently, beside her but unseen as her eyes tried to adjust to the blacker darkness.

She found them by groping over his body, but the knot of shredded cotton stubbornly resisted her blind picking.

"It will take me a week to unravel it thread by thread," she said desperately.

"My eyes are getting used to the dark," he said patiently. "We seem to be in a little galley with the bunks at that end. See if you can find a drawer."

"Yes, yes, here's one. It opens."

"Good."

His low murmurs were the antifear tonic she needed.

"Be careful. If there is a knife, you could cut yourself," he warned.

"No, this boat has a very orderly cook. All the blades are pointing away."

Finding a serated blade was easier than using it, she discovered as she cautiously sawed away at the cloth bindings.

"Hurry," he urged.

"I don't want to slice your wrists."

"You won't."

Low, furious voices from above told the prisoners below it wasn't a snap to steal a boat.

"Will they get it started?" she asked.

"With the dumb luck they've been having, they probably will."

By the time she cut his wrists free, the coughing sputter of a cold motor drowned out the mutterings of the men.

"I wanna keep the broad with us," Benny said, immediately shushed by the others.

"Hell, old man Fort isn't gonna ransom a storekeeper."

Brian ran up the ladder, forgetting his hands were supposed to be tied.

"He'll ransom my fiancée," he said angrily, "but you let that creep anywhere near her, every state trooper in the country will be looking for you."

"We're leaving her with you," Fred said in a surly voice. "Do you think we listen to him?"

"Not unless you're as eager to get caught as he is," Brian said ominously.

"Look at that fog," Mack said nervously.

"Just a little mist is all," Benny said, sulking beside the motor.

"You guys are crazy to go out in this. I'm staying here," Mack insisted.

He scampered toward the dock, scrambling up on hands and knees and panting as he bent over the boarded walkway on all fours.

"Get back here," Benny yelled.

"I can't! I can't stand up in boats."

"Wait in the van then," Fred said angrily, "but you'd better be there when we get back."

"Sure," Mack said, still fighting for breath. "I want my share. I just can't handle boats."

"Did you check the fuel?"

"Plenty," Mack assured the leader. "Plenty."

"Get below," Fred ordered Brian, "and stay there. Right now I don't care if we dump you on the island or in the lake, so don't let me see you until we get there. No lights, either. Strang, let's see if you really can find this island."

Brian backed slowly down the steps, turning to take her in his arms as if it were the most ordinary thing in the world.

Danger is arousing, she thought as their lips met for a long, demanding kiss that made her melt against him. *Well, it's okay. After all, we're engaged.*

The boat left the dock with a sideways lurch, nearly causing them both to lose footing, but Brian locked her in his arms, slipping his hands under the two jackets she was wearing, his Windbreaker and her blazer.

"I'll keep you warm," he said softly, letting his lips slide down to the hollow of her throat, his kisses filling her with a wild joy that made her forget the motion of the boat for a few moments.

Then the vessel veered again, slapping against oncoming swells with a wild, jolting movement that filled Kelly's throat with burning bile. Pushing him away, she looked around frantically, unable to see much in the unlit cabin.

"There's a head over there," he said sympathetically, guessing her problem.

I need a john, not a head, she thought desperately, but he was guiding her through the darkness until she discovered they were the same thing. There in the bitter blackness misery consumed her as the violent motion of the waves made her forget Brian, the kidnapping, even her own name.

CHAPTER THREE

Lying curled in a fetal position on one of the narrow bunks, Kelly fingered the cool cloth Brian had put on her forehead and felt his hand on her shoulder. But she was beyond comfort.

Here she was, alone in a dark hole with a warm, caring, wholly appealing man, and the incessant battering of the waves had reduced her to a subhuman wreck.

Brian wiped her face with the cloth, but his tenderness only made her feel worse. How terrible for him to be stuck with her violent seasickness. He'd never want to kiss her again.

"Have you been sick like this before?" he asked.

"On my first boat ride, when I was seven," she croaked.

"Then you know it'll pass when we get to dry land," he crooned, trying to comfort her. "Just relax and hang in there. I'm going to gather some things together to use on the island."

Surrendering to total wretchedness, she was hardly aware of the stealthy sounds he made searching the cabin, only an occasional epithet telling her when he bumped into something.

"I can't find any matches," Brian said urgently.

"Is that important?" she moaned.

"Crucial."

He seemed to be searching the confined space inch by inch, coming over to check on her from time to time, much to her dismay. Her idea of relief was a spot where she could curl up all by herself, hide her sickness from him, and pass out.

A spate of particularly vivid profanity floated down to them over the menacing howl of the wind and waves.

"How can you lose a bleeding island?" Fred shrieked.

They didn't hear Benny's answer, but the patchy bits of the outer

46

world visible through the small portholes showed a swirling fog almost enveloping the vessel.

"I gotta turn on the running lights," Benny argued heatedly.

Somewhere in the far distance a foghorn moaned, a sound heard often on the strait that Detroiters called a river, but one that never failed to fill Kelly with foreboding loneliness. The desolate wail sounded again and again, and a fresh fear nudged at her misery. A lake freighter would reduce the little boat to splinters.

"Oh, wow," she said aloud, forcing herself to sit upright, tapping some hidden reserve of strength to throw off her morbid mood.

"If you can sit up, it might help a little. Lying down aggravates seasickness."

"Have you ever been seasick?" she asked him.

"No, never."

He didn't need to sound so pleased with himself. It was only an accident of heredity, not a character weakness. Was it her doing that she'd inherited all the weak-stomached genes accumulated by generations of landlubbers?

This trip was worse than a roller-coaster ride. At least that infernal machine stopped and disgorged its victims. With a moron like Benny at the wheel, the boat could go on and on, swept around the tip of Michigan through the Straits of Mackinac, carried down Lake Huron and the Saint Clair river, whirled past Detroit and on through the Saint Lawrence seaway, out to the Atlantic Ocean, tossed from swell to swell until the hurricanes of the North Atlantic finally swamped them. Her watery visions didn't take into account how few gallons of fuel were swishing in the tank.

Kelly felt totally drained, but she tried to stand to stretch her aching body.

"Fresh air might help," Brian said. "Maybe they'll let me take you topside."

"Oh, no, please, not that. If the lake's going to get me, I don't want to see it coming."

"We're not in any danger."

"Is that supposed to be funny?"

"Lake Michigan is always choppy. I've crewed on my brother's yacht in much heavier swells without being in trouble."

How could darkness sweep over her in the darkness? She was trying to puzzle it out when an explosion of tiny yellow dots sent her off to another dimension, sinking her into a whirlwind of strangely vivid visions.

A heavy weight was pressing on her neck, forcing her face into a terrifying abyss. She struggled against it, but her arms were marshmallows spattering against a steel door that looked suspiciously like the safe in her workroom.

"Keep your head down for a minute."

Brian's voice came from the bottom of the sea, gurgling and emitting bubbles of sound.

"Hey, Kelly, don't fight me. You'll hurt yourself."

Hurt! Everything hurt. Her knees hurt; her earlobes hurt. Even her hair and toenails felt nauseated.

"Easy, sweetheart," he said gently. "You passed out, that's all. Keep your head down until the giddiness passes."

She was sitting on the edge of a bunk, her legs spread wide apart and her head hanging between them in what had to be one of the three least dignified positions a human body could assume. If it hadn't been dark, she could've expired from mortification.

She tried to raise her head, but the yellow dots swam behind her eyeballs again. Brian's hand held her down, massaging the back of her neck and producing shivers of sensation.

"Has the room stopped whirling?" he asked softly.

"It's a cabin. I know it's a cabin because the floor keeps coming up at me," she moaned, even as her frazzled nerves began to respond to his touch.

"Ease up slowly," he warned. "No fast moves."

She sat up with care, arching her shoulders back gradually to meet Brian's caressing motions.

At the end of her limbs hands and feet hung helplessly. She wanted to give them directions, but she'd forgotten how her circuits worked.

"Am I going to die?" she muttered a little incoherently, leaning to the side, letting her body go limp against him.

"No, I won't let you."

He sounded so sure she almost believed him.

"Why are they fighting up there?" she asked wearily.

"Benny's apparently lost the island."

"What if he never finds it?"

48

"Eventually we'll run out of fuel, and the coast guard will pick us up."

"That sounds good."

"I think I'd rather get away from those two right away. We'll manage all right on an island. I've made up a bundle—blankets, kettles, a few food supplies, some canned drinks, either soda or beer, I can't tell which in the dark. I just wish there were some matches." He put his arm around her shoulders and gave her a hug that boosted her spirits considerably. "I'm going to search some more."

He's such a wonderful man, she thought, imagining that her mind was a video game, trying to keep all the little cells from being zapped by yellow dots from outer space.

"What'd I tell you!" Benny shrieked from above.

"Either we've taken on a wounded hyena or that idiot has stumbled on an island," Brian said, letting some anger slip through the mask he was wearing for her benefit. "Will you be able to walk? I don't want to leave you or the supplies on board alone."

The thought of being left behind with Benny gave her a feeble spurt of energy.

"Don't worry. I won't let you leave this boat without me."

"You're coming with me if I have to carry you. It's the supplies I'm worried about. What are the chances our hosts will let me make two trips for them?"

"Zilch, zero."

"What's wrong with dropping them here?" Fred was demanding angrily.

"I can't get the boat in there."

"You said you know how to navigate."

"I'll run it right into the frigging rocks if I try to go in here. This island ain't easy. There's only one safe spot, and I ain't seen it yet."

Benny was having a great time playing captain, Kelly realized miserably. Did people really ride around in this wretched little boat just for fun? Would the trip never end?

"At least he seems to know how to handle a boat," Brian reassured her. "Hang in there, and we'll be on solid ground soon."

"Unless he drowns us first," she croaked hoarsely, not repeating herself when Brian didn't catch her words.

"See!" Benny chortled triumphantly. "I told ya. I can wiggle in and outta there, but a coast guard boat can't."

"Pat yourself on the back when you've done it," Fred said crossly.

How did he get to be a leader of men, Kelly wondered, still not sure he wouldn't toss them into the waves instead of landing them safely.

"We can swim from here," Brian said.

"Maybe you can! I nearly missed graduating from high scool because I couldn't swim enough laps," she said dejectedly. "I took the darn swimming course three times trying to pass it."

She didn't add that it had taken her most of that time to screw up enough courage to put her face underwater.

The boat motor was idling now, sounding like a washing machine about to conk out.

"He's taking us in."

Brian groped for his jacket, which had been covering her on the bed, and offered it to her.

"Put this on. You're too weak to risk a chill."

"I'm hot all over. I don't need it."

"Put it on."

"I'm going to be sick again."

"No, you're not. The minute we're close enough we have to be ready to go ashore."

That moment came with a jolting suddenness that sent her stomach crowding against her lungs.

Fred vividly cursed his partner's navigating skills, then shouted impatiently down to them.

"Come up slowly one at a time. Right now I don't much care whether we dump you alive or dead."

Brian went first, trying to make the bulky blanket-load look insignificant, carrying it with one arm, pressing it against his hip. Kelly hung on to the edge of his sweater, not entirely sure she'd won the battle with the floating darkness.

"What've you got?" Fred demanded to know.

"Blankets, some canned goods I found down there, a first-aid kit. You can look it over."

"Hey, any beer down there?" Benny asked.

"Forget it! Get over the side," Fred ordered.

Instead of the sandy beach Kelly expected, black water was swirling around the bow.

"I can't swim!"

"This is as close as we go, baby," Benny taunted her. "Glad to give you a round trip. Freddy can run this tub, and you an' me'll get better acquainted."

"Take off your shoes," Brian ordered tensely, quickly doing the same. "Put them in your pockets and roll up your slacks. I don't think it's very deep."

He couldn't know that! She hesitated until Benny moved close to her.

"I'm ready," she said, nearly panicking as she stuffed her pumps into the pockets of the Windbreaker Brian insisted she wear.

He went over first, somehow managing to land upright with the packet held above the water level.

"Hey, we forgot to give you your groceries," Benny said, handing Kelly a heavy bag, expecting that she wouldn't be able to get over the side with it.

Well, she'd show that creep! She balanced the heavy load on her hip while she eased first one leg and then the other over the side, balancing her rump on the narrow edge, as terrified of looking downward as she was of going over.

"It's only about knee-high on me, and the bottom is sandy," Brian assured her. "Just slide down and I'll catch you."

Sure, and drop your precious bundle, she wanted to say, but one of the kidnappers took the initiative from her. A rough push from behind sent her tumbling down the side, and Brian's one-handed attempt to catch her couldn't save her from landing on her knees, submerged up to her midriff.

The water was liquid ice, excruciatingly painful, beating against her breasts and back like frozen whips on her flesh.

"You're soaked," Brian cried frantically, pulling at her with his one free hand, forcing her to stand and fight through swells that were hitting the shoreline with foaming fury.

It was so dark only the breaking waves indicated that there was land ahead, but Brian pulled her toward it at a pace that stole her breath away.

They landed in a shivering heap on the sand, the supplies she'd stubbornly held breaking out of the water-soaked bag and rolling around them. The boat was already out of sight.

"You've got to get warm," Brian said, as close to panicking as she'd seen him, kicking a can of something out of his way and cursing when it bruised his toe.

Beyond the beach a forested swell of land offered some shelter from the wind, and he yanked her in that direction, tenaciously hanging on to his own bundle.

"Hurry, get your wet clothes off," he ordered.

She wanted to argue, but her teeth were chattering too much. When she didn't react fast enough, he dropped his bundle on the ground and peeled off first the Windbreaker, then her blazer. She tried to unbutton her blouse, but her fingers felt like overstuffed sausages, totally incapable of maneuvering the hard pearly knobs out of their neatly stitched holes.

"Here, let me," he said impatiently.

"You're wet too," she stammered between clenched jaws.

"You don't need to tell me that. Help me, Kelly!"

He slid her blouse off and undid her bra snap.

She pulled back in spite of her best intentions not to.

"I'm not trying to molest you! You've got to dry off fast."

With trembling hands she groped for the gem that had somehow ridden to safety between her breasts, painfully palming it and offering it to him.

"I saved your emerald."

"Never mind that now."

She clenched the gem in her fist, giving him very little help as he stripped off the slacks and panties clinging to her shivering flesh like a layer of ice.

"Here, dry off with my shirt."

He pushed the soft white garment into her hand, nearly making her drop the gem. She switched the emerald to her left palm and began rubbing her numb flesh with as much energy as she could summon.

Only vaguely aware that he was as naked as she was, she submitted when he began drying her skin vigorously with the shirt, forced into feeling how cold she was when she really preferred to be numb. Needles of pain made her resist him, but she was too drained to do more than annoy him.

"Here, slip on my sweater. It's the only dry clothing we have between us now that my shirt's wet."

"I can't take your sweater."

Why did his voice sound so far away?

"I brought two blankets. You lie down on this one, and I'll roll it around you."

"I have to put your emerald someplace safe," she insisted, carefully enunciating each word to make sure he understood.

"Never mind that."

"No, I have to."

"Give it to me. I'll put it in your shoe, okay?"

The blanket was scratchy on her legs and bottom, and she was never going to be warm again. Feeling like a caterpillar trapped in a cocoon, she wanted to squirm into a comfortable position on the lumpy ground, but all she could do was shiver and shake in the woolen tube. Brian was moving around, hanging their clothes on tree limbs, gathering her scattered provisions on the shoreline so the waves wouldn't claim them.

"You'll freeze," she said weakly, remembering he was stark naked in the chill wind coming from the lake.

"We'll need these in the morning. Damn, I wish I had some matches!"

"Brian, I can't get warm."

Her teeth were chattering convulsively, making her words come in bursts.

"Blankets aren't enough," he said, his voice hoarse with concern.

The importance of it all was slipping away, but she sipped liquid from a can he held to her lips, barely noticing what it was, forgetting she hated beer.

"Drink more," he urged.

Either her teeth were echoing or his were chattering too.

"You have to get warm," she said from a far place that was claiming her.

"Drink first. You're dehydrated."

She obeyed but was relieved when he finished the can himself and tossed it aside. Thank heavens, he was freeing her from the binding, scratchy, useless blanket, laying beside her on top of it and covering them both with something softer.

When Pompeii had its big disaster, people were petrified in all kinds of odd positions, just the way they were when the ash and lava caught up with them. That's the way they'd find her someday, she thought, frozen stiff, and she wanted to be sure her corpse didn't look silly. What was a dignified way to freeze to death? Flopping on her back, she forced her legs out straight, carefully pressing her ankles together and moving her toes to make sure they were in a neat row. Crossed hands on the chest probably looked best. Undertakers seemed to favor it, anyway. Her mind was rambling with all kinds of silly thoughts, but she couldn't seem to control it. Now she tried to sleep while she waited for her blood to congeal.

"I won't take advantage of you, at least not tonight," he whispered close to her ear.

He was rubbing her feet with his, the effect about as warming as ice cubes clacking together in the bottom of a glass. He moved his legs vigorously over hers, massaging her arms with fingers that felt like popsicles.

"You're as cold as I am," she accused him, peeping out of the haze that threatened to engulf her at any moment.

"No, only my legs got wet. I have enough body heat to warm us both eventually."

She rolled on her side to face him, forgetting the petrified people of Pompeii, surprised to feel a glimmer of warmth when her hands slid under his arms. The hair on his chest tickled her nose, proving that she had some sensations left, and her nostrils seemed to be in working order, catching just a faint whiff of male musk, reassuring and pleasant. Was he actually working up a sweat trying to get her warm?

"Try to sleep now," he whispered just when she was remembering some of the nice things about being alive.

Turning to lie cradled against him, her back to his front, she squirmed closer, selfishly trying to extract warmth from his long length, appreciating the hard, solid, lumpy ground under them because it didn't sway, dip, or heave. She was definitely going to wake up alive.

Funny, she could tell there was light on the other side of her eyelids without making the effort of opening them. Had she been unconscious or sleeping? Did it really matter?

Her nose was pressed against a solid wall of warm flesh, so much smoother and nicer than the blanket under her cheek. Somehow while they'd slept, their positions had reversed. Her breasts, out-

54

lined under the soft cashmere of his sweater, were flattened against the firmness of his back, and her stomach and legs were pressed spoonlike against him.

Umm, nice, she thought, enjoying the warmth of his back, nestling closer to the curve of his buttocks, running her hand over the jutting ridge of his hip before she remembered he was practically a stranger.

Easing one eye open enough to see the world through the fuzzy fringe of her own lashes, she decided the view wasn't worth a two-eyed effort. All she could see beyond Brian's smooth, lightly freckled shoulder were a few tree branches and a lot of sky. If there was any poetry buried in the depths of her soul, it couldn't be dredged out by the dull green, prickly-looking needles of an evergreen.

Slipping one cold foot between his warm, hairy calves, she found it amazingly pleasant to lie there and drift back to sleep.

"I promised I wouldn't do this."

Brian's lips brushed the tip of her nose then made the adventurous leap to her mouth, gently teasing and nipping until she stirred sleepily under the weight of his chest.

"Promised what?"

"Not to take advantage of you."

"Is that what you're doing?"

If it was, she had absolutely no objections.

"No, but I'm tempted."

"I can't imagine why."

Remembering the awful boat trip, she didn't even want him to look at her.

"I have to brush my teeth, wash my hair," she protested, trying to wiggle free, but he trapped her with a very strong, excitingly muscular leg.

"Cold lake water won't do much for your hair, and we won't have any safe drinking water until I can get a fire going."

"I can clean my teeth in the lake," she insisted, finding that struggling against him was almost as much fun as kissing him.

"I think not. It's clean-looking this far from shore, but we're not taking any chances. That's why I brought two kettles from the boat, to boil water."

"Brian, we stole that stuff, didn't we?" Kelly asked, relaxing under him to study the rise and fall of his chest.

"I did, but I'll see that the owners are reimbursed when we get off this island."

"When will that be, do you think?"

"Hard to say. A signal fire is our best bet for attracting attention."

"Without matches?"

"I'm a geologist, I should be able to find two stones that will produce a spark."

"That's comforting," she teased, trying to hide her discomfort at the intimacy of their situation—a discomfort that grew as she became more awake, more aware of his very satisfactory body nestled against hers. Her little shiver had nothing to do with the mild breeze fanning her face.

"You're still cold."

"No, not really. Only my feet. You make a great heating pad."

He sat, pushing the blanket to his waist with the result that her top half was exposed to the cool morning air.

"Cover up and keep warm," he said, but not before his eyes roamed over his sweater with an appreciative gleam.

"You don't need to tell me," she said pulling the covering under her chin. "I'm certainly not going to play Eve to your Adam. What are you doing?"

"Rubbing your feet. They're icy."

Taking first one and then the other between his palms, he created enough friction to send warming currents up to her knees. Vigorously at first and then more slowly, his hands massaged, separating each toe with his fingers and kneading until tingles of real warmth flowed upward—and inward.

Trying not to notice that his share of the blanket had fallen to his lap, covering a formidable bulge, she wrapped her arms across her chest and tried for a conversational tone.

"Are you sure your father will pay them?"

He released her feet so she could tuck them under her legs Indian-style, pulling up the blanket but sitting so close her knee was wedged against his thigh.

"No, I'm not."

"Brian, you can't mean that. He wouldn't let kidnappers murder you just to save the ransom money."

"Of course not," he said, sounding a trifle annoyed. "But this is something our family has discussed. Our policy is—"

"You have a policy for abductions?"

She found herself shocked and just a little bit horrified.

"It's something we've had to consider. Our decision, if you'd rather put it that way, is not to pay ransom without receiving proof that the victim is still alive."

"So if the kidnappers plan to kill you, they have to hold off so you can write a note or talk on the phone or something."

"Yes, it gives the police, FBI, and private investigators time to work."

"But no one can contact you here."

"Not unless that gang of idiots comes back."

"Do you think they will?"

"I doubt it, not for a while anyway. They're somewhere near Detroit hoping to pick up a suitcase of money."

"And if it's not that easy?"

"Either the police will follow their trail and find us, or we'll get help by signaling."

"I did write a note on the restroom mirror with soap."

"Good!"

"I didn't know where we were going, though."

"It's a clue, and it's not as if we're lost in the South Pacific. Thousands of boats sail Lake Michigan."

"In the summer."

"Freighters run until ice closes the straits. Some years coast guard icebreakers keep it open most of the winter. Don't look so discouraged. Island life won't be so bad."

"Until it snows."

"Well, it's nice today. If our clothes are dry, we've got it made."

"Anything's better than Benny, right?"

He smiled and seemed as reluctant as she was to leave their blanket and begin playing Robinson Crusoe.

"Stay under the cover while I check our clothes. Hopefully none blew away. I tried to hook everything on branches, but the wind was pretty brisk last night."

"Do you think Benny and Fred made it back?"

"Probably. The lake wasn't too rough for navigation."

He stood, totally naked, without any apparent self-consciousness, although he did keep his back toward her. Men could be beautiful creatures, she thought, not high-minded enough to look away as he walked toward a clump of trees. His shoulders and back were well developed, tapering down to a slim waist and compact buttocks. His legs were long and muscular, carrying his weight with effortless ease.

Larry had been well built too, tall and athletic with a staunchness in his stride that was totally misleading. When he hadn't been on the prowl, using sexual conquests to make him feel like more of a man, he'd been whiny and demanding, expecting her to cater to his whims and bolster his ego.

Why rehash old hurts now, she thought, pulling her knees up under her chin and wrapping the blanket tent-style around her. She'd had some good times with Larry, enjoying a courtship that began in high school and ended when they eloped on the night of her graduation. After six months of marriage she knew he wasn't the mature, self-assured man he pretended to be, but it took another four years for her to admit her love for him was totally dead, killed off by his unfaithfulness and her own maturation. For five years that chapter in her life had been finished. Why think about it now?

Her illness must have totally drained her, she decided, realizing she was desperately thirsty. The deep blue waters of the lake looked invitingly clean, but Brian didn't think they should drink from it. Certainly he wouldn't object to bathing, but remembering the icy painfulness of her dunking, she decided to hope he could get some water boiling.

After checking all the garments hanging on limbs and retrieving a few that had blown down, he walked back to her, his shirt tied around his waist but flapping loosely on one side, revealing the lean hip she remembered touching.

"Well, you certainly look like Robinson Crusoe. Are the clothes still wet?"

"A little damp. They should be dry completely in an hour or so. The sun is pretty warm for September."

"We're due for some luck."

"Here, these are dry, but you'll have to shake the sand out. Your bra fell on the ground."

"Thanks," she said, not knowing if she should be embarrassed.

At least her panties were dry; she wouldn't have to parade around with a bare bottom.

With quite a bit of shaking, her undergarments seemed to shed the sand sticking to them. She slipped into them under the blanket while he made a couple of trips to the shoreline, finding a few containers from her broken bag, missed in the darkness the night before, piling them beside the blanket with the items he'd scrounged from the boat.

"Five cans of beer, six of cola, a can opener, first-aid kit, two cans of tuna fish, four of canned peaches—they must have had a special on them—soda crackers, sauerkraut . . ."

"Sauerkraut?"

"Well, it's edible," he said with a little smile. "Lots of baked beans and a can of corned beef."

"That all came from our good-will package?"

"No, the beer and pop were in the cabin. Also cans of pâté, mushrooms, miniature shrimp, and water chestnuts, toilet tissue, paper towels, and a bar of green soap. The boat owners aren't hot dog and hamburger sailors, I guess."

"Quite a fancy breakfast menu," she said.

"How about starting with cola and crackers. You need liquids, and the soda crackers will settle your stomach."

"Oh, it's settled. I have an iron constitution as long as both feet are on solid ground."

What she wouldn't give to erase last night from his memory! And hers! She never wanted to think about it again, so, of course, that was all she had on her mind, reliving the whole awful experience. He'd even held her head while she was sick. Horrible!

"Did I say anything odd?" she asked hesitantly. "On the boat I mean."

"No, nothing."

He grinned broadly, unwrapping a stack of crackers and handing her several. She didn't believe him, but he had a nice way of lying.

The warm, bubbly cola burned her abused throat, but she sipped it gratefully. She would've preferred cold water, but Brian seemed to know what he was talking about. It wasn't necessary for her to hear horror stories about pollution being in the lake to take his word about the safety of the water. The great outdoors was alien territory to her. Her single one-week foray to scout camp had cost her parents

nine long-distance phone calls and six assorted medications including ointment for poison ivy. When they suggested she give it a
second try the next year, she sulked for six weeks and finally bought
the first and last marijuana cigarette she'd ever handled, cunningly
asking her father why all the kids brought them to camp.

Watching Brian breakfast on beer and crackers, she thought
being marooned might be a lot more fun than scout camp. There
was sand in her bra, and her ribs ached from upchucking, but the
sun was comfortably warm on her face. There was nothing but
approval in his dark brown eyes, so maybe the darkness in the cabin
had been the best thing about the boat ride.

"I wonder what time it is," she said.

"Late morning, I'd guess. Is your watch still working?"

"No, there seems to be water under the crystal, and I didn't even
make a forty-foot dive wearing it."

He took her wrist in his hand.

"You cracked the glass."

"True, but isn't it just like a capitalist to defend misleading advertising."

"Aren't you a capitalist, running your own business?"

"Tell my banker!"

"You can have the cola if I can have the beer."

"Fair enough, but I won't eat cold sauerkraut."

"I'm going to get dressed and walk around the island. Do you feel
up to it?"

"Sure."

After handing her a neat pile of clothing, he disappeared into the
woods with his, leaving her alone to shake out her bra again, the
uncomfortable little granules stuck in one cup reminding her of the
emerald. Checking first one shoe and then the other, she shook it
into her palm and let it lay there capturing magical glints from the
bright sunlight. For lack of a better place, she carefully secured it
in toilet tissue and left it in a kettle until she could think of a safer
niche.

The cuffs and waistband of her slacks were damp, and her blazer
had shrunk enough to leave the lining hanging in back, but she still
felt more human wearing her clothing. She folded Brian's sweater
and tried to decide whether a trip to the woods was an absolute
necessity. She really didn't have the slightest idea how to take care

of her basic needs without plumbing, but if cave women had figured it out, she could.

Brian returned wearing slacks and shirt, walking barefoot without watching the ground. Her shoes wouldn't last long as hiking boots, damp and stiff as they still were, but she surely wasn't going to walk around stepping on thistles and sharp stones.

He handed her a comb and shook the sand off their blankets, folding them neatly and weighing them down with canned goods.

"We have a lot to do," he said.

She couldn't imagine what, but she worked gamely on her long, tangled hair, trying to analyze the look on his face without returning his stare.

"I'm going to skirt the shoreline and decide on the best place to light a signal fire."

"You sound sure of yourself. Have you ever started a fire without matches before?"

"Just for fun I have. Don't look so worried. I've been on plenty of geological expeditions in the wilds. We'll be fine, and we'll get away from this island quicker than I want to."

Why say that, she wondered, looking up to meet his gaze. No, she wouldn't ask.

CHAPTER FOUR

Crouching down, pretending to examine a rock on the ground, Kelly tried to will away the weakness in her legs. Brian, sensibly wearing his casual suede shoes on their circuit of the rocky island, looked back at her with concern.

"Getting tired?"

"No, I just thought this rock looked promising."

She handed him the stone closest to her hand, not surprised when he tossed it away. Her jacket pockets were bulging with hard, fist-sized rocks, and he seemed confident about starting a fire.

"I'd like to have a good chunk of iron pyrite, but I should be able to get some sparks from what we've found. Don't worry about looking for more."

"Okay."

Rising reluctantly to her feet, she ran a few steps to show him how peppy she was but quickly slowed, too pooped to show off. This wasn't an island; it was a continent. They'd never get all the way around it.

"Benny was right about one thing," Brian said.

"That's hard to believe."

"The beach where he came in is the only safe harbor, but right here is where we should make our signal fire. Look out there."

They were on high ground away from the forested interior of the island, sharp-bladed dune grass whipping at their legs as they slowly progressed along the water's edge, high enough to avoid the spray. She hadn't noticed the bluish-green speck far out on the watery horizon.

"I have my bearings now," he said with relief. "That should be Beaver Island."

"It's so far away."

"Yes, but a smoky fire on this island should attract someone's attention."

"Do many people live there?"

"A few hundred maybe. There was a Mormon farming community there in the last century until someone murdered their leader. Do you want to rest a few minutes?"

"No, I'm hoping it will be lunchtime when we get back. Who murdered him?"

"They never found out. Maybe one of his own followers."

"An unsolved crime."

She didn't say what she was thinking: They could be the victims of another one if help never came.

"Let's eat now over on that rock," he suggested.

"Eat what?"

"Shrimp and crackers with a cola chaser." He pulled a can out of each jacket pocket. "Why do you think I've been handing you the rocks?"

"Because you don't have a pack mule?"

"Get over there!"

He swatted her lightly on her rear and took her hand, pulling her toward a wind-scoured boulder.

"This wind is enough to take my breath away!" she said, sinking down on the ground gratefully, cold perspiration forming on her forehead in spite of the warmth of the sun.

"You're exhausted," he said matter-of-factly. "I shouldn't have let you walk this far."

"You couldn't stop me! I'm not going to sit alone back there waiting for bears to get me."

"I'm the closest thing to a bear on this island, but I did see a squirrel. If we're here too long, we may be having him for dinner."

"Brian!"

"Just want you to know we won't starve."

He took a small packet of crackers wrapped in a paper towel from his pants pocket, handing it to her while he used the can opener.

"When was the last time you lunched on cracker crumbs and shrimp?" he teased, laying a tiny pink morsel on a fragment of cracker.

"Let's call it a canapé."

Her mouth was so dry the salty tidbit stuck to her tongue, difficult to swallow because her throat was like a sandy tunnel.

"Could I have a drink, Brian?"

"Drink it all," he said. "You need to replace your fluids."

"Don't be silly." She gulped gratefully. "We'll share it."

"No, I never drink the stuff. I'll have a beer when we get back to camp."

"Camp!" She laughed.

"The place will shape up with a little help from you."

"Am I supposed to weave a wigwam or something?"

He had a great smile, beginning with his eyes and forming one little dimple in his right cheek. Watching him she almost forgot about eating.

"This one is yours," he said, holding the loaded corner of a cracker near her mouth.

"No, you eat the rest."

"There's no way I'm going to finish them alone. They taste like iodine, and you have to take your share."

"They're delicious and you know it.

"Here." His finger brushed her lower lip as he tried to pop his offering into her mouth.

Shaking her head, she kept her lips pressed together.

"You're so stubborn I might as well be with a mule."

"We split everything down the middle, or it's no deal. You're not going to fatten me up."

"You're a tough negotiator."

"Darn right."

They ate slowly, tranquilized by the rhythmic waves slapping on the shoreline below them. Parched after the salty snack, she drank the bubbly cola too fast, coughing and sputtering as a big swallow made her nose burn.

He's not a back slapper, she noticed through her distress, accepting the remnant of paper toweling that had held the crackers.

"You okay?" he asked.

"I need drinking lessons is all."

It wasn't all that funny, but they laughed until he reached over and took the empty can from her, replacing it in the pocket of his jacket.

"Rule number one in the wilderness is save everything. You never know what might come in handy later."

He studied her face, reaching for her hand and sheltering it between both of his palms.

"And what's rule number two?" she asked, feeling lively and playful now that her hunger was appeased.

He smiled broadly and brought her fingers to his lips.

"Get to know your fellow camper."

Leaning forward on his knees, he kissed her gently, savoring the texture and tang of her lips, lightly cupping her chin in one hand while the other caressed the nape of her neck under her streaming mane of dark hair.

"This isn't in the survival manuals," she teased a little breathlessly, kneeling to be closer and laying her hands over his ears, tracing their contours with a light touch.

"We don't have to go by the book."

His breath was warm on her lowered lids as his arms circled her.

"I bet that's something you never do."

"Is that what you think?"

She stopped thinking as his hands slid to her throat, massaging the delicate hollows above her collarbone with his thumbs. Waves of sensation flowed through her nervous system as she impulsively reached for contact with his skin, sliding her hands under the layers of clothing to the lean expanse of his rib cage, feeling his body heat radiating through her stiff fingers.

"Are you warm enough?" he asked softly. "No afterchills from the dunking?"

"I'm deliciously warm," she whispered, boldly curling her fingers into the soft nests under his arms.

It was happening again, the same crazy yearning she'd felt after his kisses in the van. Being kidnapped and marooned with this man was making her react like a pinball machine gone berserk.

When he kissed her again, he slid his tongue between her lips and explored the soft membranes of her mouth, finding the underside of her tongue and teasing it until she gasped with excitement, stunned by the burning urgency of her arousal. Their aching need was mutual, a caldron of boiling desire fueled by the probing explorations of their swollen tongues and pulsating lips.

They rose to their feet in one quick movement, grinding their bodies together in an embrace that left them breathless and just a little shaken by their own raw sensuality. Aware that she'd signaled her desire with a spiritual nakedness alien to her usual nature, she buried her face against his chest, hearing the rapid beat of his heart but shying away from the hard masculine bulge she'd reveled against seconds earlier.

"Incredible," he said, keeping her in the circle of his arms and speaking with carefully chosen words. "Yesterday in the van I thought being in danger had pumped an overdose of adrenaline into my system, but I want to make love to you now more than then."

His frankness was like a dash of cool water in her face, but it was refreshing, not dampening. After Larry's sly innuendos and vague references to "fun," it was delightful to have a man admit he desired her. But how should she answer him?

"Unfortunately, I have to get a fire started," he said quickly, lightly kissing her forehead before releasing her.

You already have, she wanted to say, but things were happening too fast.

Since her divorce she'd avoided romantic attachments, refusing to surrender any of her hard-won independence for the sake of a warm body in her bed. She wasn't a bed-hopper, and she didn't have time for emotional involvements. Maybe if she ignored it, her traitorous body would stop yearning for Brian Fort, a man who wouldn't give her a second glance under normal circumstances.

They found a dirt-encrusted whiskey bottle and the remains of a man's high-top shoe, but there was nothing to suggest recent visitors to the island.

"What we need is birch bark, lots of it right from the trees," he said, assembling his rock collection on sandy ground somewhat sheltered by a land rise behind it.

"There's some driftwood on the beach."

"Anything on the ground is too damp to start a fire. We need dark, dry moss, dead needles, rotten wood that's powdery. Find as much as you can. Carry it in the big kettle."

"Yes, sir!"

She saluted sharply and marched off toward the woods with exaggerated steps.

"What will you be doing?" she called back.

"Trailing behind you so you don't get lost and gathering bigger branches to keep the fire going."

"*If* you get one started!"

"Bite your tongue, woman. Here, you take the knife."

"Where'd you get that?"

"On the boat. I carried it off in the first-aid kit. I would've taken a bigger one, but I didn't want our hosts to notice it."

It was only a paring knife, but it really helped in flaking off birch-bark fragments. Even with it she managed to break a fingernail. Gathering tinder was like a treasure hunt, and it was a pleasant challenge to fill the good-sized bail-handled kettle with enough dry scraps to start a fire.

"Can you whistle anything besides 'Hail to the Victors'?" she called out, teasing him after he finished what seemed like his twentieth rendition of Michigan's fight song.

"How about 'Yankee Doodle'?"

"Maybe you could sing instead?"

"Only in the shower."

"I'd settle for a silent sponge bath at this point."

"You've done well," he said, looking at her kettle over the armload of broken branches he was carrying. "That looks like milkweed down, and there's a feather. I didn't need to tell you what to get. Let's get that fire going."

"What can I do now?"

"You might gather some driftwood. When the fire's going strong, we'll need slower-burning fuel to give us good coals."

Here on the narrow strip of sandy beach she decided to follow his example, taking off her shoes and knee-highs, noticing a broad run in the now-sagging nylon. By the time they were rescued, her clothes wouldn't be accepted for a charity rummage.

The sand had absorbed heat from the sun, making it warm underfoot, but the wind from the lake seemed much chillier. They were living on borrowed fall weather, she knew, since winter could begin pressing in on them at any time this far north. Taking childlike pleasure in dipping her foot in sandy granules and letting them run through her toes, she had an almost irresistible urge to build a sand castle. Running to the water's edge, she tested the damp sand to see how well it packed, then decided she needed the kettle to construct a really fine castle. Of course, she couldn't play with their precious containers.

Driftwood littered the area in pieces the size of a quarter to great chunks she could barely budge. Obviously it wasn't a favorite scavenging ground for mainland artisans. Remembering the prices charged by some crafts people she knew who worked with driftwood, it occurred to her that she was surrounded by a small fortune. But the lake debris wasn't nearly as precious to artists as it would be to the castaways if it burned well enough to attract help.

Brian was still kneeling beside a small pyramid of sticks that sheltered his highly flammable bits and pieces.

"Any luck?" she asked, dumping her load, knowing the answer because there wasn't a sign of a flame.

"What I wouldn't give for a couple of chunks of iron pyrite," he said without looking up.

"You mean fool's gold?"

"Yes. It's great for starting fires. The Eskimos carry it all the time."

He discarded the rocks in his hands and picked up two more, knocking them together with a brisk stroking motion. A light film of moisture made his dark hair stick to his forehead in loose ringlets, and Kelly had an almost unbearable urge to twirl her finger around one. It was far too cool for him to perspire from his exertions; his lack of success was making him anxious, she guessed.

The spark was so tiny she didn't notice it, but a tongue of flame flared up, quickly spreading through the pile of dry tinder.

Sitting beside him, watching him patiently feed small sticks and bits of bark into the fire, she remembered how much she'd liked his hands at first sight. The nails were nicely manicured, but there were signs of hard work, roughened palms, a long scar that ran from his index finger to his wrist, a jagged break in a thumbnail that no amount of filing could smooth entirely.

"Here, keep adding bark while I break apart that limb."

Nurturing the fire, watching it outgrow the little mound and spread across the pit Brian had hollowed in the sand was fun. She loved candles and fireplaces, but the flame greedily consuming her offerings was much more fascinating, dancing hypnotically in a pagan frenzy. The more wood she pushed toward it, the more vivid the fire-pictures grew before her eyes.

Brian cautioned her to move back and took the job from her, confidently adding larger fragments of the brittle branch he'd found hanging limply on a giant evergreen.

"Will anyone see this fire?" she asked.

"There's always a chance, but tomorrow we'll build a really smoky one on the spot where we had lunch. That's our best bet, but it's getting too late to try it today. Right now we need to boil water and cook dinner."

"Faithful Friday awaiting your commands."

"Don't think you won't get some. Everyone pulls his own weight on this expedition, Friday."

"Well, what should I do?"

"Rinse both kettles in the lake and fill them with water while I find some green sticks."

Insisting that every drop of water they consumed be boiled at least five minutes, Brian insured their supply for the next day by filling their empty cans. Kelly didn't find the makeshift twig toothbrush very satisfactory, and the warm boiled water was flat and unappealing, but she shared his tremendous feeling of satisfaction at having accomplished a difficult task.

"Ready to look for dinner?" he asked when the water problem was temporarily resolved and the fire seemed stable enough to forget for a while.

"I thought I was looking at it." She gestured toward the meager stockpile of canned goods.

"That won't last long. Come on, let's visit the island supermarket."

"You're kidding!"

"Nope."

Tying the arms of his sweater, he made a makeshift carryall, then took her hand and pulled her inland.

"I saw some bearberries when we were gathering tinder."

"Berries for bear? You said there weren't any!"

"I don't think there are. I haven't seen their spoor."

"Goodness, you sound so woodsy," she teased. "Aren't you afraid wild berries will be poisonous?"

"Not these."

It was cool and dim under the trees, with occasional patches of sunlight streaking through like overheads lighting the stage in a dark auditorium. He really did find berries, still clinging to a bush, and popped one in his mouth, offering another to her. She didn't want to eat it, but did so as a sign of trust. It was mealy and pretty tasteless, dryer than she'd expected a berry to be.

"They're better cooked," he said.

"Why not cook a batch with a can of peaches, sort of balance the too-sweet and the tasteless?" she asked, helping him strip the dry red fruit.

"Now you have the idea. Let's find some salad."

"Don't we have enough food for tonight?"

"You want your vitamin A, don't you?"

Not if it means crunching on weeds, she thought, tagging after him and wondering how many excursions her battered shoes could stand.

"A Caesar's salad would be nice," she thought aloud.

"How about tossed scurvy grass and fireweed with a little shepherd's purse for a nice peppery taste?"

"And you wouldn't let me drink the water!"

Preparing dinner and eating it in courses was a long, slow process, especially since they used only the smaller kettle, heating beans by setting the can in boiling water, simmering some green leaves that proved to be edible if not exactly gourmet, and finally cooking the berries with half a can of peaches. Brian even found some leaves that made a passable substitute for herbal tea, a beverage she loved. She actually felt full.

"I guess we can hold out here for quite a while," she said, watching his face in the dusk, the low flame of the open fire giving his skin a ruddy glow.

His beard, a dark shadow on the lean, strong line of his jaw, made him look rugged, but high cheekbones and a straight, patrician nose gave his face an unusual nobility. When he met her gaze, his eyes were shadowed by heavy lashes, the dark brown depths unreadable.

"I'm not sure I can," he said softly, sitting absolutely motionless but generating sparks she couldn't miss.

He can seduce me without moving a muscle, she thought, suddenly panicky because this man she hardly knew attracted her so strongly.

She stood and busied herself, adding wood to the fire, rearranging supplies, finding a ready-made bandage for her nail in the first-aid kit. She didn't fool him for an instant.

70

"Come sit by me," he said softly.

"I thought maybe I'd get ready for bed, well, not for bed exactly, but I am sleepy. This fresh lake air has me yawning. You did say we'll have a lot of work to do tomorrow, fixing a signal fire and . . ."

"Kelly, come here."

He couldn't give her orders! This island arrangement was a fifty-fifty proposition. She moved a few feet closer, forcing him to look upward while she decided how to lay things out for him.

"Brian, you've really been so wonderful, and I really appreciate it, but . . ."

Why was he grinning like that, and what had she intended to tell him? He reached toward her with both hands, locking them on the sides of her legs, willing her closer rather than demanding it. Sinking down on her knees in front of him, she was oblivious of the heat of the fire on her back and the crackling of burning wood.

"You're too close to the fire," he said, moving until his back was against the high sandy rise, taking her hand and pulling her with him.

Playing with fire, that's exactly what she was doing, but she slid unresisting onto his lap, aware of the resinous smokiness behind her and the pungent freshness of living evergreens.

He didn't kiss her. It was like waiting for soothing unguent to be applied to a burn, and she stirred restlessly, aware of the intensity of his eyes even though his face was shadowed.

"I'm really sorry I've gotten you into this," he said slowly.

"But it's not your fault."

"If they hadn't recognized my name, they would've let us go, but let me finish what I need to say."

"Don't let me interrupt!"

The arm of his sweater was soft under her fingers, and she could imagine the fine sprinkling of dark hairs under it.

"Kelly, I don't want anything to happen unless you want it too. Say so, and I'll sleep back in the woods tonight."

"I couldn't make you leave the fire."

"That's not a problem."

"But I don't want to stay here alone. There could be bears or . . ."

She was at a loss to think of anything that frightened her on the island, but the last thing she wanted was to have him leave her.

"There are no bears."

She could detect the amusement in his voice.

"Tell me if you want me to go," he whispered, so close she could feel the warmth of his breath on her cheek.

"We can just roll up in separate blankets and share the fire," she said weakly.

"Do you think that would work?"

She didn't, and if she turned her head just a little, he'd kiss her.

"Will the fire last all night?"

Her question had nothing to do with what she was feeling.

"I wouldn't be surprised if it did."

He took her face in his hands and kissed her gently, his nose rubbing against hers, his lashes tickling her lids. How could such tiny gestures make me want him so much, she thought, giddy with the wonder of desiring a man.

Every move he made was gentle, slow, controlled, so different from Larry's self-serving haste. But tonight she wanted to consign all thoughts of her ex-husband to total oblivion.

Without talking about it, they stood and spread the softest of the two blankets on the sandy ground between the long fire trench and the land-rise, laying the second one near at hand. The air coming off the lake was cold, but their campsite was an oasis of warmth. Leaving their shoes a safe distance from the coals, they lay together fully clothed, exchanging long, promising kisses, tentatively exploring the contours of their bodies with unhurried pleasure.

Imagine, I'm making love before the late news is over, she thought dreamily, deciding that no couple in love should ever own a TV set.

"I'm sorry about my beard," he said, his voice husky.

"It's a nice beard."

She stroked his face, the stubble bristly under her fingertips, following the curve of his chin downward over his neck until she felt the wiry softness of the hair at the opening of his shirt. He turned to her then, pushing her flat on her back as he assaulted her mouth. Her tongue encouraged the deep thrusts of his until spasms of pleasure made her writhe under the weight of his shoulders and chest.

Deliberately experimenting, trying to find the places she loved to have touched, he played with her earlobes, then filled her inner ear with a damp warmth almost insanely enjoyable. She clutched impatiently at the soft wool of his sweater, wanting to feel his skin against hers.

"I want our first time to be very, very good," he said, his voice heavy with desire.

Standing, he towered above her, silhouetted by the fire at his back. He removed his clothing slowly, as though aware of how eagerly she was feasting her eyes on the revelation of his body. His toes, close to her, had tiny granules of sand sticking to them, and his legs rose powerfully to slim hips and a flat stomach. His masculinity reminded her of their fear-triggered arousal in the van, and the shiver of anticipation she felt was mixed with surprise and awe and even a little fright. What had happened to the cool, unresponsive Kelly Valentine, so sure she could live without the demands and expectations of a man? How could she possibly want anyone as much as she wanted this naked stranger?

Impatiently brushing sand from his feet with a corner of his pant leg, he stepped toward her, kneeling with his legs on either side of her quivering body.

He seemed determined to blank out her conscious thought, submerging her mind in an ocean of sensation. As though performing a ritual, he slipped each button of her blouse from its slit, not frustrated or eager when he found the nylon of her bra firmly imprisoning her breasts. Her nipples strained against the silky cloth as he caressed them with both hands, teasing the tips with devastating gentleness.

Finally she was the one who could no longer tolerate her clothes, squirming awkwardly on her elbows until he came to the rescue, easing her out of jacket, blouse, and bra until she lay before him naked to the waist, her skin glistening with the heat of her desire.

With iron control he kissed and stroked her lean midriff, moving upward and planting a circle of kisses around each breast, tantalizing her until she pulled his face hard against her, guiding one painfully swollen nipple to his lips. Stimulated to the point of screaming, she was frantic with need, hot and moist and yearning. His back was smooth under her sharp-nailed clutch, and he moved up and down, letting her feel his weight, then robbing her of it.

His voice was only a throaty murmur, but the words she could hear made her feel beautiful, desired, sensual.

When she was ready to rip her slacks and panties from her body, he slowly edged them downward, his lips and hands promising more and more until she was sure her stormy reaction would shake the island loose from its foundation.

As a lover he was merciless, making her throb and pulsate as she began to realize her own potential for joy. Swelling and burning, she felt the tension tearing her between sweetness and pain, wanting so much yet more eager than ever before to give the same.

Her cries sounded demented in her own ears as she surrendered control, the walls of restraint she'd carefully constructed for so many years tumbling down before their shared passion. When he rolled onto his back, taking her with him, she drew him into her madness, stroking and caressing him until he became a driven man.

Waves of heat peaked and flowed as he shuddered to a climax, her spasms sharp and buzzing at the same time, then spreading outward to leave her with a dazed sense of well-being.

Coming down slowly, she couldn't get close enough to him, wanting their bodies to melt into one vibrant mass. When he leaned over to find the other blanket, she didn't want anything but his flesh to touch hers.

"You'll get cold," he said, flicking the covering over her a second time when she pushed it away.

"No, I'll never be cold again," she said impulsively, feeling that the warm glow of her contentment could keep them both cozy.

The fire was burning low, and he sat up reluctantly.

"I'd better feed the fire."

Even in the brief time it took him to renew the blaze with wood from the pile they'd gathered earlier, she missed him. Her arms felt empty and her loins ached. Back beside her again, he rained tiny kisses on her face and breasts, burying his fingers in the thick hair that fell back from her forehead. If what she felt was lust, she regretted every moment of her life spent without it.

Moistening the tip of one finger, she pushed the blanket aside and made lazy circles around his nipple, wondering if he felt anything like the tingles she experienced when he caressed her breasts. She took the dark knob between her lips and was gratified when she felt

74

him shudder, increasing the pressure until he moaned and clutched at her.

"Have your way with me, little sorceress," he growled roughly, lying in suspenseful agony while she teased and stroked him, hardly recognizing herself in the daring, passionate woman she'd suddenly become.

For the first time she was able to remember Larry's cruel taunts and not feel inadequate. No man could ever hurt her again by calling her frigid.

Much later, cradled against him under the rough blanket, she listened to the strong, even beating of his heart, thinking it was the most beautiful music she'd ever heard. The sky above them was a sea of stars, as distant and remote as her femininity had been until this night. Now she knew she could be a blazing inferno of feeling, just as each tiny pinprick of light was a brilliant, fiery sun.

Brian was sleeping, his breathing low and regular, but she'd never felt more wakeful. His knee, locked between her thighs, was growing heavy, his chest hair was tickling her nose, and the ground under her hip was stony and hard. She barely noticed. His skin was moistly exciting against hers, faintly salty with a musk that was still driving her wild. When she finally slept, her dreams were fantastically erotic.

"Good morning."

"Oh, is it winter?" she asked sleepily, shivering when she became conscious of her icy feet.

"Feels like it."

His lips were cold when he kissed her, but where their bodies were pressed together, the chill of the night had been defeated. Unfortunately that didn't include her backside, which had come uncovered. She felt like she'd been sitting on a cake of ice.

"Oh, warm me up," she moaned.

"Where are you cold?"

"You'll laugh if I tell you."

"Then I'll find out for myself."

He ran cold hands down her back, resting them on her generous buttocks and enjoying her little shivers.

"Are you massaging or spanking me?" she grumbled, unwilling to admit she was warming up very nicely.

"Umm, I hate to get up," he said, pressing closer, trapping her legs under his, demonstrating his idea of starting the day right.

Their joining had none of the passion and frenzy of the previous night. In fact, it was almost companionable, a sweet expression of lingering contentment. Afterward they lay locked together for a long while, each mulling over the force of what was happening.

"Is it too much to hope you're on birth control pills?" he asked wryly.

" 'Fraid so. I stopped taking them a year before my divorce."

Only his sharp intake of breath indicated that her previous marriage might bother him a little.

"Actually I tried to get pregnant for a while, but nothing happened. The doctor said I might be too tense. So probably there's no worry now."

"I wasn't worrying. How long were you married?"

"Does it matter?"

"No, I suppose not." He sounded irritated.

"I hate to talk about it," she said quickly, "but just for the record, I married Larry the night of my high school graduation, and the more I grew up, the more I regretted it. I've been on my own for years now. I like it that way."

"I see."

"What do you see?"

"That you're a beautiful woman who's been going to waste."

"Oh, thanks." She propped herself up on one elbow and glared at him. "You make me sound like an undiscovered natural resource."

"No man in your life?" he asked, ignoring the bite in her words.

"No one I'd buy an emerald for," she said with forced reserve, remembering only too well the beautiful stone that had thrown them together.

He laughed.

"What's so funny?"

"You are. If you want to know about my love life, ask."

"I don't."

"Then who did you think the stone was for?"

"It isn't my concern."

"You don't care if I'm engaged, married, living with someone?"

76

Of course I care, you fool, she wanted to say, tightly clamping her lips shut instead.

He rose a little stiffly, remarking that he felt every one of his thirty-three years after sleeping on the ground two nights, hurrying toward the neat pile of supplies, then dashing back under the covers with her.

"Here, it's yours now."

He was offering the brilliant green stone to her.

"I can't take that."

"Why not? You saved it from Fred and the boys."

"Don't be silly. You have plans for it."

"Had plans. I was going to give it to a lovely woman who means a great deal to me."

"Then I suggest you give it to her."

She started to get up but he held her down.

"My mother."

"Oh, really, you don't have to make up stories for me."

"Is it so impossible that I'd want to give my mother something special on her sixtieth birthday? She isn't that keen on getting older."

"That's really why you were ordering a pendant?"

"October nineteenth is her birthday."

"Well, that's really sweet of you. If we ever get off this island, I'll get it made in time."

"You're not paying attention. The emerald is yours now. I knew you should have it as soon as I saw your eyes."

"Brian, I can't take it."

"Then let's toss it in the lake for good luck."

He started to get up.

"Don't be crazy!"

"Darling, it's yours now. Do you want to make a wish on it or put it in a setting?"

"I won't be paid," she said stubbornly.

"I don't pay women."

He flushed angrily, leaving the blanket in angry strides and tossing the stone back at her. Scooping up his clothes, he disappeared into the woods.

CHAPTER FIVE

She couldn't lie there pouting. Without the warm length of his body to snuggle against, she felt bereft. Her clothes were less than twenty feet away, but dashing to get them she grew a suit of goose bumps that made her feel like a Thanksgiving turkey before defrosting.

Shaking each garment violently, trying to whisk out the sand that had invaded during the night, she dressed with a distaste for her soiled clothing exceeded only by her shivery need to get warm. For the first time she really understood what a wind-chill factor was. The gusts that roared off the lake were laced with needles of ice. Yesterday the island had seemed like a warm, unspoiled paradise. She couldn't help feeling deprived by the falling temperature.

The slapping of the wind and the chattering of her teeth made her deaf to Brian's return. She jumped when he came up behind her and wrapped his arms around her, even though he'd been in her thoughts at that very moment.

"You're shaking," he said. "You'd better wear my Windbreaker."

"Absolutely not! You're not going to be a hero for my sake."

"You're mad at me," he said, holding her close, giving her a chance to warm up in his arms. "You should've stayed in bed and let me bring your clothes to you."

"I can manage on my own," she said crossly.

"You're angry, and I'm sorry. You accidently trampled on one of my hang-ups, and I shouldn't have overreacted."

"I don't know what you're talking about."

She struggled halfheartedly to break away from his arms but wasn't sorry she failed.

"Do you have any idea how many women have . . ."

"Have what?" she asked when he didn't finish his sentence.

"I don't know how to say it without sounding conceited. Just understand that my father's money makes me pretty eligible. Some women want my name; other will settle for the money. I'm not interested on those terms."

"Well, you certainly laid that out plainly enough," she said, furiously twisting away.

"I want to give you a small gift. I feel rotten about getting you into this mess. You act like I was trying to pay you for sleeping with me."

"I can't see the difference between paying me and easing your conscience. You know I don't blame you for Fred and Benny and Mack and the island and . . ."

Breaking free, she ran toward the woods, determined not to let him see how hurt she was.

"Kelly, wait!"

"Don't follow me!" she cried angrily. "Can't I have a few minutes of privacy?"

"Have all you like!"

She hated answering a call of nature behind a tree; she hated the bitter blasts of air that reached her even among the thick foliage. Most of all she detested Brian Fort for ruining the afterglow of their wonderful, uncomplicated lovemaking. She wandered farther away from the campsite to delay facing him, staying far longer than she'd intended, moping and shivering as she tried to sort out her feelings.

"Kelly!"

"Too bad, Mr. Fort, you blew it," she hissed under her breath. "I'll freeze before I'll be your bedwarmer again."

"Kelly, answer me!" he called more urgently.

Standing silently behind a massive pine tree, she refused to respond, needing time to pull herself together.

"Kelly, dammit, where are you?"

He was plunging noisily toward her, snapping twigs and thrusting aside branches.

"Kelly, if this is a joke, it's not funny!"

Stiff with cold, she moved reluctantly toward the sound of his voice, coming upon him as he turned to go in the opposite direction.

"I thought there weren't any bears in the woods," she said.

"The only bear you need to be afraid of is me if you pull this disappearing act again."

"I have a right to some time to myself."

"You don't have a right to scare me."

"Why were you scared?"

"I feel responsible for you, that's why!"

"No one appointed you my guardian."

Their voices resounded through the quiet woods.

"I've never met a woman who needs a man more than you do."

His words were like a slap in the face, unleashing a flood of anger.

"A man is the last thing I need cluttering up my life, giving orders, making demands. The day I need you, Mr. Fort, I'll know I'm senile!"

"Your trouble is you're too damn beautiful," he said, shaking his head.

"Oh, sure, try to manipulate me with compliments. I know every trick in the book."

"What book are you talking about now?"

She realized he was enjoying their quarrel, and this only made her angrier.

"You have your life, I have mine," she said through tight lips. "Hopefully you'll be able to return to your hoards of admirers soon."

She intended to stalk back to the campsite, but he caught her, holding her by the shoulders at arm's length.

"So you are interested in my love life?"

"Not at all! Let me go."

"First you're going to wear my jacket. You're so cold your lips are blue."

"No, I'm not."

"I wouldn't mind a wrestling match if there was time, but we have a signal fire to build."

"Force is your solution when anyone disagrees?"

"Kelly, you're going to succeed in making me really angry."

"Am I supposed to tremble and beg for mercy?"

"No, of course not," he said wearily. "Look, will you compromise? Your blazer doesn't shut out the wind like my jacket does. At least wear my sweater under it. We both suffer if one of us gets sick."

"Okay," she said reluctantly, longing for warmth but hating to give an inch.

She refused his help, working her jacket over the bulky sweater sleeves with difficulty but appreciating the faint warmth retained from his body. The sweater hung over her hands, serving as a makeshift pair of mittens when she curled the wool around her fingers.

"Ready for breakfast?" he asked.

"Two eggs lightly over?"

"I saw a bird's nest on a spruce limb."

"Even I know it's too late in the season for birds' eggs."

He walked beside her, draping his arm over her shoulder.

"Can you imagine anything dumber than fighting between Robinson Crusoe and Friday?"

"No, I guess not," she admitted, not resisting when he hugged her close.

"Listen, darling," he said, bending so his breath warmed her ear, "let's get things straight before we get on with trying to survive."

"You don't need to say anything."

"I want to. You have a right to know. I'm not married and never have been, even though I've lived with women several times. None recently. I travel a lot, and sometimes I'm gone on geological surveys for months at a time. My life-style makes me a poor risk."

"This doesn't have anything to do with me."

"Darn it, it does."

He stopped and faced her, taking hold of one sweater-covered hand to keep her there.

"I don't know why, but it's important that you know last night was special to me. It wasn't just the danger or being alone with a lovely woman. I care about you. I'm not ready to make promises or commitments, but you mean something to me, Kelly. I just need time to figure out what."

"I'm . . . I'm glad you told me," she said hoarsely, feeling her eyes fill unexpectedly.

Turning her back, she wiped at them with one sweater cuff, hating the strange weakness that made her feel weepy.

"Hey, we've got work to do," he said with forced heartiness, planting a noisy whack on her backside.

"Brian, I don't like that!" she protested, quickly stepping ahead of him.

"You're not supposed to."

Hurrying hand in hand back to the beach, they were cheered by the faint warmth of the sun. At least they wouldn't freeze today.

Breakfast was a cold meal of crackers, pâté, and peaches with water left in the kettle from the previous night. What was left they used to wash and clean their teeth, emptying the large kettle to haul hot coals to the signal fire site. Brian carried it, taking what he hoped was a shortcut through the woods, while she followed, carefully balancing two pop cans of boiled water. A can of tuna bulged in one blazer pocket, and she hoped to keep the crackers from crumbling in the other. Both of them had a blanket folded lengthwise over their shoulders, taking them along in anticipation of a cold wind on the rocky ledge.

Cutting through the woods made the trip shorter, although Kelly would've been in trouble relying on her sense of direction to get there and back to the beach. Brian was worried about the coals dying, carrying his two best stones in his pockets but hoping he wouldn't have to start another fire from scratch. She wondered how their water would taste after using the kettle as an ash bin.

"We've got our work cut out for us," he said, his jacket and slacks billowing in the fierce wind.

"Does it have to be here?"

"We'll at least try this spot once. There's always a chance our fire on the beach will be seen at night, but a good pillar of smoke right here has a chance of being seen on Beaver Island. We've got to try everything, Friday."

She knew he was right, but the wind was doubly strong on the unprotected rise, and she didn't see how they'd keep a fire under control.

Leaving the kettle of coals and their meager supplies in the woods, they hunted for dry kindling and branches, working in silent haste as the wind showed no sign of abating.

They assembled an impressive pile of dried sticks, bark fragments, and dead branches, but Brian sent her for more fuel while he tried to ignite what they had with the coals.

"Get as many boughs as you can break off," he said. "If we throw them on a roaring hot fire, we'll get all the smoke we need. Wet leaves and moist sticks from the ground will make a good smudge too."

Her lightweight leather pumps were creaking from wet woodland walking, and her body was utterly exhausted, protesting the abuse it had suffered in a dozen different ways. Most annoying of all, she was getting a pimple on her chin, a hard, blind blemish that taunted her with its throbbing. She hadn't had one like it in ages, and it hurt her pride more than anything else. So much for cold-water skin care!

She piled an impressive load of greenery near at hand and settled back on her heels, watching anxiously as Brian struggled with the feeble fire. Then, so suddenly that it startled him as much as it did her, the wind fanned the flames through his pile of dry brush, blazing up so violently they had to retreat.

Standing as close as he dared, he threw handfuls of damp fuel on the inferno, finally grateful to see a column of thick gray smoke blowing downwind of them.

Her face was smudged, and he looked as tired as she felt, eagerly gulping water from one of the cans. Lunch wasn't quite the adventure it had been the day before. The wind was erratic, occasionally gusting toward them, giving them lungfuls of pungent smoke. Their eyes were red-rimmed and watery, and they retreated into the woods to avoid the searing billows.

"It's a good fire, huh?" she asked, trying to sound cheerful.

"Perfect for signaling," he agreed, sinking down with his back against a broad tree trunk.

"Can we go back to the beach now?"

"I'd like to, but we'd better watch until it burns down. We want to attract attention but not by starting a forest fire."

"How can we prevent it if the wind takes over?"

"That's what the blankets are for, beating out fire."

"Oh." She thought they had a more important function.

"But we can use them to cover up while we watch. It certainly isn't getting warmer."

Brian guided her between his outstretched legs, letting her use his firm torso as a back rest, covering them both with the blankets and holding her against him.

"Someone should see all that smoke," she said for his benefit, wondering if even their island could be seen from such a great distance.

"Are my hands cold?" he asked, sliding them under her layers of clothing after vigorously wiping them on the corner of a blanket.

"A little but don't stop," she said sleepily, snuggling closer as his thighs tightened against her hips.

The blanket tucked under his chin reminded her of playing cowboys and Indians in a homemade teepee when she was young, a game her more sophisticated older sisters considered tomboyish. Brian snapped the elastic on her bra, trying to open it with stiff fingers, mumbled an apology, and cupped each breast in his cold hands, content to rest them across the swelling mounds, feeling the nipples harden between his fingers.

"I need something to keep me awake," he said.

"We have to guard against forest fires," she said wryly, squirming even closer until the hard pressure of his masculinity nudged her lower back.

"It seems to be going all right," he said, but she wondered if he meant the fire.

"Do these pine needles seem pretty soft to you?" he whispered in a husky voice.

"Softer than sand, but I can feel them pricking me through my slacks."

"Let me spread the blanket."

"I don't know if we should."

"Please."

"You think I'm easy."

He laughed and squeezed her breasts.

"That's the last word I'd apply to you."

"Brian, the fire!"

A sudden violent gust of wind swept a burning branch away from the fire, showering sparks in its wake. Brian ran toward it, stamping his feet and swinging the blanket frantically at every errant spark, checking and double-checking to be sure none had escaped into the heavily wooded area.

"I'm afraid we'll have to keep watching it," he said breathlessly, coming to stand beside her when he was sure the blaze was under control.

They sat closer to the fire, risking an occasional puff of smoke to take advantage of the warmth. The ground was harder here, and she got up to give her bottom a rest, pacing restlessly and returning to the blankets and Brian in a short time.

"How did you get into the jewelry business?" he asked, sitting cross-legged under the blanket and stroking her knee.

"I've always liked to make things. After my divorce, I had a little money, so I began gradually, teaching myself and taking courses when I could. I started selling at art shows and was lucky. My jewelry caught on, and I finally got enough financing to start my own business."

"Winning prizes every step of the way."

"Now, how do you know that?"

"I'm interested in every phase of gemstones, so I subscribe to all the trade papers."

"My helper at the shop wondered why you came to me. So do I."

"I told you. I saw your picture, winning an award. They had a nice spread on your entries."

"My work doesn't show up well in photos," she said skeptically.

"No, but your face does."

"You're putting me on. You didn't bring an emerald to me because of a picture."

"Not entirely," he said, smiling, "but I'll admit I was curious. You looked so young and vulnerable, but your work was outstanding."

"I'm twenty-eight, and I don't appreciate being called vulnerable. I can look after myself."

"I'm learning what you do and don't appreciate," he said quickly, reaching over to tweak her nose in an annoying way. "Why pick Ann Arbor to start your business? The university?"

"That, of course, and I did so well at their summer art show. There's a good market there for my kind of work."

"Doesn't running a business interfere with making jewelry? You must be spread thin trying to do both."

"I manage very nicely," she said irritably. "How much longer do we have to baby-sit with this fire?"

"Depends on the wind. What else is there to do here?"

"I'd like to boil some water and wash my hair."

"That's impossible."

"I'd like to know why."

"I have to use the kettle to take coals back to camp, and it's much too cold to get your hair wet."

She knew he was right, but the man made her furious sometimes.

"You're gorgeous as you are," he said, catching a long tendril of hair the wind was whipping across her cheek. "Easily the most beautiful person on the island."

His lips were cold and hers were chapped, but they played games with them, nipping and caressing, keeping their desires at bay but unwilling to forgo the pleasures of being close.

"Where do you live?" he asked.

"I have an apartment over the shop."

"And where's home originally?"

"Downriver Detroit."

"Where?"

"Wyandotte. My parents still live there. So do two of my sisters. Another's been living in Lincoln Park since she got married."

"Older or younger?"

"I'm the youngest of four."

"And the only entrepreneur taking on the world alone?"

"If you must put it that way, yes. They're all married, but only Jackie's home with children, two little boys. My father was thrilled to get male offspring."

"And the other two?"

"Are you really interested in my family history?"

"Yes, I really am."

"Well, Joanie, the oldest, married a vet, but she can't stand the smell of his office, so she keeps on working for a credit union. That way her husband can't draft her to help in his clinic."

"And the third?"

"Jill and her husband run a wine shop. They'd like to have their own winery some day. He makes the most fantastic dry white in his basement, just for them and their friends, of course."

"J, J, and J. Why are you K?"

"Oh, my folks are Jack and Janette. They liked the idea of a family full of J.V.s, but by the time I came along it seemed trite, I guess."

"So they started down the alphabet?"

"If they did, I'm as far as they got."

"Let me guess. Jackie is the next youngest."

"How'd you know?"

"Great deductive reasoning worthy of Holmes himself. Your father kept getting girls. He named Jackie after himself, and Kelly was supposed to be a boy for sure."

She laughed, warmed by his hand nestled between her thighs, appreciating the way he figured out her father's system of naming his offspring.

"You said you crewed for your brother on a yacht. Is he the only other child in your family?" she asked.

"If you can call him a child at two hundred pounds, yes. I didn't think you'd remember anything I said on the boat."

"Oh, I remember every bit of that trip," she said with mock horror. "If we're rescued, I'll have to go through all that again on the boatride home. I'm sure the lake is getting rougher every day."

"Maybe help will come by helicopter. This island's not safe for navigation, especially when the wind is up."

She wasn't cheered by the prospect of a helicopter rescue. So far Brian knew only that she had a weak stomach. What would he think when he discovered she was terrified of heights, too? She was such a normal, unneurotic type when she didn't have to travel!

"What does your father do?" he asked conversationally.

"Both my parents are teachers. Mom has third grade this year, and Dad's at a community college."

"In Wyandotte?"

"No, neither wanted to live and teach in the same district. We've always lived in Wyandotte, but they've never run the risk of getting their own kids in their schools."

He has a gift for listening as if he really cares, she thought, shifting her bottom restlessly on the hard ground, terribly, terribly aware of the hand stroking the soft flesh of her thighs. Maybe he was only warming his hands, but he was keeping her hot all over.

"I think the fire's about had it," he said after a long silence.

"Can we leave now?"

"Let me stir it around a little just to be sure."

Transferring hot coals to the kettle using two green sticks was a tedious process, but so was looking after their simplest needs, she was discovering. Most irksome of all was looking at the huge body of deep blue water surrounding the island, so inviting to the eye and forbidding to the body. How she'd love to soak and soak and soak some more, but the temperature of the water made it unfit for any kind of bathing. Her hands were red and chapped just from rinsing kettles and filling them with water.

On the way back they found a few more red berries, quickly picking them and wrapping them in the empty cracker wrapper. Brian kept racing ahead, wanting to begin a new fire at the campsite while the coals were still hot enough.

For dinner she sliced water chestnuts into some slightly bitter greens Brian found, eating the warm vegetable substitute because her stomach was growling.

"What'll we do when our canned goods are gone?" she asked, pretending that the lukewarm beans were roast beef.

"Look for edible roots, fish, set traps for small game. We won't starve, but I think we'll be rescued before it comes to that."

She stirred the syrupy peaches and berries with a clean stick, cooking their third course in the small kettle. They ate with their fingers, sharing the same utensil, finishing one course before they could warm the next. Not even the substitute for tea, her favorite part of the meal, could wash away the fuzzy coating in her mouth. The peculiar taste of the green leaves kept coming up.

Measured by the amount of work they'd done, the day was the longest in her life, but Brian had another project for them.

"How does a bed of evergreen boughs sound to you?" he asked.

"Prickly."

"Not with a blanket covering them. We need some padding between us and the ground."

She couldn't argue with that, but it was dusk already and the woods reminded her of a cartoon where trees with arms tried to snatch anyone who came near. After gathering bark, twigs, branches, berries, weeds, and driftwood, not to mention smooth stones to heat as footwarmers, she'd had it with nature's treasure hunt.

"Brian, do we have to?"

"I know you're tired, sweetheart," he said, holding her against him for a moment of rest, "but it will be well worth it."

Her hands were sticky with tree sap and her fingers felt raw from trying to break off stubborn, leathery limbs.

"This had better be good, Fort," she grumbled as they shaped armloads of prickly branches into a bed-shaped rectangle.

"I don't expect any complaints."

"You sound pretty sure about that."

The blanket covering them smelled like the inside of a chimney, but the fragrance of the boughs helped neutralize it. Kelly pressed her feet against the still-warm stones at the end of their nest, hugging her arms across her chest. Except for loosening her bra and waistband, she hadn't undressed for bed, nor had Brian. The temperature had dropped noticeably, and the wind blew relentlessly, carrying a promise of wintry weather to come. He unzipped his jacket and pulled her head to his chest, wrapping his legs around hers.

"Warm enough?" he asked.

Surprisingly she was, and it felt wonderful after a day of icy hands and numb toes. Cuddling so close to him, she was perfectly content until she started thinking too much.

"Do you think anyone saw the smoke today?"

She rose on one elbow to watch him in the firelight, her worries increasing when she saw his face tighten into a frown.

"It's at least a possibility. We had a good column, and someone on Beaver must have looked in this direction. I really don't know if we're close enough to be seen from there."

She refused to ask the obvious: if the smoke had been seen, where was their help?

"Well, I guess I can stand you a little while longer," she teased instead.

"Can you stand this?"

He kissed a sensitive spot under her ear, drawing her into his arms. When he began exploring under her clothing, his hands were much too cold for pleasure, but she trapped them under her arms, sharing her body heat until his fingers were cozy.

"Are my hands warm enough now?" he asked, shifting his weight to get closer, dislodging a few boughs on his side as he did.

"Have you noticed our bed is falling apart?" she asked.

"Just rearranged a little. I didn't promise you a featherbed."

"Maybe we can work on one tomorrow. There must be some feathers lying around. We've found everything else."

"The only thing I want to find right now is this."

He slid his nicely warmed hand over one breast, caressing it tenderly and lightly fingering her taut nipple.

89

"I enjoy you," he whispered, his lack of urgency pleasing her.

With a little wiggling she managed to slip her hand under the back of his waistband, finding a little dimpled indentation at the end of his spine and teasing it with one finger. Giggling unexpectedly, she was reminded of Saturday night at the drive-in movie, double-dating with her best girl friend who anxiously compared notes with her at school on Monday. She never stopped being self-conscious with another couple in the car, but necking had been fun then, a little tentative stroking and self-conscious groping, but exciting in its newness.

"What's funny?"

"Oh, I was just thinking about my social life in high school."

"Tell me about it."

Shifting his position again, he cupped her breasts, tempting her to wiggle even closer.

"My best friend ordered some sexy underwear from a Hollywood mail-order company. She wore it to the drive-in and deliberately let her boyfriend discover it. He must have thought she was a fallen woman or something. He never called her again."

"What else happened while you were in high school?"

"I nearly lost my pom-poms before the homecoming game. I would have been swished out of the squad if someone hadn't told me they were in the boys' locker room. No comments, please! Some joker stole them and hid them there."

"What else did you do?"

"Oh, I painted scenery for the plays, and I was class treasurer my senior year. We gave the school a new flagpole. Just the usual stuff, you know."

"No, I don't know. I never went to high school."

"You skipped it?"

"Not exactly. I went to a prep school. I was programmed for Harvard after that, but I threw my dad a curve and insisted on Michigan."

"Did he mind?"

"Sure, but he survived."

No one at the drive-in ever caressed her breasts quite so nicely. She couldn't withhold a sigh of satisfaction, realizing what was happening between them. They were petting like two people just getting acquainted, talking softly and not making demands. After their heated lovemaking of the previous night, they needed time to get to know each other. Because he understood this, she yearned for him with an aching tenderness.

"Do you like this?" he asked, kneading her nipple between two warm fingers, stretching and pulling with gentle little tugs.

"Oh, yes."

He was making it hard for her to answer, directing all her attention to the delicious sensations darting through her. She hadn't known such little gestures could give so much pleasure.

He played her spine like a lyre, making silent, sensual music vibrate through her system as she curled on top of him, letting her hand roam under his shirt, delighted by the contrast between his smooth rib cage and the springy mat of hair that disappeared under his loosened slacks.

They never undressed completely, but she'd never felt more thoroughly loved. Her skin, where it was accessible, sizzled under his deft hands, and she felt wholly unrestrained, free to touch him without hastening to a conclusion.

Their joining was a quiet one, almost motionless until the final moments, but so deeply satisfying Kelly felt her concept of self changing. She was a minute speck under an endless sky, a frail bit of humanity clinging to a desolate strip of sand, but together they were the center of the universe. Nothing they did was insignificant nothing they felt was trivial. Quietly, caringly, they rocked their island cradle until oblivion claimed them, locked as they were in each other's arms.

"Kelly, darling, time to wake up."

All the boughs seemed to be under her feet and head. Her hip ground against hard-packed sand and stones when he rolled away, sitting up and fastening his clothing with fingers grown stiff with cold.

"Button up," he urged, reaching for his shoes and hardly feeling the numb toes he pushed into them. "Winter is here."

"So much for the morning news," she said with early-morning grumpiness, blaming him for the North Pole blasts that made her duck her head back under the blanket, uncovering her feet as she attempted to escape the cold.

"Get up or you're asking for trouble, Friday," he warned, stomping his feet to get circulation.

"There's no hurry."

"Lying there will only make you colder. Get up and move around. Help me with the fire. I had to feed it twice during the night."

He knelt beside her, tentatively running one finger over the sole of her foot.

"Oh, don't, I'm ticklish there."

"I hoped you were."

Grabbing her ankle, he tickled the ball of her foot unmercifully, making her laugh until she was afraid she'd wet her pants.

"Please stop! I'll get up! I'll do anything!"

"I thought you'd feel that way. We need water, fuel, and a miracle, sweetheart, not necessarily in that order."

She sat pulling the blanket under her chin and staring uneasily toward the lake.

"Is the lake too rough for a boat to get here?"

"Not necessarily. We should try another signal. If anyone spotted it yesterday, there's a chance a boat will come this way for a closer look."

"We have to spend another day on that rock?"

"No, we'll build our fire here in case a boat does come."

She had more questions, but she held them back, knowing it wasn't fair to ask for reassurances he couldn't give.

"Look, it's blowing so hard the trees are moving!"

"Don't worry, this is only a moderate gale, maybe thirty to thirty-five miles an hour. We won't blow off the island."

It was beginning to look like that was the only way they would leave it.

The forest seemed to murmur, and the sound of slapping waves was magnified. Even over the high wind every sound was distinct, and the tangy scent of the pines was sharper.

"Where's the sun this morning?" she asked, reluctantly pulling on her battered shoes and rising, hugging her jacket tightly across her chest.

"Under that dense cloud cover." He tried to sound lighthearted. "Even the sun is embarrassed by our abandoned behavior."

"Don't be silly. Where will we go if it rains?"

"I've been wondering the same thing." He kissed her forehead. "After we build the fire up and have breakfast, we'll work on a wind and rain shelter."

"I knew we'd end up in a wigwam."

Tramping in the woods for her duty call, she would've been delighted to visit even Mack's cousin's bathroom. She'd even use it without first putting tissue on the seat.

She ran back to the beach, grabbing at likely-looking branches as she went, realizing that they'd used most of the easy-to-obtain dead wood close to their campsite. Her small armload wasn't a very impressive contribution, but without an ax the supply was limited.

Brian was nowhere in sight, and she tried to convince herself it was silly to miss him while he was off in the woods for a few minutes. How would it feel to be separated from him all day every day? Feeling an emptiness that had nothing to do with hunger, she wasn't as eager as she'd thought to see a boat fighting its way shoreward. Either she'd stay here with him, miserably cold and wet, or she'd go home and be miserable in comfort without him.

He'd never said anything about not seeing her again, only that he wasn't interested in marriage. What if she were pregnant? She rubbed her abdomen, now flat and firm, and wondered how it would feel to carry another life inside her. Single women raised children all the time today; it was no big deal.

But it was a big deal. She didn't want her life changed, not after the struggle she'd had to get her business started. But if she was pregnant, she'd have Brian's baby and probably love it to distraction.

Well, she probably wasn't. Kicking at a fragment of driftwood, she began the chore of hauling water for their breakfast. There was enough water in front of her to give everyone in the world a lifetime of morning baths, but she could only heat a few dribbles at a time.

Brian came into sight carrying an armload of wood, his hair tangled and his face reddened by the relentless wind, looking as disheveled and grubby as she felt, and she ached with longing to be clean and groomed and glamorous for him.

He was just able to stir up enough sparks to get the fire started again, sacrificing a few precious scraps of paper toweling to encourage the feeble flickering.

"Imagine what a difference it made to primitive people to be able to start a fire," she said wistfully, warming her frozen fingers over the struggling tongues of fire.

He laughed softly, his pleasant tone carried away by the wind. "What we need is a good cave."

Bats and creepy, crawling things lived in caves, not to mention hibernating bears. She'd be just as happy taking her chances in a makeshift wigwam.

They ate cold leftover stewed peaches and berries, then prepared a warming pan of island-style tea, sipping from opposite sides of the kettle rather than trying to pour it in small pop-can openings. Touching the kettle warmed their hands, and Kelly began to believe they could survive another day. The nights didn't worry her.

The wood supply wasn't really running short; they only had to carry it farther, each trip burning up calories that wouldn't be easy to replace if they were marooned much longer. Well, her sisters kept telling her to reduce her backside. Think of all the money she might've wasted on a health spa when a little starving would do just as well.

"Have I told you you've been a good sport?" he asked, taking her latest load from her and leaning forward to brush a kiss across her nose.

"Not recently."

"You are. I can't think of anyone I'd rather be shipwrecked with."

"You're a prince when it comes to seasick fellow-travelers."

"Well, don't be sick again on my account."

His smile reached his eyes, forming tiny laugh lines, making her want to feel his lashes flicking over her lids again.

A good-sized branch shifted in the blaze, bombarding them with sparks, making them retreat and frantically brush at their clothing.

"Soft woods do that," he said. "I could chop some good birch logs if I had an ax."

"Next time we're marooned, we'll bring one. Do you think they've contacted your father by now?"

"Almost certainly they have, unless they backed out for some reason."

"Maybe Benny sank the boat or Mack took off without them in the van."

94

"Your guess is as good as mine. Next we'll burn our bed," he said, kicking a protruding branch back into the center of the fire.

"Must we?"

"Sorry, love, we need some nice black smudge. Our boughs are pretty much flattened anyway. We can always pick more."

The evergreens threatened to smother the fire, but it struggled on, throwing off billows of thick black smoke that were driven away by the wind. They went to the edge of the woods to escape it, wrapping the blankets around their shoulders.

"We'll be all right, even if we aren't found for a while."

"Sure we will," she said, wanting to please him even if she did have doubts.

"Look at me."

She focused on his chin, now dark with heavy bristles, not wanting him to see how shallow her optimism was.

"I'm falling in love with you," he said softly.

"I look pretty good here with nothing but trees, huh?"

"Don't be facetious. I'm very serious."

"I'm sorry. It's easier to be flip than admit how much that means to me."

"It does mean something to you?"

"Oh, yes, a lot. I . . ."

"What?"

"I don't want to be rescued if it means never seeing you again."

"What gave you the idea that you wouldn't?"

He looked unhappy enough to shake her.

"Your world is so different from mine."

"You sound like a snob."

"Me?"

"Passing judgment on my way of life before you know anything about it. Assuming rich is bad and the middle class has a monopoly on virtue."

"I don't do that."

Her protest was a little unsure. After all, hadn't all the great fortunes originally been gathered by robber barons exploiting the underprivileged? That's what her father taught in his political-science class.

"Then look directly at me."

Was it possible to be hypnotized by love? When their eyes met, she felt herself being swept into an emotional whirlpool, wanting to lean on him, depend on him, be his woman.

He kissed her and the spell was strangely shattered. She felt passionate yearning, an aching need to be close to him, but nothing less than an equal partnership could satisfy the woman she was now. Love might bring them together, but neither of them could ever be fettered.

CHAPTER SIX

"We haven't begun to tap the natural food resources on this island," Brian said cheerfully, poking and scraping the ground with a long stick.

The small inland clearing was close to a huge spruce with heavy, low limbs strong enough to support loose foliage. They'd invested most of their afternoon hours hunting for a promising rain shelter. Their nest under the spreading branches was far from waterproof, but greatly preferable to the open beach during a storm. By criss-crossing dead limbs on the existing ones, they'd managed to build a roof of sorts over their niche, but Kelly was too tired from tramping the woods and lugging branches to be interested in Brian's search for edible plants.

"Maybe I'll find some groundnuts," he said, still slicing shallow trenches in the ground-covering of decayed leaves and needles. Some people call them Indian potatoes."

She'd never known anyone who'd even mentioned groundnuts, let alone called them Indian potatoes. He must be acquainted with a bizarre crowd.

"They lie in strings just under the surface. You can eat them raw or cooked, just like a potato."

"You can eat them raw! Where'd you learn all this nature lore?"

"I've done a lot of camping. I told you I'm a geologist."

"But don't they go down in mines and look at rocks?"

"And explore wilderness areas for mineral and petroleum resources."

"Is that what you do for a living?"

"You're finally asking?"

Did he think she wasn't interested in what he did? Her cheeks flushed as she tried to explain.

"I just thought—I assumed—you were in your father's line of work."

"Do you know what that is?"

"Not exactly. I've heard of him. A financier or something?"

"Or something. But I do have interests of my own, exploring for mineral wealth being the primary one. That's how I became interested in gemstones."

She deserved the cool formality in his tone.

"I'm sorry. It just never occurred to me that you have to work."

"How did you imagine I spend my days? Partying, racing speedboats, chasing women? I didn't realize I have a playboy image."

"Oh, Brian, stop that. I said I'm sorry. How can I know how you live if you don't tell me?"

"Ask."

"All right, I'm asking!"

"Maybe we'd better gather our dinner first. Unfortunately there's no arrowroot here either. You can cook and eat those roots all winter."

"You don't really think we'll be here all winter!"

"Of course not, but it doesn't hurt to explore ways of surviving."

"Oh, I give up."

She stormed across the clearing into the thick woods before realizing she didn't know the way. Returning to him in embarrassed silence, she found him grinning broadly.

"See, you do need me, independent lady."

"How warm will your bed be without me tonight?" It was a cheap shot and she knew it.

"Would you do that, freeze yourself just to irritate me?"

He moved closer, taking both her chapped hands in his rough, stained palms.

"I believe you would," he said softly, answering his own question. "How about a truce? We'll feast on our one can of corned beef, then move here for the night."

"What if help comes while we're hiding in the woods?"

"No one will come after dark."

"How much daylight do we have left?"

He glanced at the sky, now a solid mass of heavy gray clouds. "Hard to tell on a dreary day like this. Come on, Friday, we want to get back here before it's pitch dark."

Had they really walked so far? The prospect of repeating the trek in a short while made her feel even more exhausted, and there was water to haul, wood to gather, and a meal of sorts to prepare. To think she'd once been fascinated by native American culture! The average squaw used to do all this plus grow food, raise children, make clothes, skin game, and, of course, obey her brave's every command. Kelly laid the fantasy of the natural life to rest with Sleeping Beauty and knights on white horses.

"I've heard of fishing with yarn unraveled from a sweater," he said, keeping her hand locked in his as they ducked and seesawed between the trees, following the easiest if not the shortest route back to the beach.

"You're enjoying all of this!" she said, astonished at the realization.

"How can I possibly deny that when you've shared it all with me? Has it been so terrible for you, Kelly?"

She only had time to shake her head, then he was kissing her—quick, sweet little pecks that smarted on her weather-raw lips and a long, slow embrace she could feel all the way to her toes. He was her only real source of warmth on the whole wind-ravaged island.

She wasn't surprised that he made her ears buzz and her toes vibrate, but the volume grew louder, a hum building to a grating roar that tore them apart and sent them running toward the beach.

"It's a chopper," he yelled as he ran, dragging her forward, both of them stumbling in haste.

Frantic that the machine might leave before they could be seen, she sprinted by his side, not even noticing how much her feet hurt in her fragile, battered shoes.

They came bursting out of the woods within yards of a tall sandy-haired man who was examining their meager supplies with his back toward them.

"You're a welcome sight," Brian called out, attracting the man's attention.

"Brian Fort?" he asked in a heavy drawl.

"Yes, and Miss Kelly Valentine."

"Pleased to meet you, sir, ma'am," the helicopter pilot said over the noise of his machine, offering his hand.

"How'd you find us?"

"I'd better tell you later, sir. I'd like to get going right away. The word on the weather is all hell's about to break loose. Anything you need here?"

"The emerald," Kelly cried, remembering the precious gem stuffed inside the empty can weighted down with stones. She ran to retrieve it.

"Leave the rest," Brian ordered, pulling her toward the helicopter, instinctively ducking and getting ready to board before he felt her weight dragging on his hand.

"I've never been on one of these," she screamed, most of her words drowned out by the noise of the machine.

"Tell me about it later," he yelled impatiently.

She couldn't believe they were going to fly over the dark, ominous expanse of the lake in such a small thing. Crowded between the pilot and Brian, she couldn't see where it was any sturdier than a carnival ride. At least in amusement parks the monstrous little capsules stayed in one area. They didn't whip out over a lake so deep lost ships and bodies might never surface.

Without realizing it she was clutching Brian's hand, her fingers squeezing so tightly he finally winced and tried to ease her grip.

"You'll be all right, darling! You won't get sick in this."

He had to shout to be heard, but she was too frightened to worry about what the pilot thought.

"Relax! We'll be home soon."

It wasn't just airsickness she was worried about. Her stomach gave an agonizing lurch when they took off, but she hardly noticed it, sure as she was that the frail-looking blades wouldn't be able to lift them above the water.

The lake was really going to get them this time, roaring and swelling as the thin-shelled craft fought the wind and finally won, gradually rising above the angry waves, buffeted by galelike winds but gamely heading for shore. She didn't see this, though. She elected to meet her end with eyes clenched shut and lips tucked painfully between her teeth.

Brian gave up trying to shout comfort, tightly gripping her fingers in self-defense.

Didn't that pilot ever shut the motor off? she thought ungratefully, finally realizing they were firmly anchored on solid ground again.

"I don't know the whole story, sir, but your father knew exactly where you were. We're at the Pellston Airport now. He has a private jet warming up for you."

"I can't thank you enough," Brian said sincerely. "We'll see that your boss hears what a great job you did."

"I was lucky. Twenty minutes later would've been too late."

"Too late for what?" Kelly finally regained the use of her vocal cords.

"To get us off that slab of sand before the storm hit," Brian explained, taking her toward a terminal building under the protective shelter of his arm.

"Where did he say we are?" she asked hoarsely.

"Pellston."

For a town she'd barely heard of, it had a decent-sized air depot, a modern facility with two wings, well lit and inviting.

"There are people in there." She stopped abruptly.

"Well, sure," he said, sounding puzzled.

"Brian, look at me. No, don't. No self-respecting scarecrow would wear these clothes."

"You look like you've been through a lot, and you have. Don't worry. You can freshen up in the restroom. Here, take my comb."

"Freshen up! I need a total overhaul. I'll just wait out here."

"Don't be silly."

Silly! She was so weak and nauseated from the flight she could hardly stand, and he thought she was silly for not wanting to face strangers looking like a skid-row reject.

There was a plane waiting for her. An airplane. She'd never flown, sure that the ordeal wouldn't be worth the time saved. Buses and trains weren't as speedy, but they rolled along on good solid earth, smoothly eating up the miles, delivering anxiety-free passengers without holding patterns or landing crashes.

"I think I will use the restroom."

She could take a bus home, but she didn't have a cent with her, nor did Brian since his billfold had been stolen. Her parents would come for her. They must be frantic with worry. Her mother used to be able to manufacture a migraine if one of her daughters was an hour late getting home from a date. Even her father must have noticed something was wrong, although the rest of the family tended to shelter him from domestic crises. He was much too busy studying the international situation for the family to bother him with internal affairs.

She left the restroom, deciding nothing that was wrong with her could be remedied with green liquid soap. Feeling like an aging hippie, she approached an older man sitting in a wool tweed topcoat, convincing him that she'd return his twenty cents as soon as she made a collect call to her parents. He loaned her the right amount of change, looking as pleased as a missionary who's just saved another soul with a bowl of rice.

The phone rang and rang until the operator broke in, suggesting her party wasn't home and could she place her call later?

How could they be out when their youngest daughter was in the clutches of crazed kidnappers? Was this their bridge night? No, it couldn't be Friday already. They were supposed to be frantic with worry, and they were out gallivanting around. She didn't want that much independence.

The man beamed at her when she returned his coins.

"We can board," Brian said coming up behind her.

"I called my parents. I'm sure they'll want to come for me."

"Kelly, we're hundreds of miles from your home. Come on."

"Really, they won't mind. I haven't seen them much lately, and the ride will give us a chance to catch up on family news, you know."

"You're afraid of getting airsick," he said flatly.

"Well, actually, you're not going to believe this."

"Try me."

"I've never been in a plane, and I'd rather start with something a little larger, say a 747. So why don't you get on the plane, and I'll meet you later?"

"You've never flown? Look, there's nothing to be afraid of, darling."

"I'm not exactly afraid."

Terrified was more like it.

"Let me speak with the airport manager. He's standing by to see that we're all right. Maybe he can get something for your motion sickness, then you won't have a thing to worry about."

"Not a thing," she said miserably, sitting down to wait as far as possible from her benefactor in the topcoat but still wondering if she could borrow his dimes again.

Jill would come for her; what were sisters for if not to help each other? And if Jill was still working at the store, Jackie owed her a favor for all the free baby-sitting she'd done over the years. Or she could threaten to tell Joanie's husband the truth about who accidently let that howling sheepdog out of its kennel last year.

"Are we in luck," Brian said, bringing her a glass of water and handing her two small white tablets. "The manager's wife gets motion sick, and he'd picked up a prescription for her during his lunch break. They're flying to Hawaii for Christmas, and she wanted to be prepared. Lucky for us, he didn't have time to take it home. Well, swallow these, and we can get on the plane."

She'd never forgive her parents for not keeping a vigil by the phone. How could they abandon her?

The sky was pitch black now with rain blowing across the runway in wet blasts.

"The weather is terrible," she said with a glimmer of hope. "We'll never to able to take off."

"Planes fly in rain," he said, "and the worst disturbance is still over the lake."

A man in a yellow rain slicker walked to the plane holding a striped golf umbrella over the two of them. The plane looked like a miniature version of the ones she'd seen meeting friends or relatives at Metro Airport, and it simply wasn't possible that she was going to ride in the thing.

"I think I'll call my parents' house again," she said firmly.

"No time. We're taking off in a few minutes to get ahead of the rough weather. Anyway, I'm sure my parents have told them you're safe. They'll probably be waiting when we land."

"Well, you just go on without me," she insisted. "I'm perfectly capable of getting home on my own."

He laughed.

"The only question is whether you're going to walk onto this plane or be carried."

He tightened his arm around her waist, and she believed he'd actually force her to board.

"You've no right to make me fly."

"I won't argue that, but it's time you learned to travel comfortably and conveniently."

"I won't be comfortable!"

"Before you know it, we'll be landing in Detroit."

Here she was, in the middle of every girl's favorite fantasy, flying off in a private jet with a rich, handsome, splendidly attentive man, and her heart was pounding in terror.

Strapped in a seat with a pillow behind her head and his hand resting on her thigh, she felt like the victim of a mad scientist who was only waiting for liftoff to use her in his crazy experiments.

"Comfortable?" he asked softly.

"Tomorrow I walk barefoot on hot coals. It will be a treat."

How could he sit there and laugh at her?

"Relax. The pills will probably knock you out."

The sensation of racing down a dark runway was bad enough without the screeching noise and the bolts of lightning visible through the small window.

"We'll get hit by lightning," she protested. "Make the pilot turn around and go back."

"He knows what he's doing, and you're safer then you'd be at home in the bathtub."

That was the one topic that could distract her.

"Brian, I'm so filthy. Will anyone see us when we land?"

"Everyone who sees you will be so glad you're safe, it won't matter how you look."

"You say awfully nice things, but you should've left me back on the ground."

"Not a chance."

He explained about air pockets and turbulence, assuring her that no auto in the world was as safe as the plane, but her fingers were clenching the armrest so tightly he had to pry them loose.

"The pills have had time to work, and your worries are over."

"Ha!"

Miraculously she did sink into a drug-induced stupor, hardly aware of their landing or Brian's voice insistently trying to summon her back to consciousness. Finally feeling firm ground under her feet, she wasn't sure if her dream had improved or the real nightmare was over.

"Darling, we were so worried!"

A slender woman in a wool pantsuit and short fur coat collapsed on Brian's neck just inside the terminal, hugging him and giving his

104

back nervous little pats, not unlike a mother working on a hard-to-burp baby.

"You're okay, Brian? Not hurt or anything?"

A silver-haired man reached around the woman and took Brian's hand, shaking it vigorously, while a third person, a heavyset version of Brian, pumped the other hand.

"I'm fine, fine," Brian kept saying, not quite able to convince them.

A familiar voice pierced the fogginess of her brain, but Brian had his arm around her again, talking rapidly to the family that surrounded him.

"Mom, Dad, this is Kelly Valentine, the jeweler who was marooned with me."

She'd always been proud of her profession, but that seemed a formal way of introducing the woman he'd been kidnapped with. The woman he'd made love to, for that matter.

"Welcome home, Miss Valentine," Damon Fort said. "My wife Louise and son Brad."

The demands of courtesy met, he turned eagerly to Brian.

"You won't believe how we located you."

"Tell me."

"Apparently that gang of scoundrels had a falling-out. They were asking for a million dollars without giving us any proof that you were still alive. After a number of calls, each one more hostile than the last, I got one from a different man who said he was willing to settle for less, twenty-five thousand, to tell us where you were."

"Your father is such a good judge of character," Mrs. Fort said.

"I gambled and arranged to pay him in person after asking him some questions about you. It cost me twenty-five thou, but he came through with a map showing the island."

Kelly wondered morosely what her share came to.

"Did you see the guy?" Brian asked curiously.

"Not very well. He had some rigmarole worked out to get the money at Hart Plaza at night, but he did have a bushy beard."

"Benny!" Brian's laugh startled them. "That boy wasn't so dumb after all. He pulled a fast one on the other two and headed for his Canadian love nest."

Somehow several people got between them, distracting Brian

105

with a barrage of questions. She heard the same familiar voice working its way closer, calling her name.

"Kelly, over here, Kelly."

She followed on the fringe of the group engulfing Brian, gulping air to clear her head.

"Kelly, here!"

It was her mother's voice, but she saw her father first, something suspiciously like a grin spreading across his thin, scholarly face, the lights of the terminal exposing the spot on the top of his head where the hair had thinned to a few struggling strands of graying fluff.

She was in his arms in an instant, collapsing against his narrow chest while her mother did a war dance around them in her eagerness to determine the state of her child's health.

"Did you get enough to eat? Are you hungry? Did they hurt you? Did you get seasick going to that island?"

"Give her a chance, Janette."

It was the closest thing to a rebuke her father had ever directed at his wife.

The crowd around Brian was drifting farther away, and she panicked, afraid they'd be separated forever.

"Miss Valentine, how was it alone on an uninhabited island with Brian Fort?"

All she noted about the speaker were black bangs and owlish glasses, but the woman's voice had an irritating edge.

"Who are you?"

"Mary Barnes, Channel Twelve news. We have our camera here, Miss Valentine, if you'll just say a few words for our viewers."

"I don't want to be on TV looking like this," she said, forgetting that appeals to her father were apt to be overlooked, tabled, or forgotten.

"She's not talking now," he said resolutely, tucking Kelly under his arm and guiding her away from the milling crowd.

"Jackie and Jill were coming too," her mother said, getting into the act by grasping her hand, "but Billy brought the flu home from nursery school, and it seems to be going through their family, and . . ."

"Just a minute, Mother."

She broke away from her parents, seeing Brian do the same.

"Don't leave," he said.

"That woman is from a TV station. I don't want to talk to her."

"No, don't, not until we tell our stories to the police."

"Are they here?"

"A couple of detectives are. I told them to come out to our place for our statements."

"My parents are here. Come meet them."

"Sure, but things are pretty hectic here. Ride with me and have them follow us."

"Brian, I can't go to your house. I'm a wreck. I need clothes, a hot bath, a shampoo."

"My mother will have clothes you can wear, and I'll personally draw your bath and wash your hair if you'll let me."

"Not in your parents' home!"

"I live in a guest cottage on the grounds."

"I didn't know that."

"There are a lot of things you don't know about me. Come on."

"I can't leave my parents. They want to know all about it too."

Her mother had caught up, curiosity giving her attractively round face a positive glow.

"Mr. Fort, I'm Kelly's mother, Janette Valentine."

"It's a pleasure to meet Kelly's mother," he said gravely, turning to shake her father's hand and exchange pleasantries with him.

"I suggested to Kelly that you follow us to our place. We have to give our statements to the police."

Was her father frowning at the thought of entering a robber baron's lair, or did he have an early class in the morning?

"I think we'd better take our girl home," he said in the voice he used to explain term-paper requirements and announce exams.

"Surely even the FBI will understand how exhausted she is. Tomorrow will be soon enough." Her mother was used to making decisions.

"Every minute we delay lessens the chance of catching the kidnappers. You don't want your daughter's captors to go free, do you, Mrs. Valentine?"

How could Brian get her mother's number so quickly? Nothing worked better than a challenge to her family honor. The offenders had to be punished.

"You'd better go on with Mr. Fort, Kelly," her father said, again surprising her with his decisiveness.

Why hadn't he been firm enough to forbid her marriage to Larry? Of course, she wouldn't have listened, but it would've been nice if he'd tried. She was pleased that for once he wasn't conserving all his energy for his causes.

"Dad, you came all this way to meet me."

"I'll go with you," her mother offered.

"Out of the question, Janette. You need a good night's sleep to handle that rowdy class of yours. You've lost enough sleep over this."

Miracle of miracles, her father was taking charge. By some quirk of reasoning did he blame his wife for the kidnapping? Kelly tried to imagine some flaw in her largely maternal upbringing that might have cast blame on her mother.

"You'd better go along and do your duty, dear," her mother said, giving in with uncharacteristic grace.

"But I want to go home."

"And we want you, Kelly dear, but Mr. Fort is right. You have to tell the authorities all you know immediately." She bent near to kiss her. "Your skin is so chapped. It must have been terrible on that island."

Brian whisked her away before she could give her mother any details to share in the teachers' lounge the next morning, steering her out to a dark Lincoln parked in the loading zone in front of the terminal. His parents were in the front seat waiting. Apparently Bradford had satisfied his curiosity or done his fraternal duty and gone his way. Two men in dark suits hovered near the fender, apparently having chased away the press and curious onlookers.

"Are they the police?" she asked.

"No, they work for my father. Get in."

She wanted to ask if they were bodyguards but not in front of his parents. Whatever their job, they got into a second car and followed the Lincoln driven by Mr. Fort.

"This whole experience must have been terrible for you, Miss Valentine," his mother said politely.

"I won't forget it in a hurry."

She felt like a used rag doll on display in a velvet-lined case, wanting to relax against the plush seats but feeling too out of place to enjoy being comfortable. Brian squeezed her thigh, chuckling when she brushed his hand away.

"How did you happen to be in the jewelry shop during the robbery, Brian?" his mother asked.

"I stopped in before the game."

"But the game was well underway when the robbery took place."

"I was running late. One of the quirks of fate, Mother."

He found Kelly's hand on her lap and moved it to his thigh, stroking it lightly.

"What I mean is why weren't you at the stadium by then? Grant and Jim were worried when you didn't show up. They called the house after the game, and, of course, by then we knew you'd been kidnapped."

Was there some kind of accusation in her voice, a suggestion that her son had gotten into trouble because he wasn't where he was supposed to be? She smirked until Brian squeezed her hand too hard.

"I was looking for your birthday present, Mother."

Oh, good move, Kelly thought. Return the guilt to the parental court. Then she felt a little ashamed. She really was being a snob, feeling antagonistic to a woman she didn't know at all. Brian couldn't be as nice as he was without loving, sympathetic parents.

"We had an earlier appointment, Mrs. Fort, but Brian was held up by an accident on I 94. He didn't want to go on to the game without explaining. It's unusual to find people as considerate as he is."

"He always thinks of other people," his mother said proudly. "Did you have enough to eat on the island?"

Her questions weren't so different from the ones Kelly's parents had hurled at her, and she let Brian answer them uninterrupted, wondering how much he intended to tell them about their relationship. But what was there to tell? They'd felt a strong attraction, and living on the island had thrown them together in a way that couldn't happen in ordinary circumstances.

Opening an ornate iron gate with an electronic control, Mr. Fort drove onto the estate, following a tree-lined roadway to their riverside home. Kelly had a fleeting impression of a sprawling Tudorstyle house with broad steps leading to a dock on the river. She was startled when Brian turned her over to his parents, saying he was going home to take a shower.

"Brian has the guest house. He travels so much it became a

nuisance to keep his apartment in town," his mother explained. "Now you'll want a nice warm soak. Those policemen will just have to wait."

A maid in a dove-gray uniform and white apron led Kelly to an upstairs bedroom with adjoining bathroom, turning on the water in the tub then leaving the room, returning with a lovely pink nightgown and a warm burgundy robe. It wasn't an outfit Kelly would have picked for a police interrogation, and when she glimpsed the designer label in the gown, she gasped. It was the kind of garment she'd only read about.

The pills were wearing off, leaving her with a metallic taste that two glasses of water didn't wash away. The matronly maid with a slight Scandinavian accent turned off the water and stood at attention by the full tub. Was she supposed to help guests undress?

"That's all, thank you," Kelly said, trying to sound as dignified as Mrs. Fort but spoiling it with a grin.

"If you'd like to give me your clothes, ma'am, I'll see about cleaning them," she offered.

"They're ready to be burned, but I'll leave them in the other room. Thank you."

Without her three semesters of Swimming I, she wouldn't have dared step down into the massive sunken tub. The bubbles were shoulder-high, covering the deliciously slippery, scented water, and she bravely slid downward until her head was momentarily submerged. Now she remembered why she hated putting her face underwater, but it was well worth smarting eyes to rinse off completely. Even after scrubbing vigorously from head to toe, she wasn't entirely satisfied, resoaping her hair and standing in the shower stall for a final drenching rinse. Cleanliness wasn't underrated.

The gown felt like liquid silk, as different from the scratchy blanket on the island as satin was from sandpaper. She hated to cover it with the robe, wishing Brian was with her to see how good she could look. Her blow-dried hair was a gorgeously clean mass of waves swept back from her forehead, and her red cheeks looked more healthy than chapped.

A soft rap on the door made her pulse race, but it was only the maid inviting her down to the breakfast room for a late-night supper.

110

"These gentlemen are eager to talk to you," Mrs. Fort explained when Kelly had returned downstairs. "I've invited them to join us for a little snack. We were so excited about finding Brian, we forgot how hungry the two of you must be."

In the soft light of the room his mother showed few signs of her approaching sixtieth birthday. Her few wrinkles made her face look gentle, and the loose skin on her neck was the only giveaway. She'd changed from the suit and high-necked blouse to a flowered caftan in shades of bronze and gold. Mr. Fort was was casual in a beige sweater and Black Watch plaid slacks, but Brian wasn't there at all. The two policemen looked tired in gray and brown suits they'd probably worn since early morning.

Brian's entrance was the signal to sit around a glass-topped wire-legged table with matching ice-cream-parlor chairs. The rest of the house had seemed very formal from the glimpse she'd had, but this room was lovely and relaxed with brightly flowered orange and yellow wallpaper and baskets of hanging ferns. The window overlooked the river. From where she sat Kelly could see the lights of a long ore boat going north for a cargo of iron taconite. It was a common sight on the waterway, but not one she'd ever enjoyed from a house on the river.

Under the policemen's courteous but professional questioning, they remembered countless details about the kidnappers.

"Definitely amateurs," the older of the two detectives said, finally persuaded to cut into a slice of thick pink ham on his plate. "Benny Strang, age around thirty, employed at Little Joe's Restaurant, planning to escape to Canada. Apparently involved with a woman there."

He repeated pages of facts between bites, asking them to verify each one. They agreed pretty well on the details, Brian able to add a few things he'd heard while she raced in and out of restrooms.

"The station owner found the note you left on the mirror, Miss Valentine. Clever the way you did it."

She appreciated his praise until he described the forest of toilet tissue and the owner's first reaction. He made it sound like a cheerleader's trick on homecoming night. So much for glory.

Mr. Fort roared with laughter. She could like that man.

The police left, complimenting them on how much they'd learned about their captors. She felt Benny really deserved the credit.

"Kelly, you must be exhausted," Mrs. Fort said, apparently just deciding to use her first name. "We must have a toast, then off to bed."

They polished off the decanter of dry red wine, but the men were only humoring her. Brian's father stole him away for a late night talk. Kelly had to be satisfied with a good-night smile.

The comforter had been folded back, showing genuine baby-blue satin sheets that must have been ironed on both sides to look so sleek. Even a thirty-three-year-old bachelor had to behave himself in his parents' house, but she tried to remember if he'd given them any clues about their feelings for each other. She fell asleep imagining she was back on a sandy beach beside her castaway lover.

CHAPTER SEVEN

"Good morning."

He kissed her shoulder, sliding the strap out of his way and caressing the soft curve. As she uncurled and reached for him, he pressed his mouth against her palm, sliding it over her delicate veined wrist to the inside of her elbow where he gently kissed the sensitive skin. When she moved responsively he lavished his attentions on her shoulder again, bending closer so she could finger the nape of his neck, finding his hair surprisingly soft.

"You're all dressed," she accused him.

"Not by choice." He brushed her slightly parted lips with his. "I have to fly to Chicago."

"Chicago!"

She sat up abruptly, forgetting how much she wanted him to see her in the clinging pink gown. Certainly he was on his way somewhere, dressed in a dark pinstripe suit, his shirt immaculately white above the vest. With a gray-patterned tie he looked conservative enough for a bankers' convention, but so handsome she was slightly awed.

"Don't look so stricken. With a little luck I'll be back late tonight."

"I'd better get dressed and go home," she said, scrambling for the edge of the bed to cover her disappointment.

"There's no hurry. I thought you could stay here until I get back."

"I can't do that."

"I don't see why not."

"What would your parents think? No, I'd better leave right now. Can you drop me somewhere near a bus stop?"

"No. Slow down. You can spend the day getting acquainted with my mother, then move over to my house this evening. I'd love to come home and find you under my covers."

"Brian, you're crazy!"

"Why?"

"How could I handle that? Should I say, it's been nice chatting with you, Mrs. Fort, but I'm going to sleep with your son tonight?"

"I told my parents we've become very close. They certainly don't pass judgment on the guests I bring to my own home."

"You mean you bring women here right under your mother's nose?"

"I've never had a woman living here with me, if that's what you mean. I had an apartment in the Lafayette Towers for a long time, but I gave it up when I went to Indonesia for six months."

"Well, I can't stay here."

Looking anxiously around the room she wondered where on earth her clothes were. Ragged as they'd become, they were hers and she needed them.

"My mother can hardly wait for you to come downstairs so she can start clucking over you like a mother hen. I'm afraid my brother and I aren't very satisfactory chicks. She hoped for grandchildren when Brad got married, but his wife's too busy practicing law to have babies."

"You're just saying that."

"No, she can't wait to help you recover from your ordeal. She canceled her volunteer work at the hospital just to be with you today."

"Well, it's nice one member of your family is free today," she muttered, frustrated because she couldn't find a trace of her clothing in the closet or the drawers.

"Are you looking for something?"

He knew darn well she was.

"My clothes."

"That's one way to keep you here, barefoot and"—he came up behind her and slid his hands down her sides—"sexy."

"Brian, take this seriously. I have to get back to my store. I can't make a living with the door locked, if anyone even bothered to lock it."

"Wait until tomorrow, and I'll drive you home."

"I can't wait here. I'll call one of my sisters to come get me."

"I couldn't sleep thinking about you last night. I don't know if I can take another night alone."

"No one's making you fly off to Chicago."

"I'm scheduled to appear on the program at a convention. It wouldn't be fair to cancel now."

"Well, I have obligations too. My helpers don't know whether they still have their jobs. I have orders waiting to be picked up."

"Okay, I'll let you go this time, but you don't have to take a bus. I'll leave orders for a car to be available when you want to go."

"I can't take one of your cars."

"You have an awfully long list of things you can't do. Can you kiss me good-bye?"

"Yeah, I can handle that."

She grinned and moved against him, feeling wicked kissing a man wearing a three-piece suit while she was still in a nightgown. He cupped her bottom none too gently and kissed her soundly.

"That's probably all I can stand if I'm going to catch my flight," he said, taking a deep breath.

"Won't the plane wait for you?"

"Not this one. We used a friend's jet last night. Our business doesn't warrant keeping our own. I'm catching a commercial flight."

"So, you're one of the peasants after all?"

"Have I ever pretended I wasn't?"

He had her there. Brian Fort was the most natural-acting, unassuming person she knew. Maybe because he was so terrific, he didn't have to pretend anything.

"I can stand one more kiss," he said invitingly.

He drew her close, sliding his hand between her thighs and arousing her quickly, making her gasp in surprise and longing. Could she really be wishing they were back on that island?

"I want you to think about what you're missing all day." Brian broke the spell, kissing her quickly and retreating to the door.

"You're terrible!"

She tried to pretend her agitation was anger.

"I'll call you. If you need anything before you leave, just ask. And you can change your mind about staying. With a little luck I can be back by two A.M."

"I'll be sound asleep in my own bed by then."

115

"Above your shop?"

"That's where I live."

He winked wickedly, stripping off the gown with his eyes, and left. She'd forgotten to ask where her clothes were.

The phone was an ornate model that matched the French provincial decor of the room. The white furniture and woodwork were set off by wallpaper that picked up the pale blue of the sheets and the deeper shading of the wool carpet. Jackie's phone was busy, but if she still had flu in the family, Kelly didn't want to risk catching it anyway. Joanie was tied up in the manager's office, so she decided against leaving a message. Her sister took her career seriously and might not want to be bothered at work.

Jill answered the phone at the wine shop, exploding into a barrage of questions.

"What's Brian Fort like? Did you sleep out in the open? Weren't you freezing? For goodness' sake, tell me all about it, Kelly. Did the crooks . . . ah . . . threaten you?"

"Threaten yes, rape, no. Great, yes, and yes to your questions. Jill, can you come get me?"

"Where are you?"

"Still at the Forts' in Grosse Pointe, but I really have to get back to Ann Arbor."

"You spent the night there?"

"Yes, the police questioned us here. It was too late to go home, and now Brian's left for Chicago."

"Brian? First names, huh?"

"Of course first names! We were marooned on an uninhabited island. Can you come?"

"Todd just left to do some errands, but I expect him back soon. I'll come as soon as he gets here."

"I don't know if there's a street number. It's on Jefferson on the river side."

"Oh, you don't have to tell me where it is. Jackie and I drove out and located it."

"You mean you were out sightseeing while I was in mortal danger?"

"Well, there was nothing we could do to rescue you, and Joan had already driven past it with Mom."

"Oh, great! My family, the tourists."

"If you want me to come, tell me how to get past the gate."

"I don't know. It operates electronically. Just honk your horn, and someone will open it."

"Don't you dare meet me at the gate," she warned. "We couldn't even get a glimpse of the house from the road. If I'm coming all that way, I at least want to see the outside of the place up close."

"I'll be waiting for you in the house."

She walked into the bathroom and surveyed the pool-size blue porcelain tub, deciding to take a shower before someone offered to draw water for her. She didn't have enough nerve to go home without leaving evidence that she'd bathed, but darned if she'd take another bath for one in a tub built for two.

Toweling dry she took advantage of the steamy full-length mirror on the door to see if she'd lost any weight. Her waist had the nipped-in look she liked, her stomach was flat beneath a lean midriff and nicely rounded breasts, and even her thighs looked trim. But from what she could see, her bottom still drooped, two fleshy pads defying exercise and starvation. She pulled on the robe impatiently.

The knock was soft but insistent. She answered, hoping it was a maid with her clothes, but Mrs. Fort herself stood there, looking a little wan in a bright yellow satin negligee.

"May I come in, dear?"

Dear? Either Brian was right about his mother's maternal overflow, or she was being patronized.

"Of course."

She started to say all the civil things guests say to their hostesses, but the older woman waved her off rather impatiently.

"Please, Kelly, not before my coffee! I try not to confront another human being before noon, but I want you to know you're welcome to stay here as long as you like, here or in Brian's house."

"He put you up to this?" she asked, deciding candor was the best course.

"It was his suggestion, but the invitation comes from me. Brian has defied my best matchmaking efforts for years, so I encourage his friendships wholeheartedly. Of course, it is unusual for Brian to have a friend here."

She flushed, conscious of having said too much.

Kelly could almost see the older woman planning a wedding.

117

What had Brian told her about their time on the island? She wanted to throttle him!

"Thank you for the invitation, Mrs. Fort, but I really do need to go home now. I know Brian will be gone all day, and I have to check on my store. The robbery, you know. Do you know where my clothes are?"

"Ingrid's been working on them, but there's not much hope, I'm afraid. One knee of your slacks is worn through, and the blazer seems to have shrunk away from its lining. She did find this in your pocket."

It was the emerald, free of its toilet-tissue wrapping.

"It's the gem Brian brought to my store to be set," she said, feeling compelled to give some explanation. "Would you give it to him, please?"

"Of course, and I'll send some clothing, if you feel you really must leave. Nothing you need return. You do have time for breakfast, don't you? Our chauffeur, Harry, brought Brian's Mercedes up to the house, so it's ready whenever you need it."

"Thank you, but it won't matter what I wear home. My sister's coming for me in an hour or so. Can someone open the gate? I told her to honk."

"Harry will watch for her and open it. Sometimes it's such a nuisance, living with all this security. And it didn't keep Brian from being kidnapped, did it?"

"No, but that was just a crazy fluke, and it was probably harder on you than on him," she said sympathetically.

"He certainly doesn't seem any worse for the experience, In fact, he's positively glowing."

Kelly smiled, realizing Mrs. Fort would've loved to heap motherly comfort on her son after his ordeal, but he didn't even have chapped lips for his mother to fuss over.

Ingrid proved to be the same maid who drew her bath, on duty again in her dove uniform with a fresh, crisp apron. Kelly was tempted to ask how many hours she worked every day, but Mrs. Fort's kindness made her reluctant to come on like a union agitator. Probably the return of the lost son had thrown the whole household off schedule.

"I'm afraid this is the best I can do, miss," she said rather apologetically, offering Kelly her pathetic outfit, cleaned and pressed. "Mrs. Fort said to keep any of these if you like them. May I draw your bath now?"

"Thank you, no. That's all for now."

The maid looked a little disapproving, so Kelly quickly added, "I took a shower."

The forest-green slacks were the softest wool flannel she'd ever felt, fully lined and exquisitely tailored. She couldn't resist slipping into them although she felt like an orphan being dressed by the rich folks. She'd only seen Mrs. Fort's figure concealed by bulky fur and flowing robes, but one thing was obvious: the older woman had a pair of hips that made Kelly feel like a blimp. She couldn't begin to force the side zipper over hers.

The knee on her slacks had been patched with iron-on tape, something she hadn't seen since she gave up touch football. Her underwear and blouse had been laundered and seemed serviceable, but the blazer was a total loss. Ingrid hadn't even tried to stitch the limp lining back into the sleeves. She tucked in her blouse and left the assortment of fine wool and cashmere sweaters on the bed, which she couldn't bring herself to leave unmade. Childhood conditioning triumphed! Her mother always made beds, even in motels, insisting there was something degenerate about rumpled sheets and displaced blankets.

A slender black woman, in a navy skirt and white blouse, was setting the table in the breakfast nook, looking more like an airline stewardess than an old family retainer.

"Good morning. I'm Mrs. Wilcox, and breakfast will be ready in just a few minutes. Mrs. Fort said to serve your coffee, and she'll be joining you in a moment."

She even sounded like an airline hostess, or at least the movie or TV version of one. Kelly's drug-dazed first flight hadn't left her eager to check out the service on a real commercial flight.

"Would it be too much trouble if I had tea instead? It's all I really want. You needn't bother cooking for me."

"It's no trouble at all."

The woman said exactly the right things, but somehow Kelly felt she'd flunked the guest-servant test. Obviously Mrs. Wilcox was used to a better class of visitor. Would a little haughtiness help? She sipped her tea in tight-lipped silence, resisting the urge to ask about the number of domestics employed in the Fort household.

"Kelly, dear, I'm sorry to keep you waiting. I've reached the age where I can't face a boiled egg until I do my morning exercises. Oh, weren't the clothes satisfactory? I'm sure I can find something else."

"They were lovely, but I'm afraid you're a size or more smaller than I am. You're in marvelous shape."

It was envy, not flattery, but the older woman beamed.

Mrs. Fort wanted to know everything that had happened from the robbery to the rescue, obviously dissatisfied with her son's abbreviated version.

"They held a gun on you the whole time in the van?" she asked, horrified by this detail her son had omitted.

"Well, the leader had it beside him. We were never in any danger of being shot, though."

She decided to skip the part about Brian grabbing Fred, then getting his hands tied in back of him.

Describing life on the island was much harder. How could she gloss over the warm, wonderful togetherness without actually lying?

"Wasn't it terribly cold? You were so far north, and the wind off Lake Michigan must have been fierce."

"We had blankets, and Brian made fires by hitting stones together. He knew everything that was edible, although I didn't care much for wild berries and weeds."

"You ate those? How could he be sure they weren't poisonous?"

"Brian seemed to know."

Door chimes sounded, but no one in the breakfast room moved. It was Ingrid's job to announce visitors, which must have been inconvenient when she was upstairs.

"A Mrs. Pacinni, ma'am."

"My sister," Kelly said, wondering how her overly eager chauffeur had managed to round up her husband and speed through downtown traffic from the southern suburb to the northern in record time.

"I'm blocking a Mercedes," she said, understandably breathless since she'd just broken the crosstown record. "Will someone need it?"

"Oh, no, my son left it for Kelly, but she's decided not to use it."

Her sister's expression told her she must have left her marbles on the island.

"Mrs. Fort, my sister Jill," she said a little belatedly, since her sibling had already accepted an invitation to join them for breakfast.

Mrs. Wilcox seemed to approve of Jill's style of giving orders, describing how she wanted her eggs and toast with an attention to detail worthy of the queens of France. Just because she had a cleaning woman half a day on Fridays, she didn't need to boss domestic help as if she were Scarlett O'Hara.

"Jill, I'm ready to leave anytime," she hinted broadly, only to be ignored.

"I love Tudor style," Jill was saying. "Is that chest in the entryway genuine Jacobean?"

"My mother-in-law was proud of that piece," Mrs. Fort said. "Kelly was just telling me how they survived on the island. I had no idea my son could make a fire with stones."

Jill wasn't that easily put off. The island adventure could wait. She wanted to know how it felt to live with museum pieces and bask in the attention of a domestic staff. Before she finished the last bit of congealed egg on her plate, she knew more about the Fort family history than Grosse Pointe's most ambitious social climber.

"How could you be so obvious!" Kelly shrieked at her sister when the metal gate came down inches from the back bumper of the cherry-red Citation. She curled and uncurled her fists, wanting to punch her sister for the first time since she'd brought out Kelly's naked baby pictures to show a new boyfriend.

"Tell me," she insisted. "How could you?"

"I was only being friendly. Is there some rule you can't be friendly with rich people?"

"Asking Mrs. Fort if she has stock in her own name isn't being friendly!"

"I handled that just fine. Women today are very conscious of financial independence. I wanted to know if she was well off without her husband. I'd ask any woman the same question."

"Her father was head of a steel empire. Her finances are none of your business!"

"She didn't seem offended. Anyway, you could thank me for leaving the business and rushing over to drive you all the way home. Why didn't you take the Mercedes?"

"I didn't want to."

"You probably wouldn't know how to drive it."

121

"If I can drive my Bug, I can drive anything!"

"You don't have to get hostile. It's a long drive to Ann Arbor."

"You hate eggs, you never eat breakfast, and you're on a diet. I have your number."

"Oh, stop being a drag. When will either of us get inside a genuine mansion again?"

Good question, Kelly thought dejectedly.

Sulking with Jill was like keeping an ice cube cold by sitting on it. She didn't notice Kelly's silent brooding, so it didn't dampen her enthusiasm.

"What is he really like?" she asked, zipping through midmorning traffic on the freeway. "I can't imagine being marooned with a catch like him."

"He's very nice," Kelly said, giving up on the silent treatment.

"Nice! He's gorgeous and rich, and gorgeous and famous, and . . ."

"Please stop, Jill! I'm just too tired for this."

"Did you sleep together on the island?"

"Jill!"

"Well, it seems likely. He's a virile bachelor. You're pretty sexy when you're not on your independent-woman kick."

"A few minutes ago you were using women's consciousness as an excuse to ask Mrs. Fort embarrassing questions."

The expressway traffic was light, and Jill made good time, but an hour with her was beginning to seem like a day before they finally reached the Ann Arbor campus exit.

"Thanks. I owe you gas money," Kelly said crossly, getting out in front of her closed store.

It wasn't until her sister drove away that she realized she didn't have a key to her own business, and she couldn't get in her apartment either. The window at the top of the fire stairs in the alley was always locked. If she hadn't been so annoyed by her sister's attitude, she might've remembered to borrow some change for the phone. The police must've locked the place and kept the key.

In her bedraggled jacket, patched pants, and dilapidated shoes, she looked like a refugee from a major disaster, and her eyes filled involuntarily with tears. She had so many responsibilities and no way to get on with them. Worse, all she could think about was waking up in Brian's bed, feeling him crawl in beside her on satin sheets, wanting him more now than she ever had on the island.

"Ms. Valentine, I read about your rescue!"

The stocky policeman with his sandy mustache was more welcome than Santa Claus on Christmas eve.

"Oh, am I glad to see you, Officer Michaels. I'm locked out, and, oh, did you get your ring?"

"I helped myself and put my check in your register. I'm officially engaged."

"Congratulations! About getting into my store . . ."

"I picked up the key at headquarters, thinking you'd be here pretty soon. We need an official inventory of what was stolen and a description of the suspects. Even though the big boys are working on this, we have local sources who won't open up to strangers."

"Yes, yes, I'll give you all that, but I need a little time," she said wearily, suddenly feeling the whole impact of the past days.

"Time's what we don't have," he said, turning sternly professional on her. "If you'll stay here, I'll let the detectives know you're back."

Funny how detached she felt inside the shop she loved. The cases were largely empty, their gray painted bulk looking shopworn, and the whole place had a musty smell from the damp cold in the old walls. She turned up the heat far higher than the acceptable level and hurried up the narrow bare steps to her apartment to change clothes.

The second story was one huge room, partitioned only for a bathroom that overlooked the alley. Her front view of the busy street was framed by three identical narrow windows, and the ceiling was covered with old, ornate metal squares, the layers of paint now thicker than the tiles. She'd made the unpromising studio apartment livable with warm colors, a rusty-orange carpet, and white wallpaper with yellow, orange, and olive stripes. Her Salvation Army furniture was covered with afghans still bright years after her maternal grandmother had made them. The only good piece of furniture in the room was her double bed, terribly inviting now under a green and white quilt salvaged from her paternal grandparents' estate. Securely wrapped in the down covering, she probably could sleep for a week.

The door buzzer rang before she had time to do more than slip

123

into red plaid Pendleton slacks and a matching sweater, trying for a cheerful look she didn't feel.

The detectives were congenial but curious, asking more questions about her stay on the island than about the criminals. Before they were through she gave up trying to sort relevant questions from nosy prying and answered everything in a dull monotone.

No, she didn't know when Mr. Fort would be available to answer their questions. They'd have to find that out for themselves. They hadn't even given her time to go to catch her breath, but she didn't tell them that.

Alone, finally, her mind buzzed with things she should do. Locking the door of the store, she went to the phone on her desk and located the numbers of her three student helpers. Before she could pick up the receiver, the phone rang.

"Ms. Valentine, this is Darcy Shapiro from *The Michigan Daily*. Congratulations on getting back safely. May I come to your store now to ask you a few questions?"

How typical that the student newspaper was ahead of the local paper, she thought wearily, wanting so much to refuse the eager young reporter. But the *Daily* had been her friend, giving her a great write-up when she opened and always putting her advertising copy in an advantageous spot. She owed them. No point in putting it off.

Before the *Daily* got there, the local and two Detroit papers had contacted her, each one more insistent than the one before. The rest of the day became a blur of questions and answers. After the press finally left, she couldn't remember a single thing she'd said.

Cheryl called twice, both times in the middle of interviews, and Kelly had to put her off, promising to call the moment she was free. Before that time came, Cheryl appeared in person.

"You look like a baby bird that tried to fly too soon," she said. "Is there anything I can do?"

"Yes, call the others and tell them it's business as usual tomorrow. Just follow last week's schedule unless there's a conflict with someone's classes. And put a small display ad in both papers to let people know we're open. Just say Valentine's Treasures is open as usual and mention our hours."

"Don't you want some time off?" her helper asked.

"I've had my vacation." Kelly smiled wanly. "And here I am,

thanking you again. If you can take care of the calls, I'll check the register, make a deposit, and inventory the stock in the safe."

Her receipts were safe between the jars of chemicals, and a count of the spilled and disordered jewelry confirmed that nothing was missing. It was late in the evening before her work was done, and she dragged herself up the stairs vowing not to answer the phone again for a week. But, of course, she couldn't do that. Brian had promised to call.

Her apartment phone was only an extension of the shop's, an arrangement that had been less expensive than separate numbers at a time when every penny counted. Tonight she fervently wished for the privacy of an unlisted number. It was well after ten before the calls tapered off, her friends and relatives asking more questions than the police and press combined. She'd told her story so many times she didn't even believe it anymore.

The milk in her fridge smelled funny, the cold meat was brown, and a half grapefruit was as dry as tumbleweed. She settled for a can of soup and fell asleep on the couch watching the late news. If she was part of history as recorded on television, she was too tired to know it.

Her neck was stiff, and the corner of the afghan she'd unconsciously wrapped around her legs had slipped to the floor. She awoke puzzled because she was warm, not cold. Struggling for alertness, she remembered turning the heat way up to get rid of the musty smell in the store. Unfortunately one thermostat controlled the whole building, and her apartment felt like July during a heat wave. She had to run downstairs to turn it down and open a window to bring the temperature to a livable level.

The bedside clock said two o'clock—Brian's ETA. Funny how the nonflyer was suddenly using an air terminal term, she thought, wide awake now and more interested in the phone than her bed. It was nearly dawn when she fell asleep again, having reluctantly set her alarm to ring for a business day.

All three helpers were scheduled to work that day, running in for their short shifts and bubbling with questions whenever Kelly let them get her alone. This wasn't often. The shop was doing a landslide business. Although more conversation than money passed over the counter, they made a lot of sales. When Kelly was finally alone after closing for the day, she couldn't help but notice how rapidly her stock was diminishing. She'd have to call all the artisans who left things on consignment and beg for more of their output. And she desperately needed more help out front so she could be free to finish some good pieces before the holiday rush. As tired as she was, she worked for a while finishing the long-neglected silver bracelet and added it to a tray in the safe. Tomorrow she'd talk to Cheryl about increasing her hours, but the only practical solution was to hire a full-time person and let the other two college girls go. She couldn't afford one full and three part-time workers, but Cheryl was too valuable to lose. She dreaded firing the others, although one girl was too shy to sell effectively and the other was a little unreliable.

As late as it was when she finally went up to her apartment, she still had to eat something. Unfortunately grocery shopping hadn't been on her crowded agenda that day. In fact, she wondered if her poor, neglected old VW would start. Her battery was almost over the hill. She ended up laying out tuna and Saltines with a glass of orange juice. She'd eaten better on the island.

Brian still hadn't called.

The tuna stuck in her throat, and she threw the stale crackers away. Darn him anyway! Why say he was going to call if he didn't mean it? The island seemed as remote as outer space, and she wondered how she could've hoped their idyll would continue in the real world. Jill was right: Jefferson Avenue was a tourist attraction, a life so remote from theirs that a gap the size of the Grand Canyon existed between Brian's world and hers.

She reached for her alarm before realizing the noise came from the phone.

"Hello."

"Darling, did I wake you?"

"I think you must have. Is it morning?"

"No, just past midnight. I'm sorry to call so late."

If he was so sorry, why not wait until morning? She grumbled a meaningless response.

"You heard about the fog, didn't you?"

"What fog?"

"O'Hare was socked in all last night. My flight was canceled, so I found a hotel room and caught up on my sleep."

"You slept twenty-four hours?"

No wonder he sounded so jolly; he'd been on a sleeping binge.

"Twelve at least. Then I contacted a few people in Chicago so the day wouldn't be a total loss. Just my luck, the plane I finally took had mechanical problems, and I had a two-hour layover in Kalamazoo."

"Where are you now?"

"Metro Airport. Do you want to pick me up?"

"I'm not sure the car will start."

She wasn't even sure she had enough energy to get down to the alley and try it.

"You're having trouble with my Mercedes?"

"No, I didn't take it. I'm talking about my VW."

"Oh, if you don't have my car, I'll rent one and be there in an hour or so. How do I get to your apartment?"

"Through the store, but Brian, I don't think I can stay awake another hour. Today was terrible, reporters and customers and people I hardly know asking a million questions. And last night I fell asleep on the couch and couldn't get back to sleep. I'm really tired."

"Poor kid, you do sound exhausted. Would you rather I didn't come?"

"No, I want to see you, but I have to be up by seven to open the store."

"You're opening tomorrow?"

"Of course. I was open today—or was it yesterday?"

Her eyelids were so heavy they ached, and her stiff neck had gotten worse, not better.

"I was sure you'd take some time off to rest."

His voice was heavy with disapproval.

"I can't afford vacation time," she snapped. "My employees need their jobs to stay in school, and the rent comes due whether I'm open or not."

"I'm not criticizing," he said with a marked attempt at patience. "Only worried because you need more time to recuperate from the island."

"If you're worried about my rest, why call in the middle of the night?" she asked, angry because he'd waited so long to phone her.

"I tried three or four times today, but your line was always busy."

"A lot of people called."

"I have a good idea. I have to see my attorney in the morning,

127

so I'll stay at the Plaza Hotel and meet you there at the RenCen for lunch around one. Any problem with that?"

"No, where should I meet you?"

"How about the art gallery? I still need a birthday present for my mother. You can help me choose a painting."

"But the emerald . . ."

"See you at one. Go back to sleep, darling."

She slept through her alarm, awaking with only half an hour to get down to the store. Had she really talked to Brian last night, or had she wanted him to call so badly she'd imagined it? Rushing to get ready, the details came back, convincing her the call had been real.

How could she let Brian think she didn't want him to come? After a few moments of tragic despair, she decided she'd done the right thing. What kind of reunion could they have in the middle of the night when she was totally exhausted? He had a lot of nerve asking her to drive all the way to Detroit after midnight, even if he did think she had his car.

Racing downstairs, she tried to figure out how she'd get away before noon in order to meet him at one. How heavy would the traffic be going into Detroit at that time of day? She'd allow an extra half hour, but Krista was scheduled to come at eleven. If that girl was late again, she really was through.

Would her car start? She'd better try it before opening the store. If she was still the local freak, it could be her only opportunity all morning.

Her little Bug looked forlorn, alone in the alley with two battered metal garbage cans and a pile of railroad ties that had been there as long as she could remember. The rust spots eating away at the yellow paint made her car look like it had measles, and she wondered if it'd see her through another winter. The obsolete little Bug was on the borderline between being collectible and being junk. Today it was definitely leaning toward the latter.

When she turned the key in the ignition, all she got were clicks. Further attempts didn't even get that much response. She'd have to play the helpless female to get a battery installed in her car before noon. The worst part of owning a car was having to depend on the mechanics who serviced it.

By the time she finished talking to the owner of a local gas station, she'd even convinced herself her whole future depended on having a battery in her car by eleven. He agreed the trip to her alley was a legitimate auto-club call.

Worst of all, Cheryl didn't show up for work. Kelly called her room to see if she'd overslept or forgotten it was her morning to work, but there was no answer. She didn't have a morning class, and it was totally out of character for her to miss work. By ten o'clock Kelly was more worried than angry, handling the brisk morning trade and trying to forget about the ring she'd planned to begin.

"Kelly, I am so sorry!"

Cheryl came into the store with a rush of words, not even noticing the pair of students dawdling over a gift one was buying for the other.

"I'm getting married!"

Kelly blew the sale in her haste to talk to Cheryl, steering her back to the workshop and demanding to hear more.

"Duane and I, we're doing it as soon as he graduates. I dropped out of the university this morning. That's why I'm late. It took longer than I thought."

"You dropped out?" Kelly was horrified.

"He's graduating this spring, and he's almost sure to be drafted by a pro team. It was still early enough in the semester to get some of my money back, so I did."

"But you were so excited about being a dental assistant."

"Now how can I do that and get married? Anyway, I'm not all that crazy about being up to my wrists in mouths all day.

"You're making excuses. You're giving up a career you really want."

"Friend, I don't want anything but Duane. He's buying a diamond and bringing it to you for a setting. Now can't you congratulate me?"

"Of course I can," Kelly said contritely. "I just can't believe you're giving up your education. I hope you won't regret it."

"The only thing I regret is that I have to quit working for you."

"Oh, no! Aren't you going to stay in Ann Arbor?"

"Oh, you bet I am. I even have a place to stay with some girls in an apartment, but I've got to find a full-time job."

"You've got one!"

"You're kidding?"

"No, relying on part-time help has become a real pain. I need someone I can depend on full time. If I don't get time to work on my own jewelry, I won't have a thing to sell for the holidays."

"That's the second-best offer I've had this week. I'm yours till the wedding."

"Can you start today?"

"Why not?"

"Great. I have to go to Detroit. Krista is due at eleven and Hayley at three. I'll decide what to do about their hours later. I hope you won't regret quitting the university, Cheryl."

"I've been thinking about learning a trade, the jewelry business or something fun," she said grinning.

"Well, you've come to the right place for on-the-job training. I have to change clothes."

"Why? You look fine."

"I thought I'd wear a skirt."

"Are you going in to get your silver supply?"

"Did I say that?"

She ran up to her apartment before Cheryl could ask more questions.

The RenCen, as Detroiters called the glistening five-tower Renaissance Center complex, always intimidated Kelly. The interior seemed designed for giants, and she purposely wore her highest spike heels, a silly gesture since they didn't add enough to her five and a half feet to make her feel less like a dwarf. Walking into the concrete, multileveled jungle, a complicated maze of shops, open-air restaurants, fountains, and even a small lake, she always felt it had been built for a race of superpeople. Looking upward from the sky-lit court, she felt transported into some future century, an illusion enhanced by great hanging mobiles and massive clumps of foliage. Her favorite area was a colorful little open restaurant with bright yellow umbrellas over the tables. She sincerely hoped Brian planned to eat there. She'd heard of the revolving restaurant at the top of the highest tower, but there was nothing in the Detroit or Windsor, Canada, skyline that she wanted to see badly enough to ride the elevator to the top floor.

High heels were a bad idea; she'd forgotten how vast the place was and how hard the concrete floors were. She located the art gallery from directional guides, skirting the kind of massive pillars she'd always imagined Samson destroying in the temple.

The gallery was carpeted and had only glass separating it from the broad corridor. Brian was there, his eyes on the entrance, not the works of art on display.

"You're not going to buy your mother a picture! The maid showed her the emerald. She's expecting that for her birthday."

"Hello. How are you?" he said wryly. "So nice to see you again."

"If you bow and kiss my hand, I'll scream."

"I'd rather kiss something else."

"Be serious, Brian. Your mother knows about the emerald. I can finish a setting for it in time."

"You probably neglected to tell her I gave it to you."

"I didn't accept it."

"My mother wouldn't want me to be an Indian-giver. Do you suppose there's a private corner somewhere where I can kiss you?"

"In public?"

"You're right. Let's go up to my room."

"Here?"

"Didn't I tell you I stayed here last night? Dad keeps a room for business purposes. I borrowed it last night, but it's still vacant."

"You lured me here under false pretenses."

"I did promise you lunch, didn't I?"

"Yes, and I'm starved. I didn't have time for breakfast."

"First, what do you think of this?"

With his arm on her shoulder he guided her toward a delicately executed watercolor of children playing in a meadow by the woods. The chubby-faced, bare-legged trio reminded Kelly of Berta Hummel's delightful tots, but they were more than imitations of the famous German nun's creations. Each had an individual personality, and the dynamics of the small group could be read in their expressions and actions.

"It's really very good, isn't it?" Kelly asked.

"Mother is crazy about kids. She'll love it."

"But the emerald . . ."

"That wouldn't be a surprise, would it? And it'd only remind her of the kidnapping. I think I'll get this picture."

She wandered among the oils, acrylics, and watercolors while he arranged to have the painting delivered, enjoying the display in an absentminded way.

"Let's go."

"Can we eat at the place with yellow umbrellas?"

"I had something else in mind."

"Not the restaurant that revolves?"

She wasn't quite sure how the tables moved, but she was willing to leave bird's-eye views to the birds.

"No, although we can go there if you like."

"Oh, no, whatever you had in mind is fine."

Anything was better than the top of the highest tower.

He had her in an elevator before she had time to think of an excuse. Her stomach got off on the second floor, but they shot upward, alone in the moving cubicle.

"I thought we weren't going to the top of the tower."

"This is one of the small towers. Here we are."

"What is this?"

She whispered automatically, sure that any louder sound would be a serious impropriety in the elegant dining room they entered.

"The Michigan Club."

She'd heard of an exclusive club in the RenCen, but no one from her part of the world had ever been there. The waiters were dressed to perform in a symphony orchestra, and the garb of the waitresses was just as dignified. They functioned as a team after greeting "Mr. Fort" by name, and Kelly couldn't tell if the women were minor league players or members of the first team.

"Where would you like to sit?" Brian asked.

"Over there."

She pointed, not consciously defying her mother's edict against it.

"Wouldn't you rather sit by a window?"

"I think that table looks cozy."

"We'll go for cozy then."

The waiter led them to a table covered with white linen, and she wondered if Brian's status had suffered from her table selection. The window seats were the ones occupied by men in custom-tailored suits and women in clothing that had never seen a rack. At least she didn't have to analyze the smog content on the horizon as she ate.

132

The menu didn't have prices. She never wanted to be so rich she had to pay for anything without knowing the cost.

"The French-dipped sandwiches are good," Brian suggested.

"I'll have quiche," she said just to show him she could handle the high-class luncheon menu without his help.

He ordered wine from one waiter and food from another, while a third deftly placed crystal goblets near at hand. Another brought wine for Brian to taste, and he approved it. Kelly wondered what they did with wine customers didn't approve. Did the waiter have to drink the whole bottle himself, or did they recap it for another, less discriminating diner?

She sipped her water, wondering what the slice of lemon in it signified, afraid to try the wine until she'd broken her long fast. She really had to get to the supermarket. Their meals on the island had been bountiful compared to what she'd had since returning.

"How are you, really?" he asked, moving the stem of his goblet between his thumb and finger.

"Rushed but recovering. The police and the press swamped me yesterday."

"I have to meet with the Ann Arbor police today. I don't know what they can do that the FBI can't, but their chief was insistent."

"When did you talk to him?"

"This morning. He left a stack of messages with my mother."

"You picked a good time to leave town."

"I'm sorry. I should have been here to take the heat away from you, but this conference was planned a year ago."

"I understand. You had to go," she said with more sympathy than she felt.

A different waitress brought huge spinach salads. Kelly wondered how one tipped an army.

"I should have taken you with me."

"Without clothes? My island outfit is in the trash bin."

"Didn't my mother loan you some?"

It hurt to admit his mother was a smaller size.

A waiter stopped to ask if the wine was satisfactory, and another brought their meals. The help seemed to outnumber the diners. By the time Brian signed the check, cash being too crass for the clientele, they'd managed to discuss absolutely nothing for the better part

133

of an hour. No wonder, when they'd hardly been unattended for a moment.

Were they friends or lovers, fellow adventurers whose paths had crossed briefly or two people held together by deeper ties? Was he serious about going to his hotel room? She certainly wasn't interested in being an afternoon quickie.

"I have to pick up my luggage," he said.

When she saw he'd checked it on the main floor, her relief was slightly tinged with some other feeling. The key he turned in was for a room on the 59th floor. People probably got nose-bleeds having sex that high in the sky.

"Where's your car?" he asked, carrying a matching gray briefcase and suitcase.

"In the parking lot, fortunately. Are you coming with me?"

"Of course. I have to see the Ann Arbor police, remember?"

She opened the front of her VW to stow his cases, wondering if his silence on seeing her car was charitable.

"Aren't you going to tell me I have a rust problem?" she asked, opening the door on the passenger side for him.

"I can't believe you haven't noticed."

"Well, most men feel some compulsion to point it out."

"A lot of men are interested in your car?"

"My father, my three brothers-in-law, the smart guy who services it, my landlord. He doesn't think it's classy enough to park in his alley. Gives the property a bad name."

Embarrassed by the car's condition, she overdid it, putting the VW down herself so he wouldn't.

She slid behind the wheel, trying to remember how to get to the right freeway. Her mind was a blank. If she followed the river all the way south to Wyandotte, she could pick up Ford Road and go out to the airport. From there she couldn't miss I 94. Of course, that route would take just about twice as long. Or she could gamble and get lost. Or ask Brian. She was still debating with herself and fumbling with the key when he kissed her.

"You weren't this jittery when Benny was threatening you."

"I had you to protect me, didn't I?"

"I'm still here."

"To protect me?"

"Do you need protecting now?"

134

"This is a crazy conversation."

"I agree."

His kiss was more filling than a dozen lunches, and suddenly he didn't seem like the proper, worldly stranger who'd taken her to the Michigan Club.

"For a while there I thought you didn't like me anymore," he murmured. "I was ready to drag you out to the parking lot and feed you edible weeds from the cracks, if that's what it takes to make you warm up."

"Have I been that cold?"

They kissed hungrily, moving their mouths with demanding eagerness until Brian cried out in pain.

"I banged my knee on your dash," he said, rubbing it and grimacing.

"The police chief is waiting for you."

She did remember the intricacies of the inner city expressway network, following a route through deep cement canyons and high overpasses, past decaying rows of houses in once livable neighborhoods and the belching smokestacks of an industrial valley. Reaching the open countryside beyond the airport where the traffic started thinning, she didn't have to concentrate so intently.

Brian was coming home with her, but for how long? Would he dash off somewhere else after doing his civic duty, or did he plan to do something about the promise in his kisses? On the island everything had seemed so simple, but how could she walk through her store, past Cheryl and her customers, with a man carrying a suitcase? Before she could even consider her love life, she had to solve her excess-help problem, help Cheryl put jewelry in the safe, cash out, make a bank deposit, and talk to her new full-time helper about hours and salary.

By the time she got back the afternoon would be practically over. She'd better check her order book to make sure she wasn't in trouble with a customer. Her monthly ad copy was lying half-written on her desk. What duties could she pass on to Cheryl to give herself more working time?

"You really concentrate when you're driving," he said, "but isn't it hard on your lip?"

Embarrassed to be caught gnawing her lower lip, she giggled nervously. He rested his hand on her knee, fingering the nylon of

135

her panty hose, edging up her honey-gold and brown plaid skirt until she pushed his hand away.

"Not while I'm driving," she said. "I'd hate to wander across the median."

"If I can affect you that much, I'll gladly behave myself for a while."

Everything seemed less complicated when he asked to be dropped off at the police station, yet she couldn't deny the emptiness that flooded her as he walked away.

CHAPTER EIGHT

Resolutely closing the door between the store and her workshop, Kelly left the retail business in Cheryl's care. She had to engrave initials on a heart pendant and bring her books up to date, not to mention paying some bills before her credit went skidding off into limbo. The few remaining afternoon hours went much too quickly, and thinking about Brian made her a model of inefficiency, flitting from job to job, wasting time because she couldn't keep her mind on what she was doing.

When she spoiled a second check, writing the wrong amount even though the electric bill was right in front of her, she tore it up impatiently, giving up on that job. It was closing time, and she rushed Cheryl as much as possible, deciding to hide the receipts in her jar instead of checking them and going to the bank.

Why hadn't she asked Brian what his plans were? If he came back, she couldn't even offer him a drink without going to the store. But if she did go shopping, would he find her place deserted and leave? A soft tap on the front door made her heart race. Since the robbery she couldn't look at the door without wondering if a friend or enemy was behind the CLOSED shade.

"Do you open for just anyone?" Brian kidded.

"Not for men with bushy beards. How did you get here from the police station?"

"I rented a car."

That must mean he was going home.

"Oh, that's convenient."

"More convenient than carrying five bags of groceries three miles on foot. Can I unload from the alley?"

"Sure, I'll unlock the back door."

"I hope it's all right to park beside your car."

137

"Officially I'm entitled to two spots because I pay rent for the upstairs too. You didn't need to bring groceries."

"When have you had time to shop?"

Good question.

They both made two trips up the stairs, and Kelly couldn't shake off the feeling that this was a charade. Brian Fort couldn't be here in her apartment, playing house as if he enjoyed it.

Another thing she hadn't done recently was clean her apartment. She tried to remember how messy the bathroom was. Had she taken her panty hose off the towel rack?

"Brian, you've brought enough food for a month."

"No, only for the weekend. We're going to San Francisco Monday."

"We? Meaning you and me?"

"Yeah. By the way, is there a laundry where I can get my shirts done in one day? I don't want to bother going home for more."

"Back up! You're going too fast. I can't possibly leave Monday, and if you want your shirts washed, you'll have to take than to a Laundromat."

"I can do my own shirts if I have to but I'm not going to San Francisco without you. Come here."

"Shouldn't these groceries be put away?"

She edged around her all-purpose card table, evading his grasp.

"Forget the groceries. I just spent the afternoon in a room full of envious cops, anyone of whom would give a month's pay to be marooned with you. I deserve a reward."

"For what?"

"For not bragging."

"Oh!"

She threw a package of paper napkins, hitting him squarely but harmlessly in the face.

"Now," he said, lunging and catching her, "tell me you're only interested in my steaks."

She couldn't tell him anything. A tight feeling in the back of her throat made her speechless, and her breasts ached to be touched. Everything she'd felt on the island had been real, not an exaggerated fantasy heightened by adversity as she'd feared.

His kiss was full of tension, hard and urgent, sucking away her resistance until she clung to him, the hot yearning in her body a sweet form of torture.

"I've been thinking about this since I made you get on the plane in Pellston," he said.

"Why did you stay away so long then?"

He laughed softly.

"I came into your room after my father went to bed, but you were sleeping so soundly, I didn't have the heart to wake you."

"Oh, dear, I was probably snoring."

"A gentleman doesn't tell."

"You should have."

"Told?"

"No, woken me up."

"I didn't expect to be fog-bound and rejected."

"I didn't reject you!"

"You surely weren't waiting in my bed."

"You never got there anyway."

"If I'd known you were waiting, I would've rented a car and driven all night."

"That would be crazy."

"Is this crazy?"

He slid his hands under her clinging knit top, finally bringing relief to her aching breasts, his soft caresses on top of her bra giving her excruciating pleasure. Fingering his biceps while he touched her, she felt power in his hard muscles, absorbing his strength so she could be everything he wanted in a woman.

"There's only one thing wrong with this," he said softly.

"What?"

"The ice cream's going to end up as a puddle on your floor."

"I love ice cream."

"Then let's salvage it."

She'd neglected to toss out the browning cold meat, now showing specks of green, and the dead grapefruit had somehow hidden itself in the butter-keeper. A half-bottle of her brother-in-law's home-made blueberry wine stood in lonely isolation in the appliance, leaving plenty of room for the contents of Brian's bags. Why did her hands shake putting them away?

"How hungry are you?" he asked, neatly folding the empty sacks.

She usually wadded grocery sacks and tossed them in her ten-gallon crock, lined with a plastic bag to serve as garbage can and wastebasket.

"We had a big lunch."

He hung his suit jacket and vest on the back of a kitchenette chair and walked toward her with slow, measured steps, his easy smile making her feel warm and damp, inside and out.

"You keep your apartment warm," he said.

"The heat tends to rise. I can run downstairs and lower the thermostat."

"No, warm will be nice. I'd like to feel your skin slippery against mine."

She was slippery enough already to melt through the floorboards. Every pore in her body was pulsating as he stood beside her bed, rolling the quilt back in layers until it lay neatly across the footboard. Last Sunday had been her day to change sheets, and naturally her mother's yellowing old castoffs were there, the crude mend down the middle showing plainly.

"Mom gave me all her old sheets," she explained weakly.

"You think of the darnedest things to worry about," he said, gruffness concealing a much stronger emotion.

He walked to the far side of the bed and pulled his tie loose, folding it neatly and laying it on her bright yellow dresser, an early thrift shop find.

On the island they'd rushed for the warmth of the blanket, not even undressing when the weather turned frigid. Watching as he unbuttoned his white shirt was exciting in a way she didn't understand. She wanted to do it for him, but her eyes were greedy to watch every move he made.

He folded his shirt as neatly as if he planned to wear it to a formal banquet in a few minutes. Before he unhooked his trousers, he rolled his belt into a coil and laid it beside his tie.

She loved men's legs, especially his, covered as they were by a dark sprinkling of hair. He knew enough to take his socks off before his pants, avoiding the silly look men had in white jockey shorts and dark stockings. After sliding his shorts over lean hips and thighs, he bent and took them, neatly folding them too. She wished for a sculptor's skill so she could mold the perfection of his body in clay and cast it in bronze, the twentieth-century man in the flower of perfection.

"You won't be cold without your clothes," he suggested softly.

"No, I won't be, will I?"

She unconsciously locked her hands across her breasts, crushing her throbbing nipples. With fingers that felt double their usual thickness, she raised her jersey top over her head, shaking back the streaming tendrils of hair it displaced. Piece by piece she tossed her discarded garments onto the bed between them, not surprised when he folded each one and laid it with his.

"Stop there," he said.

Wearing only her panty hose and the uncomfortably high heels she'd been too busy to change, she stood motionless, watching him come toward her. Standing behind her, he made little whirlpools of heat on her back, rubbing circles with the palm of his hand until her skin was charged with electricity. Pulling her back against him, he kneaded and stroked her breasts, feeling her heartbeat become more erratic.

With deliberately teasing slowness he rolled her panty hose over her hips and down her legs until they bound her ankles together. If she took a step she'd surely fall, but his body was a brace, a wall of hot flesh that made her tingle wherever she touched. When he bent to taste her breast, she clutched at his back, off balance and bombarded by pangs of yearning.

"I'm falling," she said, managing to kick off one shoe, which only put her hopelessly off balance.

"As long as it's for me."

Who would believe he could nip with his teeth and produce only the most exquisite sensations? He knelt then, removing the other shoe and freeing her from the tangle of nylon.

"It seemed a little late to take precautions this month," he said, backing her onto the bed and leaning over her.

"Did you tell your mother anything about us?" she asked.

"A little. Curiosity is one of my mother's dominant traits. What I didn't tell her, she probably guessed. It was a small island, and I certainly didn't come home with my tail between my legs. She remarked on how cheerful I looked."

He nuzzled her ear, sending flashes of heat coursing through her.

"That's terrible!"

"You don't want me to kiss your ear?"

He didn't stop.

141

"No—yes. I mean, your mother must think I'm . . ."

"A loose woman?" He shifted onto his elbows and smiled into her face. "You're inventing things to worry about."

"Meaning what?"

"Meaning I love you, but sometimes you stew over the darnedest things."

"Say that again."

"You stew . . ."

"Not that part!"

"I love you, Kelly."

He kissed her deeply, exploring her mouth with a thoroughness that left her gasping for air, the pulse in her throat beating to the rhythmic thrusts of his tongue.

"Oh, I love you so much," she whispered, burying her face in his chest to hide the nakedness of her desire for him.

"Look at me," he said, taking her face in his hands and staring at her, his eyes smoldering with emotion.

He moistened his lips with his tongue, a tiny nervous gesture that endeared him to her with heart-rending intensity, then stretched his length beside hers, drinking in the beauty he saw with avid eyes. At first he only touched, willing her stillness while he explored with gentle wonder, but when she reached for him, loving the warmth of his skin under her hand and the firm contours of his body, he began a shower of kisses, bestowing them from her forehead to her toes until the vibrations deep within her built to a frantic ache.

Just when she thought no greater peaks of arousal were possible, he took one swollen breast in his mouth and drew out sensations so sweet she quivered with expectation. When he parted her thighs, she strained toward him, trembling as he slowly joined his body to hers. His words of love seemed to flow through her, the incredible throbbing of their union making them one in spirit and purpose until sudden fiery contractions made her cry aloud, her voice echoing against the metal ceiling and nearly drowning out his deep sensual gasp. Their collapse left them both trembling and shaken, unwilling to pull away from their perfect union.

"Nothing has ever felt so good," he whispered, finally falling to her side and running his fingers through her hair fanned out on the pillow.

Limply savoring the tiny explosions still shuddering through her,

142

she held his fingers to her mouth, kissing each one in turn, then reaching for his other hand.

"I didn't know it could be so wonderful," she murmured.

"Then you see why you have to go to San Francisco with me," he said, laying one leg over hers and making lazy circles on her stomach with his palm.

"That's blackmail," she moaned, wiggling as close as she could.

"Sweet, loving blackmail. Can you blame me for not wanting to be away from you?"

"Stay here with me."

"I intend to. All night and all day. Right here in your little hot studio."

"I can turn down the heat, but I can't stay in bed all day."

"What about tonight?"

"I'm yours."

She ran her hands over his chest, trying to memorize each knot of muscle, tormenting his navel with her little finger until he restrained her with fierce kisses.

"You set a wicked pace," he said grinning.

"I don't have a sunken tub, but I'll wash your back."

"Don't do that."

"What?"

"Mention my family's possessions as a subtle put-down."

"Did I do that?"

She was genuinely puzzled.

"Maybe not intentionally, but you enjoy sounding Bohemian, don't you? Above luxuries, dedicated to your work."

That hurt.

"I really don't give a damn about your possessions or your money," she said angrily, "but if you're going to call me a snob again, you can take your neat little piles of clothing and get out of here."

"Would you really like that?"

"I'd hate it."

"Good."

He sat on the edge of the bed.

"Are you going?"

"Yes, to the bathroom to fill the tub."

She threw a pillow at the back of his head.

"That's one time too many."

He swung the fat pillow across her face, stunning her, but only for a moment. She jumped out of bed, running for the bathroom but not reaching it before he walloped her shoulders and backside.

"I won't come out unless you promise to put the pillow down," she called through the door, bent double from laughing.

"I will if you'll wash my back."

"Okay, it's a deal."

He was waiting for her beside the door, capturing her in his arms and kissing her soundly before he let her go.

"I've changed my mind about tropical temperatures," he said, wiping the perspiration from his forehead with the back of his hand. "Where's your thermostat?"

"Down in my workshop on the wall by the safe. The nightlight's on."

Even without additional heat blasting up from the furnace in the basement, the bathroom was hothouse-warm. She quickly scoured the old-fashioned claw-foot tub while he was gone, dumping in the last of her bubble bath and turning the water on full blast. The whole tub vibrated under the rush of water coming through the pipe, and soon there was plenty for both.

"Where are your towels?" he asked, watching from the doorway.

"In the chest right behind you."

He found her largest bath towels, two of them alone almost a full load at the Laundromat, laying them across the wash basin.

"You forgot washcloths," she said.

She left to get some, sorting through her supply to find two without ragged edges. When she returned he was leaning back in the bubbles, easily filling her big tub.

"What made me think you're a gentleman? You've left me the faucet end."

"I'm not even going to let you in until you keep your promise."

"What promise?"

"What promise? Ha! Scrub my back. Your memory is better than that."

He handed her a sliver of bathsoap from the metal holder that hung on the edge.

"It's about used up, isn't it?"

She took it from him, going to a drawer in the kitchenette to get another.

"I can see you don't do much entertaining in your bathtub," he teased.

"None, actually."

"I'm glad."

She soaped his back, standing and leaning over him to do it, slapping at his hand when he tried to fondle her breast.

"When I scrub backs, I'm all business."

"Get in here."

"Oh, are you ordering me into my own tub?"

"Will you come if I am?"

"No."

"You always want to deal?"

"That's the way I operate."

"Okay, get in here, and I'll cook the steaks."

"The best deal I've had all day."

"You're sure of that?"

"Well, the second best, anyway."

She stepped gingerly into the water, watching with wariness as he worked the cake of soap between his hands until they were almost hidden by the lather.

"You're not going to wash me," she squealed, bringing her knees up and wrapping her arms around her legs. "No one's ever done that!"

Her mother belonged to the "throw them in the tub and let them soak clean" school.

He only smiled, leaning forward to lather her cheeks and neck, then sliding his still soapy palms over her shoulders and breasts, making lazy circles around her nipples, then piling sudsy bubbles on the tips before he rinsed her.

"I feel like your personal rubber duck," she said, squirming and squealing when he slid his toe under her bottom.

"No, you don't," he said, giving her a devilish grin as he worked the soap between his hands again. "Kneel with your back to me."

"Oh, no!"

"There are easy and hard ways to do everything."

"Okay, but no tricks!"

"Is this a trick?" He massaged the soap into her back with a heavenly touch, both soothing and arousing, then worked lower, kneading and rinsing until she felt like melting into the water. By the time he finished her toes, teasing the cracks between them with sudsy fingers, she was able to share in the pleasure he felt in intimately bathing her, feeling alive and cherished in every pore.

They dried and powdered each other, laughing and teasing until the scented powder in the air made them sneeze. He kept his word and cooked the steaks, a towel tied around his waist, the white marks from the powder mitt showing on his back and shoulders. After slipping into her best nightgown, a shimmery green silk and lace one Jackie had given her a year ago for Christmas, she set the table and poured wine from one of the bottles he'd bought. When the steaks were done he put on a shirt, leaving it unbuttoned.

"I should pay for half these groceries," she said.

"Leave it on the dresser."

"I'll probably have to write a check."

"I don't take checks."

"I'll go down and get the cash from my secret hiding place."

"Kelly, you don't keep cash on the premises, do you?"

"If you can find it, you can keep it."

"Let's eat."

"You're handy to have around," she said, cutting into her steak with a ravenous appetite. "Do you do windows?"

"I'm an all-around worker. My price is high, though."

"How high?"

"Your promise to come to San Francisco with me."

"Brian, I'm just swamped with work!"

"No help?"

"Well, I just hired one of my helpers full time, but my stock is terribly low. I absolutely have to make more jewelry."

"I'll take you to a wholesale import store in San Francisco. You can stock up at a good price."

"That's not my style at all."

"Don't be offended. The place I know has some unusual gemstones plus pearls, coral, the fast sellers."

"My business is based on fine handcrafting. Anyway, I don't have a lot of capital to risk."

146

"I can give you a loan."

"No, Brian. Don't do that to me!"

"I'm not sure what I did."

"This business is all mine. No sugar daddies. No silent partners. I'll succeed or fail entirely on my own."

"You're something else."

"I'm serious."

"That's what makes you so unique. Do you want to visit the import mart just for fun?"

Did she! But he was assuming she'd go.

"How long would we be gone?"

"I can take care of my business in two days."

"Counting Sunday?"

"No, counting Monday and Tuesday. Wednesday we'll fly back."

She sat there weighing two plane trips and four lost work days against being with Brian.

"You don't think you can stand my company that long?" he asked.

"I can more than stand it," she said softly.

She washed the dishes while he dried, then changed the sheets while he ran her electric broom. Setting a fresh bottle of wine and two glasses that had once held dried beef on a metal steamer truck that served as her coffee table, she settled down next to him in front of her black and white TV, barely watching some show that involved a lot of car chases.

"Here's to us, darling," he said, handing her a full glass of pale amber wine.

To us. "Are you trying to get me tipsy?"

"What do you do when you're drunk that you don't do sober?"

"Giggle a lot and fall asleep sitting up."

"Then I'll strictly ration every drop you drink."

"How do you really feel about everything that's happened?" she asked.

"Very, very lucky."

"We could have been killed, couldn't we?"

"I'm talking about meeting you, not the kidnappers."

"Oh."

"I think I'm in love with you."

147

"You think so?"

"It's not my field of expertise, but all the signs point in that direction."

"What signs?"

"You do like things spelled out, don't you?"

"Yes, always."

"I think about you every waking moment and dream about you at night. When I'm with you I'm wild to make love to you, and when we're apart, I'm still wild to make love to you. You're too damn independent and too hip, but you're so desirable I can overlook your big bottom."

"And my independence?"

"I'm a little worried about that."

"I love you, Brian."

"But?"

"You're sure there's a but?"

"I'm sure this relationship isn't going to be easy. I hate panty hose hanging in the bathroom."

"I suppose I could hang them in the basement."

"I like ice trays full and leftovers wrapped in plastic."

"And you probably make lists, read books from start to finish, and wear seat belts in town."

"I don't wear pajamas. Is that a redeeming quality?"

"It will go a long way. Are you planning to live here?"

"Not exactly."

"Meaning?"

"I don't exactly live anywhere, darling. I'm gone more than half the time. And I'd sure like to take you home with me once in a while."

"I have to live here, Brian. I work here. If I'm gone a week, things will start falling apart."

"I said it wouldn't be easy."

"You wanna give it a try, huh?"

"I don't have a choice."

"That's flattering."

"It was meant to be. I can't get enough of you."

He swallowed the last of his wine, put the bottle away, and rinsed the glasses. She took a long time in the bathroom, flossing her teeth

148

and examining the blemish on her chin that was finally fading. He was lying on his stomach in bed, his face hidden against her best green candy-striped pillow case. Shutting off the light, she crawled in beside him, luxuriating in the warmth of his body and the way it felt when she snuggled close.

"Brian?"

For a man who couldn't get enough of her, he sure conked out fast.

CHAPTER NINE

"Want me to answer your phone?"

"Oh, what fiend is calling this early?"

"I'll find out."

He rose on one elbow and groped on the nightstand.

"No, don't," she cried, finally awake enough to realize what a bad idea it was for him to answer her phone.

She changed her mind too late. He was saying good morning in his rich baritone voice.

"Who is it?" she asked in an urgent whisper.

Her mother had been calling three times a day, checking to make sure she was replacing the vitamin C, A, and D in her system, suggesting she get a medical checkup, and prescribing remedies for chapped cheeks, lips, and hands.

He muffled the mouthpiece with his hand.

"It's a female. That's as far as I can describe her."

Kelly took the phone with trepidation, but broke into a smile at the sound of Cheryl's cheery salutation.

"And a very good morning to you, Msssss. Valentine. You've been keeping secrets!"

"Oh, Cheryl, when you left there wasn't anything to tell."

"If I weren't in a frantic rush, I'd wonder about that. Who is he?"

"Later."

"I just wanted to be sure you can get along without me today. One of the girls at the apartment offered to help me move, since the team's way out in Iowa today."

"Don't tell me you won't be glued to a tube at kickoff time?"

"Yeah, her tube. That's why I'd like to move this morning."

"No problem. You're not on the schedule anyway. Krista wanted to work this morning to make up some of the hours she missed. Don't give the store another thought today."

"Well, have a nice, nice day," Cheryl said, teasing Kelly with the overused phrase they both hated.

Brian was lying on the cord, forcing her to wiggle across his chest, lay the receiver on the stand, and try to move him. Before she succeeded, she was caught.

"Are you trying to keep me a secret?" he teased. "Hide me under the bed when company comes?"

"Of course not." She finally freed the cord and replaced the receiver. "Well, maybe when my mother comes."

"Mama won't approve?"

He snuggled closer, wrapping his legs around hers.

Should she try to explain her mother? She ran her fingers through the curly whorls of hair on his chest, deliberately teasing his nipples, trying to distract him.

"You can let your fingers walk on me all day, but I still want to hear about your mother."

"She'll overreact."

That was putting it mildly.

"How? Hysteria? Righteous indignation? A shotgun and a preacher?"

"All of the above."

"She's done this often?"

"Never, actually. But I brought a friend from the art school home for Thanksgiving dinner once, and she showed him all five thousand pictures from my three sisters' weddings."

"Was he inspired?"

"He roared with laughter all the way home and sent my mother a mum plant the next day."

"I guess I missed the punch line."

"Besides being witty and supertalented, he's gay."

"Thank heavens. I thought I'd have to fight a duel."

"Would you do that for me, duel at dawn in the alley?"

"I'd rather duel with you right here."

"Let me see the clock," she said suspiciously.

"Here it is."

He set the cold metal timepiece against her cleavage, laughing at her shriek.

"I have lots of time. I think I'll clean the apartment before I go to work."

"I just heard you say someone else is working this morning."

"Krista, but she's a little dippy. I'll have to help her open the safe and carry out the stock."

"And then?"

"We'll see."

"Tell me you don't like this," he said, moving his mouth against hers, "and I'll let you go."

His good-morning kiss made her toes tingle, and she rolled into his arms, the time forgotten.

"I thought you were going to sleep in the bathtub last night."

"All I did was brush my teeth, and you went to sleep."

"Um, you look great for a woman who just woke up."

"You've seen a lot, have you?"

"A fair number."

He kissed her chin, dropping his lips to the hollow of her throat. Uncombed, his hair formed little ringlets, jet-black against the paleness of her arm when she hugged his head closer.

"Take this off," he said, tugging her gown over her hips.

"A fair number, huh?"

"Oh, well, if you're not interested."

He made a big production of rolling on his side away from her, taking most of the quilt with him.

"Brian, it's cold! How low did you set that thermostat?"

"Very low. I'm saving you fuel."

"You're freezing me."

"It's warm by me. Come closer."

"On the island you shared the blanket with me."

"I still will."

He turned quickly and flung it over her, making her a willing prisoner against his warm body.

The phone rang again.

"Ignore it," he said.

"I will."

On the seventh ring she couldn't stand it.

"I have to answer."

It took two more rings to get untangled enough to reach for it.

"My mother never gives up with less than ten rings."

He groaned in mock agony and found a nice soft spot to stroke while she talked.

She listened with increasing irritation.

"Krista, you *asked* to work today. It's too late to get Cheryl."

Irritation turned to anger as Kelly listened to the girl's excuse.

"Everyone enjoys having friends visit," she said, ignoring his snicker, nearly losing the cool reserve in her voice when Brian parted her legs, "but this is the second Saturday in a row."

"Slave driver," he hissed, softly fondling her bottom and making it extremely difficult to concentrate on the call.

Krista's answer was so snippy, Kelly knew there was no point in hedging.

"I don't think I can use you anymore, Krista. If you have any hours coming, I'll mail your check."

Hot spasms were making the job of firing her employee almost impossible.

"No, it's too late to apologize."

Brian hung up the phone for her, sliding his hands under her gown and working it up to her neck. She hugged him close, but she couldn't help glancing at the clock. With no help coming that morning, she thought of a hundred things that needed doing.

"Do you want to set the timer?" he asked. "Five minutes for foreplay, three minutes to . . ."

"You're terrible!"

"Is it so terrible to want your full attention?" he asked softly.

"No, it's wonderful."

But she couldn't relax, not even knowing that he sensed her tension, as they made love gently and quickly until he shuddered to a climax in her arms.

"I like it better when you're with me."

His rebuke was gentle and loving, but it hurt.

"I'm sorry. I just seem to have so many things happening lately."

"Leave the shop door locked today. Stay in bed with me till noon and pretend this room is an island."

"It's so tempting."

"If you aren't tempted, I'll worry about losing my old fatal charm."

"You are a charming man."

She nuzzled his face, loving the scratchiness of his morning beard and the hard boniness she could feel high in his cheeks.

"I want to make our love wonderful for you. I don't think any man's done that."

"Makes me sort of a secondhand virgin, doesn't it?"

"Didn't anyone ever teach you bed manners?" he asked, nipping at her nose in a mock bite.

"My mother must have slipped up there," she said, scrambling to leave the bed, trying to pull her nightgown down before she stood up.

"You know, Kelly," he said with a grin, "no one amuses me like you do."

"Clowns amuse, stand-up comedians amuse, performing seals amuse."

"No, no, you're certainly out of your class in that group. Come here, I'll prove it."

"Too late!"

"It's never too late for more loving."

"This morning it is. I have a customer coming to pick up an engraved bracelet, and my help's let me down again. I have to hustle."

She didn't enjoy racing around trying to get ready with Brian propped up on both pillows eyeing her dolefully.

"Really, you look like a puppy that needs petting," she said, bending to snap her bra, feeling more self-conscious dressing in front of him than she had undressing the night before.

"You're right about the petting part. Hand me my briefcase, would you?"

"Are you going to stay in bed all day?"

"No, only until you turn up the heat. I just want to check the time on our tickets."

"Our tickets? You bought plane tickets before you even asked me?"

"What kind of woman would turn down a trip to San Francisco?"

"A working woman! Get your own briefcase."

He bounded up so quickly he startled her, catching her in his arms and falling backward onto the bed with her as his prisoner. Crushing her mouth with hard, heavy kisses between savage war whoops, he succeeded in pinning her to the bed, straddling her and holding her down with his weight.

"Listen to me, woman! You're walking on that plane with me tomorrow morning, or I'll throw you over my shoulder bottom-side-up like a sack of potatoes and load you that way."

"If you have caveman fantasies, you have the wrong woman," she said, struggling against him without much success.

"My fantasy right now is the two of us walking along Fisherman's Wharf, me popping little pink shrimp in your mouth, showing you one of my favorite cities. Being alone with you. No phones, no jobs, no rushing off."

"No wood to gather, no water to boil, no berries to pick?"

"They weren't such bad days, were they?" he whispered, rolling to her side and stroking her cheek with one finger.

"They were wonderful because you were there."

"I need to hear things like that from time to time, you know."

"Sometimes I feel as if you're up above me, not needing anything you don't already have."

"So you do your hard-boiled career woman bit to test me?"

"No, it's not like that."

"Then someday you're going to have to talk about that ex-husband of yours."

"He doesn't mean a thing to me now."

"No, but he left you with a bundle of mistrust. Trust me, Kelly."

"I'll try. I just don't understand. Why me?"

"You're beautiful."

"How many attractive women do you know?"

"Thousands."

"Smart women?"

"Quite a few."

"Amusing women?"

"The list gets shorter."

"But there is a list. So why me?"

"Damned if I know! I have to cook my own dinner, threaten you to get you on a plane, and compete in bed with your business."

"I sound terrible."

"You are! But you'd better wear a little more clothing if you're going to work."

"You do understand?"

"I do. I don't like it, but I understand. Now get going."

He helped her up and went back to bed, pulling the quilt under his chin.

"Don't forget the heat. Try for something between an equatorial jungle and the North Pole."

"Yes, sir!"

Somehow, between working in the morning and being with Brian the rest of the day, she didn't get around to packing until the last possible moment early Sunday morning, not helped at all by his frantic urgings.

"I like to check in at least a half hour early," he said, sitting in his three-piece pinstripe suit while she rushed around in her slip trying to remember everything she might need.

"You're not helping me, Brian."

"Tell me what to do. I will."

"Just be quiet and let me think! You're sure I won't get motion sick on a big plane?"

"I've flown a million miles and never seen passengers use those little bags."

"They give out bags?"

"Utility bags are standard conveniences. Maybe people use them as doggie bags. I've never paid much attention."

"So you might not've noticed if someone did get sick?"

"I would've," he said firmly, getting up to pace, moving his cases a few inches closer to the stairs and straightening his perfectly positioned tie.

"Oh, I need some money. I'll just run down and get it."

"You don't need money."

"I never leave home without cash."

"Kelly, we're late. Never mind."

He followed her down to the early morning dimness of her workshop.

"It was your idea to stay in bed so long," she pointed out.

"You didn't argue."

"I'm almost ready."

She took her painted jar off the shelf and plucked out all the bills, shoving them into her shoulder bag.

"That's where you keep your cash? Why not in the safe?"

"Ha! Fred made me open the safe, but he never thought of opening all my jars."

"You have me there," he grumbled, "but please hurry, Kelly. I'll put my cases in the car and come back for yours."

"Your car or mine?"

"I can turn the rental in at the airport. Are you stalling so we'll miss the plane?"

"No, just let me use the bathroom."

"You did, ten minutes ago."

"Traveling makes me nervous."

"The terminal has restrooms. The plane has them, assuming we don't miss it."

"This is so crazy," she said, finally seated close to him in the rental. "I'm leaving an inexperienced helper to run my business, while I jet out to San Francisco."

"You said Cheryl is very competent. Fasten your seat harness."

"She is, but she's never run the whole business before. What if there's another robbery?"

"Your seat belt, please, so we can get going."

"You mean you won't drive through town without wearing one?"

"We're headed for the state's busiest expressway, not a ride on South State."

"Where did you live when you were a student here?" she asked, trying to take her mind off her business and her fear of flying.

"In a fraternity house. I had an apartment while I did my graduate work."

"A fraternity. I should have known."

"You have objections to fraternities?"

"I just don't appreciate some of their dumb stunts. Male peer bonding at its worst."

She finally fastened the seat belt, and he backed away from the building.

"Psychology 101?"

"No, all I took were art courses."

"I'm an Episcopalian too. Do I lose points for that?"

"Fort is French, isn't it? I've never met a French Episcopalian."

"I'm hardly a full-blooded Frenchman. One sixty-fourth is more like it. The first Fort in Detroit was a fur trapper, we think. He

157

married an Indian, or at least conceived several children by her and took responsibility for them when he wasn't trapping beaver."

"How wonderful to know so much about your ancestors! My mother's parents were Irish-Hungarian and German-Scotch."

"And your father's?"

"Well, Italian obviously, with a little Swiss-French and maybe Dutch. We're not sure about my great-grandfather."

"You're making that up."

"No, not at all. You have no idea what a hard time we have deciding which ethnic festival to attend in Wyandotte. And of course, my German great-grandmother was really born in Russia, so I don't know if that counts for anything."

"We have something in common," he teased.

"What?"

"We're American-type mongrels."

"Yeah, we are. I forgot to mention Pennsylvania Dutch, which is really more German, but it sounds so colorful I like to mention it."

When they were close to the airport, a bulky silver shape streaked across the highway. The wheels of the plane seemed perilously close to the car tops, and Kelly closed her eyes, expecting to hear the roar of a crash.

"You can open your eyes now."

"That one sure looked close."

She had a sudden urge to bite her nails, a habit she'd kicked in ninth grade when a forward on the junior varsity basketball team said her fingers looked like unbaked bread sticks.

"It's a perfect day for a flight. No storm warnings, not much wind. Even the Rocky Mountains are relatively free of clouds."

"How do you know?" she asked.

"I checked on TV while you were in the bathroom."

She'd forgotten about the Rockies, those jagged, treacherous peaks that turned people trying to cross them into cannibals. Of course, that had been before airplanes. Now all she had to worry about was crashing into one. Undoubtedly there wouldn't be survivors.

Their flight was on schedule according to an official-looking board behind the attendant who weighed their luggage and made it disappear. Brian elected to carry his briefcase onto the plane, and she wished she'd thought of bringing her makeup case. Now if her bag ended up in Afghanistan, she wouldn't even have a toothbrush. Of course, if the plane didn't get across the Rockies, it really wouldn't matter.

"Come on," he said, still rushing her. "They'll be boarding soon."

She made it through the metal detector, but her shoulder bag didn't. A burly policeman rushed forward to supervise the search of her purse, his stoical expression cracking when her antique compact, which was made out of hammered tin and studded with rhinestones, rolled across the counter.

"Where'd you get that thing?" Brian whispered as he hurried her away from the slow-moving line.

"When we cleaned out my grandmother's house," she hissed, not sure whether to laugh at his discomfort or get angry.

"Figures. Did you have to bring it?"

"It's a very handy pocket mirror."

"I'll bet."

They boarded through a covered loading dock that reminded Kelly of the entrance to a fun house, but she wasn't having fun. Only Brian's grasp on her arm kept her from bolting to safety, and the first thing she did was check for the paper bags.

"Do you want a window?" he asked.

"No, you take it. Please."

"Just relax, sweetheart. The Detroit–Chicago run is so routine to the pilot, it's like biking across campus."

"Chicago?"

"We change planes there, of course."

"You never mentioned changing planes!"

"I didn't think of it."

Two takeoffs! Two landings! Why couldn't she die in peace right away?

"It's not just motion sickness you're worried about, is it?"

He sounded so kind and understanding, it was worth a shot.

"Go on without me, Brian."

"No way. How can we have a relationship if I have to leave you behind all the time?"

"I'll ride trains, buses, cars."

He shook his head.

"Bikes, motorcycles, ox carts?"

"You know, psychiatrists have made a lot of advances on your problem. I'll bet you could get over your fear of flying with a little professional help."

"You want me to see a shrink?"

She felt like a bug trapped on a glass slide, even though she knew her attitude was silly, childish, and medieval.

"Only about your fear of flying."

"It's just a little nervousness, nothing I can't handle," she said, trying to find her seat belt and hoping no one sat in the third seat.

She *would* handle it too! If Brian thought she'd quiver and quake, he was traveling with the wrong coward. When everyone else was screaming and cowering in their seats, he'd see how calm and dignified she really was. She forced herself not to look for oxygen, parachutes, and emergency exits, made eyes at the male flight attendant, and pretended to yawn. If that wasn't being cool, what was?

When the plane started to taxi for takeoff, she changed her mind. It couldn't spoil her image if she just noted the nearest exit.

Her legs were iron rods riveted to the floor, her hands were claws fossilized on the armrests, and her brain was malfunctioning like a computer with hiccups.

"You can take your seat belt off and relax now."

He didn't have to do it for her!

"What do you usually do on planes?" she asked stiffly.

"Work, read *The Wall Street Journal,* nap if it's a long flight, have a drink. We're on a lunch flight after Chicago."

"Well, don't let me stop you. I'll just read."

"Those are things I do when I'm not with the lady I love."

He leaned over and brushed her cheek with his lips.

"Did I tell you we're staying at a friend's house?"

"No, you didn't. I thought we'd stay in a hotel."

"So you brought all your cash to cover your half?"

"If you like."

"I don't like. Let me do things for you, darling. It gives me pleasure. Anyway, you'll like the house. It overlooks the bay."

"Won't your host be surprised to see me?"

"The owners are in Switzerland. We'll have the place to ourselves. You won't have your middle-class morals put to the test."

"You'll have the place to yourself, if you make cracks like that."

"I apologize, but I made you mad enough to stop digging your

160

nails into the cover of your book. See, flying's not so bad, if you don't think about it. Pretend you're riding in your own car, which by the way isn't as safe as this plane."

"I knew you'd point out poor Pippen's flaws eventually."

"I wasn't attacking your car, only quoting safety statistics. The airways are much safer than the highways. Pippen's a crazy name for a car, isn't it?"

"Sometimes you sound like my father!"

"I'd love to be your authority figure."

"Oh! I'm going to the restroom."

He was wrong about motion sickness on planes. By the time she got back, he was anxiously watching the aisle.

"I *was* sick!" she whispered, weakly triumphant.

Physical weaknesses were somehow more excusable than irrational fears.

"Congratulations. We have a two-hour layover. Somehow I'll get some pills for you."

He did. Leaving her in a coffee shop to sip weak tea, he maneuvered his way through the channels of airport officialdom and returned with two pills in a paper cup.

"You're getting your own prescription in San Francisco," he said wearily.

She slept over the Rockies, trailed behind Brian in a daze at the terminal, and fell asleep again in a cab. The driver carried their bags to the front door of a three-story Spanish-style home with outside walls that looked like lemon ice cream in the drizzling rain. She shivered when cold drops ran from her hair down her cheek, but at least Brian was proving himself human, having a devil of a time unlocking the two locks on the door.

"The housekeeper has Sunday off," he grumbled.

"Only one day a week free?" she asked, revived by the rain. "I don't think my father realizes how wretched the lot of American domestic help is. Last year he studied government employees in Luxembourg for two weeks, while Mother went to the Netherlands on a singles tour."

"The same mother who yells 'preacher'?" he asked dryly, ushering her into a wide flagstone entryway.

"She expected the singles to be unmarried teachers and widows.

161

Anyway she got a bargain rate and a chance to observe nightlife in Amsterdam."

"How'd she like it?"

"Better than the bike tour along the dikes. Her seat got sore."

Kelly slipped out of her damp shoes, wondering if it was the pills she'd taken that made everything seem unreal.

"Look out here," he said, guiding her into a vast room carpeted in pale blue.

A huge bay window overlooked the water, the long expanse of the Golden Gate bridge clearly visible through the haze.

"Spectacular, huh?"

He took their coats to a closet in the entryway and returned to find her slumped down in an oversized black velvet armchair, one of the dozen or so pieces upholstered in that fabric. Black-and-white photographs, most of still-life arrangements enlarged to the size of the average pool table, covered most of the wall space. The whole setting totally overwhelmed her.

"I like your mother's breakfast room better."

"So do I." He laughed. "Let's find some coffee."

Seated at a wooden-topped counter under a hundred or so polished copper pans and utensils hanging from a special rack, she took in her surroundings with a glimmer of real interest.

"Who owns this house?" she asked.

"Friends of my parents. They own several cheese factories back in the hills. They sent Dad the key to use the house while they're traveling."

"Very hospitable."

"Not when you consider I'm here to decide whether to finance a large expansion program for them."

"More cheese factories?"

"No, a chain of rental outlets. I'll be meeting with their son, who's in charge now, and some company officials in the morning, then I have some investigating to do."

"What does a geologist know about cheese?"

"Not a darn thing, but I do know money. Dad has to be in New York this week, so I was drafted."

"What does your brother Brad do?"

"He spends money. I think his team lost a quarter million last year, but his wife makes a lot."

She felt wide awake now.

"What do I do while you investigate cheese?"

"Shop, go sightseeing, relax."

"You were going to show me San Francisco."

"We have three wonderful evenings, darling."

"Doesn't it make you uncomfortable to walk into a house where the people aren't home?"

"No, I don't think anything about it. The Schneiders spend most of their time at their ranch near the factories anyway."

"I would too, if my living room was decorated with five-foot black-and-white pictures of cheese and grapes."

"I think he's an amateur photographer. Do you want instant coffee or tea?"

"Tea, please."

"I know a wonderful little French restaurant with an open patio roofed by grapevines."

"Won't we get wet?"

"The rain will stop."

They showered together in an orange tiled stall, lathering with chunks of green soap that smelled suspiciously like her father's favorite cheese, then made leisurely love on slippery black sheets, falling asleep and not waking until the room was dark.

"Do you really want to go out for dinner?" he asked.

"No, not really."

She parted his hair with her finger, dropping lazy kisses on his eyelids and the end of his nose.

"Wanna see the rest of the house?"

"What's the alternative?"

"A pillow fight."

"I'll see the house."

She found fresh pink panties in her suitcase and slipped into them, putting on her warm red quilted robe and brushing her hair with vigorous strokes. His dressing gown was a plush burgundy with silk trim that made her feel like someone's little sister.

Except for the color scheme, which largely tried to duplicate the makings of a fruit salad, the rest of the house was conventional enough until they reached the third floor.

"It's a gym," she said.

"An exercise room. They bought so many machines they had to reinforce the floor."

"And you're thinking of loaning them money?"

She walked up to a weight bench upholstered in black and picked up a dumbbell from a nearby rack.

"Maybe. What would you like to try?"

It was a medieval torture chamber done in chrome and plastic with mechanical monsters to punish every muscle in the body. Brian threw aside his robe, revealing a pair of running shorts.

"You dressed for this. I didn't."

"Here, let me hang up your robe."

"All I'm wearing are . . ."

"I noticed."

He flopped down on his hands and toes on a thick plastic mat large enough for a wrestling match and began doing pushups, his arms flexing and straining under the impact of his weight.

"Is this how you keep so trim?"

"Right," he said, hardly puffing.

Well, she certainly needed some exercise. Her only serious attempt at keeping in shape had been to run across campus every morning during the summer before she dressed for work. When the fall semester students came back, she'd gotten out of the habit.

Walking gingerly over to a relatively innocent-looking treadmill-type contraption, she found the on button, set it for the slowest speed, and began running. Funny how a person could get out of breath going nowhere. Her bare breasts bobbed uncomfortably, and she decided a runner did need proper apparel. Meanwhile Brian had done enough pushups to qualify for Michigan's football squad and was lying on a boardlike thing lifting weights with his legs.

"Watching me won't do you any good," he teased.

"No, but I enjoy it."

She swooped over him and planted a wet kiss on his mouth.

"You won't get out of this that easily," he warned her.

She fought with an elastic gadget while he lifted weights, then rode the exercise bike, too conscious of her scantily clad bottom hanging over the edge of the seat to enjoy it. To keep in the spirit of things without having to deal with more machines, she did some toe touches while he ran on the treadmill and kept his eyes on her.

"Is this why you brought me to San Francisco?" she finally asked, sitting down to rest on the mat because chairs weren't part of the equipment.

"No, this."

He dropped beside her, his bare torso slick with perspiration, finally allowing himself the luxury of a little panting as he cupped her breasts.

"Pooped?" she asked.

"Don't count on it."

He pushed her backward, straddling her thighs and sliding his hands up and down, massaging her torso, sending wake-up messages to sluggish cells.

"Roll over," he ordered, and she did, enjoying the vigorous massage, flexing her shoulders and tightening her buttocks as he used his fingers with telling pressure, leaving her for a second and returning with some slippery lotion he applied in generous globs.

"Now your front," he ordered, his voice growing husky.

She was putty under his marauding palms, writhing and squealing when his thoroughness made her throb.

"Now my turn," he whispered, collapsing on his stomach beside her, handing her the bottle, and slipping out of his shorts.

She loved his shoulders, slippery with lotion under her fingers, and, following his example, she massaged his flesh energetically, pummeling and slapping when that seemed the thing to do, growing shyer when he rolled on his back between her legs.

"Don't stop. It's up to you," he said, fondling her breasts as they glistened provocatively above his chest.

He trusted his aching need to her, and she didn't disappoint him, riding the tornado that engulfed them, clutching at the wiry hair on his chest as though this unsubstantial handhold could keep her from washing overboard. At the last moment he crushed her against him with his legs and arms, eyes shut and lungs gasping for air.

Without realizing it she etched a trail of jagged scratches, horrified when she saw his blood on her fingertips.

"Oh, Brian, I've hurt you," she cried, hot tears flooding her eyes.

"If that was pain, my nervous system has its wires crossed."

"But I scratched your shoulder."

"Kelly, don't worry. Kiss me instead."

It was a blubbery kiss, salty with the tears of total depletion, but they reveled in it, tenderness completing their union.

They stood for ages under the warm spray in a little shower cubicle off the weight room, too beat to reach for the soap until their bodies slowly rallied. She loved him for not wincing when she bathed his scratches with liquid soap.

He washed the plastic mat while she gathered their clothes and went to the bedroom to slip into her favorite shorty pajamas, pink and white checks with little bows on the legs. She wasn't worried about looking childish.

They feasted on thick grilled cheese sandwiches, and the rain didn't stop.

The sound of water running in the shower woke her first, and she rolled over to the side still warm from Brian's body, pressing her cheek against his pillow. Minutes without him passed slowly, and she finally crept through the partially open bathroom door, watching silently as he lathered his face with a brush.

"Good morning," he said, catching a glimpse of her in the mirror.

"Hi."

She pressed against his back, wrapping her arms around his waist above the towel, loving the scent of his clean skin against her nostrils.

"If I cut my throat, it's your fault."

He moved the razor over his cheek, leaving a path in the thick white lather.

"Not many men use a brush and shaving mug, I'll bet," she said, releasing him for his own safety.

"I have a tough beard."

She watched, pleasantly interested, until he finished and roughly slapped a tangy aftershave on his cheeks. Everything he did seemed to fascinate her.

"I hope you're having fun," he teased, stripping off the towel around his waist and tossing it into a hamper.

When he left the room, no whiskered globs of cream or dabs of toothpaste gave evidence he'd used the facility, only the lightly scented, steamy air.

"You're unbelievably neat," she said, following him back to the bedroom.

"Mother never liked us to leave a mess for the maids," he said, smiling. "If you do any shopping today, will you buy me some shorts, shirts, and socks? I never did get to the Laundromat."

"If I do some shopping?"

"Well, if you'd rather do some sightseeing . . ."

"I'd rather be with you."

"Tonight you will be."

He nonchalantly stepped into his shorts and shook out another white shirt.

"Are all your shirts white?" she asked.

"Most of them."

"You probably know how devastating you look in white."

He looked surprised but pleased.

"I'm certainly willing to have you tell me."

"Come here. I will."

"Tonight. But look, darling, this city has plenty to do. Golden Gate Park has more than you can see in a day. Be sure to visit the Japanese tearoom and the Oriental museum. I'd get a car for you, but parking is such a nuisance. It's easier to use cabs."

"What about popping shrimp in my mouth on Fisherman's Wharf?"

"We'll do that this evening if you like."

"Where will you be all day?"

"Several different places this morning, then I have a lunch date."

"Date?"

"Appointment. With two bankers. And this afternoon I have to tour cheese plants."

"I could do that with you."

"Don't think I wouldn't like to have you, but I'll be with a group of bores and won't inflict them on you. Here's the key if you leave the house, and this should be enough for a good tour of the city and my shirts."

He handed her a discreet little wad of bills, tied his shoes and necktie, and slipped into a brown vest and jacket. She'd never met a man who could look so sexy in a three-piece suit, and she didn't want him to look that good for anyone but her. She laid his money on the dresser, determined not to use it.

"You're pouting," he accused her.

"I am not."

"Aren't I worth waiting for?"

167

He nuzzled her ear and kissed her quickly.

"What about breakfast?"

"No time. The maid should be in. She'll fix something for you if you ask."

"I can manage myself."

"I'm pretty sure of that."

The cable car was out for repairs, and she didn't care for the abalone steak she ordered for lunch. Or maybe it was eating alone in a nice restaurant that felt so blah. But it was fun to wander along the wharf, and she made up for her half-eaten lunch by indulging in delicious shrimp and sauce sold outdoors in little disposable cups. She walked and walked, viewing the old whaling ship from a nonwatery vantage point on the shore, then found a cab to return to the house.

Mrs. Ducas, the daily woman, was friendly but a little intimidating, offering a variety of services from cooking dinner to washing clothes.

"Mr. Fort does need some laundry done, if you don't mind my using your machines."

"I've done that already, ma'am."

So she had. All their soiled garments, including her panties and hose, had been laundered and laid in the dresser drawers. Brian's shirts looked suitably bleached and starched. There went her chance to do one useful thing with her day.

On impulse she picked up the phone in the bedroom and called Cheryl at home, writing herself a note to leave money for the call. It was past closing time in Ann Arbor.

"How'd it go?" Kelly asked with forced cheerfulness.

"Pretty well, but not good enough for long-distance phone calls," Cheryl teased. "Everything's under control, boss lady, and I sold that silver bracelet with the turquoise inset."

"Good girl!" she said, but the urgency of replacing her stock nullified her pleasure. "Did Ronnie Dirk bring a consignment?"

"No, he called and said he was saving all his enamel work for the Christmas craft show at the Detroit Armory."

"Bad news! Well, keep up the good work. See you Wednesday."

"Now have a good time and don't worry. Business is booming, and I made the deposit and locked up just the way you showed me."

"That's not why I called. You know I trust you."

"You just miss the business so much?"

In a way that was true.

Brian didn't get back until after six, running up to the exercise room to work out and shower. She didn't change out of her best black dressy dress to join him.

The vine-covered patio was all he'd promised, but the garlic in the food made her burp all evening, nearly strangling to conceal it from him. They went to enjoy the city afterward, wandering the strip, letting themselves be drawn into an exotic nightclub where the two-drink minimum was served immediately, four cocktails sitting side by side in damp glasses with the ice melting. Brian didn't seem especially interested in the professionally sexy strippers performing on shoulder-high runways, and Kelly was bored when the initial shock wore off.

"Now you've seen San Francisco at night," he baited her.

"A big turn-on," she cracked.

"Not for me. I'd rather watch you riding the exercycle."

Tuesday she toured Golden Gate Park, lunching at a teahouse and enjoying the still mild breezes whipping through the lush setting. She bought a garment the clerk called a happy coat for Joanie's Christmas present and a sake set for Jill, enchanted by the little handleless cups meant to serve the fermented rice drink. She did decide against trying to dress her nephews like Japanese cherubs.

Tired of being a tourist and wanting to save some of her money, she went back to the house early to take a nap, but worries about her shrinking stock and the upcoming holiday rush kept her awake. She went to the third floor, exercised until she was ready to drop, and took another shower.

"We're invited to a cocktail party," Brian said when he returned in late afternoon. "I hope you don't mind that I accepted."

"What can I wear?"

"That black dress is fine. Makes you look sexy and untouchable."

"Like an ice princess?"

"More like an active volcano!"

The house they entered later was large with broad, steep steps that had to be murder on the handicapped, only to find themselves in a ballroom left over from an era when nothing was too ostentatious for the nouveau riche. Three chandeliers illuminated an improbably ornate, gymnasium-sized room, their lights reflected on a gleaming hardwood floor.

"I feel like Cinderella," she whispered.

"Does that make me a pumpkin or a prince?"

He guided her toward a group of people in evening dress, keeping his hand possessively on her waist. At least Brian had worn his dark business suit instead of rushing out to rent a tux, she thought, trying not to be awed by the jewelry collections displayed on both sunken and bulging bosoms. She really hadn't realized anyone still wore brocade, at least not seriously. Trying to store up some details to relate to her ever-curious sisters, she missed something a man near her said.

"I'm sorry," she said, leaning closer. "I didn't hear you."

"Mr. Roat asked if you're enjoying his city," Brian said.

Mr. Roat was also patting her bottom.

"Yes, of course," she said woodenly, moving away.

"His city?" she hissed when they escaped from that group.

"He does own more than his fair share of it."

"I'll just bet he does."

"Do you dislike him because he's rich?" he asked seriously.

"No, because he's an overbearing ass."

She was greatly pleased when he laughed.

The cocktail party included a buffet worthy of Diamond Jim Brady and an endless flow of small talk that lasted until Brian spirited her away at midnight.

"Just like Cinderella," he teased.

"I don't see a pumpkin."

"You'll have to settle for the prince."

In the morning he left her at the import mart after introducing her to the manager, needing time to finish some odds and ends of his business before their flight. She bought a garnet ring, an opal pendant, some earrings with tiny chips of turquoise, and several jade pieces including a necklace and bracelet, spending the last of her cash but adamantly refusing Brian's offer to use his credit. Trusting her judgment, she was sure the pieces, mostly fashioned in Taiwan, would sell quickly, but it wasn't the same as offering her own work to the public.

She'd forgotten about motion-sickness pills, but Brian hadn't, securing a prescription from some doctor he met in the course of his business.

"Are you going into the cheese shop business?" she asked sleepily, having dutifully taken her two pills half an hour before boarding.

"It's got to be a secret between you and me."

"Who do I know who would care—besides you?"

"No way," he said firmly. "Not a chance."

"They were nice to let us use their house. Won't you feel bad turning them down?"

"Not as bad as I'd feel a couple of years from now, on the carpet with my father's board of directors for a million-dollar loss."

No wonder he hadn't had much time for her in San Francisco. Being responsible for that much money was a job she'd detest.

She swallowed two more pills at O'Hare Airport and spent the trip home in a stupor.

CHAPTER TEN

"Was that flight so bad?"

"I can't remember."

She yawned but couldn't cover her mouth. One hand was tucked in the crook of his arm and the other clutched the strap of her shoulder bag, trailing it beside her leg only inches from the floor. Emerging from the tunnellike dimness of the passenger tube into the hustle of the terminal helped clear the cobwebs from her brain, but she felt a little dazed, clinging to Brian because she couldn't remember where the exit was.

"How many pills did you take? I don't think your eyes are focusing."

"Just a couple."

"Two in San Francisco and two in Chicago that I saw."

"For goodness' sake, Brian, if you kept count, why ask?"

"I still think you should get professional help."

"Going to a psychiatrist isn't going to cure my weak stomach."

"You didn't take four pills to calm your stomach."

"Don't we have to get our luggage?"

"In a minute. Why don't you sit while I rent a car?"

She couldn't argue with that idea. The fuzzy haze in her mind was gradually clearing, and she wondered if he ever drove his own car. He seemed to use vehicles as casually as she used tissues.

Why, she wondered as they watched suitcases, backpacks, and assorted containers inch out on a circular conveyor belt, was the airline so casual about returning luggage? A thief could stand there and grab his choice, risking only an outcry from the owner. In English detective stories, the delight of her free time when she had any, there was an elaborate ritual for repossessing one's trunk. Here

172

in crime country they just tossed the whole planeload on a moving line, first come, first serve.

It was unlikely anyone would snatch hers, however. A souvenir of her long-past high school graduation, the blue imitation leather was flaking off the corners, and the travel stickers she'd used to cover the grazing on the sides looked tacky. It was a measure of Brian's chivalry that he handed her his executive-type briefcase and claimed her case along with his.

"Let me get you a cab now," he said, leading the way up to the exit.

"I thought you rented a car."

Had the pills short-circuited her hearing?

"Darling, I've got to go home. There's my report to my father, and my own work has been piling up. Do you want to come with me?"

"You know I can't. I have to get back to the store."

"That's why I'm putting you in a cab. Wouldn't it be silly for me to waste time driving you to Ann Arbor, when I have to come back in this direction immediately?"

"Logical," she said, trying not to feel let down, "but will a taxi go that far?"

After buying the imported jewelry, tucked safely in her purse, she didn't have enough money left to pay the fare to the terminal exit.

Brian talked to three drivers before he found one willing to drive to Ann Arbor. Small wonder, when some of the aging vehicles looked like they'd been through World War II.

"Here," he said, pressing a wad of bills into her hand. "And don't tell me you won't accept cab fare."

"Since I'm flat broke, what choice do I have?"

"None."

He bent his head and kissed her, a quick little buss that only whetted her appetite.

"I'll call you," he said before shutting the door of the taxi.

He didn't say when.

Considering that he was driving a car with no springs, the taxi driver made amazingly good time, and Kelly was willing to endure a few bumps and bruises to get back to the store before closing time, eager to see how things had gone in her absence. The cabby deposited her luggage on the curb a good hour before the shop day was supposed to end, but the shade was drawn, the SORRY, WE'RE CLOSED sign legible from the street.

"Damn," she whispered, handing the driver a larger tip than she thought he deserved after he dumped her suitcase on the curb.

Why would Cheryl close early on a Wednesday afternoon? This time Kelly did have her keys, but anxiety and anger made her awkward in using them, almost forgetting to use the one first that turned off the burglar alarm. She didn't relock the door, but she didn't raise the shade either. Something was definitely strange. She'd been so positive that Cheryl was reliable.

The note she found was brief and didn't explain a thing.

KELLY—CALL ME IMMEDIATELY! CHERYL

As if she wouldn't anyway! "Immediately" was underlined three times, and there was a postscript giving her new phone number. On second thought, Kelly snapped the lock on the door, not wanting a customer to wander in before she could hear the reason for her helper's desertion.

The phone was answered on the first ring.

"Kelly, I thought you'd never get here."

"Why is the store closed?"

"The police told me to lock up and go home."

"The police! Cheryl, what's going on?"

"When I went to open up this morning, there was a threatening note written on the front window with some kind of red paint."

"What did it say?"

"It said 'You'll get yours' and it called you a four-letter word. It will only scare you if I say it."

"I won't be any less scared if you don't say it."

Cheryl said it, and it was the kind of word Benny would use. But Benny got money, and the others didn't. It didn't make sense, no matter which of the kidnappers was threatening her. What could anyone hope to gain? She didn't even consider the possibility that one of the trio wasn't involved. The threat was no student prank.

"You called the police right away?"

"You bet I did! And they didn't even try to hang it on the frat boys. They took it seriously, Kelly. They didn't want me alone in the store, so what could I do?"

"I'm sure you did the right thing. What did they do?"

174

"A lab crew took samples of the paint, then the police had it cleaned off. I guess they hope it's a clue to finding the kidnappers."

"I know they'd like to be the ones who do."

Kelly bit her thumb, not knowing what to do next.

"More bad news, Kelly."

"Great! Let's have it."

"Hayley has mono. Health service sent her home for a rest. Should I come in tomorrow morning?"

"Yes, do come. I'll talk to the police. They can't put me out of business just because someone sprayed my window."

"Keep the door locked. Open it for customers you think are safe. Sorta like letting people into your house on a dark night. You're sure before you turn that key."

"That would really help business."

"Business has been good. I can say that much. Everybody in the state's heard of Valentine's Treasures. Maybe the threat came from jealous competition."

"Or from a crank who gets his kicks scaring women."

But neither of them believed these explanations.

Officer Michaels showed up three minutes after she called.

"I'm supposed to drive you to headquarters," he said.

The trip was largely a waste of time. She couldn't add a thing to what the police knew already, and she wasn't reassured by their concern.

"Leave the store lights on and the shade up all night," the detective in charge directed, nearly driving her up the wall with his habit of pulling dead skin off his lips. "We'll keep a close watch all night. Is there an outside light in the alley?"

There was, and she wondered if he knew how high her light bill would be. Lord, she'd left without writing that last check to the power company. What was the grace period on that utility?

Officer Michaels escorted her home, checked doors and windows, and directed her to lock the door at the bottom of the stairs.

"I can't stay in my apartment all evening. I have work to do."

"Better let it wait. We're taking this threat very seriously. The chief would like it better if you'd go somewhere else. Couldn't you stay with a friend or relative until we investigate further?"

She'd turned that suggestion down in the dingy little green-walled office at headquarters, and the fact that it was nearly dark outside wasn't going to sway her. She hoped.

"Won't I be safe with Ann Arbor's finest watching over me?" she asked sarcastically.

Officer Michaels flushed.

"No, I'm sorry. That was nasty. I'm just on edge, is all."

He showed his forgiveness by carrying her suitcase upstairs, waiting until she gathered her account book, mail, bills to be paid, and checkbook to lug upstairs. If she wasn't allowed in her workshop, she could at least put her business in order. She'd promised to mail Krista a check—not that she deserved fast service.

"You'll set the burglar alarm?" the policeman asked.

"The instant you leave."

"Leave the lights on and the shades up."

He repeated all the instructions so thoroughly, she began to doubt her own ability to follow them. Surely she'd omit some telling detail and find herself at the mercy of the villain, just like the heroine of a silent flick.

Dear God, she really was scared after he left! Looking around her workshop she grabbed a box half full of sacks, dumped the contents on her desk, and filled it with potential weapons: a heavy tray she used to catch filings, a container of sulphuric acid used in pickling metals, the lead pan she used for the same purpose, steel tongs, a wickedly sharp pick, and heavy metal-cutting shears. She debated whether to move her torch upstairs, but decided she was more likely to set the old building on fire than singe an attacker. There were lots of tools and jars that could help her defend her stair-top refuge, but she had a hard time imagining she'd actually come to that. Nevertheless, she carefully arranged her small arsenal on the floor upstairs, deciding she felt a little more secure. If an intruder broke down the locked door below, she'd have plenty of time to get ready.

Brian's grocery shopping had been imaginative, although the selection had dwindled considerably. After changing into an old flannel nightgown and her quilted robe, she opened a can of crab meat and made a salad with the somewhat limp lettuce that was left. Apparently terror didn't affect her appetite; she was still hungry when that was gone, so she made an omelet with sharp cheese and drank two cups of tea.

Before tackling her bookwork, she rearranged the table so she could sit directly facing the stairwell. This put the fire exit at her back, so she reconsidered, angling the table so she could keep an eye on both. Only a thin sheet of glass stood between her and anyone athletic or tall enough to grab the bottom of the retractable stairs. She'd tried reaching it herself from the hood of her car, and it wasn't that tough to do.

Figuring Krista's wages three times, she got three different answers, jumping and dropping her pen when the phone rang.

"Why didn't you call me?" Brian asked angrily.

"Was I supposed to?"

"Good lord, Kelly, I know what happened! The police called here all day trying to get me. Unfortunately I had a few stops to make and just got home a few minutes ago. Are you all right?"

"I'm locked in with more security than Fort Knox."

She told him all the measures the police had suggested, plus her own defensive tactics.

"So you're sitting with one eye on the window and one eye on the door, a box of tools and chemicals handy to hurl down the stairs if necessary. And you're not a bit scared? I'm on my way!"

"Brian, you don't have to come all this way. The police are watching, and this place is locked up so tight I don't even know if I can let you inside."

"Sure they're watching, once every half hour when they make their rounds. I'll ring your door buzzer three times, then once, then three times with pauses in between. Got that? Three-pause-one-pause-three."

"What about"—the phone went dead in her ear—"all your urgent business?"

The sink needed scrubbing, her dishes were stacked on the drainboard, and the dust showed even on her brightly painted furniture. Brian had insisted on coming and didn't deserve a clean apartment, but she was too agitated to concentrate on her books anyway. After scribbling off a check to the electric company, she threw herself into a frantic bout of housecleaning, needing activity to keep from going wild every time the floor creaked or a street noise invaded her sanctuary.

The first buzz nearly gave her a heart attack, but she quickly remembered Brian's secret signal, relaxing and dashing down the stairs, fumbling with the old-fashioned key in the door she never locked. Her hands were shaking so much! All her self-sufficiency was a farce. She wanted to be in Brian's arms.

He repeated the signal impatiently, running the sounds together so she had a moment of doubt. Maybe he'd been attacked and someone else was ringing.

"Where are your police now?" he asked angrily. "I've been standing here five minutes!"

She relocked the door, trying to tell him not to test the door handle so vigorously or he'd set off the burglar alarm.

"Are you all right?" he asked, crushing her against him.

"If the police go by now, they're going to see us," she said breathlessly between kisses, hearing his heart pound in the same crazy tempo she felt.

"Let's get out of this goldfish bowl."

He used his body as a moving shield, hurrying her through the workshop and up the stairs.

"I don't like this fire escape," he said, going to the window. "Anyone can come up that way with a little effort. It's a good thing I have a man in the alley tonight."

"You have what?"

"One of my father's men is in the alley and one in front. We notified the police."

"You're really taking this seriously!"

"Aren't you?"

"Yes, but I thought the police could handle it."

"In an eight-hour shift you might get a half hour of attention. For tonight I'm here. Tomorrow we'll make other arrangements."

"What other arrangements?"

"A place to stay where you won't be so vulnerable."

"Brian, I pay rent for this apartment whether I live here or not. I can't afford to move somewhere else."

"Kelly, listen to me."

He sat on the edge of the bed, pulling her down beside him.

"All of this happened because of who I am. We think . . ."

"Who's we?"

"My father, his security men, me. We think the two kidnappers who were left empty-handed are behind this. Remember, they think you're my fiancée, thanks to my big mouth."

"You had a good reason for saying that at the time. Benny wanted to . . ."

"Well, yes, but they must think they can get to me through you, and they're right. If anything happened to you, I . . . I don't know what I'd do."

"But why threaten me?"

"I can't get inside Fred's mind, and he's the most likely suspect, but he probably wants revenge. Maybe he thinks we cheated him, paying Benny instead of him. Maybe he thinks we'll pay him to leave you alone. I just don't know."

He looked tired, with dark shadows under his eyes and a weary droop to his mouth that made her want to kiss away his concern.

"Maybe he just wanted to get in a cheap shot and won't be back," she suggested.

"That's a big maybe."

"I'm frightened, but they didn't kill either of us when they easily could have. Why try now when the police are looking for them?"

"We just have to assume they're dangerous," he said wearily.

"Are we going to stand watch all night?"

"No."

He pulled her against the front of the suit he'd worn all day, pressing his lips against her hair.

"Did you get your urgent business done?" she asked.

"No, and I was crazy to send you off alone in that broken-down cab."

"Yeah, I agree there."

She slid his jacket off his shoulders and tossed it on the couch, slowly unbuttoning his vest and then his shirt until she could rub her cheek on the downy firmness of his chest. Slipping out of them, he tossed both garments on top of his jacket.

"They'll get wrinkled," she said, moving to hang them up.

"I don't give a damn."

Peeling off her robe and somewhat shabby gown, he carried her in his arms to the top of the quilt, touching her urgently as though reassuring himself that she was all there, every part safe and waiting for him. Throwing his pants and shorts on the floor, not even removing his socks, he penetrated her with quick, hard thrusts, clutching her breasts with his eyes tightly clenched, an expression of pain contorting his features. She was pinned under his weight, unable to lift her hips to ease his assault, clutching at his thighs in an unconscious effort to slow him.

Not like Larry, she begged silently, then the unbelievable happened: the force of his need exploded through her, carrying her with him until he collapsed in the circle of her legs.

"Forgive me," he murmured when he could speak, sheepishly rolling aside to lie spent beside her.

"There's nothing to forgive, my love."

"I haven't done anything that clumsy since I left prep school. I was so worried driving here. If one of those creeps had . . ."

"Since prep school?" she asked in mock horror. "What a precocious boy you must have been!"

"Forget that and let me hold you," he whispered.

"Wait."

Slowly, deliberately tickling his toes, she pulled off first one dark sock and then the other, hanging them on the knobs at the ends of the footboard.

"Why'd you do that?" he asked with a soft laugh.

"I want you to wake up in the morning and remember how sloppy you were."

"Do you like me sloppy?"

"I adore you sloppy."

"I'll leave the cap off the toothpaste and wad napkins in my leftover coffee."

"You'd do all that for me?"

"If you love me, I will."

"I do, but I love you the way you are. Just don't try to change me, darling."

"As if I could!"

He laughed and worked the quilt over both of them.

He grumbled anyway when he had to wear his dirty socks the next morning, leaving before she went down to help Cheryl open but promising to return soon. The first person to enter the shop wasn't a customer.

"He's a man Brian hired to protect us," Kelly explained to Cheryl, drawing her aside in the workshop.

"A private eye! How exciting!"

"Well, just ignore him. Business as usual."

"At least he's not wearing black socks," Cheryl said, surveying the casual outfit of their guardian. "Knock off twenty years, let his hair grow a couple of months, and make him smile. Then he could pass for a student."

"Well, let's hope he doesn't scare away the customers," Kelly said. "I'll try to be back before lunch."

"If not, I'll send Sam Spade for sandwiches."

Brian insisted she wait inside the store until he arrived at the front door with his car. She dashed out feeling like a counter-espionage agent.

"Did you buy everything you need?" she asked cheerfully, teasing because he'd tabled all their morning business claiming he needed to buy fresh clothing. "I like you in a blue shirt."

"I bought it for you. Also mesh underwear, but I draw the line at white socks with a suit."

"Um, I'd like to see that."

"White socks with a suit?"

"No, mesh underwear."

She pinched his earlobe.

"Ow."

"Brian, don't you think this is unnecessary? I mean, consider it in the light of day. Any idiot could have painted a few nasty words on my window. No one bothered me last night."

"I thought we'd settled it. I need an apartment here, if only to keep a supply of clean shirts. As soon as the kidnappers are caught you can move back over the store, if that's what you want."

"Of course it's what I want. It's terribly inconvenient, living away from my workshop. Sometimes I get an idea in the middle of the night and run right down to work on it. Besides, I don't want you paying my rent!"

"Did you ask for an apartment?"

"No."

"Do you want one?"

"No, of course not."

"Then you'll be living there as a favor to me. I can't work if I have to worry about that place of yours. It's a miracle thieves haven't stripped you clean a dozen times."

"Well, they haven't." She pouted.

"Then live there for me. Please."

She'd roll over and play dead if he asked in that tone of voice.

"We're halfway to Ypsilanti."

"It's not easy to find a nice apartment in this town."

The complex he finally entered was solid brick with tasteful trim, substantially built without the temporary look most apartment developments have. A matronly woman with overly bright red hair met them by the door of number eight.

"Mr. Fort, I'm Henrietta Jordan."

"Mrs. Jordan, Ms. Valentine."

The front room was pleasantly spacious with a raised hearth in front of a red brick fireplace. The kitchen was small but functional with a larger room beside it that could be a breakfast room or formal dining room, depending on the occupant's wishes. They completed their tour after seeing the three bedrooms and two complete baths.

"It's much too big, Brian," she said softly when the woman walked across the living room to demonstrate a window crank.

"It'll do though, won't it?" he asked absentmindedly.

"You've already decided to lease it," she accused him, "but I don't have time to clean a five-room apartment with two full bathrooms."

"We'll have a cleaning woman, of course."

"Now, Mr. Fort, how do you like it?"

"Very nice. Exactly as described, Mrs. Jordan. You do have the papers ready?"

"We rushed them through. Is ten thousand earnest money satisfactory?"

"Of course, but we want immediate possession. I'll have some furniture delivered this afternoon. You can make arrangements to have someone here?"

Earnest money! Tenants made security deposits.

"You're buying this!" she accused him unhappily.

"I told you decent apartments are hard to find. I didn't spend all my time buying clothes."

"But . . ."

"A good condominium is an investment," he said casually.

He whisked her through a huge furniture store, buying a queen-size bed with coordinated dresser and chest, a second bedroom set, a three-piece living room set, and a kitchen table and chairs, giving her as large a part in the decisions as she was willing to take, but making up his own mind immediately when she hesitated. She stubbornly opposed the purchase of a thousand-dollar coffee table, but he bought a set of three other occasional tables before she had a chance to check the price.

"This all has to be delivered this afternoon," he repeated to the manager, who, of course, had given them his personal attention. "And get your decorator working on drapes. Anything quiet and tasteful."

"I'll handle everything, Mr. Fort."

"You don't want to meet with her, do you, darling?" he asked Kelly.

"Him or her. Decorators don't have to be women! No, no, I certainly don't."

It was one thing to visit Brian's family home and know that he lived in a wealthy setting, but to actually see him buy a condo and completely furnish it in a few hours was staggering. She couldn't take it in.

"Mother is loaning us Mrs. Wilcox for a few days. She'll stock the kitchen and bathroom and get things put away," he said in the parking lot. "Then we'll have a daily woman come to clean two or three times a week."

"What is this 'we' business, Brian? I thought you were going to find a small place for me to hide. You're setting up housekeeping!"

"I'll love playing house with you," he said.

"But shouldn't you ask me how I feel?"

"How do you feel about me?" he asked, standing beside the passenger door of the Mercedes facing her with a mischievous grin.

"That's not the right question!"

"Let's have lunch and then I'll help you move your clothes. Oh, you'd better drive. I want you to learn to handle the Mercedes."

"No, no, no. You've gone too far! I will not use your car. I have my own."

"I had it hauled in for a total overhaul while you were in the store. When my mechanic gets through, you can drive it. Until then, use mine when I'm gone."

"That does it!"

She stalked off, not caring that they were miles from her store and she didn't have cab fare in her purse. He caught her before she'd begun to cool off.

"Kelly, I know I'm being high-handed, but time is the one thing I don't have. I have to leave for Philadelphia in the morning, and I have seventy hours of work to do before my flight. My ulcer is burning and . . ."

"Your what?"

"Nothing important. I just . . ."

"Brian, do you have an ulcer?"

"A minor one."

"An executive-type, high-pressure, stress-related ulcer?"

"Well, I guess you could call it that."

"I love your ulcer!"

She threw her arms around his neck and kissed him so vigorously he nearly tipped over backward, ignoring the catcall from a semi driver waiting for the traffic light to change.

"Ulcers turn you on more than emeralds?" he asked in grinning puzzlement.

"It's such a relief to know you're vulnerable somewhere. Do you have any idea how hard it is to be crazy about a man who handles everything perfectly?"

Laughing and swinging her, he made a gesture at the truck driver, whose comments were becoming obscene.

"Let's go before I have to punch out a truck driver," he said, grinning broadly.

"You said you'd fight a duel for me."

"In the car!"

"About Mrs. Wilcox," she said when he got in beside her to drive. "I really can do things myself."

"Nonsense. She's coming this afternoon."

"I don't think she likes me."

He only laughed.

"Next you'll be telling me she's an ex-policewoman."

He looked a little startled. "How did you guess? She worked for the Detroit police until her husband talked her into quitting. He works for us too."

"Another woman who gave up her career for a man!"

"Actually, we pay her more than the city did. She's mother's personal bodyguard."

"I thought she was the cook!"

"She likes to keep busy. Mother isn't much of a challenge. For her a trip from Grosse Pointe Woods to Grosse Pointe Farms is a big production."

"Doesn't she travel with your father?"

"Sometimes. I do most of the running now, when I'm not away on a job of my own."

"Who hires you, exactly?"

"Governments, corporations, individuals."

"But you don't have to do geological work?"

"Not for the money, no, but I do have to have something that's my own. How can I explain it?"

"Like my store?"

"You've got me there."

He patted her hand.

The sheets still had the package creases, and the furniture smelled new, a varnished, polished scent that wasn't unpleasant, but wasn't homey either. In one way she was glad Brian had left after moving some of her clothes. She wouldn't feel right sleeping with him when Mrs. Wilcox was using the room right beside theirs. The woman was a marvel, organizing a trunkload of domestic necessities with off-hand efficiency, as professional in this assignment as she would be on the police force, Kelly suspected.

Alone in the big bed, she missed Brian terribly. Her back ached because her period had started, and she couldn't think of anything more soothing than cuddling against his warm back and bottom. Of course, it was a relief not being pregnant; the vague let-down feeling that oppressed her was only a reaction to everything else that had happened.

Sorting things in her mind kept her awake for a long time. She still hadn't mailed all her bills, and it was obvious her business required at least one part-time clerk in addition to Cheryl. If she advertised in the *Daily* she'd be swamped with applicants, every one of whom would use up some of her valuable time. She'd call student services at the university and ask them to send someone.

What a pleasure it would be to work at her bench, taking raw silver and working it into a design that was uniquely hers. Even the time-consuming finishing would be a sheer joy to do. Working on her jewelry was better than a tranquilizer, giving her time to think things through even when she was totally absorbed in a process.

Mrs. Wilcox became her driver and her shadow, insisting it was

Mr. Fort's orders, leaving her only when she was in the protective watch of the detective in the store. She was constantly conscious of her guards. When she worked in the back room, the detective paced from one part of the store to the other, watching her and the door. She tried to ignore him, but it was hard.

Brian didn't call until Saturday night.

"Darling, I haven't had a free second," he said contritely. "How are you?"

"Okay. Mrs. Wilcox and your detectives never let me out of their sight."

"Any word from the police?"

"A patrol car spotted someone fooling around in the alley last night. They scared him away but couldn't catch him. He disappeared somewhere on the campus."

"Don't take any chances. Please. For me."

"No, I won't, but do you really think I need someone all the time?"

"There's an alternative. I have to go to Paris next week. Come with me."

"Paris, France?"

"The City of Love. We'll leave Tuesday."

"I can't be ready that soon."

"Why not?"

"Well, I need clothes—and a suitcase. And a passport. I'd need a passport!"

"You don't have one?"

"The only foreign country I've visited is Canada. You don't need a passport to get through the tunnel."

"You take the tunnel?"

"It's faster than the bridge."

"No, it's not. When traffic backs up it's a bottleneck in there. The air gets bad too. You'll do anything to avoid heights, won't you?"

"No, not anything."

"We give a lot of support to our congressman. He'd rush your passport application through for me, I think."

"It's not the passport, Brian," she admitted. "I'd love to go. I'm dying to be with you. I just have so many problems right now."

"What problems?"

"I have to hire new help. The furnace broke down, and my

landlord tried to fix it himself. It's still not working right, so I have to get him on Monday morning. And my shelves are a disaster. I have to call every artisan I know and beg for consignments. Most of them work craft shows before Christmas, so I'm not very optimistic. And there's my own work, too. But I do love you."

"Lock the door and forget it all. Come to Paris with me, Kelly. I want to make love to you in the city where Napoleon loved Josephine and . . ."

"Stop, please." She felt weepy and miserable.

"Okay, you know what you have to do."

"I wish I could explain."

"No, you don't have to."

"It's still a hand-to-mouth business. A bad holiday season could force me to close. And I'm paying Cheryl a full-time salary."

"Trust her to run it."

"There's so many things I have to do myself, and she seems distracted lately. Not her usual bubbly self."

"You don't sound so peppy either. Are you sure you're all right?"

"My period started."

"Oh."

Did he sound disappointed, or did she imagine it? Her own feelings about being pregnant were so ambiguous. She never really let herself believe it could happen.

"I love you," he said softly.

"You're all right? Your ulcer isn't bothering you?"

She didn't want their conversation to end, needing to hear warm and intimate words from him.

"I've got an ache that has nothing to do with ulcers, but you're the only medicine I need."

"Will I see you before you leave?"

"No, I'm going on to New York from here. There's no way I can squeeze in time to come there."

"I'll miss you so much."

"I miss you already."

"Oh, Brian, I wish I'd known you forever. I wish I'd been in backseats with you in prep school."

"I can hardly handle you now. You would've totally bewildered me fifteen years ago."

"Where are you staying in Paris?"

"I haven't checked with my secretary yet. I'll let you know."

"You have a secretary? I didn't know that! You must have an office."

"Yes, in my father's suite downtown."

"You never told me."

"It never came up."

"It's so odd that I never knew."

"We've only known each other two weeks, sweetheart."

"It seems like much longer."

"I'm going to hate Paris."

"I hate it already because it's taking you away."

"Good night, darling."

She hung up feeling like an infatuated high school girl, lingering over The Big Call. Instead of working the way she should, she was moaning over Brian, as restless apart from him as a tigress in heat.

After Brian left for France, she assured Mrs. Wilcox she could manage alone. Her bodyguard was cordial but unmovable. Mr. Fort wanted her there.

His mother was harder to reach by phone than the President, even using the family's private number that Brian had given her. Or was she avoiding Kelly?

"What a pleasant surprise, Kelly," she said, finally accepting a call.

Hardly a surprise since her servants had been given thirteen messages in three days.

"Mrs. Fort, I appreciate having Mrs. Wilcox so much," she fibbed, "but there's no need for me to deprive you any longer. You can tell her to leave."

"Oh, no, Brian would be furious with me. Since that note arrived he's had two more men working on surveillance."

"Watching out for me? What note?"

"Oh, dear, I had no idea you didn't know. Brian got a note from one of the kidnappers."

"Saying what?"

"It was vague. Only that we owed him money, and he'd see that we paid one way or another. My husband had a terrible time persuading Brian to go to Paris, but he finally convinced him the agency men are more effective when Brian isn't trying to supervise them. I've never seen my son so agitated."

It was a gentle rebuke, but telling.

"Don't you think the note was an idle threat?"

"No, we can't assume that."

Kelly was so upset she called her own mother.

"Are you feeling all right, Kelly?"

"Of course, Mom, fine."

"Well, it is a little unusual for you to call me at school. My class is studying animal life, and one of the boys brought a garter snake to show. I had to bring him with me to the office, so he won't chase the girls around the room with it."

"Oh, I thought you might be on a break. I'll call another time, Mom. I'm really sorry."

Her mother detested snakes. She could almost see her warily eyeing the little boy, trying to keep his pet at a safe distance without giving away her fear. It was the wrong time for mother-daughter confidences, and what could she say, anyway, that wouldn't upset her parent?

"But you must have had something important . . ."

"No, I just miss you sometimes."

"Oh."

She hung up on her flustered mother, feeling better for no particular reason. If her mother could deal with four daughters, an absent-minded husband, and creepy fourteen-inch reptiles, she could handle her own life. Sometimes she really liked her mother.

Brian stayed away ten days. Kelly hired a student who stole from the register, and Mrs. Wilcox continued to refuse to go home. Her next new helper at the store knew everything, driving both her and Cheryl crazy. Kelly let Cheryl practice her management skills by firing the girl. Giving up on university referrals, she ran an ad that brought fifty-two responses and finally hired a pleasant, chunky girl named Jane who didn't get on anyone's nerves.

By the tenth day Kelly realized Cheryl was as miserable as she was.

"How's Duane these days?" she asked tactfully.

"Oh, he has Rose Bowl fever, like all of them," she said bitterly.

"Maybe they'll go and win for a change."

"Yeah, if they don't let the players loose in Disneyland first. And the coach puts the cheerleaders off limits."

A bitter Cheryl was a surprise.

"Want to tell me?" Kelly asked kindly.

"I wish there was something definite to tell. It's just a sort of vague feeling. I don't know."

"You're not getting along with Duane?"

"Oh, we get along fine, all five minutes a week. There's just something wrong, and I can't put my finger on it."

"Wish I could help you, but I don't know enough to keep my man from jetting off to Paris."

My man, that had a nice ring—but so far she hadn't heard a word from Paris, not even a postcard saying "Wish you were here."

CHAPTER ELEVEN

October's gift to Ann Arbor was a string of marvelous Indian summer days played out against a background of vivid red and yellow foliage. The campus world moved outdoors, with joggers, bikers, and strollers swarming like locusts around busy tennis courts and crowded lawns. Touch football games sprouted like dandelions in spring, while fledgling botanists moved clumplike from tree to tree guided by earnest young teaching fellows in white lab coats.

Kelly took to the road, wondering how she'd survived so long without her morning run, loving the uninhibited feeling of pounding across the campus in her navy knits. Betty, as she now called Mrs. Wilcox, ran slightly behind her but was never the first to call for a rest. First names notwithstanding, Kelly still felt repressed by her bodyguard, imagining that children in bygone centuries must have felt the same way about their governesses.

The prospect of a second weekend without Brian made her run to the edge of exhaustion on Saturday morning, returning to the condo for a long, bracing shower that didn't really do a thing for her spirits. Except for a few hours of assistance from Jane, who was too new to be much help yet, she had the full responsibility for the store that morning. It was the first home football game since the kidnapping, and the town was a solid mass of excited fans and sun-loving students.

The store was a beehive of activity, making the morning hours fly. She sold the garnet ring to a divorced father who came in with his somewhat pouty coed daughter—a gift obviously being used as a parental apology for months of neglect. The pieces she'd bought in San Francisco were attracting attention and selling fast, and she wondered if she could find a regular source. As much as it went against her original concept of the store as an outlet for fine handcrafted pieces, she could see that commercially made stock was becoming a necessity. Business was just too good.

Jane left, pedaling off on her skinny-wheeled bike to meet some friends at the stadium, leaving Kelly to close the nearly empty store. The last customers left, a young couple, both blond, who looked more like brother and sister than lovers, and she noticed with relief that it was time to lock the door. Before she could move to do it, a man entered, darkly handsome in a subdued plaid sportscoat and navy sweater, his shirt collar a dash of white against his tanned throat. He nodded at the bored security guard in the corner, who greeted him with deference, and waited for her to speak.

"Brian!"

She was in his arms, oblivious to the interested gaze of the guard, kissing him with all the bottled-up fervor of the lonely days without him.

"Does this mean you missed me?"

"I thought you'd never get back!"

"Don't ever think that."

He stepped back, dismissing the man, so sure he didn't need protection himself she wanted to shake him. He watched intently while she pulled the shade and locked the door, taking her in his arms again before she could get rid of her keys.

"Um, you taste good," he whispered, running his hands down her spine and fondling her bottom, straining against her with impatient urgency.

"After all this time, you'll have to court me," she said, wiggling free and ducking behind the counter.

"It will be a pleasure."

He stooped beside her as she opened the sliding door of a case, leaning forward to plant a noisy kiss on her cheek.

"Can't they wait?" he asked.

"No, you can! Do you want to help me take trays to the safe? Mrs. Wilcox—Betty—will be coming soon."

"No, she won't. I sent her home. I'm your bodyguard for the weekend."

"You are, huh?"

"You're stuck."

She headed toward the back room with her hands full, bending over the safe.

192

"I thought you were helping me!" she shrieked when his hand snaked under her skirt.

"Your idea, not mine."

"Was it your idea not to tell me you'd received another threat?"

"You wheedled that out of my mother."

He had enough grace to sound uncomfortable.

"She assumed I knew. After all, I've been depriving her of Mrs. Wilcox all this time. Doesn't that woman ever get a day off?"

"She prefers to accumulate them and take weeks at a time. Are you accusing me of exploiting my employees?"

"Would I do that?" she asked with mock sweetness.

"How's the condo?"

He trailed her out to the display case and took the trays she handed him.

"Empty. Lonely. Too big."

"It won't be tonight," he promised. "Are you ready to go?"

"I have to check the register and make a deposit. And I have to engrave the back of a locket."

"You have to do that now?"

"My customer will be here when we open Monday. If I don't do it now, I'll have to come back."

"Okay," he said wearily, "how long will that take?"

"I also have to solder a new clasp on an antique brooch."

"You'll be here all day. Can't that wait?"

"I wish, but she's one of my best customers. She bought my stuff when I was working the art shows and told a lot of her friends about me. She wants to wear the brooch at a faculty wives' affair on Monday."

"Come upstairs with me first," he murmured into her ear. "I'm suffering from jet lag, and I may collapse before you finish all that."

"Poor darling," she said with exaggerated sympathy, burrowing her hands under his sweater, over the smooth cotton that covered his back. "Why don't you take a nap on my bed upstairs? I'll come up the minute I'm done."

"You want me to suffer."

He opened the first three buttons of her blue Oxford-cloth blouse, letting his fingers wander between her breasts.

"Brian, if I hurry I'll be done in no time. Won't we enjoy the weekend more if I don't have to come back here?"

"You have me there."

"You can put some sheets on the bed. They're in the bottom drawer of the yellow dresser," she called up the stairs.

"I'll get you for this," he promised.

Unfortunately everything seemed to take a little longer than she'd expected. The receipts were over by eight dollars and thirty-two cents, and she had to decide whether a customer had been short-changed or her new helper had forgotten to ring something. Her register was not the computer type and had old-fashioned rolls of tape. The tedious job of comparing bills of sale with tape entries turned up a forgotten sale, but it took ages. She counted the cash and checks and stuffed them in her bag for night deposits, then crept up the steps as quietly as the creaking boards would allow to check on Brian.

He was sound asleep under her quilt, his clothing neatly hung and folded. He wasn't missing her, but she missed him, longing to crawl beside him and run her lips over his closed lids and relaxed mouth.

But if she gave in to the temptation, she'd never get her urgent orders filled. Maybe it would be a good idea to teach Cheryl how to solder.

All she had were full sheets of solder; she had to cut one into little paillons with heavy shears, catching the bits on white paper and putting the extra ones aside for other jobs. Each little paillon had to be hammered into a thinner oblong before using, and she wondered if she really had the patience needed for her craft. This was the first time she'd ever questioned her aptitude for the intricate work she did, but it was also the first time she'd tried to work with Brian sleeping above her, his presence disturbingly inviting.

The back of the old-fashioned enamel brooch, a charming pin with handpainted roses, was an unfamiliar alloy, and she had trouble cleaning it to properly flux with the solder. Her impatience made her fingers seem clumsy. She checked on Brian again, then sat down on the swivel chair by her desk, forcing herself to relax from the tips of her fingers to her toes, not starting the engraving job until she felt limp and relaxed. It took all her self-discipline to finish before hurrying up the stairs a third time to join Brian on the bed.

Leaving her clothes beside his, neatly folded, she crawled under the quilt, snuggling against him with a sigh of happiness, glad to be

194

in her familiar, if somewhat dusty, apartment. His quickly furnished condo didn't really seem like home.

"About time," he grumbled, pulling her close.

"How would you know? You've been sound asleep."

"Is that what you thought when you peeped in and left again? Raising my hopes for nothing!"

"If you were awake, why didn't you say something?"

"I don't want to be sandwiched in between jobs. I want your full attention."

"Tell me about Paris. I've never been to Europe."

"You'll see it yourself someday, if we can get you there without using ships or planes," he said sarcastically.

"That's mean."

"I can sympathize with the stomach business," he said, patting hers, "but it's not much fun traveling with a terror-stricken hostage."

"I wasn't a hostage when we went to San Francisco."

"No? You weren't exactly eager to go."

"Did you come here to argue with me?"

"Partly. Where else could I find the stubbornness of a mule in the body of an angel?"

"Not in Paris, I hope."

"I told you, love is one thing I never pay for."

"That darn condo makes me feel paid for."

Leaning on one elbow, he looked into her eyes, greener when she was agitated.

"Asking you to stay there has nothing to do with the way I feel about you. Because of my family's assets, your life may be in danger. The least I can do is give you protection. If you won't forgive me for insisting on it, we're in real trouble."

"There's nothing to forgive," she whispered miserably. "I just can't get used to being dependent."

"You've been married. Weren't you dependent then?"

"Yes, and it nearly ruined me. Sitting home stewing in my resentment, waiting to see if Larry would honor me with his company after work or hang around singles' bars hoping for a conquest."

"Neglected once and afraid to risk it another time?" he asked.

"I don't know. I'm not a ladies' magazine psychologist. After the divorce I made up my mind to be my own person. I'm stronger now than I was, but I get edgy when I feel myself losing ground. I know you can spend more in five minutes than my whole store is worth, but it represents more than a livelihood to me."

"Survival as an individual?"

"Something like that."

He leaned over and kissed her, drawing it out until she slid her leg between his, grinding against him with slow, sensual gyrations. The shades were drawn, but slivers of sunshine framed their poor fit on both sides, giving the room an unreal haziness.

"Tell me your favorite fantasy," he whispered, running his hands up and down her spine with unhurried enjoyment.

"Only if you'll promise not to laugh."

"I won't. I take fantasies very seriously."

"I like to imagine a knight, home from a long siege. He's weary and bruised, but he comes to me first because it's been so long. I send his page away and peel off his armor myself, then lead him to a big wooden tub."

"What happens there?"

He found a sensitive spot under her ear and sent tingles down her neck.

"I wash him and rub his skin with scented oil. Then we make love on a huge bed with steps leading up to it and embroidered curtains hanging all around us."

"I think you left out some of the best parts."

"You can use your imagination. Now tell me yours."

She shivered closer, burying her face in the hollow of his throat. "Nothing so romantic."

"Tell me anyway," she murmured, loving the feel of his chest against her chin.

"I'm in a huge house with all kinds of dead ends and stairs leading nowhere."

"Like the one some crazy person built in California?"

"Something like it. I know the woman I've always wanted is somewhere in the house. I hear her laughing, teasing me to find her."

"What are you wearing?"

"Nothing. I'm naked and I need a woman badly, but she's the only one I want."

"Do you catch her?"

She slid lower and teased his nipple with her lips.

"You're rushing my fantasy. Not easily. She runs and hides."

"Is she naked too?"

"In the better versions, of course. Every time I start to make love to her, she swings away on a chandelier or disappears down a trapdoor."

"How athletic!"

His hair was silky under her cheek, and she ran her hands through it lazily.

"No, just elusive, but I do catch her."

"You only want a woman who's hard to get?"

"You're looking for a man you can mother?"

"Freud didn't know everything! What happens when you catch her?"

"Let me show you."

He rolled on top of her, trapping her between his elbows and stimulating her nipples with his tongue, gently fondling one swelling mound, then moving to the other with increasing urgency. She covered her breasts with her hands, leaving nothing but her fingers for his teeth to nip, then wiggled into a ball, evading his gentle efforts to reclaim her.

"You like your women evasive," she taunted, wrapping the quilt around her torso while he struggled to free it, then unexpectedly flipping it over his head. She nearly got away, but he caught one ankle, taking full advantage of her awkward rear-in-the-air pose to tumble her back into his arms. They rolled and tussled, making mock assaults and laughing uproariously when one or the other scored an advantage. Feeling the impact of his strength but knowing how restrained his efforts were, she teased him unmercifully, letting him think he'd subdued her, then escaping for another breathless round.

Her skin was as moist as his from the exertion, and she used her slipperiness to wiggle free yet another time, miscalculating the urgency of his desire. He caught her on the edge of the bed, her feet on the floor, ready to slip to freedom. Pushing her shoulders back, he was ready to claim his prize with overheated vigor. As excited and breathless as she was, she wasn't quite willing to surrender. The bed rocked as if an earthquake had hit, and for one panicky instant she wondered how the ceiling of her shop would fare. Then Brian was towering over her, straddling her hips and grinning in anticipation. She squirmed and thrashed, but only to show him she was in his power, reaching for his neck to pull him closer. He took hard-won possession inch by inch, feasting on her warm flesh with his eyes and lips, guiding her hand and shuddering under her caresses, entering her with a gentleness born of his love, not their mock battle. Lying joined in utter stillness was incredibly exciting, a throbbing that gradually built to a pounding crescendo she wanted to last forever. Never too lost in himself for words of love, he made her feel loved and cherished, supersensitive to the sensations hammering through her when his self-control gave way to frenzied thrusts. His pleasure was her delight, a joy so mutual the concerns of the world shrank to nothingness for these precious moments.

"Give up?" he asked at last, collapsing on his back and pulling her on top of him.

"I'll never surrender," she hissed, nipping his shoulder and loving the salty tang of his skin, escaping one more time to huddle invitingly under the quilt.

They awoke in darkness, the quilt somewhere on the floor, shivering against each other.

"Want to take a bath?" she asked lazily.

"No, let's go home and take a shower."

"I am home."

"Dammit, Kelly, are we going to quibble all weekend?"

"Well, sex in the afternoon certainly makes you testy. Or is it having to fight for it?"

"You'll see how testy I am if you're not dressed in three minutes," he said.

She deliberately walked to the bathroom and locked the door, not coming out until she'd had a warm, leisurely bath. Then, with all the dignity she could muster clutching a too-small towel around her torso, she walked out to confront him.

He was gone.

"Brian, are you down there?"

Her voice sounded shrill echoing down the stairwell, and forgetting the splinters waiting on the steps for bare feet, she raced to the workshop.

"Afraid I'd left?" he teased, showing an inordinate amount of interest in the assortment of files mounted over her workbench.

"And leave me unprotected? No such luck!"

"You weren't at all worried?" He stared at her pointedly. "I like your outfit."

He made a sudden lunge, snatching away the towel and chasing her as she tore up the stairs.

"Peace!" she begged, collapsing on the bed and snatching at the quilt.

"Let's go home," he insisted.

"Where's home?"

"Wherever the two of us are together."

"I can buy that," she said, returning his gentle kiss with a lump in her throat, before she got her things together and they set off for the condo.

He drove her to work on Monday, leaving to see if her car was ready. After a few minor skirmishes, he'd agreed she should have it back. His concession wasn't much, she knew; they hadn't talked about the return of Mrs. Wilcox.

Some time later he returned, knocking for entrance on the back door of the store. "Look outside," he said.

She left her project a little reluctantly, since her work didn't lend itself well to interruptions.

"Is that my car?"

"Would you call that color emerald green?"

"You had it painted!"

"Before you get mad, have a little pity. Let me feel good by doing something for you."

"Oh, you're impossible!"

She thanked and kissed him so enthusiastically he actually blushed.

Except for lunch, they both spent the day in her workroom. He swept, straightened, and cleaned for her, restlessly trying to keep busy and making her bite her lips in frustration, finally agreeing to leave the store in Cheryl's care and go home early.

They dined on Ann Arbor's famous pizza, went to an early movie, and ended the day in the nicest possible way, cuddling together on the oversized bed.

"I'm going to Philadelphia tomorrow," he said.

"For long?"

"Only a day or two. It wouldn't be worth the flight for you to come. I probably couldn't spend an hour a day with you anyway."

"See why I need my own business?"

"Sell it," he said seriously, hugging her closer.

"How can you ask that?"

"Make jewelry but do it when I'm not around. You can sell your stuff anywhere. I'll find a jeweler to handle all you make."

"If I did sell the store, how often would I see you?" She sat up, pulling away from him.

"At least when I had time for you, I wouldn't have to spend it hanging around your workshop."

"When you have time for me? Do you realize how flattering that sounds?"

"I didn't mean it the way you're taking it. I'm scheduling every possible moment I can with you and then some. I should've left on an evening flight tonight."

"Maybe it's not too late. I'll call the airport and see if there's a plane you can catch."

She started to leave the bed, but he caught her arm.

"Don't be angry. I'm not asking you to give up your work, only the retail store. You could even keep the building just to use as a work place."

"Oh, sure, do you know how high Campus Town rent is?"

"You'll probably make just as much money concentrating on your own work. Sublease the front part, if you like."

He tightened his arm around her, but she pushed him away.

"You're the practical businessman. You have it all figured out. I'm surprised you haven't made arrangements with my landlord, the way you bought this condo without even telling me."

"I took you to see it."

"Letting me think you planned to rent it!"

"Forget I mentioned it," he said angrily, turning his back on her as if he meant to go to sleep.

"I don't forget things that quickly."

She wiggled closer to her edge, smarting from his high-handed attitude. How could he make a suggestion like that when he knew what the store meant to her? She'd built it up from scratch, doing every possible bit of the work and taking pride in the results. And business was good, better than good. It was every storekeeper's dream to sell faster than it was possible to restock. But she had a few more ideas on that too, and Wednesday she had an appointment with a design professor who, hopefully, could give her the names of promising students who might want to partially finance their education by making jewelry.

His hand on her shoulder was so tentative, she was afraid to acknowledge it.

"Kelly."

"What?"

She made her voice gruff so he couldn't tell how close the tears were.

"Come here."

"Why?"

"Because my hotel bed is going to be awfully empty, and I want to hold you."

"You don't understand about my store, do you?"

"I try, but I've never had to compete with a woman's business before. Forget I mentioned selling it. Please."

"You won't ask again?"

"I'll try not to."

He cradled her head on his chest, stroking her hair away from her face. His body hair tickled her nose, and she sniffed.

"Don't cry."

He sounded alarmed.

"I'm not. My nose itches."

"Promise to miss me while I'm gone."

"I will."

She didn't even have words to tell him how much.

"Is Mrs. Wilcox coming back?"

"No, I didn't think it was fair to mother to keep her here indefinitely."

She breathed a deep sigh of relief. School was out.

"The agency protecting you at the store will send a woman here in the evening. Let them know your exact schedule, and they'll meet your car in the alley behind the store every morning and see that you get away safely in the evening. You shouldn't have any car trouble while I'm gone. I had yours totally overhauled."

He probably spent more than the VW was worth, she thought, realizing what it meant to be a bird in a gilded cage. But the warm

201

feel of his arms around her helped banish some of the troublesome thoughts.

Four days later she got a phone call from him.

"Where are you?" she asked.

The pleasant red-haired female detective tactfully left the kitchen where Kelly was talking.

"Grosse Pointe. I have to ask you something."

Why did her stomach do flip-flops? She knew before he asked she wouldn't like the question.

"Come to Colombia with me."

"Columbia, South Carolina? Missouri?"

For all she knew there could be dozens of towns named Columbia.

"Colombia, South America. I'll be there at least three months, Kelly. Come with me."

If a gorge the size of Grand Canyon had opened at her feet, she couldn't have been more stunned.

"You'll be gone three months?"

"Three or more," he said.

"You don't have to go?"

"No, not in the sense that someone's pointing a gun at my head, but I've been angling for this chance for three years. I'll be covering some pretty rugged territory, but the corporation is sending me with a crack crew. You can come along."

"That means being gone during the holiday rush."

"Yes, it does."

"Emeralds come from Colombia," she said, weakly stalling. "Does their government like Americans?"

"No government likes Americans very consistently."

"I don't know what to say."

"I'm leaving next week. Getting all your papers in time will be a hassle, but I can do it if you decide by tomorrow."

"So fast?"

"I'll be busy all day tomorrow, but I can be there by seven. Give me your answer then."

To go or not to go, that's the question, she thought with a notable lack of originality, still undecided five minutes before Brian was due

202

for dinner. Her friendly detective was ready to slip out the door when he arrived. The agency was noted for its discretion.

"Hi," he said, opening the door with his key at the same moment she turned the handle to let him in.

He filled the doorway, moving aside to let the guard go.

"I missed you," he said softly.

She belonged in his arms, but the days apart loomed between them.

"I missed you too." Her throat was closing fast.

He was wearing a smart charcoal topcoat over a suit designed for presidential receptions. His business dress was always a little intimidating until she remembered him in less formal garb, preferably with his pants off.

Her grin was forced, but he couldn't know that, crossing the space between them and engulfing her in his arms. Their kisses were hungry ones, greedy and wet, expressing the misery of their separation, not the joy of reunion.

"Let me hang up your coat," she said.

"I'm finally getting you trained?"

It was his invitation to banter, but she didn't feel up to it, instead taking his overcoat and locating a wooden hanger in the front closet.

"I have a roast beef in the oven," she said, "and baked potatoes. A salad . . ."

"The menu sounds fine, but I'm mostly interested in dessert."

Because she'd slipped her shoes off and left them in the kitchen, he seemed taller, his lean muscular frame looking magnificent in the charcoal suit she hadn't seen before.

"New suit?"

"No."

"I never have seen your whole wardrobe, I guess."

"And I've never enticed you into my sunken tub."

"Do you want to change before dinner?"

"Always trying to get my clothes off."

As a joke his remark fell flat, but he went into the bedroom. She didn't follow.

"Not much selection here," he said, coming into the kitchen in a navy terry robe and clogs he'd recently purchased to keep there.

"Well, that's the gypsy life for you."

They weren't good at small talk, at least not with each other.

"How's the protection working out for you? Any problems?"

"They're very nice people, but do you really think it's still necessary to have full-time guards?"

"Yes, I do."

"Have you gotten more threats?"

He hesitated, making a ritual of pouring their wine.

"Not exactly."

"What does that mean?"

"There hasn't been a demand for money or any more notes, but we did have an incident."

"Well, tell me!"

"We have a couple of dogs running loose on the estate at night. They're well-trained, and they won't eat anything our caretaker doesn't give them. Unfortunately his wife's cat isn't that well-disciplined. Someone threw some poisoned liver over the fence, and she ate it."

"The cat died?"

"Afraid so." He put his arm around her. "Of course, it might not be related in any way. There are kooks who poison animals for their own twisted reasons."

"That's so horrible."

There were times when they enjoyed a companionable silence, communicating with their eyes and gestures, but tonight wasn't one of those times. She picked at her food until he commented on it, then forced herself to swallow a few bites. He ate without pleasure, hardly tasting his food.

"I'm waiting for you to tell me," he said. "I wasn't going to ask, but you're driving me crazy."

"I just don't know what to say."

"Or don't know what excuses to give?"

"In San Francisco," she began slowly, "you never did feed me shrimp on Fisherman's Wharf."

"I thought we had a good time."

"We did—wonderful. But for every hour you spent with me, you were gone ten."

"Surely that's an exaggeration."

"Well, I didn't keep a chart, but it seemed like that."

"What are you getting to?"

"Colombia. What would I do there? Would I be by your side, following you to work, helping you do whatever you do?"

"I'd keep you with me as much as humanly possible."

"What does that mean?"

"I'll be working in some primitive areas. There may be some days when you'll be safer staying back in a village. Or you can stay in Bogotá and shop. The emeralds are magnificent and cheaper than anywhere else in the world. You can help put together an investment portfolio."

"Act as your agent while you're tramping the wilderness, you mean?"

"Yes, but there are other things to do. You can spend a week shopping the Cannera 7. Their wool has natural oils that make it great for waterproof ponchos, and they even have a Hilton where you can meet other foreigners."

"Listen to you, Brian. You make it sound like a swinging singles tour. Next you'll be telling me the night spots where women can go alone."

"You know the alternative."

He sounded as miserable as she felt.

"You'll really be gone for three months?"

"At least."

"But what are you offering me? A chance to hang around hoping you'll drop in for a quickie once a week?" She knew she'd hurt him with that one, but she couldn't hold the feelings in.

"Camping out on the island was a breeze compared to some that I'll be doing, Kelly. We'll be better equipped, but the terrain is rough. And I won't be working alone."

"Will the other men have women along?"

"Almost certainly not. That's why you'll have to stay back part of the time."

"All the time, you mean."

"No. I want you near me."

"Near! Not with!"

"What do you want me to say, Kelly?"

"Say you won't go."

"I told you how long I've worked for this chance."

"Then go!"

"There's no choice. I signed a contract."

"In Philadelphia?"

"No, I flew to New York before I came back."

"I never even know where you are."

"This is all a smoke screen, isn't it? Make the whole idea seem like a bummer, so you can hide in your little shop. What kind of life can you have if you're scared witless every time you see an airplane?"

"Not your kind of life, obviously!"

"Dammit, Kelly, take a risk for once in your life! I want to make love to you in a sleeping bag in the mountains and scrub your back under a waterfall in the wilds. I want you to be mine under a scratchy Indian blanket in a jungle hut; I want to show you off to South American millionaires at the Jockey Club."

"You want! You want me all gift-wrapped in a cozy little love nest whenever you have time to break the ribbon."

"Love nest! You make it sound like I want a mistress! I love you. If it makes you feel better we'll get married before we leave."

"If I ever get married again, it won't be to make me 'feel better'!"

Her temples were throbbing, and she couldn't even remember when her headache had started.

"Okay, let's get to the bottom line. Are you coming or not?"

"No, I'm not going to sit around alone in some foreign country hoping for a glimpse of you every ten days. My busy season is coming, and I have to work."

"Okay, it's your decision."

He left the table and slammed the bedroom door, dressing before Kelly could load the dishwasher with shaky hands. When she heard the outside door bang, she broke down, weeping copiously, sitting at the kitchen table with her head on her arms.

She didn't hear him return.

"I can't leave you alone," he said hoarsely from the kitchen door.

His topcoat, jacket, vest, and shirt were all unbuttoned, and his tie hung loosely on his bare chest.

"You don't have enough sense to button your coat," she sobbed brokenly.

"I don't have enough sense to stay where I belong—with you."

"Don't go."

"The situation is too touchy. The least that can happen is they'll sue my ass off. Worse, a complicated deal with one of my father's associates is involved."

"So there are things even you can't control?"

"Not at this point."

She blew noisily on an orange paper napkin and hoped her nose didn't turn the same color.

"How's your ulcer?"

"Lousy."

"I'll fix you some warm milk."

"I hate warm milk."

"I've never seen you so mad."

"That's because being with you makes me so happy."

Arguing was easier than enduring the longing that passed between them like radio waves carrying disaster signals. Her eyes were swimming with fresh tears, and he came closer, bending over to blot them with his white handkerchief.

"It's not exactly the end of the world," he said miserably.

"Of course not. We're reasonable adults. We can handle this. When I stop blubbering," she added under her breath.

He looked so vulnerable, with a slice of bare skin exposed between so many layers of clothing. She gently touched him above his belt.

"Where does your ulcer hurt?"

"Don't try mothering me," he said gruffly. "I don't even like it from my mother."

"I suppose you'll get mad just because I worry about you," she snapped, running her fingers under his belt to caress the soft spot where she thought he was hurting.

"What you're doing isn't mothering," he said hoarsely, taking her in his arms and kissing her as if the world would end when he stopped.

In the morning the world was intact, but Brian was gone, leaving before dawn without shaving or showering. He called every day, but she didn't see him again before he left for Colombia.

CHAPTER TWELVE

"You work with unusual materials," Kelly said, trying not to wrinkle her nose in distaste.

Unusual was hardly enough to describe the collection of pigeon feathers, paper clips, old leather shoe tongues, acorn caps, unpolished side-of-the-road type stones, and tin can lids cut into bizarre shapes. The lanky blond art student fingered the bib of his overalls and challenged her with an insolent stare.

"You're very creative," she went on, "but I'm afraid this isn't quite the type of jewelry our customers buy."

"Look, lady, it's no big deal to me. This stuff sells faster than I can make it. I heard you needed consignments. I gave you your chance."

He slapped the cover back on his coat-box display case and banged out the door. Fortunately her word-of-mouth appeal to the university's art students had brought in some good items. She'd bought outright an assortment of fine copper enamels and took some unusual wooden novelty pins on consignment. For the most part students worked with inexpensive materials, but she wasn't desperate enough to fill her cases with junk made of hairpins and crushed eggshell.

Gradually, by working twelve or more hours a day, she was making headway. Pre-Christmas sales were running better than ever, helped by the combination of free publicity from the kidnapping and Cheryl's gift for selling. Kelly was able to spend most of the day in her workshop, often running out for a sandwich and returning for an evening session.

Her round-the-clock security force shadowed her everywhere, finally getting on her nerves so much she called Brian's father, asking him to discharge them. He was kind, courteous, understanding, and absolutely adamant that they remain on duty until the kidnappers were caught. His disarming courtliness made her forget to suggest another use for the detectives: finding the trio of criminals. According to Officer Michaels, her inside source, Fred had served time in prison for check fraud, Benny had a juvenile record, and Mack did very minor jobs for some very mean people. How could three such unsavory characters disappear?

Followed by David, a big silent bear of a man who was the least intrusive of all her keepers, she dashed through her personal Christmas shopping. A month earlier she'd mailed Brian's gift, a silver tie clip she'd lost sleep finishing. She couldn't remember him wearing one, but she wanted him to have something more personal than a store-bought, manufactured gift. His gift arrived two weeks early, a lovely poncho in muted, hand-dyed shades of brown and tan. She wore it like a security blanket, fingering it often and wondering if Brian had touched the same fibers when he selected it. Or had he just pointed and said wrap it? A man who bought a condo and furnished it in a matter of hours was perfectly capable of picking up a phone and ordering a gift charged to his credit card.

His correspondence wasn't much more personal. The first postcard to arrive said: "Missing you. Love, Brian." The second gave a weather report and said he'd be out of contact for a few weeks. A postcard collector might have appreciated his correspondence, but she longed for a long, newsy letter saying how much he loved her.

If pre-Christmas enthusiasm largely bypassed her, she did renew her sense of wonder in fashioning fine pieces of jewelry. After her divorce she'd used her work to dispel the emptiness and sense of failure in her life. Now she concentrated just as intensely to fight the aching loneliness left by Brian's absence.

Her father drove to Ann Arbor to fetch her for the family celebration, giving her security people a holiday break. She planned to stay with her parents two nights, so she packed her aging suitcase, using the unneeded space for gifts: a silver pendant for her mother, earrings and the San Francisco gifts for her sisters, Scotch and cigars for her brothers-in-law, and a coveted volume on political theory for her father. He tended to leave any gifts other than books under the tree until her mother got sick of seeing them and put them away. Gifts for her red-haired little nephews were the most fun. She bypassed educational and electronic toys in favor of a racing car set and a sturdy drum, a reminder of the Christmas when Jackie had put her foot through Kelly's new drum.

Because she went home for Christmas, she didn't get Brian's call until the night she returned to the condo.

"Darling, I miss you!" he said, or at least that was the way she interpreted the jumble of static that reached her ear.

"I miss you too. When are you coming home?"

"A few more weeks."

Or had he said months? It wasn't a very satisfactory conversation, but she held the receiver a long time after the connection was broken. How could she go on living if jungle snakes swallowed him or he fell off a cliff? She should be there to protect him. Remembering that she hated all kinds of reptiles even more than her mother did, she was still sure her presence could act as some sort of charm to ward off misfortunes. A thousand times during the long, miserable weeks without him, she'd been ready to hop on a plane and wing her way south, but it was too late to join him. Why couldn't she fall in love with a shoe salesman who watched football games on the tube all weekend or a good old home-boy who wouldn't cross the bridge to Canada if they were giving away Cadillacs? She almost envied women who spent all day Saturday popping corn and beer tabs; at least they had a man to warm the sheets before they crawled into bed.

Mentally slapping herself, she put aside the phone.

A brick crashed through the charming bay window of the condo living room at 3:17 A.M. that night. Her guard, Florence, a wiry wisp of a woman, tore into Kelly's bedroom waving a purse-size revolver, nearly losing her job by giving her client a heart attack. Kelly didn't have time to explain how raw terror affected her bladder. Six hours later Benny was in custody.

She really didn't believe in the invisibility claimed for trick mirrors. A detective ushered her into a nondescript room, pointing toward a scene framed by one of the deceptive one-way mirrors. It was disappointingly unlike the lineup she'd expected. A bulky man who looked like a slug with human features stared belligerently at the square of glass. Benny had shaved his beard, revealing pasty white cheeks and a weak little chin. His grayish-blue sweat shirt was filthy.

210

"Well, Miss Valentine?" the policeman asked with a hint of suppressed excitement under his habitual air of boredom.

"That's Benny," she said decisively.

Nine days later she was back in the same room, her decisiveness considerably shaken by session after session of questioning. Fred and Mack had also been picked up. The prosecutor's office wanted an airtight case. Ann Arbor's force had bagged the infamous Fort kidnappers where agencies with more clout had failed. Could the two weary, gray-faced men behind the glass be the same nasty characters who'd robbed her store and dumped her on an island?

Fred's hair was long and stringy, making the thin spot on top more noticeable. His lips were drawn into a sneer that didn't fool anyone; he was scared witless. Mack seemed to be suffering from a compulsion to blabber. His lips moved continuously, but whether sounds came out, Kelly couldn't tell. How many men had a primitive, ridged forehead and bushy brows like his? Probably millions, she thought dejectedly, her confidence shaken by the thoroughness of the questions she'd answered since Benny's capture.

"I remember that mole on Fred's neck!" she said triumphantly, finally coming up with irrefutable evidence that she was fingering the right man.

"Is he one of the men who came into your store?"

The detective seemed tense and impatient, knowing he was as well as she did. She certainly wouldn't want his job. She bit back a snotty answer.

"Yes, and Mr. Fort will confirm it."

Mr. Fort would confirm everything, and he'd be at the airport in fourteen hours and thirty-seven minutes by her latest calculation. He'd rushed through his final reports, leaving the minor details to a local geologist who'd been on the expedition. The police thought he was being extremely cooperative, cutting short his trip to aid the cause of law and order. Kelly knew an even better cause. Blessedly free of her security force, she left the condo shortly after midnight, allowing more than two hours to arrive at the airport in her VW.

Brian's plane was late, an hour and twenty-eight minutes and counting, due to a foul weather tie-up slowing a connection. The airline attendants were hiding from Kelly, sulking in some hole with the outgoing luggage just because she insisted on a mile-by-mile progress report. If Brian came home safely she'd never again let him fly alone. Far better to plunge to a fiery death with him, hands clenched, saying good-bye to each other when the dreaded impact came.

A harassed-looking man in an airline uniform peeked out, saw her, and disappeared again. Three minutes later Brian's flight was announced. Kelly had been waiting so long to hear those numbers she couldn't believe it when the call came over the public address system. A desk worker ventured out, and she dashed to him for confirmation.

She couldn't go beyond the metal detector without a ticket. Pacing, bobbing her head around the security checkpoint, and throwing pathetic glances at the guard on duty burned up a lot of energy, but it didn't make seven minutes seem less like seven hours. How long did it take to open the door of an airplane? No other passengers were coming. Had there been a last-minute disaster, a crash with a fuel truck, or an explosion on board?

Brian was one of the first passengers through the barrier, swooping down on her before she recovered from the glorious shock of seeing his beard. The lower part of his face was totally covered by a short but dense growth, strikingly dark against the deep tan of his upper visage.

A crowd swirled around them, cutting short the sweetest kiss of her lifetime. With their arms locked around each other, they hurried from the terminal. When they were outside she suddenly remembered his luggage.

"What I couldn't mail, I gave away," he said, holding her locked against his side. "Where's your car?"

She was so excited she couldn't remember.

He laughed heartily, but he wasn't even chuckling ten minutes later, when they were still searching the series of parking areas under lights dulled by driving snow. When they found a familiar-looking mound and brushed away enough of the icy covering to identify it, she apologized profusely.

"All I could think about was meeting you," she said weakly.

"I wouldn't have it any other way."

His beard had collected snow that melted against her chin, but his lips were warmly wonderful.

"Let's go home," he whispered.

It was easier said than done. Her snowbrush with the broken handle was a poor weapon against the continuing onslaught of snow, and she soon soaked her gloves trying to help.

"Get in and start the car," he ordered. "Turn on the defrosters to clear the windows."

When he finished scraping, his hair and beard were matted with half-melted snow, and visibility outside was practically zero.

"Let me drive."

She didn't argue.

Snow was drifting furiously across the expressway as they vied for space with tenacious trucks, afraid to go slow and be rear-ended, unable to drive fast with no clear vision beyond a few feet. Brian drove with dogged concentration, speaking only once to say planes were much safer.

She wanted to kick him.

When he saw a freeway exit, he took it, driving through billowing snow that seemed less menacing away from the exposed highway. The first motel they passed had a VACANCY sign. They checked in to celebrate his homecoming in an Ypsilanti motel. The student on duty, thinking they weren't going to get their money's worth that night, warned them that checkout time was noon.

Neither of them worried about overstaying their time. The maid respected the DO NOT DISTURB sign, finally asking the desk clerk to ring their room the next afternoon so she could clean.

"Is the room available for another night?" Brian asked sleepily.

It was.

Awakening slowly in the late afternoon, Kelly thoughtfully fingered his beard, glad she'd seen him without it but delighted by the soft, springy growth. She wanted to feel its tickly texture on her neck and breasts again and lose her lips in its midst. Absorbed in admiring him, it took her a while to realize one of the sensations making her edgy was simple hunger. Somehow they'd forgotten about breakfast and lunch.

"Hungry?" he asked, either reading her mind or feeling as hollow as she did.

He tickled her ribs and tummy with his beard, playfully refusing to let her evade him.

"Hanging around you, I should get really skinny."

213

"You are. You've lost weight."

He confirmed it with his hands, snickering when he patted her bottom.

"Well, you've lost it in most places."

She slapped his hand away.

"I didn't know we'd be staying here," she said hesitantly. "So—you know. We're going to have to worry for another month."

"I won't worry. As long as I'm not an unwed father, I don't care."

"What?"

She sat upright, eyeing him with a mixture of surprise and skepticism.

"Don't tell me you've never thought about the possibility?"

He sat up and faced her, taking both her hands in his.

"When I do, I bang my head against so many brick walls. Your traveling, my store, your life-style, my . . ."

"Stop there!" He squeezed her hands. "Do you love me?"

"You know I do!"

"Then we'll work out the small stuff." He coughed and had to wait a minute. "I love you, Kelly, and a few days ago I would've traded the whole country of Colombia to have you in my sleeping bag."

He leaned forward and kissed her love-swollen lips with a fervor that made her senses swim.

"How about it?" he whispered, his lips tickling her ear.

"How about it? What kind of proposal is that?"

"What do you want, gypsy violins, bended knees, flowery words?"

He caught her earlobe between his teeth and gently nipped it.

"Violins aren't necessary."

"Okay, you asked for it."

He pulled her to the edge of the bed and slid onto his knees on the carpet, clasping both her hands in his.

"Is this the proper form?" he asked.

"I've never seen it done without clothes," she said, giggling.

"Do you want me to get dressed?"

"No, please don't!"

"Sure you're ready for this, no giggling or interruptions?"

"Oh, yes, quite ready, sir."

"Beloved Kelly Valentine, could you find it in the kindness of

214

your heart to accept this humble, unworthy slave as your lawfully wedded husband? No—don't answer yet."

He kissed her knee with exaggerated passion, stopping to cough.

"You sound congested," she said unromantically.

"It's nothing. Be quiet. Where was I? Yes, to become my help-mate, my beloved, the light of my life, the object of my desires. How'm I doing?"

"Splendidly. Is there more?"

"Definitely. Where was I? Oh, yes, to wash my fevered brow and soothe my wounds, to press your trembling body against my coarse, unworthy person, to . . ."

He coughed again.

"Shouldn't you quit while you're ahead?" she asked, barely suppressing her mirth.

"And have you think this proposal is one-sided? I haven't gotten to the things I'll do for you."

"What will you do for me?"

If he did much more, she was going to be on the floor with him. Who'd ever suspect a kneecap was an erogenous zone?

"I can't improve on the old way of saying it: love, honor, cherish."

He stood and offered her his hand, pulling her into his arms and kissing her deeply.

"I've never heard it said more beautifully."

"Does that mean yes?"

His hands traveled down her back, cupping her bottom and lifting her against his hard masculinity.

"Yes, yes, yes. Darling, I missed you so much it was like being half-dead."

His knee parted her thighs, and she instinctively wrapped her leg around one of his, letting her other toes grope for a precarious hold on top of his foot.

"I really didn't think this was possible," she gasped, awestruck by the sensations rippling through her as they slid together.

"Anything's possible if you want it enough," he said hoarsely.

"Especially our marriage," she moaned, clinging to his neck, almost fainting with excitement, not a trace of doubt in her voice.

"Of course, there are hard and easy ways to do things," he laughed breathlessly, straining to support her whole weight but finally lowering her to the bed and finishing what he'd begun with deep, unhurried thrusts, carrying her from plateau to plateau until she ached for the explosion to release a series of shuddering contractions.

Their passion was a plunge in the river of love, waves still washing over her as they clung together in damp ecstasy.

"This deal has some neat fringe benefits," she whispered into his hair, locking her arms around his head so he wouldn't stop stroking her breast with his tongue. She never wanted to come down from the high she was riding, and his tender mouth kept arrows of fire flying to the very center of her being.

She found a whole new vocabulary to express her love for Brian, vowing fervently to bring nothing but happiness to this man she adored.

They started talking about the wedding over juicy porterhouses in the motel dining room.

"I know a judge who will marry us in his chambers as soon as we get a license," he said, laying down the steak knife and watching her chew a bit of slightly pink meat.

"A judge? We can't be married by a judge."

"Why not?"

"Brian, my family would never forgive me! I eloped over ten years ago, and they're still disappointed that I didn't have a wedding. It's Joan's turn to be matron of honor, and my mother simply doesn't recognize any marriage not performed in a church."

"Tell them you have to get married fast."

He casually cut another piece of steak and put it in his mouth.

"That's a terrible idea!"

"Why? I'm going to make an honest woman out of you. They can't object to that."

"That's not the point."

She forgot about eating and sat unconsciously trying to punch holes in the cloth napkin on her lap.

"Be honest with me," he said, still eating, coughing and taking a sip of wine before he went on. "If you could have any kind of wedding in the world, what would you choose?"

"A garden wedding with a lattice arch and big baskets of spring flowers, tulips and daffodils."

"No way am I waiting till summer!"

"You didn't let me finish. The flowers aren't the important part. I want to be surrounded by everyone I love, my family, my friends. I want them to see how happy I am. I want them to know you're the only man I'll ever love. What we have is so special, it has to be shared."

He stared at her now, food forgotten, his wistful smile making her knees feel watery.

"You're baiting a trap with beautiful words," he said softly.

"What do you mean, baiting a trap?"

"I can see the ground falling away under my feet. You'll want armies of bridesmaids and a fleet of groomsmen in tails. The guest list will be phone-book size, and you'll end up dancing all night with third cousins and horny old men instead of doing a solo for me like a good bride should."

"Maybe I should wear a red satin dress with slits up the sides instead of a white wedding gown. After all, I am a wicked divorcée."

"The only thing wicked about you is your tongue when you want your own way. Can we talk about this back in the room?"

He glanced around at the dozen or so other diners, obviously all motel guests since it wasn't an evening for casual socializing. The wind-driven snow blasted against a half-shuttered window, confirming the wisdom of staying another night.

"Are we going to yell?"

"No, we'll have a calm, rational, sensible discussion, then I'll turn you over my knee and spank you until you're reasonable."

"The day you do that, Brian Fort, you can zip yourself into your sleeping bag and spend the rest of your nights on a frozen peak for all I care."

He laughed softly.

"I'd never use physical force, sweetheart. Verbal warfare with you is too much fun."

"You make me furious when you sit back so calmly superior and let me blow off. You started this fight. It was your idea to get married."

A woman at the next table was glancing curiously in their direction, trying not to be obvious.

"Truce?" he asked, coughing into his napkin. "I'd like to finish my steak."

"Well, I'm still hungry too," she mumbled.

After dinner he bought a newspaper and discovered a small weight room available to guests. He was enthusiastic until he remembered his clothing situation. Instead of lifting he did pushups in their room, stripping first because the weather was too fierce to bother shopping for fresh clothing.

"I don't see why you can't keep track of your own wardrobe," she said coolly, pointedly ignoring his naked exertions and sitting cross-legged on the bed in the same navy slacks and ski sweater she'd worn to meet his plane.

"That's why I need a wife."

"I knew you must have some ulterior motive."

She called Cheryl to explain her situation and ask about the store, trying to ignore the rasping of his breath as he jogged in place, afraid he was overdoing it because it usually took a lot to make him short of breath.

"Sounds like you're getting old."

He might forget their quarrels after a few minutes, but when she was mad, she stayed mad.

"My chest is tight," he said, finally quitting. "My cold seems to be getting worse."

"You do look a little sickly," she said unsympathetically.

"I'm going to take a shower. Want to join me?"

"No, I don't think so."

The hot steam of the shower loosened the congestion in his chest, and she could hear his hacking cough over the noise of the water. On impulse she dialed room service and ordered a hot brandy drink for him and a half-liter of white wine. The service was fast, probably because the only other guests in the motel were snowbound travelers, there through necessity, not for partying. She rapped on the bathroom door, warning him not to barge out naked while the waiter was there.

"Maybe it is a good idea to marry you," he teased hoarsely, seeing the drinks when he emerged wrapped in two towels.

"Get under the covers," she ordered. "This will stifle your cough."

"The sheets are cold."

"Your drink isn't. You shouldn't have exercised if you didn't feel well."

He arched his brows and sipped his drink gratefully. "You're talking like my mother."

"No, that's common sense talking."

"Except for a scratchy throat I'm fine. I sure would like a bed warmer, though."

"Too much like mothering. I'm going to take a shower."

They watched television under a pile of blankets and spreads gathered from both double beds in the room, but Brian was still cold, his teeth chattering even though he tried to conceal it from her.

"I'll try to reach a doctor," she offered.

"No one is going to come out on a night like this."

"I can take you to the hospital emergency room."

"No. Going out in this storm won't warm me up. Besides, it's only a cold."

She lay awake most of the night listening to his shallow breathing and bouts of coughing, not at all liking the hot feeling of his skin or the restless way he tossed. He woke often but absolutely refused to consider medical help before morning.

In the morning she drove him to an Ann Arbor clinic, insisting he see the doctor on call and waiting until he was finished.

"A two-hour wait for a shot in the rear," he whispered disgustedly on the way out.

"You could've waited until it turned into pneumonia and had a lovely rest in the hospital."

Once all four Valentine sisters had been home sick at the same time with nasty cases of viral flu. Kelly wondered many times during the next two days how her mother had survived. Undoubtedly she'd made her decision to finish her degree program and get a teaching certificate during that hectic siege or one like it.

As patients went, Brian was the pits, holing up in the condo with all the grace of a bear walking on hot coals. Kelly squeezed fresh orange juice for him; he strained the pulp out. She greased his chest with her mother's favorite chest-cold salve; he washed it off complaining of the menthol smell. She ordered him to bed; he spent the afternoon coughing into the phone. When she threatened to go to the store and leave him to suffer in solitude, he was charming and contrite—for at least twenty minutes.

The wedding discussion was temporarily tabled.

On the third day, a damp, dismal January Friday with the recent snow turning to gray slush in the streets, she went to work in the morning, making him promise to take his pills, drink hot herbal tea, and stay inside. When she returned at noon with a sack full of groceries to fix his lunch, he was gone.

He was back before she could put her purchases in the refrigerator and cupboard.

"Am I in trouble?" he asked, poking his stuffy red nose around the kitchen doorjamb.

"You're lucky you're too big to spank," she muttered. "Brian, you promised! You look terrible. You sound terrible."

"If you don't stop mothering, I'm going to change my mind about getting physical."

His threat wasn't very effective when he had to cough for two minutes after making it.

"Drink this," she ordered.

"Not more of your mother's cough medicine?"

"It's only whiskey, honey, and lemon. You're not a baby, for goodness' sake."

"I'd prefer a good shot of Scotch. Did my father call?"

"I just got here myself."

"I tried to beat you home." He grinned sheepishly.

"Your promises aren't worth a whole lot, are they?"

"If you interpreted my mumble as a promise, that was your mistake. You were giving all the orders."

"You don't like taking them from a woman, do you?" she teased.

"Never tried it, but if you order me into bed so you can rub my back, I'll give it a try."

"You don't deserve a back rub. Why did you go out?"

"Civic duty."

"Ah, the police caught up with you."

"I had to go to the jail to make a formal identification."

"Our friends wouldn't be there if you waited till Monday?"

"Oh, they'll be available ten years from Monday."

"Only ten years?"

"Vengeful creature, aren't you? Don't you have a soft spot in your heart for the men who brought us together?"

"Not really."

He came up behind her as she dumped a can of soup in a pan, running his hands over her hips.

"Not chicken soup again," he moaned.

"Beef noodle, you'll love it. Mack really didn't want to be involved. He isn't quite as guilty as the others, is he?"

"He wanted the robbery loot and the ransom money as badly as the others. Something interesting's going on with them."

"You are feeling better, aren't you?" she asked, wiggling free of the hand that was investigating the zipper on her slacks.

"Is this a nose you could love?" he asked, blowing it more noisily than necessary.

"Not a chance! Tell me about our matchmakers."

"They're trying to outconfess each other."

"You're kidding. They all admit they're guilty?"

"They're scrambling to cooperate."

"In return for a lesser sentence, I suppose?"

"Partly. Fred and Mack would like to see Benny broiled over hot coals—very, very slowly."

"For getting the ransom money himself?"

"That and getting them caught."

"Benny did that? Here, stir the soup. It will give you something to do with your hands."

"I liked what I was doing."

"Stir and tell."

"I might as well be in jail."

"Brian!"

"Okay. Benny took off for Canada, and the other two holed up with Fred's woman somewhere in southern Illinois."

"Then they came back here and tried to scare us?"

"Remind me never to tell you a joke. You want the punch line before the story. Does this stuff have to boil?"

"No, take it off and divide it. Do you like celery in your tuna salad?"

"Any way you like it."

"I like celery, but tell me about the kidnappers."

"Benny made it to his girl friend's in Canada, but she had some other guy living with her. Benny scared him off and really beat up the woman, but he forgot about her brothers, two mean lumberjack types. When the brothers saw what he'd done, they cornered him in her cabin and started working him over, but the sister had found out about the twenty-five thousand."

"Benny showed it to her?"

"I guess he wanted to be friends when he was through knocking her around."

He sat across from her and sipped the soup before continuing.

"Too hot. Anyway, the woman wanted cash, not blood. The brothers took it all, kept a share for their trouble, and gave the rest to their sister. Well, you can imagine Benny was pretty upset. He got back to the States, robbed a gas station in northern Michigan, and stole a car. Some woman he'd met when he had a restaurant job hid him in Romulus."

"Right near the airport!"

"Anyway, he felt cheated because he'd ended up with nothing, so he decided to hit us again."

"The threats, the poisoned liver, all that was Benny? What did he expect to gain?"

"Extortion money. In his simpleton way he figured that I wouldn't let him have you on the boat because I wanted you. If he could get to you, I'd pay for your safety. Only he didn't expect to find an army guarding you. It took him a long time to learn about the condo."

"But why try to poison your dogs?"

"Ninety percent spite and ten percent wishful thinking. He had some vague idea about robbing our house some night."

"Wow! When you're his favorite victim, he doesn't give up. But you said he was responsible for getting the others caught."

"Well, you know how he was caught. Trying to attack you here was pure stupidity. Three people saw the car, and that man walking the dog got his license number."

"Yes, yes, I know that. Officer Michaels was one of the policemen who picked him up after the car was spotted."

"Benny somehow arrived at the conclusion it was all his brother-in-law's fault. He was the one who offered to let him help rob your store."

"I bet he really had to twist his arm."

"Honey, there's nothing rational about Benny."

"Did he know where the others were?"

"No, but he knew friends and relatives of Mack's, and one of them knew Fred's ex-wife. She'd left him because of the woman in Illinois and was glad to give her name and town to the police."

She got up and sat on his lap, burying her face against his shoulder.

"You'll get my virus."

"It's a little late to worry about that. When will the trial begin?"

"Not for months, if there is one."

"If?"

"The court-appointed defense attornies know there's not a chance of an acquittal. Unless they're incompetent, and they're undoubtedly not, they'll plea bargain."

"Plead their clients guilty?"

She sat upright and rested her arms on his shoulders.

"In exchange for a lesser sentence, yes."

"It doesn't seem right."

"You're eager to be a witness for the prosecution?"

"Good grief, no! But isn't it our word against theirs?"

She stood and started clearing the table.

"No, a dozen people remember seeing Benny the morning of the robbery because he hung around so long. Your policeman friend saw them in the store. The service attendant remembers them because of the mess you left in the restroom, and Benny made a crude pass at the restaurant owner's wife when he went across the street for hamburgers."

"So that wraps it up for us?"

"I hope we can avoid a sensational trial. Do you want to be the star attraction in a three-ring circus?"

"I certainly don't."

She brushed aside long strands of hair, uncut since he'd left for Colombia, and kissed the back of his neck.

"Can I have my back rub now?"

"How about tonight? I was going back to the store for a while."

"I can't stay here another night, darling."

He caught her palm and kissed it.

"You're still sick! Certainly you don't have to rush to work on a Friday afternoon?"

"I knew you wouldn't like it." He smiled tentatively. "It's the only chance I'll have to go over some things with my father before he leaves for New York Sunday. Come back and stay in my house this weekend."

"Oh, why not!" she yelled in exasperation. "If I don't watch you,

you'll end up at the Mayo Clinic. I'd hate going to Minnesota in the winter just to rub your back."

He laughed, then coughed so hard she spooned more medicine between his reluctantly parted lips and left him propped up in front of the TV while she prepared for their trip.

Four hours later he was coughing in the delightfully cozy living room of the guest cottage he called home.

"I'm in love with this room," she said, curled in an overstuffed chair in front of a blazing fire.

"My mother decorated it," he said, sniffing miserably into his third tissue in five minutes. "She was inspired by a hunting lodge in the upper peninsula. She did forget the moose head, though."

"Thank heavens! I can't imagine spoiling such beautiful paneling with a dead animal head."

"Mother's sentiment exactly. She'll be here any minute, you know."

"Did she say so when you called her?"

"No, but she zeroed in on my cold when she heard my voice this morning."

"Your serious virus!"

"Just watch. She has concoctions as awful as your mother's chest rub and cough medicine."

"I brought some along."

"Lord save me from mothering women!"

"You know you brought me along to nurse you."

"Like hell I did."

Fifteen minutes later Mrs. Fort arrived with two maids carrying enough food for the winter, including a full crock pot.

"When Brian called this morning, I could tell how sick he was. I made some of my mother's vegetable pepper soup. It's wonderful for chest colds and congestion. I won't stay for dinner, but you see that he eats a big steaming bowl, Kelly."

"I certainly will," she said, repressing a smile.

"I told your father business can wait until morning, Brian. You're in no condition to sit in the library huddled over piles of papers all night."

Kelly pretended to ignore his I-told-you-so smirk, while Mrs. Fort sent her helpers back to the main house.

"Sit down, Mom."

"No, I really shouldn't."

"My infection has been neutralized by a horse-sized shot and enough antibiotics to cure an epidemic. You won't catch anything."

"I wasn't worried about that," she said stiffly.

"You'll like what I have to tell you."

"Well, just for a minute. You should boil a big kettle of water and put a towel over your head to inhale steam."

"Mom, I'm firing you."

"What?"

"I've finally found someone just as bossy and overly protective as you are. Kelly and I are getting married."

Kelly had guessed his intention, but she hadn't anticipated his mother's teary enthusiasm.

"Brian! Kelly! I'm so happy for you."

She hugged each of them, snatching one of Brian's tissues to pat her eyes.

"When?"

"Very soon," Brian said, grinning at his mother. "Next week if I have my way."

"You won't run to Las Vegas and get married in some horrible marriage factory like your brother did?" she asked in horror.

"We certainly won't," Kelly assured her. "We haven't reached a decision yet, but my mother will be crushed if she can't see me married in a church."

It occurred to her that Mrs. Fort probably didn't know about her divorce. She was glad she hadn't said "married this time in a church." Brian could do as he liked about telling her.

"I completely agree with your mother. Brian's only joking about next week, of course." She was talking to Kelly now, recognizing an ally when she saw one. "We planned my wedding for nearly a year. There's so much to do, you know. Oh, I do hope your mother will let me help."

"It seems only fair. She's had her turn three times with my sisters."

"A year is ridiculous," Brian said, storming out of his chair, "and I was serious about next week."

His coughing took some of the assertiveness out of his words.

225

"I wasn't suggesting you wait a whole year, dear, but weddings require a great deal of planning. First you must reserve your dates, and a good caterer is hard to book. There are gowns to order and guest lists to make. I can suggest a few places for your bridal registry, Kelly, once you've picked your china and crystal. Now don't let me be an interfering mother-in-law, but anything I can do to help will please me so much."

"Mother, stop!"

Brian finally managed to stifle his coughing and get through her enthusiasm.

"This wedding is not going to be the social event of the season!"

"Well, if the Durbans and the Dormans and the McVees come back from the Bahamas, we can't offer them lemonade in the church basement."

"Why the devil should they come back to Michigan in the winter?"

"Yelling makes your cough worse, dear. Of course, our best friends will want to come to your wedding. Heaven knows they've waited long enough for it!"

"Mother, you're the only one who's been waiting for my wedding!"

"Brian, I really think we should discuss the guest list when you're feeling better."

"This discussion isn't about guest lists. We're having a very small, very quiet wedding. It's all decided."

"By you," Kelly said softly.

Mrs. Fort heard her.

"Kelly, please tell your parents we want to help in every possible way. I'm so thrilled and so happy."

She brushed Kelly's cheek with dry lips, glared with motherly disapproval at her son, and left.

"I'm going to pour a triple Scotch and go to bed," he said.

"What about your mother's soup?"

"You can soak your feet in it for all I care."

She smiled indulgently and wished him a good sleep, which only annoyed him more. Surprisingly, she wasn't the least bit perturbed. Poor baby, he felt rotten, and the wedding trap was closing.

The soup was delicious, thick with vegetables, rice, and chicken, skimmed free of fat, and seasoned liberally with herbs and pepper. Kelly enjoyed it very much.

Throwing another log into the fireplace, she settled into a comfy corner of the couch to read *The Detroit News*, delivered every day whether Brian was there or not, but the hypnotic dancing of the flames captured her attention and lulled her to sleep.

"You didn't have to sleep on the couch."

Brian bent over her, brushing her cheek with the back of his fingers. He'd obviously had his triple.

"How do you feel?"

"Hungry, miserable, and sorry, not necessarily in that order."

"The soup is delicious. I left the crock pot on low."

"Still want to mother me?" His words were slurred and the Scotch fumes were unmistakable.

"Maybe, if you say please."

"Okay, I say please. And darlin'."

He slipped to his knees beside the couch and wiggled his hands under her thighs.

"What?"

"Have the wedding your way, but have it soon. And please, don't pay too much attention to my mother. Cobo Hall is out!"

"You're making me very happy."

"Happy enough for a back rub?"

She drew a steamy tub, fed him hot soup while he soaked, warmed his flannel pajamas in the oven, and gave him a long, gentle back rub underneath the covers. By the time she came back with a shot glass of her mother's cough concoction, he was snoring noisily, propped up on several pillows. She quietly crawled in beside him, her rest not at all disturbed by his congested snore.

CHAPTER THIRTEEN

Brian was still sleeping when she crept out of bed and boiled water for tea in the snug little kitchen. Everything in the small two-bedroom cottage was a delight, particularly the view from the window over the sink showing ancient snow-frosted spruce and oaks. Knowing he was supposed to meet his father at the big house at nine, she made a phone call, then poached an egg for him, toasted bread, and topped both with warm milk.

"Breakfast, sweetheart," she said cheerfully, setting the tray on his nightstand.

"What are you doing out of bed?" he grumbled.

"Fixing you a nourishing breakfast, good for your tummy."

"You're overplaying the nurse bit, Kelly. Just because I let you get away with it last night, don't press it. I don't usually drink a triple Scotch on an empty stomach." He clutched his head and his stomach at the same time. "Actually it was two triples."

"Is that why you were so mellow and sweet last night? How do you feel now?"

"Terrible. If you really want to do your good deed for the day, go to the medicine chest in the bathroom and bring me all the pill bottles you find."

"Um, as soon as you finish your milk toast. Maybe you won't need pills if you eat."

He swallowed several bites with a sour expression.

"I hate eating in bed. I keep expecting someone in a starched cap to show up with a bedpan. Only the desperately ill should have meals in the sack."

"Well, you can eat wherever you like for the rest of the day. I'm going to Wyandotte."

"Oh," he groaned, setting aside the tray. "I suppose you're off to make wedding plans. What's your price for a few quiet words in a judge's chambers?"

"We've settled that nonsense, and I'm holding you to it, Scotch or no Scotch," she said, standing over him with her arms crossed. "I'll get your stomach pills and something for your head."

"You're not really leaving me?"

"You want our wedding to be soon."

"Yes, but can't you wait until Monday to start planning it?"

"My mother works Monday through Friday. So do I, although you wouldn't know it lately. I have a lot of paperwork to get ready for my tax man. Besides, I owe it to my parents to tell them we're getting married. You told your mother."

"Much to my regret. I'll get my own pills. At least come back tonight. You can drop me at my office on your way home Monday morning and keep my car."

He started to get up, but she sat beside him blocking his legs.

"I have an idea for our honeymoon, Brian."

"I have a few too." His leer was the closest he'd come to a smile that morning.

"No, this one is serious."

"You think mine aren't?"

"Listen! People are always tired after a wedding. It's a bad time to pack bags and travel."

"Any time is a bad time for you to travel, Kelly."

"Couldn't we come here afterward? Spend our first night as husband and wife here? I just love this cottage, and it's so secluded by the woods."

"That idea tops milk toast."

He leaned over and kissed her, missing her lips and hitting her chin.

"So you see, if we do that, I don't want to stay with you until we're married."

"You stayed with me last night!"

"But nothing happened! All we did was sleep. I want a honeymoon in a place with no memories. I want to start fresh after we're married. You understand, don't you, darling?"

He sank back on the pillows and groaned.

"Are you telling me no sex till our wedding night?"

"Well, darling, think. What's so special if we get up together in the morning, get married, and go to bed again at night? There's no anticipation."

"I stored up plenty of anticipation in Colombia. I've got more than enough left."

"It's not the same thing. This would mean so much to me."

"I think I still have a fever. Don't you want to take my temperature?"

He coughed a little for emphasis.

"Please, Brian."

"If you say no, what can I do? But I want that wedding to take place in two weeks."

"That's not possible! Invitations have to be printed and mailed. Doing everything even in six weeks is practically impossible."

"Six weeks is out of the question. Three is my final offer, three weeks from now."

"But Brian . . ."

"Three weeks, take it or leave it."

"You have things to do too! Picking your best man and groomsmen and ushers."

"I'll draft my brother. He's enough."

"I have to include my three sisters, and you don't know how many friends I owe. I've been a matron of honor three times and a bridesmaid . . ."

"Kelly, I'm not participating in a wedding where all the bride's friends line up on one side and the groom's on the other, like two teams squaring off for the big game."

"I thought you were a conventional person."

"Just because I wear white shirts and black socks to work doesn't mean I want a cast of thousands in my wedding."

"That's easy for you to say. You only have one brother. My sisters have to be in it. I can't pick one and not the other two."

"Can't we just forget this whole conversation? Come back to bed with me, and we'll start fresh in a couple of hours."

"Brian!"

"Okay, I'll drag two other unfortunates into this to make the sides even. Three phone calls will take six minutes. What else do I have to do?"

"Order your suit and have it fitted, make out your personal

invitation list, help me pick china patterns and whatever, buy gifts for your attendants, go for premarital counseling . . ."

"Go for what?"

"Our minister always counsels couples before he marries them."

"Kelly, no, no, no! I don't have that kind of time."

"It might be interesting."

"Why don't we just live in sin? Come back to bed and rub my back."

"Too late. You told your mother."

"Does this mean you're not going to take a shower with me?"

"Yes! My sister Joan will be here to give me a ride in minutes. Are you going to put your pants on or hide?"

"Why do you need a ride? You know you can use my car anytime."

"We're not married yet."

She kissed the end of his nose.

"Do I have to shave my beard for this affair?" he asked petulantly, following her to the living room window a while later.

Just a sliver of river showed, and the big house was screened by the dense growth of trees, cleared only to allow a single lane drive to meander past the front of the cottage.

"Don't. I love your beard."

She ran her fingers through it, tipping her head for a proper good-morning kiss.

"You're asking for trouble, you know," he said grimly. "Two mothers with wedding fever may be more than you can handle."

"Aren't you making this sound more complicated than it is? You've never been married."

"No, but I've served time as best man and groomsman. Families get a little crazy over tying the knot. One of my friends was offered a hundred thou at the rehearsal dinner to call the wedding off and leave town alone."

"Who'd make an offer like that?"

"The bride-to-be's father."

"You made that up! Anyway, my father will adore you. He likes all his sons-in-law. Well, Todd does get on his nerves when he gives wine lectures, and . . ."

He leaned over and kissed the back of her neck, parting her hair and pushing it forward over her shoulders.

231

"And?" he murmured.

"Oh, never mind. Brian, I'm leaving in a few moments! Leave my bra alone. Will you be around this week?"

"I'm not sure, but I want you to take this."

He handed her a folded check from the pocket of his robe.

"What's this?"

"You and I are paying for our own wedding."

"My parents won't go for that. It's a put-down, don't you see? Like saying they can't handle it."

"That's not my intention at all. My mother is going to offer to pay for the reception."

"How do you know?"

"I could see the guilty look on her face as soon as she started talking wedding. If she doesn't come up with a guest list of six hundred, I'll eat that check. And she can't in good conscience ask your parents to entertain everyone she's known since grammar school."

"Oh, Brian, I don't know how to handle this."

She looked at the check and whistled.

"That much for a wedding? You're mad!"

"Have you ever poured champagne into six hundred of Mother's best friends?"

"You're just trying to discourage me. Where could we possibly have a reception that big? The Polish Legion Hall is the biggest private place in Wyandotte, and I bet it doesn't hold four hundred. We'd have to rent the hockey arena."

"I'm trying to warn you."

"I have in mind a nice, moderate wedding, family and close friends."

"Mother has a thousand close friends. You'd better plan on the Waverly Hills Country Club. We're members."

"My mother's used the Bingo Gardens twice and Fernando's restaurant for Jill's reception because her husband's cousin owns it. She won't feel comfortable at a strange country club."

"We'll have something in common then. I'm not comfortable with any of this wedding business."

Joan's gas-guzzling old station wagon crept up the drive and stopped.

"Should I hide? I didn't put my pants on."

"You won't shock my sister in pajamas and robe."

"Good. She's a beauty like you, I see."

"We're all envious of her, actually. She's the tallest. Brian, you don't have to leer."

What she didn't tell him was that Joan's brisk, no-nonsense attitude compensated for her practically perfect 36–22–32 figure. He'd find out. She entered the house with her best pretending-to-be-bored expression and introduced herself to Brian before Kelly could do the honors.

"It's a pleasure to meet you, Brian," she said, offering her hand with the polished manner that had made her the highest-ranking woman in her branch of the credit corporation.

"You're our matron of honor," Brian said, holding her hand much longer than necessary.

No one ever pulled the rug out from under Joanie, but she'd met her match in Brian. Her mouth actually fell open until she pulled herself together and started asking businesslike questions.

"Well, congratulations," she finally said, again offering her hand to Brian and flushing when he kissed her loudly on the cheek instead.

Kelly tried not to giggle.

"I'll get my bag and we'll go. Brian has a meeting with his father in eleven minutes."

It was his turn to look uncomfortable. Damon Fort had a fetish about promptness.

"Let me tell Mother and Dad before you say anything," Kelly warned her sister in the car before they fell into a companionable exchange of family news.

The two-story brick house with decorative green shutters had seemed desperately crowded when all four sisters lived there, doubling up in bedrooms never meant to serve as art studios, music rooms, rock concert halls, social centers, or menageries for stuffed animals. Now her parents seemed to bounce around in it, wallowing in the free space available for their interests—in her father's case, bookshelves—but delighted when as many of their brood as possible came back to fill it with noise and warmth.

Catching her mother before she dashed off to sing in the church choir, Kelly told her the news.

"I'm stunned. You're going to marry Brian Fort. I'm simply

stunned. I never thought . . . I mean, I thought . . . well, I didn't think he'd . . . Well, this time you will have a proper wedding, won't you? I knew something strange was happening when you called me at school. Of course, you will get married in church this time, won't you? Imagine, you're going to marry Brian Fort."

"Mother . . ."

"Something good comes out of everything, even that terrible kidnapping. I do hope you'll be happy with him, Kelly. He seems like a nice man, even if he is rich."

"Mother, stop! I have to talk to you. We do want a church wedding, but Brian insists we get married in three weeks, three weeks from yesterday."

"Oh, that's not possible, Kelly. You can't plan a church wedding in three weeks. Oh, you don't mean one of those little get-togethers with no guests and a piece of cake afterward?"

"His mother has six hundred friends."

Even her mother was speechless at that.

"At least that's what Brian told me."

"If it was summer, we could use the park. A wedding on the waterfront would be nice. We've never done that. But February! A February wedding. No one gets married in February."

"You could have a big heart-shaped cake for Valentine's Day," Joan suggested.

Coming from her, it was an amazingly fanciful idea.

"Joanie, I love it. Tiny red hearts, napkins with cupids, heart-shaped bouquets," Kelly said.

"We invited a hundred of our own to Jill's wedding," her mother wailed, not distracted by hearts and flowers. "Where can we have seven hundred people?"

Probably her father was still paying for the last wedding in the family, Kelly thought. No wonder fathers were eager to have sons. She made her decision. It hurt her pride, but she'd have to accept Brian's check. She couldn't possibly expect her parents to pay for a reception for that many people, and her own capital was tied up in her business.

"Money isn't a problem, Mother," she tried to say tactfully.

"Oh, no, I know what you're suggesting, Kelly, and the answer is no, absolutely no. We gave your three sisters lovely weddings, and we'll do the same for you. I don't care how rich the groom's family

234

is, the bride's family pays for the wedding. If it's not fancy enough, that's too bad."

"No, Brian's family won't be paying a cent. Brian gave me this check. He insists on helping because his mother has such a long guest list in mind."

The figure on the check left her mother temporarily speechless.

"No," she said, slowly recovering. "It's still out of the question. Your father won't even consider it."

Backed against a wall, Mrs. Valentine called on a higher authority. Joan was dispatched to rouse him in his study, going with ill grace because she resented being ordered around like a five-year-old.

"Kelly, you're getting married again. That's nice," he said, coming into the living room with its yellow-white woodwork and painted fireplace.

Her father seemed about to shake her hand but decided against it, giving her a kiss instead.

"And the groom's mother wants to invite six hundred people!" her mother cried hysterically.

Even her father blanched at that.

"And that's not the worst! The groom wants to pay for the wedding himself."

"Well," her father said slowly, obviously torn between teaching extra night-school classes for the next ten years to pay for it himself and facing his wife's hysteria, "that's an interesting suggestion."

"It's insulting! Jackie's wedding was beautiful, all those gorgeous spring flowers from our garden, and they still talk about Joanie getting married the day after Christmas. Even Jill's wasn't so bad, considering she insisted we go to that cousin's restaurant. Sour wine! But the ceremony was very nice. We both have good jobs. We'll do Kelly's wedding too. That's final."

The voice of authority was silent.

The church choir had to manage without their strongest soprano, and Kelly's father completely forgot the important point he was making in a letter to *U.S. News & World Report* as the family conference raged. Jackie and Jill were summoned, for what purpose Kelly wasn't sure. Her mother sent them out in the kitchen to make sandwiches when they enthusiastically endorsed the use of Brian's check.

"Lots of couples today pay for their own weddings," Jackie said, never willing to leave a room without the last word.

"We'll send you a bill for yours," her mother snapped, not one to overlook a challenge.

"Did Mrs. Fort actually say she wanted six hundred guests?" Joan asked, bored but allowed to stay in the room because she hadn't taken sides yet.

"I'm taking Brian's word."

"Call her."

"No, I'll call her," Mrs. Valentine decided. "If we're going to let her son in our family, it's high time we had some words."

Kelly appealed mutely to her father, but he'd managed to get his hands on the morning newspaper and had dropped out of the debate.

Her mother insisted on calling from the bedroom, holding the slip of paper with the Forts' private number between her thumb and forefinger like an X-rated comic she'd found in one of her student's desk.

Sure that no one could talk to a complete stranger for fifty-three minutes, Kelly finally crept up the stairs and inched open the door of her parent's bedroom, feeling about ten years old again.

"Louise, here's my daughter now. . . . Yes, I'll give her your best. . . . Such a pleasure talking to you. . . . Yes, lunch next Saturday at the Red Lion. . . . I'm so excited too. I'm sure my little grandsons will be wonderful ringbearers, but without your help, what would we do for a flower girl? I don't know a single little girl who could do it."

"A friend's granddaughter," her mother whispered to Kelly.

Kelly sat on the end of the lavender chenille bedspread and waited for the closing cordialities to end. Not for nothing had her mother been on the teachers' negotiating team for seven years. Her district's contract was one of the best in Wayne County.

"Well, we compromised," her mother said gruffly, wanting Kelly to know she hadn't backed down without major concessions.

"What are the terms?"

"The wedding is totally ours at our church, except I'll use Louise's friend's granddaughter as the flower girl. Louise hoped she could scatter rose petals in your path."

Had Kelly ever heard Mrs. Fort called Louise?

"I'll buy that. What did you have to give her?"

Kelly had been raised on a diet of collective bargaining.

"The reception."

"You're going to let his mother run the reception?"

"No, just help. She thinks it's only fair Brian pay for it, since he's causing us both so much distress trying to plan a wedding in twenty days. I'll have to use my personal business days and my emergency days. God forbid there should be any funerals for the rest of the school year."

"Distress" had been Mrs. Fort's word.

"We're each inviting a hundred and fifty of our most intimate friends to the church, and the rest will be invited to the reception only. Louise says a lot of weddings in Grosse Pointe work that way."

Her father had disappeared, and her three sisters were in the kitchen quibbling about who would drive her home. To Kelly's surprise, none of them was trying to get out of it. They compromised and all three rode along in Joan's wagon.

"Have you thought about colors?" Jackie asked. "Jill and I still have the dark green dresses we wore at Joan's Christmas wedding. Be nice to wear them a second time."

"Why not?" Kelly said, thinking quickly. "Do you still have the patterns? Joanie could wear the same style in a lighter green."

"I'll even make it, if she buys the material and watches the boys while I work on it," Jackie volunteered, willing to do almost anything for time off from mothering.

"Green doesn't flatter me at all!" Joanie moaned.

"Good," Kelly said. "For the first time I'll look better than you."

What sister could argue with that?

Tired as she was, she drafted her sisters for one more job: They all carried a load of her clothing and possessions from the condo to her apartment over the store.

"The kidnappers are in jail, so I'm not staying here under guard anymore," she explained, loving them when they pretended to believe that was the only reason for the move.

The phone rang while she was in the bathtub that evening, and she couldn't get to it in time. Twenty minutes later it rang again.

"When you didn't answer at the condo I finally started trying there," Brian said. "How could you leave me at a time like this? My

237

mother has me dressed in a top hat and tails and honeymooning in Bermuda."

"Not really?"

"I got rid of Bermuda and the top hat by agreeing to her plans for a rehearsal dinner."

"I had a day of heavy bargaining too. How do you feel?"

"Better. Scotch is the best shot for a virus, I've decided."

"Depends on which end you want to ache. I don't think a conclusion like that will put any doctors out of business."

"Sassy as you are, I miss you."

"When will I see you?"

"Not next week. I have to go to Chicago."

"Oh, Brian, all you do is go."

"Yeah, that is what I do. Next weekend I'm going to court you."

"How?"

"All the ways we've missed. Flowers, wining and dining, dancing until the wee hours. The theater, the symphony, basketball, hockey. What do you like to do?"

"Anything with you."

"That's not an answer. You're right, you know. About anticipation. We have a lot of getting acquainted to do. I don't even know if you like baseball."

"I don't follow it, but I like going to the ball park."

"Good. I like to go to a couple of Tiger games every season, and I love White Sox games."

"Why?"

"Those Chicago fans are wild."

She didn't like being reminded of his trip.

"I love you," he said in a husky voice.

"I love you too."

Saturday morning she got a dozen red roses and an apologetic phone call. Brian had to fly to Dallas.

Sunday morning the wedding fell apart.

"The invitations went out yesterday," her mother cried into the phone. "Seven friends helped me address them. I practically had to promise the printer his son wouldn't be held back in school in order to get them done on time. Three hundred invitations to the church and reception both, and another six hundred twenty-two for the reception only. I had to invite people I don't even like to give our side a good showing. And now this!"

"Mother! What?"

"They ripped out the pews! The front pews, not the back pews where it wouldn't matter so much. No, the front pews! Half of Grosse Pointe is coming, and we're supposed to borrow metal chairs that say Diefendork's Funeral Parlor."

"You're talking about the church where I'm getting married in thirteen days?"

"Do I care if they rip out Mount Carmel's?"

"Why'd they do it?"

"Slave labor! Your father's writing a letter right this minute."

"To the church council?"

"No, to the governor. Taking work away from men who need it to exploit prison labor. Tomorrow morning the men who kidnapped you may be working on those pews."

"No, they haven't been tried yet. Mother, listen, let me get this straight. *Your* minister sent all the front pews to the prison to be refinished. When will they be back?"

"Four to six weeks minimum. He didn't even tell me. I walked into the nave and there they were, gray metal chairs with the funeral parlor's name stenciled on the back. I mailed the invitations! People will come there. They'll have to sit. Those chairs were old in World War II. They should have been donated to a scrap drive then."

"We'll have to use the funeral parlor chairs."

"Never!"

"But, Mother . . ."

"Don't worry. This family is handling the wedding. We'll have nice seats."

Three days later her mother called back to announce her sacrifice: She'd agreed to stay off the teachers' negotiating team for two years if the school board let her borrow the new chairs from the high school cafeteria.

"Upholstered seats and back," her mother said, seesawing between dejection and elation. "Brand new so there shouldn't be much gum on them, but I'll check anyway."

Whatever had made Kelly think she wanted a big wedding? That night she got a dozen yellow roses telegraphed from Dallas and another apologetic phone call.

239

Saturday morning all three sisters tramped into her store loaded with heirloom-preservation boxes. She tried on their three wedding dresses and their mother's. Joan's she liked best, but the bust was too big and the waist too small. Jackie's was too tight in the shoulders, and Jill's had a big stain on the skirt that had defied the cleaner's best efforts. Their mother's had a surprisingly low neckline and had twenty-two yards of ballerina-length fabric meant to be worn over long-discarded hoops.

"How can you possibly not be able to find a dress? You're getting married in a week." Joan always zeroed in on a problem.

"I'll make you one," Jackie said. She loved making generous offers, forgetting her offsprings' demands on her time.

"Don't be so fussy," Jill added.

The three of them took her shopping and made her buy a dress that cost three and a half times more than she'd budgeted. And white shoes were as plentiful in February as peacocks in the Arctic.

Finding a dress wasn't the only holdup. Unless Brian came back soon, she wouldn't even know what size to make his wedding band. His ring and her clothing were her responsibility, she decided, pinching to avoid using his money.

The shop buzzer rang early Sunday morning. With a cautiousness learned the hard way, she peeked out the side of the shade, then couldn't open the door fast enough.

"Remember me?"

He swept her into his arms, hungrily kissing her with the door leaning against his back, open to the swift wind blowing off the street.

"The kiss is familiar," she gasped, losing her fingers in the hair at the nape of his neck.

"You mean all the anticipation hasn't improved it any?"

He knocked the door shut and kissed her again, holding her cheeks between cold hands and taking possession of her whole mouth. The cold made his aftershave seem especially fragrant, and she pressed her nose against his cheek appreciatively.

"You smell so nice, like a winter flower," she murmured.

"Let's go upstairs," he suggested hoarsely.

"I'm still waiting to be courted."

"Can't it wait? Sweetheart, you won't believe what I've been through missing you all this time."

"Won't I?"

"You don't sound sympathetic."

They went up the stairs side by side, the narrow space between the walls requiring quite a bit of squeezing.

"You've got to sit on the couch," he said, laying an unfamiliar sheepskin-lined suede jacket across a chair, looking great in a navy cashmere sweater and matching slacks.

"Well, if you say so. Are you going to start the courtship now?"

"Yes, if you'll forgive me for giving my business to another jeweler."

"What do you mean?"

"I wanted to surprise you with this."

The emerald was easily twice the size of the one she'd hidden from the kidnappers, simply but beautifully set in rich yellow gold. The flat surface of the stone with its pure deep depths reminded her of a magic pond with a mysterious light that only hinted at the wonders concealed within. Her throat tightened when he sat beside her and slipped it on, brushing her fingers with a light kiss.

"Brian, it's incredible!"

"I bought it in Colombia. I hope you don't mind an emerald instead of a diamond."

"There's nothing I'd rather have."

"I have an official wedding band too. Oh, and a little sentimental gift from the groom to the bride."

He dangled a delicate pendant from a chain, opening the clasp and reaching behind her neck to fasten it, lingering for a long kiss before he lifted it on his finger for her to see better. A familiar green stone was mounted in a setting of gold wires.

"Your mother's emerald!"

"No, it's always been yours. You could've designed a more imaginative setting yourself, but I wanted to surprise you."

Saying thank you took a long time. Sitting on his lap, exchanging kisses and hugs, tenderly petting and cooing, Kelly was sure no woman had ever loved a man more.

They wandered hand in hand on the campus, saw an old Bogart film at the student union, ate a leisurely dinner, and drank beer at a campus hangout until the town closed up for the night.

"How'm I doin', courtship-wise," he asked, holding her in his arms outside the door of her store.

241

"I've never had a nicer day."

"It doesn't have to end now. I don't have to do a thing until nine tomorrow morning."

"Anticipation," she whispered.

"I hope you can handle all mine."

"When will I see you again?"

"Not until the rehearsal. I'll have to meet you at the church."

"I forgot to ask where the dinner is."

"The top of the RenCen."

"Oh, no!"

Her stomach lurched just thinking about that elevator.

"No, I'm only getting back at you for sending me to the condo alone. It's not there. Mother lined up a little French restaurant across the river in Windsor with a private room upstairs. I haven't been there, so we'll have to trust her."

She forgot to ask if they could take the tunnel instead of the bridge. She was so happy it didn't really matter—much.

The hardest thing about weddings, Kelly decided, awakening in her old room at home on the big day, was having to depend on so many strangers. Everything, except for showing up at the church, was being done for her, and if anything went wrong she wouldn't even know about it. An army of florists, bakers, caterers, and bartenders were preparing for the most important day of her life, and she had to sit idly, trusting them to do their jobs right without any supervision from her.

No, that was the second hardest part of her day. Not being with Brian was the hardest. She woke up with a warm, burning ache, wanting to squeeze her legs together to make it go away, knowing she'd suffer until the time when they could be alone as husband and wife.

Everything was quiet in the house, her parents tiptoeing and talking in whispers as though trying not to wake an ailing child. She forgave them their zealousness; in a way this was the last morning she'd belong to them. She'd be Brian's wife in a way so complete and fulfilling, all her past life was erased.

The rehearsal had gone well, the two fathers apparently enjoying a lengthy conversation about international monetary reforms and the mothers conferring on last-minute details with the intensity of generals preparing for battle. Brian's brother and friends rode him unmercifully about losing his long-cherished single status and spirited him away early for his last fling. He pretended reluctance at being parted from her for his bachelor party, but went off glowing.

Her mother arranged for a favorite beautician to open her shop early for prewedding hair styling, having her own hair done at seven A.M. to allow plenty of time for fidgeting. Kelly declined the service, preferring to wash and blow-dry her recently styled hair herself, letting it fall in loose shoulder-length waves as she usually did. Cherishing her time alone, she soaked in the tub until the skin on her toes puckered and lingered in her room long after there was any need to be by herself. She felt shy with her own family and longed for the day to be over, nervously refusing food except for the tea and toast her mother insisted she eat.

The four sisters dressed at the church, using the nursery room, laying their gowns on the cribs and playpen, skirting around toy boxes and wooden trucks as they helped each other, then dashing to the restroom to view themselves in the only full-length mirror in the building. Joan stooped to arrange Kelly's floor-length skirt, and Jill stepped on hers, leaving a small smudge and a ripped hem on the matron of honor's dress. Jackie rushed through the church and finally appropriated a little sewing box the altar guild used for emergency repairs, stitching frantically on the damp spot that fortunately had sponged clean.

The flower girl was a delicate, wispy blonde, a five-year-old with the calm self-assurance of an octogenarian, who gravely consulted with Kelly on how many rose petals to throw in each handful. Her nephews eyed the stranger with male aloofness but showed off every time their mother turned her back. When they started bopping each other with their little white satin pillows, she confiscated their props and led them to their Grandfather Valentine, an unlikely but surprisingly effective guardian.

No one mentioned Brian. Was he there? Was he ready? To avoid long and tedious delays in getting to the reception, nearly an hour's drive away, the photographer assembled the wedding party at the front of the church before the guests began arriving. Her mother suffered, only her social efficiency persuading her to break the old taboo against the bride and groom seeing each other before the ceremony. Kelly needn't have worried. Brian stood beside her, took her hand, smiled on demand, and made conventional responses if someone spoke to him—but he wasn't there. They were two strangers going through a charade. Duly immortalized on film, they separated with weak smiles meant to be encouraging.

When her father came for her, he looked grayer, tired, and a little wistful, but his smile was beautiful.

"This is it, baby."

He was uncomfortable calling her a pet name, but he patted her hand warmly to let her know the things he'd never say in words.

In a filmy veil and the gown of a princess she moved between two walls of people, a paper doll with a painted smile, the organ processional blowing her forward. Then Brian smiled at her, a broad joyous grin, the man she loved waiting for her, stepping forward to take her from her father. Darkly handsome in gray formal wear, he offered his arm and his heart at the same time.

The ceremony washed over her like an incoming tide, inevitable but rightly so, the traditional words wholly adequate for what she was feeling. Jackie and her husband had labored for weeks writing their own vows, but to Kelly no words could be more meaningful than "love, honor, and cherish."

"I now pronounce you husband and wife."

Falling into his arms, she responded to his kiss with all the bubbling intensity of her nature, a little stunned when he stopped and led her to their damp-eyed parents for quick hugs, then down the white-carpeted aisle.

Brad drove them to the country club, acting as their chauffeur in the big Lincoln, the two brothers chatting casually as if the whole world hadn't changed. Brian kept her hand between both of his, exploring it with his fingertips, caressing her wrist and palm, straightening the pair of rings.

She liked Brad. He was witty, lighthearted, and impractical, dreaming of athletic glory for his team while his own paunch comfortably overlapped his belt. His relaxed air made Brian seem more intense; it was hard to believe Brad was the older.

The country club was a huge brick Tudor-style mansion with the snow-sprinkled acres of the golf course behind. She felt like Cinderella again, alighting from her carriage with her prince, but destined to rush away disenchanted at the witching hour.

"If you don't stop looking so scared, I'm going to tickle you,"

Brian threatened under his breath, helping her manage the flowing skirt of her bead-bedecked ivory lace gown.

"I most certainly am not scared!"

"You should be! Hoards of people are going to ogle you for hours. Every male in the bunch willing to give his eyeteeth to be me tonight."

"The groomsmen are supposed to be the ones who make suggestive remarks."

"They had their turn last night."

He stopped just out of hearing of the doorman waiting to open a heavy iron-studded door for them.

"Did they keep you up all night?" she asked with concern.

"I slept a couple of hours. Don't worry, my anticipation won't be dulled by my revels."

"Does that mean you won't get drunk and fall asleep on me?"

She was actually thinking of Jill's disgruntled wedding-night report. Her sisters would wait in vain for her to kiss and tell.

"If I do, feel free to revive me with ice water."

"Brian!"

How could so many people be there ahead of them? Someone whisked their coats off their backs, and both mothers descended, leading them to huge windows on the far side of a massive room. On one end artificial logs were glowing in a castle-size fireplace, while the other was lined with white-covered tables laden with food. The cake sat in state on a separate table, giant heart-shaped layers with pink frosting, rosebuds, and hearts.

". . . not a formal reception line," her new mother-in-law was saying. "Just the parents and the bride and groom."

What did one call a mother-in-law? "Mother" sounded all wrong, but she'd never have enough nerve to call this elegant woman Louise. She turned to Brian for a clue, but he was talking to her mother, obviously struggling with the same problem, avoiding the use of a name.

She toyed with the possibility of Mother Fort, giving up when people started streaming past, introducing themselves, congratulating one or the other, wishing them happiness, hugging, and kissing. Brian seemed to get far more hugging and kissing than the situation warranted. He was going to reek of overly potent perfume by the time she got him alone.

Waiters circulated with long-stemmed goblets of champagne, Brian accepting one for both of them and turning from the well-wishers for a moment to silently toast her with his eyes.

She detested Brian's cousin Nell at first sight, an auburn beauty with large teeth and cold eyes, but adored his aunt Freddie and uncle Willard, a delightfully warm couple who teased Brian about his beard and welcomed Kelly into the family with bear hugs.

Brian accepted more champagne for them, but it wasn't making her sparkle. She was mortified when she forgot the name of an old friend from high school.

"I looked at her, and my mind went blank," she whispered to Brian, her cheeks flushing scarlet.

"It can happen to anyone," he assured her, forced to turn back to another guest.

The flow of people did peter out eventually. If that was informal, she'd hate to try a formal line. Someone shanghaied Brian, and she gravitated toward a familiar green gown, embracing Jill like a long lost friend.

"Can you believe this?" her sister whispered. "There's enough mink in the cloakroom to carpet the Silverdome."

"I'm exhausted."

"I give up on those kids!" Jackie said, joining them. "Bobby snitched a half-full glass of champagne someone set down, and Billy's run off with the flower girl's basket on his head. If my husband can't help watch them, they're on their own."

Joanie joined them, complaining her feet were killing her, and they filled their plates at the buffet, finding chairs in a corner to eat in peace. Kelly felt like an overstuffed dove among three parrots, and she couldn't even identify some of the stuff on her plate. Whatever had made her think weddings were romantic, and where was Brian?

Her mother rushed over, scolding them for not circulating, and hurried on to visit with some teachers from her building.

"She's on cloud nine," Jackie said.

When the band started playing, people gradually backed away until a circular area in front of the musicians was clear, and a cry went up for the bride and groom to dance.

A thousand eyes would be watching, and they'd never danced a step together! Panicking, she wondered where the restrooms were, but Brian found her too quickly, laughingly whisking her out in front of everyone and twirling her around with an excess of enthusiasm, moving much faster than the music.

"You're high!" she accused him when he hugged her closer, forgetting to move his feet.

"On anticipation, not champagne," he teased, dancing again but giving her up when his brother cut in.

She danced continually with dozens of partners until her mother-in-law rescued her, looking tired but altogether pleased.

"We have more gifts here," she said, frowning. "Do you have any idea where you'd like them sent, dear? Harry will deliver them to the cottage or Ann Arbor or wherever you like."

Kelly almost groaned, staggered as she was by the outpouring of gifts that had kept her sisters busy helping her unwrap all week. Just writing thank-you notes would take a year!

"I'm not sure. I'd better ask Brian," she said.

"Where will you be living, in the cottage?"

"No, in Ann Arbor, I'm sure. Brian has the key."

She hurried away, but not to find her new groom. They hadn't talked about where they'd live, but, of course, they wouldn't stay so close to his parents. She couldn't commute to work from Grosse Pointe every day.

Why did such a simple question give her so many misgivings?

"This is probably your last chance," Brian said, sneaking up behind her and wrapping his arms around her waist, "to sneak away with me without having to carry me."

"You weren't going to get drunk!"

"I just kept finding champagne glasses in my hand."

"Do we dare go?"

"We're expected to leave. Good Lord, woman, this is our wedding night. The party will go on without us."

"I want to say good-bye to my parents."

"Two minutes. I'll get your coat."

His mother was so thrilled with the reception, it wasn't necessary to say more than thanks and good-bye. Her father hugged her, an unusual display of affection, and said he'd met an interesting man from the State Department. It was his grave way of showing approval, she knew, as she soundly kissed his cheek and told him to go home if he was tired. He didn't seem very peppy.

Brian was waiting, and so was the car, driven by one of his father's men.

"I'm much too drunk to drive," her groom admitted, hugging her against him.

Brian fell asleep on her shoulder, and the driver didn't try to make conversation.

The room was light enough for her to see her dress spread over a chair in the corner, and the dark outlines of Brian's shoes, jacket, and trousers were visible on the floor. He groaned and turned toward her, his face a pale blur above the crinkled but still starchy front of his dress shirt. When he saw her eyes surveying him, he groaned again.

"I'll bet this hangover is the least of my problems."

"No, I understand. Champagne sneaks up on you."

"The trouble is," he recalled with difficulty, "I was drunk when I agreed to that bash."

"That's not why you agreed?"

"No? I had two triple Scotches under my belt when I gave in. I haven't been hung over so much since I was an undergraduate."

She pressed her face into the pillow, but couldn't suppress a sniffle.

"Darling."

He brushed away her hair and kissed the nape of her neck with dry lips.

"Please look at me. I'm not pretty, I know, but let me see your face."

She agreed unwillingly, keeping her eyes downcast.

"You were right about the wedding," he whispered, caressing her cheek with unsteady fingers. "In spite of my bachelor party and that wretched reception and making an ass of myself, it was the most beautiful day of my life when I saw you come down the aisle like an angel and Venus all wrapped into one."

"You mean that?"

"Yes, and I'll prove it after I finish being sick."

"Brian!"

He was staggering toward the bathroom, slamming the door and locking it with a resolute click.

She couldn't bear to lie there alone, so she grabbed the wrap of her filmy white peignoir and gown set and ran barefoot to the cottage kitchen, fumbling around until she managed to start coffee in the automatic coffeemaker.

The shower ran full blast for an awfully long time, so she set the table with orange juice, coffee, tea, and toast. Going back to the bedroom to find slippers for her cold feet, she nearly bumped into Brian coming out of the bathroom wrapped in his terrycloth robe.

"Darling, I'm sorry."

"It's okay. We'll be married a long time."

"Forever won't be long enough. If our kids ever ask about our wedding, will you lie for me?"

"That's a lot of ifs. Coffee's ready."

His face was pale, making his beard seem more vividly black, and the shadows under his eyes gave him a vulnerable look. She longed to cradle his head against her and finger the unruly ringlets left by his dousing in the shower, but she wasn't quite ready to forgive him that fully.

After downing three glasses of orange juice and drinking his coffee steaming hot, he smiled at her sheepishly.

"Any chance of an old married couple going back to bed?"

"I think I'll clear the table. My husband is a bear when it comes to neatness."

"Your husband is a bear, period. Forget the table."

He came up behind her, lightly touching her shoulders through the transparent fabric.

"Your gown is lovely."

"I'm glad you like it."

She rinsed the orange juice glasses.

"Pretty soon you're going to think this whole thing is funny," he said close to her ear. "You'll have something to hold over my head when we're old and gray, the way I botched our wedding night. Did you undress me, by the way?"

"I helped. Am I supposed to stay mad that long?"

She couldn't help grinning.

"No, please don't."

He reached around and untied the sash, slipping the outer layer away from her body and kissing her shoulder.

"I'm almost crazy with anticipation, and that's all your fault," he murmured in her hair.

"Oh, your mother wanted to know where our gifts should go. I told her the condo."

"We have to store them somewhere," he said, capturing her between his arms and cupping her breasts with tentative little squeezes.

"Won't we be living there?"

"Not for long."

He slid the straps from her shoulders, slowly working her gown down over her breasts and hips until it floated to the floor in a cloud of filmy whiteness hugging her ankles.

"Where will we live?" she asked, standing completely passive as he explored the curve of her spine with gentle fingers.

"If your cooperation is any indication, I'll be spending the rest of my life in this kitchen. Haven't you punished me enough?"

"Not nearly enough."

She turned and met his lips, nibbling and teasing until he scooped her into his arms and stalked into the bedroom, dropping her face-down on the bed and planting a no-nonsense swat on her bottom.

"You said you'd never get physical!"

"I said I wouldn't get drunk too. How could you marry such a liar?"

"Is that what you are?"

He threw his robe across the room, missing a chair, giving her a chance to roll away.

"Not intentionally, but building all this anticipation was your idea."

"Was it a bad idea?"

"I'll show you how bad!"

They were trembling with eagerness, starved for each other and so hypersensitive the slightest touch was intoxicating. With a foot of space between them, he lightly fondled her breasts, feeling their weight in his hands and teasing her nipples into hard knobs with his thumbs. Light-headed, basking in his tenderness, she trailed her fingers over his torso, loving the silky hairiness of his chest and the little circles of smoothness around his nipples, letting one hand slide over his flat stomach to tease the edge of the bristly growth on his groin.

Moving closer, he moaned in ecstasy, caressing her with eager hands, raining kisses on her face, her breasts, her feverish torso. She could feel her control slipping away, tormented when his hand rested on her mound of damply curling tendrils, wanting to be under his skin, to merge with him. The pleasure of his touch was excruciating as her heart raced and her flesh burned.

She cried out in joy when he bent over her, gently pulling on her nipple with his mouth while she fought with her legs to bring him closer. The tension made her ears ring, and a red-hot iron band tightened inside her.

"I love you," he crooned, no other words adequate for what he was feeling, brushing damp hair away from her forehead and pressing a gentle kiss on her brow.

"You're incredible," she whispered, meaning it with her whole heart, reaching for him with tears of happiness in her eyes.

Guiding her legs to his shoulders, he tied a lover's knot that made her dizzy with desire, their joining the deepest and most satisfying of her life. She closed her eyes to savor the intensity of her sensations, then opened them to watch the man she loved, his face beautiful as passion softened it, his body lean and powerful. He carried her with him to unexplored plateaus, feeling the convulsion that suddenly rocked her being and joining her in a climax so sweet they prolonged it for long moments, clinging together in mindless rapture.

She was lying on the edge of a sea, the waves washing the beach and exploding over her tender, secret parts. Her throat ached with sheer joy, and her loved one's head was weightless on her breast, his tongue a balm on her swollen nipples.

"Come back to my world," he whispered.

"You are my world."

Stretching and wiggling her toes, she lost him but only for an instant, finding him facedown beside her. Kneading his back and shoulders, she delighted in the firm sheath of muscle, admiring his form with words and touches, massaging the length of his spine and giving his bottom and thighs quick little squeezes until he groaned with pleasure.

Without thinking about it, she sighed with joy, melting into his arms again when he reached for her. She could feel the pulse beating in his neck, putting her fingers there while he contentedly stroked her back. Wherever they lived, her home was in his arms.

CHAPTER FOURTEEN

"I feel bad about one thing," Kelly said, lazily stretched out with her head on Brian's lap, watching the flames in the fireplace flicker in the otherwise dark room.

"Um, what's that?"

"Cheryl didn't come to the reception, and we've become good friends. You didn't see her at the church, did you?"

"No, and I spent a lot of time peeking out at the crowd. A hundred hours at least."

He pushed her hair back and rubbed her temples.

"Did you really do that, watch people coming in?"

"Sure, I was gauging my chances for an escape, but I didn't see Cheryl. Maybe she had something else to do."

"Not work. I closed the store for the day and told her to bring Duane, her roommate, or whoever she liked. She was planning to come. I'm sure of it. She even asked directions to the church."

"Well, don't worry. She probably had a good reason. How would you feel about continuing this honeymoon in Toronto?"

"I like it right here."

She snuggled closer and slid her hands between his thighs.

"Um, one of your few soft spots," she murmured.

"You're going to get in trouble!" he warned, capturing her fingers in his. "You'd need a good fur coat in Toronto. It's cold in Canada."

"Are you trying to bribe me?"

"Do I need to?"

"Well, I don't want to wear dead animal skins, and I don't want to go to Toronto on a business trip during our honeymoon."

"What happened to love, honor, and obey?"

"The word obey was never mentioned."

"I didn't pay the preacher enough," he grumbled.

"Darling, you don't have to go right away, do you?"

"I really should, and it's a great city. I'll have a lot more free time than in San Francisco."

She sat up abruptly and pulled her hand away.

"I was sure this deal included a real honeymoon, just you and me."

"Toronto is . . ."

"Too darn cold in the winter! I like it here where it's warm. Brian, it's our honeymoon!"

"Well, I can't do what we've been doing all day every day!"

"You're doing just fine so far."

"But I'm not Superman."

"We could play gin rummy."

"Okay, but for high stakes. If you win, I stay here all week. If you lose, we go to Toronto."

"No deal! You're probably a card shark."

"Afraid to take a chance?"

"This is too important to settle that way. And you make me nervous about the condo too."

"Why?"

"Well, are we going to live there or not?"

He sighed deeply.

"It's not the most convenient location for me, darling."

"It's not that far from Metro Airport."

"But it's farther than that from my office, and I usually confer with my father right here."

"Well, I can't commute to work from here."

"Sweetheart, you don't need to work. The tax bracket I'm in, I can't afford a working wife."

"You don't expect me to do nothing all day? I'd go crazy!"

"I'll keep you busy."

"Keeping track of your scattered wardrobe? Be serious."

"Would you consider a reasonable proposal, and just listen without getting mad?"

"I don't get mad that easily, but it isn't reasonable for you to expect me to spend my life sitting around waiting for you."

"Just hear what I have to say. Why not move your shop to one of the Grosse Pointes? I'll buy a building if nothing's available for rent. We can stay here awhile or get our own place in this area, whichever you prefer."

"Rent would be higher than in Ann Arbor, and it's bad enough there. You don't seriously think my kind of business can succeed in Grosse Pointe? This area is diamonds and rubies; I'm silver and turquoise."

"You'd keep busy, and I can always use a tax loss if the business doesn't show a profit."

She stood up angrily and moved away.

"You make my business sound like a hobby!"

"I *am* your husband. I do intend to support you. It'll be pretty awkward if every time we go to a restaurant, you demand separate checks."

"Oh, be cute!"

"I'm not going to Toronto without you."

"Maybe you can dress like Santa Claus and carry me abroad in your sack."

"Sometimes, Kelly . . ."

She slammed the bathroom door too loudly to hear the rest of his words. It was the only room in the house with a lock, but not an especially good place to sulk. When he knocked on the door, she turned on the water full blast to drown him out.

It was a lovely big tub, sunk into the floor with a spout shaped like a dolphin. Rather than waste the water, she closed the drain and poured a ridiculous amount of bath oil into the rush of water. They'd never really dressed that day; she was wearing her frilly gown with a warm fleece robe. She stripped and stuffed her hair into a shower cap, then yanked it off and put on her gown and robe again. She was clean, and she didn't feel like a long, restful soak! They had a problem that wasn't going to go away by itself, and it was time they fought it out, even if it meant all-night negotiating.

Watching the water recede, she picked up a brush, intending to scrub away the film of bath oil clinging to the green porcelain sides, then changed her mind. She had more important things on her mind than tidy tubs.

The house was empty, and Brian's suede jacket was missing from the coat closet. From a distance she heard the muted howl of the dogs, guessing that he'd attracted their attention by walking on the estate. It served him right if they took a bite out of his seat. How could he walk out when they needed to talk? He knew she couldn't stay in the bathroom indefinitely.

After sitting curled in a chair for the longest hour of her life, she crawled into bed, gazing miserably around the warm little room done in shades of caramel and beige. Close to tears, she snapped off the bedside light and buried her face in the pillow. When, much, much later, Brian eased open the front door and quietly made his way to the bedroom, she lay absolutely still, feigning sleep but wanting him to wake her.

She felt the mattress jiggle when he crawled under the covers, but the embrace she expected never came. His even breathing tormented her for hours before she finally managed to sleep.

An odd scratchy noise finally roused her, and she realized Brian was scrubbing the tub. Embarrassed by her pettiness in leaving it a mess, she burrowed under the covers, hoping again that he'd try to wake her. Water ran in the shower and then the wash basin, and she thought he'd never come out.

"Good morning," she said when he went to his bureau for socks and underwear instead of coming to her.

"Is it?"

He turned to face her, and she wanted to cry.

"You shaved your beautiful beard!"

"It's no asset to look like a French Canadian in Toronto," he said tensely. "Our plane leaves at five-fifteen this afternoon."

She sighed deeply, still mourning the loss of his lovely beard.

"Can't we talk about this?"

"As much as you like," he said coolly, discarding his robe and putting on his shorts, "but we are going."

"You're making all the decisions for both of us? That's what marriage means to you, a license to run my life?"

"I can give in on the small things, Kelly, even when they're as big as our wedding, but I didn't get married to sleep by myself."

"Listen to you! You make it sound like you married me just to get me to bed."

"I didn't have to do that, did I?"

There was the ghost of a smile on his face, but she was hurt, watching with building fury as he zipped his gray wool slacks.

"Well, Mother scores one this morning," she said with undisguised hostility. "She warned me men don't respect women of easy virtue!"

"You're not easy!" he said, bursting into laughter. "You're more trouble than any twenty women should be."

"Then I don't know why you bother."

She slid out of bed with all the dignity she could muster and reached for her robe, but he grabbed it first.

"Allow me," he said, holding it for her. "I have to run over and see my father for a few minutes."

"He expects you to check in on your honeymoon?"

"No, but I want to tell him I've decided to go to Toronto today. We have a few things to discuss."

"Don't let me delay you."

"When you're uptight like this, I'm not even tempted."

She slammed the pillow against the side of his head, catching him off guard, but his reactions were never slow. He caught her in his arms with the pillow locked harmlessly between them, punishing her with a kiss that ground the soft inner flesh of her mouth against her teeth.

"Stop that!" she demanded, fighting free.

"If I do, it will be because I decide to."

They'd bantered and bickered so much in the past it took her a moment to realize he was every bit as angry as she was. He yanked the pillow aside, holding her so tightly she could barely catch her breath. His next kiss was just as punishing, while he clutched her buttocks in iron fingers. When she fell backward to the bed, he was on top of her, forcing her robe into a cumbersome lump under her back. Kicking and struggling, she found a release from her anger, pounding him with her fists until he grabbed her wrists in an unbreakable grasp, subduing her with his full weight.

"Why do we do this?" he asked, his voice hoarse with misery, rolling away to lie beside her.

"We love each other too much."

"If you love me, why make things so hard?" He reached for her hand, bringing it to his freshly shaved cheek.

"Brian, listen to yourself! You're the one who wants everything your own way. I only want some say in my life and your love."

"In that order?"

"That's a terrible thing to ask!"

256

She pulled her hand away, desperately wanting his love but drained by his demands. "I thought we'd have a real honeymoon," she said, oblivious of the tears streaming from her eyes. "We had more time alone on the island than we have now."

"Don't you think I want to be with you?" He sat upright on the edge of the bed. "I just don't understand why you're so obsessed with places. You like to hole up like a little mouse. You haven't seen anything of the world yet."

"Your world, and I won't see much of that sitting alone in a Toronto hotel room."

She heard the bitterness in her voice and hated it.

"Talk isn't getting us anyplace. My father is expecting me."

The phone rang but neither moved to answer it. Brian gave in first and picked it up.

"No, it's perfectly all right. She's right here."

His voice was so pleasant, she wanted to tape it for future playback.

"Your mother," he said, handing it to her.

"Mother, hi," she said, trying to sound normal. "Is something wrong?"

Something was.

Her mother seemed uncomfortable interrupting the newlyweds, talking rapidly and giving her message in the fewest possible words.

"Cheryl called my mother because she needed to get a message to me," she told Brian after the brief call.

His cold expression didn't encourage her, but she told him the rest.

"Mother thought she'd been crying. She wouldn't say much, just that she couldn't come to work anymore. She sounded terribly unhappy, Mother said. I'm going to phone the store and see if she changed her mind."

He looked displeased, but didn't say anything, taking a red knit shirt from the closet and dressing to leave. No one answered the phone in her jewelry store, something she hadn't expected.

"I can't believe she'd just not show up. Something's seriously wrong."

"Maybe she eloped or broke up or took a better job," he said impatiently.

"Brian, I've got to know what happened to her. My store is

257

closed, and it's after ten o'clock. I just can't believe she'd let me down without an awfully important reason."

"It's not the end of the world," he said dryly. "If she was hurt or sick, she would've told your mother."

"There are different kinds of hurt," she said, her anger welling up again, bringing a bitter taste of disappointment.

"I know what's coming. You can't go to Toronto because you have to rush to Ann Arbor and check on your store and your help and whatever. You were praying for an excuse not to go, and here it is."

"It's not an excuse! My business is as important to me as yours is to you."

"So you've told me. I'm just trying to decide where I fit in."

"That is so unfair!"

"I'm through arguing, Kelly. I lost my temper, and I'm sorry for that. But I won't apologize for wanting my wife with me full time. That means Toronto or Hong Kong or Bogotá, if that's where I happen to be."

"You didn't talk like that before we were married."

She twisted her rings, nervously wringing her hands together.

"You knew how I live! Did you expect me to become a mushroom farmer so you can play store every day?"

"Play! That's your whole attitude right there. You don't take anything I do seriously. Our wedding, even our honeymoon, was just a little amusement between your all-important trips. That's all I am—entertainment when you happen to have the time."

"You're not amusing or entertaining right now. I'm going to see my father."

"Tell him for me his son runs a lousy honeymoon!"

He stayed away most of the morning, returning to find suitcases packed for both of them and waiting by the front door.

"I'll get changed," he said, waiting for her to confirm what he hoped.

"Brian, is there a plane to Toronto every day?"

"Yes, but I've made up my mind to go today."

"Can I take a plane tomorrow and join you? I could check on the store, call any customers who're waiting for orders, and tell the police it will be closed this week. I have another girl working part time. I at least have to let her know not to come in."

"Can you solve all your problems with the store and meet me tomorrow?"

"Yes."

"You're willing to fly to Toronto alone? It's a direct flight."

She was terrified but determined.

"Yes."

"It's a start, Kelly. Not the way I want it but better than nothing."

They were overly polite to each other, eating lunch, straightening the cottage, firming up their arrangements with attention to precise details, deciding she'd drop him at the airport, drive his car to Ann Arbor, then leave it in a long-term parking lot when she flew to Toronto the next day. He called the airport and changed her reservation, writing the time and flight number in neat block letters along with the name of his motel in Toronto.

"Allow at least forty-five minutes to check in at the airport," he warned.

"Yes, I will."

She could sense his skepticism, stung because he didn't really trust her to manage a flight by herself. Her cheerfulness was forced, but she became more and more determined to show him she could get there on her own.

"I'll meet your plane," he said.

"Thank you. I appreciate that."

They sounded like strangers arranging a lunch date neither intended to keep.

"One pill is enough, Kelly, unless there's a lot of air turbulence. Don't take more than two for any reason."

"Brian, I am an adult!"

"You were a zombie coming home from San Francisco."

He arrived at the terminal entrance early, even by his standards. At his insistence, she wasn't going inside to wait with him.

"There's no need for you to waste time here," he said. "You can still get to Ann Arbor before dark."

Did he expect a new set of kidnappers to be stalking her if she wasn't inside by dusk?

"Well, I'll see you tomorrow," she said, going around to the driver's side after he unloaded his cases.

His kiss wouldn't have counted as hot stuff if they'd been married

259

forty years. She wrinkled her face at his retreating back and pulled out into the road that circled to the airport exit.

To avoid having to scrounge for dinner, she stopped at a drive-in on the outskirts of town. The food was tasteless, and she wasn't hungry anyway. All the stop did was waste enough time to insure the end of the still-short winter day before she got to her street.

Her storefront looked rundown and forlorn in the early dusk. Sleeping above the store was better than going to the lonely condo, so she made her way to the apartment by the glow of the night-lights, faithfully burning since Friday although the one in her work-shop seemed pretty dim. She made a mental note to change it in the morning and promptly forgot it.

The first thing she did was phone, using the number penciled inside her directory. Cheryl's roommate tried to be helpful but couldn't tell her much.

"She was really upset, so it has to be that Duane. I guess maybe she finally found out he gets all he can wherever he can. I tried to warn her, but I just didn't have the heart to hurt her. Not that she would've believed anything bad about him. I go with a second-string center who went to high school with Duane, and he told me she was gonna get burned."

Kelly piled this bad news on top of her uneasiness about her marriage and felt like a mountain of misery was pressing down on her.

"Where is she, do you know?"

"She said something about not being any worse off in Mississippi, but I don't know if she went there. She does have a sister and brother-in-law in some small town. I forget the name."

"If you hear from her tonight or tomorrow, would you ask her to call me? I'm at my store."

The roommate had to know that Kelly was supposed to be honey-mooning. She hung up quickly, realizing how embarrassing it would be to open her store in the morning and answer dozens of questions about why she was back so soon.

She checked her address book, but Cheryl had never had a reason to give Kelly her parents' phone number. Finding her in Detroit would be practically impossible.

What was she going to do about the store? She owed Jane some indication of whether to come to work, but what could she say? She'd promised to meet Brian in Toronto, and Cheryl was the only other person who could run the store.

So many things needed doing. Another month's bills had piled up, and she found three orders on the book for work to be completed in the next four weeks. At the same time her heart ached for Cheryl. How old was she? Just barely twenty, her employment card showed. She'd find someone else, of course, but that wouldn't help her aching sense of loss or the pain of being betrayed. Kelly wished she could do something to comfort her, but some problems had to be faced alone, problems like her own.

She cried herself to sleep, feeling like a big baby but missing Brian desperately.

She was half awake when the phone rang, hating to get up because the flight to Toronto loomed ahead with dreaded sureness.

"Hello," she mumbled, trying to suppress a wild hope that it was Brian telling her not to come, promising instead to return himself.

"Kelly, I've been calling everywhere for you!"

Joan's voice had a frantic edge so unlike her usual calm tone it made Kelly sit upright with a sense of urgency. Her sister didn't even ask why she was there in her store apartment.

"It's Dad," she said. "He was carrying out the garbage cans this morning before school and just collapsed."

"Is he okay?"

"Not really. An ambulance rushed him to the hospital, and we're all here now waiting to hear. It's his heart, the doctor thinks, but so far we don't know how bad it is."

"Wyandotte Hospital?"

"Yes, he's in the cardiac unit."

"I'll be there as soon as I can!"

"Mother said to drive carefully. There's nothing you can do here, so don't take chances on the highway."

She barely heard the relayed warning.

Her suitcase was still packed for Toronto, so she threw it in the Mercedes after blindly pulling on some jeans and a knit top. Later she would hardly remember the drive, following a familiar route automatically as she imagined all kinds of terrible things. Joan knew more than she was telling; she always did. Was their father's life in grave danger? Her mother wouldn't summon her for anything less than a critical emergency.

Visiting hours had begun when she reached the massive community facility on riverside property south of the chemical plant and north of a towering high-rise. All the parking areas were crowded, and the spot she finally found seemed miles from the closest public entrance. She'd been a candy striper in high school, so she half-walked and half-ran, automatically locating the elevators, trying to compose her features and steel herself for the worst.

Her father had looked so tired at the wedding! She should have asked him how he felt, urged him to see a doctor if he wasn't well.

Her sisters and mother formed a tense little knot in a lounge near the cardiac unit, a conspicuously cheerful room with orange and blue chairs that no one enjoyed. They were sipping coffee, their eyes dull, talking about inconsequential things because speaking what was on their minds would reduce them all to impotent tears.

"Your honeymoon," her mother moaned apologetically, as though it were important now.

"Don't worry, Mother. Plenty of time for that later. Have you heard anything?"

"Doctors! They slip you little hints here and there."

"It takes a while to find out how much damage there was," Jackie said, awkwardly patting her mother's shoulder.

"How are the boys?" Kelly asked, playing their game, pretending ordinary things mattered.

"Oh, they've recovered from the champagne snitching and flower-girl chasing. They were cute in their little short pants and jackets, weren't they?"

"Darling."

The doctor finally talked to the five of them, using long words and stuffing his hands in the pockets of his cotton coat. Most of her mother's questions only confused Kelly, but, of course, she'd never shared her mother's zeal for hearing about other people's maladies.

"Does that mean he'll live?" she asked tensely, speaking for the first time, unable to wade through the maze of words.

"The prognosis is good," the grave, heavy-jowled physician said.

"That means yes?"

"It means all the signs are very favorable at this time."

"Can we see him?"

"Your mother can look in for just a minute, but he needs rest more than anything right now."

Waiting. It was the cruelest form of torture. Kelly had to see for herself that her father was still the unobtrusively loving man who'd always been a quiet but essential part of her life. She refused to leave the floor before she saw him, wanting to say so many things to him even though she knew they'd all go unspoken.

Her plane left for Toronto in two hours. There was still time to get in the car, drive to the airport, and catch the flight. Part of her yearned to be with Brian, a need so searing it made her tremble, but her mother's frightened face was a barrier she couldn't pass.

Kelly had seen her mother in an explosive range of moods from overjoyed to furious, enthralled to mournful, but never scared. Standing over her mother and patting her shoulder, Kelly was amazed at how protective she felt toward a woman who had always been an absolutely staunch buffer against the world.

"It was a lovely wedding, wasn't it? Your father looked so handsome coming down the aisle."

Kelly knew it wasn't memories of her wedding that clouded her mother's eyes.

"I'll be right back. I have to call Brian."

She found the name of the motel inside her purse, exhausting her coin supply to reach the desk clerk. Mr. Fort didn't answer his phone, she was told. The message she left for him said there'd been an emergency, and she'd have to call him that evening. She hung up, trying not to imagine how angry he'd be when he met her plane and found she wasn't on it.

Jackie went home to take care of her children, but the other three stayed with their mother, insisting she come to the hospital snack shop for an evening meal but setting a poor example by picking at their own food, hardly able to swallow.

Kelly called the motel again and again, unable to leave a number where Brian could reach her. She needed him so much.

Late in the evening she was allowed a few precious moments with her father, trying not to see the TV screen that reduced his life functions to little bleeps.

"What the devil are you doing here?" he asked, his rebuke tempered with a weak smile.

"Brian's in Toronto. I didn't have anything else to do," she said with forced lightness.

"Darn fool."

It was her father's strongest verbal judgment, and she knew it wasn't directed at her.

The doctor made a late-evening check and sent them home, cheerfully assuring them that her father was out of immediate danger and mostly needed rest to make a full recovery. Her mother cried now that the crisis was over, and Kelly went back to the house to spend the night there with her. Sleeping pills from the doctor put Mrs. Valentine to sleep, but Kelly had to reach Brian, the need becoming more urgent with every passing hour.

It was after two when he finally answered the phone in his room.

"You weren't on the plane."

His voice was flat, matter-of-fact, cold.

"Did you get my messages?"

"Yes, a whole stack of them."

"I called and called."

"But you didn't come."

It was the harshest accusation she'd ever received.

"I couldn't."

"I wish I'd known that before I left a conference early and wasted two hours at the airport."

"Don't you care why I didn't come?"

"No, Kelly, I don't. I should've expected it."

She was crying too hard to talk, aching to justify herself but so hurt by his attitude, she didn't think he deserved to hear about her father. She let the receiver drop on his silence.

For two days she drove her mother to the hospital every morning and waited there for the short visits they were allowed. Her mother's attention gradually focused on Kelly and Brian, her questions keen but not insistent, showing a new respect for her daughter's privacy.

Her father finally sent them both home.

"Take your mother home and send her back to work," he said with gentle resoluteness. "A man can't have a heart attack in peace around that woman. And you get back to your husband."

Because he so rarely gave orders, Kelly never considered disobeying him. Anyway, his face had lost its ghostly pallor, and he seemed more interested in catching up on his political journals than entertaining his hovering family.

The next morning she drove to her store, the only place she could remotely consider home. A bride of less than a week, she had a missing husband, a locked-up business, and an ache so terrible she was one numb mass of misery.

Both the night-lights were burned out.

CHAPTER FIFTEEN

After changing the bulbs and turning up the heat, Kelly perched on a high stool beside her workbench for a long while, picking up her tools, fingering points and edges, then laying them aside. Part of her longed for the solace of working with her hands, complete absorption in her work, but the futility of doing anything kept her idle. Her eyes were swimming, but crying wasn't enough to release the knot of pain in her heart and spirit. She'd turned to Brian for comfort in a time of need only to find him remote and angry, condemning her without hearing her explanation. How could she love him so much and be so wrong about his capacity for compassion and understanding?

The phone sounded shrill in the unnatural stillness of her workroom, and she eyed it with loathing, dreading a conversation with an irate customer or an insistent salesman. Only concern for her father's health made her answer it.

"Kelly, it's Cheryl. Can you ever forgive me?"

"Dear, there's nothing to forgive. I'm sure you had a good reason for not coming in."

She was starting to sound like her mother, using casual endearments, jumping to conclusions to soothe feelings.

"I had a lousy reason. I broke off with Duane, and I had to be by myself for a while. I'm really sorry about the store and missing your wedding."

"Don't worry. Are you all right?"

"Now I am. I was crazy to quit school for that fool. I hope to come back in the fall to make up for lost time."

"Good for you! It's never too late. My mother had four kids before she got her degree. Where are you now?"

266

"Home in Detroit. I've got a chance at a job here, Kelly, and if I stay with my parents I can save money for school."

"That's what you should do."

"But what are you doing back at the store? My roommate told me you wanted me to call you there. I ruined your honeymoon!"

"Not at all. My father had a heart attack, but he'll be okay. I'm just glad you're coming back to the university."

"Hey, what do I want with a man who's playing ball in Chicago one week and Dallas the next? I'm looking for a domesticated model with big, beautiful teeth."

"Good for you!" Kelly said again, meaning it sincerely.

Cheryl hadn't been able to mask her hurt with words, and Kelly couldn't hide her real feelings behind anger any longer. She wanted to be with Brian, whether he was trekking the Sahara or sledding at the South Pole, but it was too late. In his eyes she'd failed him, and the loathing and disgust in his voice had sounded like doom for their marriage.

What did women do when their lives fell apart? Cheryl was going back to pick up the pieces, but Kelly felt her whole existence had gone sour. Her jewelry store, a place she'd once enjoyed, was nothing now but a white elephant to be unloaded as quickly as possible. Without help and, more importantly, without enthusiasm, she couldn't reopen, and she was sorely lacking in both. She called Jane and regretfully told the student she was out of a job.

There was no reason to delay the inevitable. Reading through the list of realtors in the yellow pages, she found one familiar name.

"Ms. Jordon, this is Kelly . . ." She stumbled over the use of her married name. "Kelly Fort at Valentine's Treasures. I'd like to put my business up for sale. Can you come right over and list it?"

An hour and a half later the realtor pushed a legal-size sheet of paper with lots of small print across Kelly's desk.

"This is a ninety-day agreement, Mrs. Fort."

Kelly hated the extra measure of respect in the woman's voice when she used Brian's name, but she signed anyway, eager to bind herself to her decision to quit.

"And I want a FOR SALE sign on the front door immediately," she said. "A big one."

When she locked the door behind the realtor, the sign taped in front of the shade, she was free to indulge in the only thing that was left to do: cry. Blinded by tears, she stumbled miserably up the stairs and threw herself facedown on the quilted surface of her bed, sobbing uncontrollably, soaking tissue after tissue and leaving a damp spot on the bed covering, weeping until her temples throbbed unmercifully and her tear ducts finally ran dry. It wasn't true that a good cry made a person feel better. She'd never felt worse.

She was too messed up to be helped by a wet washcloth, instead soaking a big bath towel with icy water and pressing it against her face, feeling the sting in her bloodshot eyes and swollen lips. With her hair damp around the edges of her face and red, puffy eyes, she looked like the loser in a welterweight boxing match. She felt like one of life's all-time losers.

When the door buzzer sounded downstairs, the last thing she wanted was to face another human being. Ignoring it was difficult, but she wasn't interested in signing for a package or explaining why the store was closed. A long silence made her hope the caller had left, then three buzzes sounded close together. After a brief pause there was one more, another pause, and three more demanding buzzes. It was the code Brian had used to summon her after he learned about the threatening message on her window.

Had he come to say they were finished? It was the first and only thought that came to her mind, making her freeze at the top of the stairs. The pattern of buzzes was repeated, telling her he wasn't going to give up. With his car and hers in the alley, he had to know she was there.

Dragging her feet and dreading the encounter, she slowly moved down the steps and through her store, not needing to move the shade aside and peek out before she turned the lock.

Whatever he'd intended to say, he forgot it.

"My God, Kelly, you look terrible!"

Stepping back to let him enter, she averted her eyes and didn't answer, knowing her supply of tears had replenished itself.

"You've been crying."

"Very observant," she said dryly, turning her back to him, hearing him relock the door.

"What's that sign?"

"You must have read it."

"You're not planning to sell your store?"

"It seems I am."

"Kelly, look at me."

She couldn't bear his eyes on her swollen face, but he stepped in front of her, blocking her retreat to the apartment.

"Good Lord, what a mess."

"You've already told me how I look."

"That's not the mess I meant. I'm talking about us."

Too upset to talk, she clenched her lips together. Walking over to a display case, she leaned both elbows on the top, staring through the glass at the green velvet covering she still hadn't changed, thinking dejectedly that smudges on the surface didn't matter anymore. No customers would be peering through it to see her jewelry.

"Why didn't you tell me about your father?"

It was the accusation she'd anticipated and dreaded, but actually hearing it angered her so much she forgot her red, puffy eyes and faced him furiously.

"You didn't want to hear my problems."

"I didn't want to hear some feeble excuse for not taking that plane!"

"You assumed I wouldn't have a good reason!"

Where were all the clever things she'd planned to say? Her mind was one raw, searing wound. All she could do was lash out in self-defense.

"Okay, I was blind and stupid!" he shouted.

It wasn't what she'd expected him to say.

"I wanted you with me so badly," he said, speaking rapidly. "I made that plane trip into some ridiculous test of your love. When you weren't on it, I went a little crazy, more than a little. I walked the streets for hours and damn near got frostbite trying to understand you, and by the time you called . . . Anyway, you knew I'd be angry. You could have had the decency to tell me about your father."

"How did you find out?"

"It took a few hundred phone calls. I finally reached your sister at the wineshop yesterday morning."

"You've known since yesterday morning? Did you call her from Toronto?"

"No, from Grosse Pointe," he said wearily. "Can we go upstairs and talk about this. I'm too tired to stand here arguing."

"You've been back since yesterday?"

"The night before, if you have to know."

"And you didn't even try to see me?"

"Please, can we go upstairs and talk?"

"No, we can talk in my office. I like to conduct my business there."

"You don't have an office!"

"I can call my desk an office if I want to."

She stormed into the back room, sitting down on her swivel chair with her arms crossed on her chest, feeling her heart pounding.

"First tell me why you're selling your store," he asked, sitting on the edge of the desk and towering over her.

She stood and backed to the safe, unwilling to look up at him while they talked.

"The help problem is too discouraging. Cheryl isn't coming back. She broke up with Duane and went home to her parents."

"You want me to believe that's why you're quitting?" he asked, his eyes narrowing shrewdly.

"I don't have to explain anything to you."

"No, you don't," he said, moving toward her but stopping a few feet away.

"I'm the one who should ask questions," she said, "but I'm afraid to hear your answers."

"I had a good reason for not finding you sooner, but first, how's your father?"

"He'll be all right, we hope. The doctor wants to try some new drug, beta blockers or something like that. Dad sent us all home. I guess he can't stand too much mothering either."

Try as she did, she couldn't keep the misery out of her voice.

He lifted his arms tentatively, then dropped them to his sides again.

"Dammit, I can't talk to you while you're studying the floor. Come upstairs with me."

"We can talk here."

"I can't."

Before she realized what he intended, he made a quick move, grabbed her legs, knocked her off balance, and hoisted her over his shoulder, carrying her up the steps with her rear in the air and her head and arms flopping helplessly behind his back.

"You can't do this to me," she raged impotently, trying without success to kick free of his hold.

"It seems I have," he said, dumping her unceremoniously on the bed and throwing his suede coat across the room.

This wasn't a play fight, and Kelly eyed him warily, her feelings so confused she didn't know if she wanted to oppose him.

"First," he said, sitting beside her and taking both her hands in his, "I am very, very sorry about your father. I'm also furious you didn't tell me."

"I'm sorry about that," she said, unable to lie with his eyes watching her so intently. "I was hurt by your attitude . . ."

"So you wanted to punish me by laying on a heavy guilt trip. You knew I'd find out sooner or later."

"Nothing you didn't deserve," she said with hostility, pulling her hands free and edging away from him.

"Dammit, you make me so mad sometimes," he said.

She stood and turned away from him.

"And I'm not going to talk to your back," he yelled furiously, stepping in front of her and roughly grabbing her shoulders. "I had a reason for not coming sooner, and I have one for being here now."

"You always have a reason—your reason!"

Color rose to his cheeks and his face contorted with anger, warning signs Kelly was too enraged to notice. He pulled her stumbling backward onto the bed, pinning her with his weight when she tried to evade him by scrambling to the far side.

She fought him with her fists and tried to pull him away by his hair, maddened by the unfairness of his assault. When he subdued her, pinning her arms above her head with one hand and sliding the other between her legs, tormenting her with grasping fingers, she kicked out wildly, surprised when her knee connected with his groin.

Releasing her abruptly, he stood and doubled over, clutching himself in wordless agony.

"Brian, I didn't mean to . . ."

He sat on the edge of the bed, still bent with pain, reminding her of how dangerous a wounded bear was supposed to be. She slid off the bed on the far side and backed away until the second-story windows blocked her retreat. The words he muttered made her even more apprehensive.

271

"What a way to treat the family jewels! Are you trying to make me sterile?"

"It was your own fault!"

He stood and limped toward the bathroom, slamming the door so hard, it echoed in the long metal-ceilinged room.

When it seemed he'd never come out, she inched her way toward the door, knocking once and calling in a soft, tentative voice.

"Brian, are you all right?"

He laughed, a low throaty chuckle that gave her goose bumps. Maybe Jack the Ripper had made a sound like that before he pounced on his victims. She started to back away, but he opened the door before she was out of range.

"Come here."

"Oh, no!"

"I'm much too sore to chase you. Come here."

"Why?"

"Kelly, I'm not going to ravish you right this moment. Get over here."

She took a cautious step forward, melting into his open arms at his first touch.

"Have I ever forced you to do anything you didn't want to, aside from flying?"

His hands on her head were gentle, cradling her against him.

"No," she admitted, wrapping her arms around his waist, snuggling close, being careful not to bump his injured area.

"Just because I'm mad doesn't mean I'll rape you. Were you really afraid of me?"

Was she? With his hand stroking the end of her spine it was hard to remember. She mumbled incoherently while he slid his fingers under her slacks on top of the silky seat of her panties, not difficult to do since her waistband button had been lost in their tussle. The zipper parted and her slacks slid down her hips. Before she decided whether to grab them or let them fall to the floor, a sharp little pain in her buttocks made her cry out.

"You pinched me!"

"The only way this marriage is going to work is to keep things even."

He released her, laughing when she rubbed her seat.

"Put on some pants you won't lose quite so easily," he ordered. "We have places to go."

"You go wherever you like."

"If you're still mad, I'll say this once more, then as far as I'm concerned, it's a dead issue. I am genuinely sorry about your father. I should have been more reasonable when you called, and I wish I'd been here when you needed me."

"You weren't in any hurry to find me when you did hear about him."

"Yes, I was, but he was out of danger and there were a few important things I had to do."

"More important than me."

"That question is so idiotic it doesn't deserve an answer."

"Don't try to kid me, Brian. I know you live for your big-deal business trips."

"You don't know as much as you think you do."

"How can I know anything? You dish out information in such tiny little bits, I'm never sure what you're doing. It's like trying to make out what a turkey looks like by studying the wishbone."

She stepped out of her slacks and bent to retrieve them, keeping a wary eye on him, frowning and running her pinched spot to remind him what a bully he was. Her clothes were hung in two flowered cardboard wardrobes at the far end of the room, since there wasn't a closet in the apartment. She backed toward them, skirting around the furniture that blocked her way, and found a pair of comfortable old jeans folded over a hanger.

Why was she uncomfortable when he watched her dress, but not when he watched her undress? He retrieved his suede jacket, still moving a little stiffly, while she slipped her Colombian poncho over her head.

"That suits you," he said.

"I like it, thank you."

"Unique, one-of-a-kind, a little primitive."

"Primitive!"

"How many women can use their knees like a baseball bat?"

"How many need to?" she asked in a frigid voice.

"You drive," he said, throwing her his Mercedes keys when they reached the alley.

"If I do, I'll use my car," she said stubbornly.

"There's absolutely no give in you, is there?" he asked, irritably taking his keys back and walking to the driver's side of his car with an exaggerated limp.

"You're faking so I'll feel guilty," she said when he released the lock from the inside so she could get in.

He was succeeding, too. She rallied her self-righteousness, reminding herself of his harshness on the phone and his neglect, returning from Toronto and not even phoning her.

He squirmed, trying to get comfortable before finally starting the car, making her suspect it was about ninety percent acting. And he talked about laying on guilt trips! She fastened the seat buckle, knowing he wouldn't drive until she did.

Skirting the edge of town, he took an unfamiliar road, leaving behind the businesses and apartments that clustered around the university town.

"Where are we going?"

"You'll see. It's not far."

The road was paved but narrow, running past several farms and stretches of snow-clogged woods. In a few minutes Brian made a right turn onto a drive that led to a low, rambling modern house with natural wood siding mellowed to a silvery gray.

"A professor of architecture at the university designed this house for himself. He took a job in California last fall and is anxious to sell it."

"Are you starting a collection of houses?" she asked dryly.

"It'd be less trouble than collecting women," he countered.

While she got out of the car, he took a large plastic bag, the sturdy kind made for lawn rakings, from the car, slinging it over his shoulder and walking to a side door of the L-shaped house, opening it with a key he pulled from his pocket.

"Brian, don't tell me you've bought this house."

"No, I haven't."

"Why are we here?"

"You won't find out standing in the driveway yelling."

"I'm not yelling, and I'm tired of not knowing what's up."

She walked forward on the crushed gravel drive, following him into the house with excited misgivings. Compared to the brisk wintry air outside, the interior was pleasantly warm, and Brian snapped on an overhead light in a cozy family area off the kitchen.

"Look around," he invited, setting his bulging bag on a built-in kitchen counter. Even without furniture the house was lovely, the living room carpeted in a natural woodsy brown shade with muted wheat walls and a huge natural stone fireplace. A picture window overlooked a sloping ravine in back with a thick woodland behind it.

"Do you like it?" he asked, coming up behind her.

"It's lovely, but I'd enjoy it more if I knew why we're here."

"We're just visiting," he said casually. "I haven't eaten all day. Are you hungry?"

"Hungry for information!"

"Well, all I'm offering right now are frozen dinners. There's a built-in microwave we can use if we dump the contents on paper plates. Won't take long at all. You have a choice: chicken, roast beef, Chinese, Italian, or turkey."

"Chinese, if you don't want it. I don't really care."

His bag contained a kettle to boil water, a jar of instant coffee, a package of tea bags, paper cups and plates, plastic forks, and napkins. Besides the frozen meals he was cooking, there were several others he deposited in the frozen-food compartment of the fridge. He also took out a tube of toothpaste, two toothbrushes, and a roll of tissue, tossing them at her with orders to put them in the bathroom. The heavy lawn bag still bulged.

"We're camping here!"

"I knew you'd catch on," he teased.

"Brian, this is someone's house. How can you make yourself at home just anywhere?"

"Practice."

While the dinners cooked he carried in logs from a stack outside and did a passable job of building a fire, using newspapers piled in the garage to start it. They ate the bland meals sitting cross-legged in front of the fire, Kelly too consumed with curiosity about his odd behavior to notice what she was eating.

"If you haven't bought this house, how can you come in here like this?" she asked, scraping up the last dab of pepper steak. "Are we going to get arrested for trespassing?"

"Unlikely. The professor's very anxious to sell, and I'm a very hot prospect, Ms. Jordon's favorite customer, in fact. She loaned me the key so we could see it alone this evening."

"If the condo is too inconvenient, why consider living here? It's fifteen minutes farther from your downtown office."

"Did I say anything about living here?"

"You must have to Ms. Jordon."

He gathered their dishes and burned them in the fireplace, then went back to his bag and took out a thick green bundle.

"You've brought a sleeping bag!"

"Well, the floor's a little hard, but with this it beats evergreen boughs any day."

Unzipping the thick quilted sleeping bag, he spread it like a blanket in front of the fireplace, tossing a single pillow at the top.

"Of course, we'll have to share," he said, grinning.

"I can't possibly share a sleeping bag with a poor, injured man. What if I thrash in my sleep?"

"I'll take my chances."

He came up behind her, nuzzling her neck and burrowing his hands under her soft nylon slipover, unsnapping her bra with ease and reaching around to cup her breasts. Pressed against him she was satisfied that his injured parts were in working condition and not nearly as tender as he pretended.

"It's not going to be so easy, Brian. I want to know why we're here and what you're up to."

"I'm trying to seduce my wife. That should be obvious."

He kneaded her nipples, letting them stand up between his fingers while his knee found a passage between her legs, putting her off balance so she had to lean back on him to keep from falling.

"There aren't any curtains on the windows," she said.

"That's the nice thing about living in the country. With this room in the back, only the deer and rabbits can watch."

He left her for a moment to turn off the light, stepping out of his loafers and slacks before coming back to her.

"Your legs look sexy in white socks," she teased, more susceptible to his wooing than she wanted to be. The ruddy glow of the fire achingly reminded her of their first time on the island, and even though she was sure he'd planned it that way deliberately, she was warm with yearning.

His yellow knit shirt was soft under her cheek when he took her in his arms again, but she wanted to feel the shivery smoothness of his skin. Sliding her hands over the bare skin of his back she gave an involuntary shudder, telling him more than she wanted him to know. When he started inching her sweater upward, she offered no resistance, raising her arms so he could peel it away, quivering when he trailed kisses down the soft flesh of her upraised arm, burying his face in the hollow under it until his nose tickled her, making her giggle nervously.

He tossed aside her bra, and she wanted more than ever to feel his skin against hers, all hesitation gone as she worked her hand under the back of his elastic waistband and fondled the perfect globes of his buttocks, a favor he returned with more daring.

The firelight played tricks, flickering and glowing, but the expression on his face was no illusion. His features were softened by passion, more seductive than any words could be, and his eyes feasted on her, torn between her melting eyes and the hard rosy-brown tips of her breasts. She slid his shirt over his ribs, following with her lips, delighting in his firm muscles. His nipple was a tiny love point under her tongue, and she took it between her lips, driven wild by his throaty moans.

With a little help she stripped off his shirt then bent to remove his shorts, slipping to her knees and trailing her hand from his navel to the hard bone of his ankle.

"Are you really all right?" she asked softly.

"Only a little tender. Don't be rough," he whispered in a teasing voice, sinking to his knees in front of her.

"Tell me why we're here," she pleaded, torn between burning curiosity and the throbbing demands of her body.

"For this."

He found her breast, stretching his lips to take it in his mouth, his tongue worrying the tip until she cried aloud, so aroused her remaining clothes felt like a mummy's wrappings.

"Undress me," she begged, fumbling at the waist snap herself.

"Stand up."

She turned her back and faced the fire, not waiting for his help to slide her jeans down to her ankles. Stepping out of them she pretended to evade his hand, letting him catch her and make a ritual of removing her briefs. She sank down beside him because her watery legs wouldn't support her, surrendering to his feverish

277

strokes and kisses, sure that her flesh glowed with more heat than the fire.

"Tell me," he whispered, leaning over her and assaulting her ear with his tongue, "what you like best."

"You," she said hoarsely.

"That's no answer."

He gave her other choices, taking intimate possession of all that was hers, making her bold with his sensual delight. He drew himself up and parted her thighs with his knee, leaning forward to kiss her as if discovering her mouth for the first time. They couldn't be still, groping and exploring for new depths of sensation as their bodies became lubricated with the musky moisture of love.

"I love the way you make me feel," she moaned. "I love your lips and your skin and your hands. I want to melt into you."

Was it possible to die of pleasure?

The side of her face closest to the fire was warm to her touch, but the wood coals in the grate were cool compared to the flaming inferno in her loins. Totally open to his love, she felt herself slipping away, clutching at his hips to ride the roller coaster of sensation he was creating.

He took her sitting upright, his back a brace as they rocked in each other's arms, driven by raging need and deepest pleasure, absorbing the impact of their bodies with breathless urgency. Boiling together in a final steamy caldron, they held back the dam until she cried aloud, begging for more and begging for release at the same time, so overcome that tears ran unnoticed down her cheeks. Stars were in the room, explosive bursts of incredible light, as their passion swelled to a blinding conclusion. They collapsed in a trembling heap, rocked by the aftershock of love out of control.

His hip bone was a hard pillow for her cheek, but she clung to him, letting the receding waves of ecstasy flow through her, hearing his breath and feeling the life that throbbed through his body, more a part of him than of herself.

"If that's gentle, I couldn't survive rough," he crooned softly, shifting so he could cradle her head on his stomach.

Little gurgling noises teased her ear, and his natural musk was sensual perfume in her nostrils, making her wiggle higher and cling to his chest with satisfied purring, pressing her outspread legs against his slippery hips and thighs.

"Can I sleep like this?" she murmured.

"Maybe you can, but I can't."

"Um, that's a shame," she answered softly without moving.

"I didn't say I wanted to sleep."

He stroked her back, massaging her with questing fingers.

"Are you still curious?" he asked, shifting position under her weight.

"You're uncomfortable," she guessed sleepily.

"Yes, but not because you're lying on me. I love having you close."

"Why, then?"

"I have a lot to tell you. I don't think I can sleep until I do."

She slid to his side and pulled a corner of the sleeping bag over her legs and hips.

"Do you want to zip up?" she asked.

"Lie still. I'll do it."

He crawled to the end and found the tab, working the zipper strips together until her legs were in a cocoon of cotton and nylon.

"It won't be any fun with you out there and me in here," she teased.

"Do you think I'll let you hog the whole thing? Slide over and make room for me."

He maneuvered in beside her and pulled the zipper shut on his side, cuddling against her, molding his length to hers to share the crowded space.

"You don't know how often I dreamed about this in Colombia. Those were the longest weeks of my life."

"Months," she corrected him.

"Seemed like years."

With a little experimental wiggling she managed to lie spoonlike in his arms, feeling loved and cherished but not necessarily satiated. She wanted her molecules to explode with his and make them a dual person, so close that nothing could ever separate them again.

"Why are we here?" she asked, her curiosity rekindled along with other renewable urges.

"I'll answer that in a minute. Tell me first why there's a FOR SALE sign on your store."

If she didn't feel mellow enough to tell him at this moment, she never would.

"The store isn't that important anymore. I want to be with you, no matter what the cost."

"Even if it means flying with me?"

"Yes, and you were right about getting professional help," she said reluctantly. "I'm going with you, so I might as well have help fighting my fear."

"I'm very proud of you," he said, his breath warm near her ear, "and I don't deserve you."

"You don't deserve me? I thought it was the other way around."

Her light laughter held more than a little disbelief, and she snuggled even closer, taking his hand and laying it on her soft, tender breast.

"Touch me gently," she pleaded.

He did, slipping his leg between hers.

"Darling, I like flying all over the world, pulling strings, making decisions, being my father's right-hand man."

"I never thought you didn't," she interrupted unhappily.

"My brother's been a disappointment in the business," he said, "so I suppose I've been trying doubly hard to do things exactly the way my father wants."

"He must be proud of you."

He sighed deeply and fondled her breast, making her writhe with pleasure.

"Is this going to be a long conversation?" she asked, somehow managing to turn around and plant her head under his chin, rearranging his limbs several times in the process.

"Maybe. It has to do with where I'm going to keep my scattered wardrobe."

"Then sit on your hands and tell me."

She raised up on one elbow so she could see his face in the lingering glow from the fire.

"It's not easy to admit I need to grow up," he said sheepishly.

"Brian, you're the most mature man I know."

She intentionally nudged the tangible proof of his maturity, and he kissed her soundly.

"I'm not talking about that kind of maturation," he said, sounding strangely ill at ease. "Just for once listen quietly, would you?"

"Yes, sir."

She straightened, coming as close to military-type attention as she could in the confines of the sleeping bag.

"I'm thirty-three years old, and I jump when my father says jump, go when he says go, even on my honeymoon."

He spoke quickly, with obvious pain, confessing something that made him terribly uncomfortable. It was such a new idea she actually did keep quiet.

"My father isn't a tyrant. I'm not saying that," he said hastily. "He's never pressured me to work for him, and I certainly can afford not to work at all if I don't want to. My mother's father left Brad and me well off, and heaven knows, my brother lives well without gainful employment. Dad pays me exceedingly well for what I do, but I work for his approval, not his money. Do you understand what I'm saying, darling?"

"I think so," she said, touching his chest lightly. "Parents never stop being important. In the hospital my mother was scared. She really was frightened. And it was all right. In a way it was good. She was giving me permission to be vulnerable myself sometimes. I'd never realized I wanted to be like her, so strong-willed. In fact, I was sure I didn't. But parents do strange things to their kids without even knowing it, don't they? Your father wants you to be your own man like he is, but he works against you without knowing it."

"Yes, I'm sure that's true." He brought her fingers to his lips and kissed them, but his mind was still on his problem. "By making my life so satisfying and even exciting, by giving me so much approval, he's kept me dependent."

"You get nervous if you're late for an appointment with him."

"You noticed, huh?" He laughed at himself ruefully and tucked her hand between his arm and his side. "He hasn't taken his belt to my backside since I took the boat out on the river alone when I was about ten, and then he felt as bad as I did because I'd let him down by not obeying. Old relationships die hard, I guess. He doesn't say a word if I'm late now, but I feel edgy if I know he disapproves. I just never thought all this through before you came into my life."

"He's a nice man, but, darling, why are you telling me this now?"

She couldn't help wanting to pet him, pulling her hand free and running it over the firm line of his jaw.

"I went to see him yesterday instead of finding you."

He took her into his arms, pressing her close and talking into her hair.

"Kelly, I resigned. I'm not working for him anymore. He's been thinking of retirement, and I may be responsible for rushing him into it, but I'm not going to do his running and try to keep up with my own interests too. With you in my life, I only have time for one career."

"You won't travel so much?"

She moved up so her face hovered over his, searching his eyes for confirmation.

"Remember, going to Colombia was my project. I can't be a working geologist and sit on my rear in an office all the time."

"Get to the bottom line," she urged, caressing the back of his neck with quick, nervous strokes.

"It doesn't matter where my business is based. I'm opening an office here in Ann Arbor. Actually, it's a great location because of the university. I hope to pick up some energetic young talent to handle a lot of the fieldwork, but that doesn't mean I'll never handle any assignments myself. I'm talking less traveling, not no traveling —but from now on it will be only when I want to go, not when my father wants me to."

"But we can live here? We can be together here?"

She kissed him so enthusiastically his answer was delayed for several minutes.

"When I go, you go," he reaffirmed. "You'll have to get an assistant who's reliable and stock more ready-made jewelry so you're free when I need you."

"I signed an agreement to sell my business," she wailed, sitting upright with some difficulty since it meant squirming out of the sleeping bag.

"You didn't think your business was important anymore," he said, baiting her, unzipping the bag and sitting beside her.

"I was tired of being apart from you! I have to have something to do, and living here makes it perfect. I'll hire an older woman who needs a new interest. But what if Ms. Jordon sells my business before the ninety days expire?"

"Don't worry. Maybe we can buy a house from Ms. Jordon in exchange for tearing up your agreement. The worst that can happen is I'll have to pay the realtor's commission to get you out of it."

"If anyone has to pay a commission, I will. Some things aren't going to change. Do you want to buy this house?"

"That's up to you. I learned my lesson on the condo. Do you like it?"

"I love it, but it's pretty far out of town. I want to see every house in the county before we decide."

He groaned loudly.

"And I'll finally get to see all your clothes in one closet!"

"That's your idea of excitement?"

"Not really, but I'm curious."

"About what?"

He reached for her but she slipped away, running toward the wall switch and flooding the room with light.

"Whether you'll wear pink and yellow and green and salmon shirts when you're the boss."

"I'm the boss right now, and I'd sure like to know what you're doing."

"Looking at the house. Do you think my rocking chair would look good by the fireplace?"

Her laugh gave her away, and she darkened the room and streaked away just as he got to his feet. She bypassed the first two doors in the dark corridor but ducked through a third, shutting it behind her as quietly as possible.

This bedroom had a connecting bath leading to the next room, and she suppressed a nervous giggle, feeling her way carefully. Brian was calling her, and from the bathroom she could hear him opening doors, coming nearer and bellowing with mock ferocity.

"Kelly, where are you? If you don't come out you're in serious trouble," he yelled, coming into the bedroom.

Darting through the second room she reached the hall before he discovered the connecting bath. She doused the lights he'd turned on, moving with frantic excitement. The house was larger than it seemed, and she felt her way down carpeted stairs to a lower level, checking each step with her toes, almost bursting with nervousness. The heat in the house wasn't set high enough to keep her from shivering in her nakedness.

Hide and seek on Halloween night was soothing compared to this chase. With carpeting practically everywhere, she couldn't hear him coming, and her only chance was to lure him to the far end of the lower level, then sneak up the stairs again.

"Kelly, it's too cold for this. My buns are freezing, but yours aren't going to be if you don't stop this."

His threat put a knot of apprehension in her stomach, but a surge of wild elation kept her running. He narrowly missed her passing through the room, but he either couldn't find the light switch or had forgotten it. Except for a shadowy glimpse, she couldn't see her pursuer, but she took a chance, rushing up the stairs, remembering a coat closet in the front entryway.

The cold flagstones in the small entry hall made her yearn for warm slippers, but she ducked into the closet, grateful for a patch of carpeting on the floor, hugging herself and shivering more from excitement than cold.

It was so quiet she could hear her heart beating and feel a wild, alien throbbing between her legs, her artificial fear growing into something much more powerful and disturbing. Shaking with cold and longing for him, she was still determined to play till the finish, cautiously easing open the door. She had to move or be found; he'd soon think of cornering her there. She took a first step and a second, too apprehensive to notice the cold flags underfoot, listening for the slightest sound.

It was too quiet. She backed up a single step and hit a wall of flesh that reached out to imprison her with arms of steel, frightening her so badly her scream could be heard a city block. He muffled her cry with his hand.

"What on earth are you doing?" he asked, keeping her locked against him. "Trying to rouse the whole countryside so we get arrested?"

In spite of his gruff words, his voice was strangled with passion, and his manhood swelled urgently against her back. Her skin was a sheet of goose bumps, but inside she was a roaring furnace, trembling to receive him.

"Your fantasy," she whispered urgently. "You made me so happy, I wanted to give you your fantasy about chasing the woman you want all over a strange house."

"Do you know how my fantasy ends?"

"I can guess."

But she guessed wrong. She felt the world tilt under her feet as she was eased to the cold flagstones and entered with an urgency that matched her own blinding desire. Their single point of contact became a furnace stoked by flaming gases from the sun, the focus of the world in driving, demanding passion. She could feel the center of her desire swelling and tightening, holding him a prisoner of delight. He chanted her name deliriously, but she didn't even hear the guttural sounds that welled up from her own throat. She was in a bower of her own making, mating with the god of love in pagan abandon. When they exploded together she only knew that she was his.

He carried her gently to the sleeping bag, rubbing her back and legs to warm her, patting her backside and fervently kissing her cold flesh.

"You forgot to ask the bottom line, darling," he crooned close to her ear, wrapping the sleeping bag around them both.

"Where you find me?"

"Where I find you. Did I hurt you?"

"I don't think so. You're the one who's tender."

"I exaggerated."

He wrapped his arms and legs around her, whispering endearments as she sleepily clutched at him.

"Sorry, there was no chandelier," she murmured.

"You didn't need one."

COMING
IN
AUGUST—

Beginning this August, you can read a romance series unlike all the others — CANDLELIGHT ECSTASY SUPREMES! Ecstasy Supremes are the stories you've been waiting for--longer, and more exciting, filled with more passion, adventure and intrigue. Breathtaking and unforgettable. Love, the way you always imagined it could be. Look for CANDLELIGHT ECSTASY SUPREMES, four new titles every other month.

NEW DELL

TEMPESTUOUS EDEN,
by Heather Graham.
$2.50

Blair Morgan—daughter of a powerful man, widow of a famous senator—sacrifices a world of wealth to work among the needy in the Central American jungle and meets Craig Taylor, a man she can deny nothing.

EMERALD FIRE,
by Barbara Andrews
$2.50

She was stranded on a deserted island with a handsome millionaire—what more could Kelly want? Love.

NEW DELL

LOVERS AND PRETENDERS,
by Prudence Martin
$2.50

Christine and Paul—looking for new
lives on a cross-country jaunt, were
bound by lies and a passion that grew
more dangerously honest with each
passing day. Would the truth destroy
their love?

WARMED BY THE FIRE,
by Donna Kimel Vitek
$2.50

When malicious gossip forces Juliet to
switch jobs from one television network
to another, she swears an office romance
will never threaten her career again—
until she meets superstar anchorman
Marc Tyner.